ANGELINA'S FATE

Angelina's Fate

PETER TINUCCI

Copyright

Acknowledgements

I attempted to be as accurate as possible in regard to the streets and buildings that existed during the time periods each part of the story took place.

I want to thank Beth Lake, Community and Family Engagement Coordinator from Amphitheater Schools for sending me the history of the Amphitheater district. There is a wealth of information on Tucson history covered in this book that contributed to the story.

I want to thank my friend and coworker, Gabriel Skyler, for his constant help with miscellaneous Tucson history and his insights on Canyon del Oro High School. This was the school he attended. He stood by me throughout the writing of this book.

I want to thank Jacob Linhart for the discussions we had on Tucson history and his help with information about St. Mary's Hospital from the 1970's and earlier.

I want to thank my wife, Irma, for understanding my writing notes and e-mailing them to myself in the middle of the night.

And I want to thank Jacob, Jordan and Jade, my kids for their continued support and ideas throughout this project.

Chapter 1

Senior year of high school was about to begin and Angelina Tucci was very excited. Usually you don't hear about high school students being excited about returning to school but Angelina was an unusual student. Angie, as her parents called her, loved school and learning in general. She had earned straight A's throughout high school so far and will be changing schools for her senior year. The new school was the highest rated in Tucson and she had the expectation that the teachers would be more engaged with the students and her classes would be more interesting. She felt that this would make learning more enjoyable. She also thought there would be a different class of students that were at the same academic and intellectual level as she.

It was also a few days prior to Angie's 18th birthday and Angie and her parents were planning a big party at their new house. She and her parents had just moved into a much bigger house that was in an upscale neighborhood. Now they lived at 7607 N. Christie Dr. in the Catalina Foothills.

Angie is not a typical 17 year old girl. She is very polite, confident and speaks as if she grew up in a wealthy family. Her mother taught her to be a proper lady because that is how her mother was brought up.

Angie lived a relatively modest life with her parents and her Aunt Maria. Her father and Aunt Maria also were very polite, spoke and carried themselves as if they were wealthy. And her Aunt Lillian, her mother's sister, and her grandparents are wealthy and speak and carry themselves the same. Since Angie grew up around a family where the women acted like proper ladies and the men acted like perfect gentleman, she learned these same traits and mannerisms. She also learned a different vocabulary than many kids as well. All of this caused her to have quite a bit if trouble interacting with the other students throughout her school life.

This made school difficult because other students constantly teased her and called her a poor rich bitch. So no one really talked with or associated with her and she never made any friends. However Angie was just a sweet girl that worked hard to keep her grades up and wasn't wealthy. She had lived about 2 blocks east of Amphitheater High School in a small house with her mother and father and her Aunt Maria.

Angie's mother came from a wealthy family but her father was working class. What her Grandmother Kristina and her Aunt Lillian, Lilly as many called her, did not know was that Dominic, Angie's father, was also wealthy until he was 14 years old. They would never listen to Lizzy, Angie's mother, when she tried to tell them about Dominic's past. Lizzy knew from the moment she met Dominic that he was not regular working class and would eventually excel and live a better life.

Angie's Grandfather Joseph had known Dominic's story since the day he first met him and continually attempted to get his wife and daughter to feel differently but it was pointless. He could not tell them Dominic's story due to a promise he made.

Angie also loved cars and this was something her mother, Aunts and Grandmother didn't understand. At first her mother blamed her father for pushing her to like cars but it became evident her father had nothing to do with it.

Chapter 2

Angie is very sentimental and very family oriented girl and loves hearing the stories about her mother and father meeting and dating and especially their wedding. She also loves hearing stories about her grandparents, particularly her father's parents. She particularly enjoys those because both grandparents passed away before she was born and the stories make her feel close to them. When her parents tell her these stories she sits quietly with her eyes wide open completely focused on them. And she continues to love hearing these same stories over and over again, even to this day. Angie had always been attuned to her entire family and they all had a special place in her heart.

Angie was born on August 28, 1957 to Dominic and Elizabeth Tucci. They lived in a small 3 bedroom house at 315 E. Yavapai about 2 blocks east of Amphitheater High School along with her Aunt Maria. This was the house Dominic and Maria's mother bought when their father died. And after their mother died they remained living there. They couldn't afford much because Dominic worked as an auto mechanic at his best friend's father's gas station. This is the job he began shortly after his mother died.

Angie was a very inquisitive girl that always looked at her toys as if she was trying to figure out how they worked. Dominic and Lizzy observed that she was fascinated by everything. As she grew it was evident that she was trying to figure out how everything worked.

Angie's mother and father never had much trouble with Angie that needed discipline because along with always explaining why a decision was made she had a docile personality. She listened to her parents reasoning behind decisions and they tried to always include her in decision making when it was possible. She never even got as much as a slap. Both Dominic and Lizzy believed that explanations and involvement were the best methods for dealing with Angie, and it worked well.

Angie always trusted her mother and father fully. She always knew that if she had anything to ask that they would always listen regardless of the question without becoming angry. They spent quite a bit of time asking how she felt and told her that she should never feel that her feelings and emotions were wrong. They explained to her that her feelings and emotions were neither right nor wrong because that is how she perceives the world. They also told her that regardless of how she feels or questions her feelings she should always feel that she could come to them and they would try to explain and help her understand.

There were times in her adolescence when she would get angry with her mother and father so it wasn't like things were perfect. Explanations only went so far. And like every kid, there were times that she thought that she hated them. Mostly this was in between about 6 and 15 years old

Her mother and father always tried to give her enough time to herself and would always tell her that they supported her and loved her even if she disagreed. Somehow this would end up giving her time to think about why she was angry and usually she would end up telling them she was sorry.

As Angie got older she began to see her parent's points and at times she was able to determine why she felt the way she did.

As soon as Angie was able, her mother began teaching her how to do many things around the house. She learned how to do household chores such as cleaning; laundry; cooking and baking. Angie always enjoyed this. She enjoyed learning in general. She was like a sponge. She listened and then wanted to try doing whatever she was taught. This is when Angie began to appreciate Classical Music. her mother always played Classical Music when she cleaned, cooked and baked.

Angie did the same with her father. He taught her how to paint walls; how to do small repairs; yard work; etc. Occasionally her father would bring her to work with him. Angie thought that all the different tools were really cool. What she thought was even better was when she learned how to use the tools.

As her father did repairs around the house Angie would always be there watching. And when she began talking she would ask questions about why he did repairs and how he learned how to do the repairs. He told her that he had been mostly self-taught as his father passed away when he was 14. His father did teach him many things but since they had been wealthy most of the larger things like painting and yard work would be contracted out. After his father died his mother didn't make much money and couldn't afford to pay to get things repaired. So he would always try to do it himself. He always explained everything in a way that Angie understood. And just as her mother, Dominic listened to music as well when he worked. But he listened to rock, blues and jazz music.

Often Angie's parents would find her sitting on the floor with something trying to take it apart. She wanted to determine how everything worked.

Other times Angie would just want to see what is inside such as when she opened up the radio. She just took off the cover and was just looking at everything. When Lizzy came into the room she screamed when she saw this because she thought it was still plugged in. She looked at Lizzy and showed her the plug. She said, "Mother, I unplugged it first, do not worry, I just wanted to see what is inside. I am not taking it apart. Did you ever see what is inside a radio Mother? Look, it's cool." Angie turned the radio to show her mother. "See these glass things? They are called tubes. See it says on the back cover." Lizzy was amazed that Angie could read the schematic on the back cover of the radio. She knew Angie was reading very well for a 7 year old but this seemed to her to be far advanced. Lizzy couldn't wait to tell Dominic when he came home.

Dominic was surprised when he heard that Angie was able to read some of the printing on the radio schematic. Then one day he had taken Angie to Walgreens and she saw something. She said, "Father is this where you can test tubes from the radio if they do not work? She pointed to a tub tester. "See it says Tube Tester Save Money."

Dominic was impressed that she read that on the top of the tester and that she made the connection. "Yes, Angie, this is where you test tubes. And there are tubes in the TV as well and you could also test them here. And if they do not work, you can buy replacements."

"That is so cool father!" Angie said.

This was about the time that Angie's parents realized how different she was from other kids. They began to notice that she had been far ahead of other kids in reading, comprehension and deduction. She was showing signs of high intellect.

On Angie's 8th birthday her Father and her Aunt Maria gave her the cross pendant that her great-great grandmother Tucci wore; then her great grandmother Tucci wore and then her grandmother Tucci wore and that Aunt Maria wore until her husband, Enzo, gave her his mother's cross to wear. Now they were giving it to Angie. Maria only wore it until she was married. They told Angie that it was a family heirloom and they wanted her to wear it. She would be the 5th generation of Tucci's to wear it. Angie cherished this cross because it gave her the feeling of strong connection to her father and aunt's family. Angie said, "Thank you Aunt Maria and father, I love it!" It was about 2" tall 24 caret gold and was on a real gold chain and they told Angie it is a vine cross and it symbolizes the Christian's union with Christ, as related in John 15: 1-8. Angie felt like this was kind of a tradition and always felt that she would pass it on when she had children. She only took it off when she trained because it was so dear to her and she did not want to lose it. She felt it was the most important thing she had.

Angie has pictures of her Grandmother and Grandfather Tucci and Grandmother and Grandfather Hall on her desk and she has family pictures on her dresser that include Aunts and Uncles and all of her cousins. She has always felt an unusual connection to her whole family. She was positive she inherited this from her father and mother because of the unusual connection that they had from the moment they met.

As Angie grew she became more interested in anything mechanical and by 9 years old she wanted to go with her father to work to watch him fix cars as much as possible. He would bring her there from time to time and she loved it. She started asking questions about what a part was and what it did. Then she would ask how he knew when something didn't work and how did he figure it out.

When Angie went to work with her father she got to listen to hard rock and heavy metal. This is what the guys at the shop listened to. So between her parents and the guys at the shop Angie was exposed to most genres of music. But there was one genre of music that genuinely moved her and that was what she would hear when she went to church. She was always in awe from pipe organ music. Pipe organ music, just as the sound of certain drag race cars that she would soon be hearing, reverberated in her chest. And along with this she felt as if she was in the music. It felt like it came from everywhere.

This was about the time when Angie's father took her to her first drag race. It was one of her father's hobbies. Dominic always thought this was the turning point for Angie. She wanted to see all of the cars and she especially loved the nitro burning cars. The exhaust fumes burnt her eyes a little but seeing the cars more than made up for that. She had to put her hands over her ears because the cars were so loud. She loved it so much she was almost dancing. After the first time, her father knew she wanted to continue going to the races so he bought her noise canceling ear muffs.

Angie really likes cars. She drew them on her folders and dreamt of going drag racing after she graduated high school. Her father also always took her to the big AHRA (American Hot Rod Association) events. Angie loved watching the drag racing, especially when it started to get dark because you can see the flames coming out of the Nitro cars exhaust. She also thought it was so cool to be able to feel the concussions of each cylinder firing in her chest. Her father would bring her to the fence close to the starting line so she could get a front view of Nitro Funny Cars and Top fuel Dragsters. She would hold his hand and she would get very excited. Her favorite was Shirley Cha Cha Muldowney. She had obtained her Pro license in 1965 so she had just begun her pro career. At this point she did not have her famous magenta top fuel dragster yet but Angie was impressed anyway. Later in 1973 Shirley Muldowney got her Top Fuel license. This is when she began racing her magenta top fuel dragster.

At the same time her father began taking Angie to Tucson Dragway, her Uncle Jack would go as well. In 1973-1974 season Angie got to see Shirley Muldowney run her magenta dragster; Don Garlits run his dragster. And she also liked the AA/Funny cars like Connie Colletta; Don the Snake Prudhomme; Tom McEwen; Jungle Jim Liberman. She liked Super Stock racing. She always got a kick out of watching Bill Grumpy Jenkins smoke lots of others with small block Chevy v8 powered Pro Stock car when the others had big blocks. She also loved watching TV Tommy Ivo in his multi-engine dragsters exhibition races. There was one kind of car she likes the most and thought was so cool, that was gassers. She thought these cars were just raw. At this point she had already been learning about engines and how they worked. She got quite a bit more out of the racing due to this.

When they got home this was all she talked about. Lizzy was a little disappointed because Angie was beginning to really like cars and she just wanted her daughter to be like a normal girl. Lizzy didn't want to tell Angie that it was wrong, because it really wasn't, but she had dreamed of having a girl that was girly like she was all of her life.

When Angie would go to the grocery store with her mother she would always look through the magazines. What always caught her eye were the car magazines. She would page through as many as she could before her mother pulled her away. A few times she asked her mother if she could get one but her mother always told her no. One day when she was 10 years old she was with her father and she asked him if she could get one and he told her to pick one out. She ended up picking Hot Rod Magazine. She liked the "How To" articles that Hot Rod always had. She thought articles would help her to understand more about cars. In a few weeks she just about wore out the magazine. Then Angie went to her father and asked if she could get a subscription to Hot Rod. Her father said OK and sent in the money. Soon she was getting Hot Rod Magazine every month. Her mother didn't like the idea so she started buying paperback novels for Angie to read. Angie ended up enjoying crime/thriller novels.

In recent years her father would bring her to his shop to help out in the summers. She tried to learn everything she could from everyone that worked there especially from Uncle

Jack, her father's best friend. She really liked Uncle Jack and his wife Sofia.

Angie's father also taught her how to drive when she was 10 years old by using the parking area for the shop. That's how he got around her being too young to get a permit or license. He worked with her quite a bit. After she was driving automatic well enough he taught her stick shift. She got quite good driving cars in and out of the shop.

When Angie was 13 years old she had been learning quite a bit from her father and began feeling like building something herself. So the only thing she could think of that interested her was model cars. She asked her father if she could get a model car kit so she could build something of her own. Her father thought it was a good idea so he took her to buy the kit. She picked a classic 1941 Willys Gasser race car, some miscellaneous small tools, glue, brushes and little bottles of paint and a small spray can of paint for the body. This model had a blown HEMI engine with chrome valve covers and a chrome blower. She worked on the car a little here and there then her father showed her how to spray paint the body. It came out very nice for a first time build. She was definitely getting into drag racing; reading Hot Rod Magazine and building model drag cars. She would imagine that she was drag racing while she built the models. As time progressed Angie built quite a few drag cars. She built a 1951 Anglia Gasser with an Olds v8; a 1951 Henry J with a Blown 427 SOHC Ford; The Hurst Hairy Olds race car with 4 engines. Angie built lots of other kits but all were drag cars. She had the finished models displayed around her room. Then when the first 1970 Barracuda kit came out she couldn't wait to get it. This was her favorite car and the model had a HEMI engine. She searched and finely found pink spray paint that was very close to Panther Pink, (or Moulin Rouge as Plymouth called it) her favorite Barracuda color.

At this time Angie began hounding her father for another car magazine subscription. She wanted to get Car Craft Magazine. He ended up subscribing for her.

By this age Angie was stocking shelves and filling the book and magazine racks in her father's front show room at the shop. She was getting interested in all of the technical books that he sold. He had lots of Peterson Publishing books like, "Engine Swapping; Engine Annuals; a whole series on different components such as Basic Clutches and Transmissions; Basic Chassis, Suspensions and Brakes; etc. Angie began to buy these from her father with the money she made working for him.

Angie also stocked the shelves with the performance parts that her father bought. The show room was almost like a small performance parts store. So she was getting lots of exposure to performance parts.

When Angie was 14 years old Dominic had been contemplating buying his own drag car. He had been discussing it with Lizzy for some time already. Then one day a customer came into the shop with some serious car trouble. His car needed a new engine and possibly a transmission and he didn't have enough money to do the repairs. But he needed the car to get to work. He told Dominic he had a drag racing car he would be willing to give him as payment. He told Dominic it was a 1963 Nova gasser but the motor had major problems. It was bright yellow, had a twin carb tunnel ram sticking out of the hood, wheelie bars, ladder bars and a classic MOON gas tank in front. Dominic said he was interested and took Uncle Jack and Angie along to look at it. The car was in good shape but the engine did not run. This guy showed Dominic that he could turn the engine over with a wrench but was afraid to try and run it for fear it would blow up. He said it had a nasty rod knock. Dominic and Jack were both excited because the engine was a 454 Chevy and this was a new engine that was offered in 1970 and the biggest Chevy offered. This guy said the engine came from a new 1970 Corvette that was destroyed in an accident with a truck. They made a deal and Dominic took the car to the shop. He used the 1960 pick-up he bought when he started the business but determined it wouldn't be capable to safely tow the race car. So he traded it for a 1968 Chevy C20 short bed with a 396 engine; automatic transmission and much wanted air conditioning.

It took Dominic about a year to rebuild the engine and work out the other bugs in the car and Angie was at the shop the first time her father started the car. She hounded him every day so he wouldn't forget. He knew she wanted to see the car the first time he started it so she didn't need to hound him about it. He thought she was more excited about it than he was. He primed the carbs. and Jack was in the car and turned the ignition switch and it came to life. It was so loud Angie had to cover her ears with her hands but she loved it anyway. She was smiling and excited. Her father told her it was street legal so she couldn't wait to get a ride. Uncle Jack and her father worked on the carbs and timing until it was running correctly. Then her father asked her if she wanted to go for a ride. She was so excited she almost couldn't answer.

Angie loved the way the carbs stuck through the hood and the headers came out of the fender wells. She loved the way the car sounded, so loud that you could feel it in your chest.

Angie's father got her into the seat and buckled the harness and then he got in and fastened his harness. He looked at Angie and asked if she was ready. All she could do is shake her head yes, even if she said yes he wouldn't have been able to hear it anyway. He slowly drove out of the shop and onto 2nd St. He stopped at the stop sign and turned west onto Stone. He pulled away from the stop sign a little slow and when the car was straight he nailed it. The car lurched forward and forced Angie into the seat. He just did this in first gear and only for a moment. Already they were going 50 miles per hour. He slowed down, turned around and drove back to the shop. He didn't want to run into any police. Although her father knew most of them and they probably would have just wanted a ride he didn't want to take a chance. He pulled into the shop parked it and shut it off.

Angie already knew that she needed to be 16 years old to ride in the car with her father at the track and she had less than a year to wait. She also required her driver's license and a SNELL approved helmet to ride in the car with him. And since the car ran in the low 11's she needed a SFI approved jacket. They also needed long pants a shirt and closed toe shoes. This was not a problem because that's what she wore every day.

Angie went with her father and Uncle Jack to the race track and he raced almost every Sunday after that. A few times her mother and Aunt Sofia came along. When Angie turned 16 and got her driver's license her father bought her the SNELL approved helmet and SFI jacket and the next Sunday she was finally going to ride in the car! She was excited. They got to the track and got the inspection and entered and prepared the car. Angie got in and fastened the 5 point harness and put on her helmet. Her father got in and did the same. He started the car and warmed it up. Angie already loved it and they hadn't moved yet. Then her father drove to the staging lanes. Angie's adrenalin was pumping and she was ready. Soon it was her father's time to do the burnout. This is done to heat the tires. Hot rubber bites better than cool rubber. He did the burnout and some smoke came into the car and they were ready. He pulled up and staged and revved the engine getting ready for the green light. The lights came down and he dropped the clutch and the car pulled the front wheels off of the ground when he banged second she felt the front come up again but not as far. Then he banged third then fourth. When they passed the traps he hit the brakes and slowed down. At the end the pavement turned hard left and they pulled up to the timing booth to pick up their time slip. Angie's father took the slip and handed it to Angie. She couldn't believe it. This was her dad's fastest time, 11:15/124.45! (sec./MPH) It was that minute Angie decided she was going to go drag racing as soon as she had her own car.

Angie went to LA Prince Grade School; Amphitheater Middle School then Amphitheater High School for the first 3 years. Then Angie transferred to Canyon Del Oro High School for senior year.

Angie's mother and father began seeing some very positive changes in Angie when she learned that she was transferring to Canyon Del Oro High School. They sat down for a talk with her one day about this. Just as always, Angie impressed them with her reasoning and research. She told them that this new school was rated very high in the country and that from what she read, the teachers took interest in the students and that this alone would make school life easier. This was something she never thought she received at Amphitheater High School. She said it made it very difficult to do well. She also told them about all of the classes that were offered, many more than Amphitheater. She always did very well, but mostly because she studied every minute outside of school when she wasn't training, at the shop or racing.

Angie's mother and father would tell her not to get too excited about the teachers until she began school and saw for herself. They never wanted her to only think of things from only one side so they always explained that sometimes things are not what you expect and it is wise to be prepared in that case. And if things did happen to be what she thought it would make her feel even better. Angie explained that she always heard some of the kids at Amphitheater talk about relatives complaining about the teachers at Canyon Del Oro but they considered teachers getting involved with the students a bad thing. They would say it would force them to do more work than they wanted.

Angie always loved the idea of getting married at some point and having kids. But she always thought there would be time for that later. She had definite plans for her life and she was very determined to follow her dream. And dating and marriage she thought could wait.

Chapter 3

After school was out for the summer, Angie was going to the shop every day. On Saturday August 24 she saw a car at the shop with a car cover on it in the far corner. She asked her father whose car it was and why it was covered. She never saw a car there besides her father's gasser with a cover on it. He told her that a new customer just bought it and brought it in to get a full service before he started driving it. Angie asked what it was and he told her to go and take a look and that she would love it.

Angie went over to look and her father and Uncle Jack watched. They watched her lift the cover and gasp. "Oh my god!" She screamed. "That is my car," she said as she walked back over to her father. This was her dream car. It was a 1970 HEMI 'Cuda with a 4 speed, and it was Panther pink too--- her favorite color for that car! She told her father that it was her exact dream car, as if he didn't know. She couldn't believe it. She never saw one in Panther Pink other than in a magazine. Angie was in awe. She said, "One day I am going to buy one."

Little did Angie know that this wasn't a customer's car. Her father and Uncle Jack were laughing a little about it. Jack told Dominc, "Man, I want to be your daughter."

Dominic said, "What!"

"Well to get that car for my birthday. How could I not think something like that?" And he laughed a little.

"I see your point," Dominic said.

Angie never suspected. On Sunday August 25, the day they chose for Angie's birthday celebration Uncle Jack stopped over to go with Dominic to get the Cuda. Dominic drove the Cuda back and parked it in the driveway. Uncle Jack drove the truck back and parked it in the garage and went home to get ready for the party.

As soon as they drove off Lizzy and Angie left to get their nails done and to go to the makeup artist to do Angie's makeup. They scheduled this a few weeks earlier. Angie wanted her eyes done just like Suzanne Pleshette has in the Bob Newhart Show on TV. Angie didn't normally use much makeup usually just eye liner. And since Lizzy didn't know how to do dark eyes, she set up the appointment with the makeup artist. They both had acrylic nails done but Angie wanted hers short, only slightly longer that she normally kept her nails. They both had them color matched to they're new gowns. Lizzy had light beige and Angie had bright white.

Angie and Lizzy returned shortly after Dominic returned with the Cuda.

They walked into the house and Dominic glanced at them and said hello but had to look again. "Angie, you look fantastic and you are not in your new gown yet. I cannot get over it; you are incredibly beautiful with this look."

"Thank you father, could I maybe get a ride in that Cuda before you bring it back?" Angie just thought her father was driving it a little to make sure everything was right on the car before returning it to the customer which wasn't uncommon for him.

Just then her mother walked in and smiled at her father and said, "What are you waiting for Dom? Tell her."

Her father tossed her the keys and said, "Happy Birthday Angie!"

Angie said, "You are letting me take it for a drive for my birthday, how cool is that!"

Lizzy said, "No honey, it is yours! We looked for a large bow but could not find one. Happy Birthday!"

Angie stood there dumbfounded. She didn't know how to feel. It wasn't registering. "What do you mean it is mine? You are kidding, right?"

"No, we are serious." Dominic said. "I was difficult holding back at the shop, but your mother needed to be present when we gave it to you."

Angie got tears in her eyes. She couldn't believe it. She ran to her mother and father, hugged them each and struggled to get a, "Thank you, I love you so much. I am the luckiest girl ever! "Both of you HAVE to come with me for the first drive, I could not have it any other way."

They said, "OK." Lizzy was skeptical that Angie would be able to drive a car with a stick shift. She didn't know that Angie had been moving stick shift cars in and out at the shop even before she had her license.

They got into the Cuda and Angie started it. The sound was incredible! Better than she dreamed. She revved it a few times and Lizzy thought, "If she smiles any bigger her face will break!"

Angie noticed that the car smelled brand new. She looked at the odometer and it said 4000 miles. "It only has 4000 miles? It is almost brand new!"

"Are you sure you can drive this with a stick shift?" Lizzy asked her.

"Of course I do mother." She said. Dominic just grinned knowing that she could.

Angie put it in reverse and let out the clutch and killed it. She started it again and killed it again.

"Relax Angie. HEMI's have a stiff clutch. Ease out a little slower." Dominic said.

Angie started it again and eased out the clutch. This time she didn't kill it. She put it in first and drove up the driveway and turned onto the street. She drove around the neighborhood and back onto Christie Drive up to Ina Rd. She continued straight onto 1st Ave. (Christie becomes 1st Ave. south of Ina Rd.) She gave it some gas and the tires squealed a little. Then she accelerated a little hard and shifted to second, then third. "WOW!" She screamed! "This feels surreal! I cannot believe this. Never in a million years would I have surmised I would attain my dream car so soon and now I am driving it! And I begin school next week. Should I drive it there? Will it be too showy for the first day of school?" Angie didn't notice the parking permit on the lower left corner of the windshield.

"Do you not want to drive your new car to school Angie?" Lizzy said. "When I brought the last paperwork to the school I got you a parking permit. I even put it on the windshield."

"Mother! This is almost too much to comprehend! I understood that you did not want me to have a car until after I graduate. You were entirely opposed to it."

"I can keep a secret quite well. We have been searching for this car for almost a year. I was concerned we would not find this car, especially in Panther Pink." Lizzy said.

"Really? I never would have guessed. I had the understanding that you did not approve of my passion for cars."

"I did not. But I have seen how much enthusiasm you have for them and I want to support you any way I can. I love you more than anything honey."

Dominic added, "I feel likewise. I have known for quite some time that you were enthralled with cars. At first your mother accused me of pushing you to like cars but I never did. You could not wait to go racing with me, so much that you were almost beginning to irritate me. And when I opened the shop you pestered me to take you there daily. I want you to be happy. I am not concerned with what you do with your life as long as you are happy Angie."

"Wow! I am so blessed to have parents like you. This feels like a dream. I could never ask for more. I love you so much that I cannot even describe." This whole time Angie was driving around without any more clutch issues.

Lizzy was enjoying Angie driving this car. She was proud and surprised that Angie drove this car so well.

When they got back home Lizzy reminded her that the whole family would be there in the afternoon to celebrate her birthday.

"Do any of them know about the car?"

"No, we did not tell anyone, with the exception of your father telling your Uncle Jack. But he would not have told anyone. You know, your Cousin Eddy is going to be jealous."

"Probably. Uncle Carl and Aunt Lilly are continually buying things for Eddy and Shelly. I used to be a little jealous but I now know that they do not appreciate possessions in the same manner as I so it no longer troubles me."

"We know. We always taught you that you need to work for your possessions to appreciate them. And you have been working extremely hard in school and at your father's shop. You deserve the Cuda. We need to begin preparing for your party. Everyone will be arriving soon."

This year was a turning point for Angie's immediate family. Life would be changing and it was all because of the success of the shop. Lizzy was thinking how happy she was for following her heart instead of following what her mother and sister constantly told her. They always reminded her how difficult it would be to marry a lower class person like Dominic. They told her that her life will be very difficult because Dominic was not like them. He came from a poor family and poor people have poor manners and they do not appreciate the finer things in life. But Lizzy knew different. She knew that Dominic had not always been poor. And she knew that they did not recognize that Dominic had perfect manors and that he was a gentleman.

The whole family was coming. Angie's Uncle Carl & Aunt Lillian and her cousins Eddy and Shelly; Aunt Maria & Uncle Enzo and her cousins, Bella and Rosa. Angie's Grand Parents, Grandma Kristina and Grandpa Joseph were coming as well, along with Uncle Jack and his wife Sofia, 15 people total.

The new house would be full. All but Uncle Jack were going to see the new house for the first time. They were going to see Angie's new car as well. Lizzy and Dominic didn't tell any of the family that they had been looking for a car for Angie, but of course, Uncle Jack had known. Uncle Jack was instrumental in getting the Cuda shipped to Tucson from California. This was where they found the car.

Angie and Lizzy had her upcoming birthday party well planned and it would be very different from any party that they had had in the past. They were having the party catered complete with servers and a coordinator.

Lizzy and Angie had gone shopping and bought new gowns. Angie's gown was a white mermaid type that was bias cut so it would show her body shape in a dramatic but tasteful way. It was floor length and had short beaded sleeves and a V shaped neckline that would accent her cleavage. And she also had a head piece made with white roses. She was going to make an impression that everyone would remember.

Lizzy also had a beautiful gown but it wasn't as spectacular. It was a floor length beige chiffon A-line neck with thin straps and a ribbon belt. She didn't want to take anything away from Angie, this was her day.

Angie and Lizzy went and got dressed. Lizzy looked at Angie and pulled the gown at a few places to get it to hang correctly. She stepped back and told Angie that she was so beautiful.

"Really mother? I think I look very nice. I just cannot see myself as beautiful."

"I really do not know why you think that Angie. You really are exceedingly beautiful."

"Well, I do not know. Let me look at myself in the mirror." She stepped in front of the full length mirror and instantly looked behind herself and had kind of an odd expression.

"Is there a problem Angie?"

"Well, I did not recognize the reflection in the mirror mother and I glanced behind me to see who it was, but it was me."

"Let's see what you father thinks, shall we?" Lizzy said as they walked out of the bedroom.

When they came out from dressing they were surprised when they saw Dominic was wearing a black tuxedo. Dominic's expression was all Lizzy and Angie needed. They looked incredible. Dominic said, "I have never seen such beautiful women."

Lizzy replied, "Thank you Dominic, you are sweet."

"Thank you father, that means quite a bit." Angie was surprised because even though she knew she looked very elegant she still didn't think of herself as beautiful.

They had planned a grand entrance for Angie and they both were hoping that they would finally impress the whole family. Lizzy desperately wanted to impress her sister and her mother as they always poked at her for marrying poorly. They didn't like that Dominic was not wealthy. Lizzy had thought about finally being able to tell her sister and mother about Dominic's unfortunate past and why he did not act like a typical poor person. He was refined, polite and a perfect gentleman. And her sister and mother would never listen to her when she tried to tell them, but she had a very strong feeling that sometime during the party she would finally have the opportunity.

Angie just wanted to impress her cousin Shelly. Shelly always dressed very girly and elegantly just as her Aunt Lilly and Shelly never understood why Angie only liked to wear jeans and cowboy boots or gym shoes. Shelly had thought it was because Angie was poor and that was how poor people dressed.

Since Angie didn't grow up wealthy as her cousins had, she had to work hard for everything she had. Because of this, unlike her cousins, she appreciated what she had. Angie loved her cousins and in fact her whole family. She treasured every minute they were able to visit. Aunt Lilly didn't share some of the wisdom with Shelly and Edward that her mother had taught, so her kids never learned to value things as Angie did.

Angie wondered how her cousins Shelly and Eddy would react to their new house. They now were living comparably to them. However, she never had much thought about the reactions from her other cousins, Bella and Rosa. They were Aunt Maria's kids. Aunt Maria is Dominic's sister and she had lived with her Dominic after her grandmother died. Aunt Maria had the same life lessons from living poor just as Dominic did. And she, just as Lizzy and Dominic had done, passed these on to her kids.

Everyone arrived almost the same time and as each drove into the driveway they wondered who was there that owned a Pink Barracuda as none of them had seen this car previously.

They were all talking about the Barracuda as they walked to the front door. As they got to the door they were greeted by Lizzy. Everyone called her Elizabeth as only her side of the family didn't use nick names, they only used full names. She greeted everyone as they came in. She then took everyone on a tour to show them the new house.

Lilly, Maria and Kristina complemented Lizzy on her beautiful gown and how beautiful and elegant she was. But this was as usual. She always looked elegant at family events as usual.

As Lizzy showed them the house, Lilly, Lizzy's sister, asked who owned the Barracuda.

Lizzy replied, "I will let Angelina tell you."

Lilly immediately blurted out, "Angelina has a boyfriend?"

Lizzy again said, "You need to ask Angelina."

"All right, if you will not tell us. You never want to tell me anything that is going on in Angelina's life." Lilly was being sarcastic as they each knew most everything there was to know about each other's families.

Maria listened but knew Angie did not have a boyfriend. She was suspecting it was Angie's birthday gift from her parents. But she did not want to suggest this so not to spoil the surprise. Maria has very strong intuition, sometimes bordering on premonition.

Lizzy finished the tour and everyone thought the new house was very beautiful.

Lilly asked Lizzy, "How does it feel to finely live in a proper house?" Lilly always was a little condescending because she felt Lizzy wasn't living up to their family standard. Now they lived in a proper house. Lizzy and Lilly grew up in an upper class style of living. Their mother always paid people to cook for parties, clean, do laundry, etc. They had grown up living in a 4589 square foot home at 4801 N. La Lomita that was on a 2 acre lot with horses and a stable and bordered by government land. It always appeared that they owned the Santa Catalina Mountains. She always liked to remind Lizzy that she didn't marry well enough for her liking. So her question was more of a poke than a real question.

Lizzy tried not to let this bother her as she really loved her sister, but deep inside it did bother her. She just figured sooner or later she would be able to show Lilly that she was wrong. Lilly loved her sister just as much but still couldn't keep from poking her about her financial position.

But with Dominic's business doing so well it will be a little difficult for Lilly to poke at her much now.

Everyone was talking in the Arizona room. This was Lizzy's favorite room. It was almost like being outside but the room was enclosed with very tall windows and it faced the Santa Catalina's. It reminded her of her parents' house. And now she was living in the Catalina Foothills again just as when she grew up. Lizzy was thinking that now she could start poking at

Lilly about how this house was comparable to hers but had a much larger lot, and was now living in the Foothills again. But Lizzy did not find humor in teasing like Lilly did, although it was true. Lilly, her husband Carl and the kids lived in a house a little further west in the foothills at 4831 N. Camino Luz. Lizzy never thought much about who lives better. Even though they lived for quite some time in a small house that wasn't in a very good neighborhood, she was always happy, but she always questioned in her mind if Lilly was really happy.

Angie's cousins Bella, Rosa, Shelly and Edward were talking and wondering where Angie was. Bella went to Aunt Lizzy and asked, "Aunt Elizabeth, where is Angelina? She is not here."

"Angelina will be here shortly Bella." Lizzy answered.

With everyone gathered in the Arizona room Angie made her entrance. She walked very gracefully into the room. Kristina saw Angie first and shrieked, "Angelina? I cannot believe it! You," she stuttered from shock, "you are absolutely stunning!" Now everyone turned around to see what Kristina was talking about. Almost everyone was in shock, except Maria had a very strong feeling that Angie would dress very eloquently for her 18th birthday. After talking with Lizzy and hearing that they both bought gowns for Angie's birthday, Maria was certain that Angie would be dressing unlike she had done in the past. But she couldn't believe how beautiful Angie looked. Shelly stood there with her mouth open. Lilly noticed and said to Shelly, "Close your mouth Shelly that is not polite." She closed he mouth. Bella and Rosa just smiled as their mother had told them Angie was going to do something very different. No one could believe the transformation; Angie wore a huge smile which just accentuated her beauty. Everyone had an opportunity to tell Angie that they couldn't believe how beautiful she looked.

Angie appeared as if she just stepped out of a fashion magazine. She could easily be an outstanding model. Shelly went over to Angie. She had to work to keep her mouth closed. She found it difficult to come up with words to say. She had never seen Angie dressed like this. Well, no one had ever seen Angie dressed like this. Everyone was shocked by both her beauty and the fact that she wasn't wearing Jeans and a blouse or sweater. Shelly finally composed herself enough to say, "Angie, because of your looks maybe I should address you as Angelina. You do not look like the Angie I know and you are so graceful. I never expected to ever see you like this. If you went anywhere like this you would be the only person anyone would see. You are absolutely beautiful!"

The way Shelly had always looked at it, Angie was a tomboy. She didn't like girl things. Shelly always wore dresses and Angie wore jeans. She liked to look elegant just like her mother. If she wore pants they were never jeans and she felt like she wouldn't be found dead wearing a t-shirt or sneakers. Her nails were always long with a perfect manicure and she was always graceful when she moved. Shelly loved her cousin but did not want to be like her. She and Angie had spent many hours discussing how each of them dressed and their interests. Shelly couldn't understand Angie. Angie would tell Shelly that wearing dresses and having perfect nails just didn't fit for one that does auto repair. It was very clear to Angie. Although Angie did wear dresses and paint her nails, but only for special events like weddings. She just didn't care to wear that type of clothes very often. But Angie and Shelly still discussed the cloths that they wore and how Angie thought Shelly was so beautiful. Shelly always wondered why Angie knew so much about dresses, jewelry, nails and those types of things but didn't like to dress that way very often.

Angie had a little different relationship with Bella and Rosa. The way Angie dressed wasn't a problem for them because their mother and their Uncle Dominic had the same values. Unlike Shelly and Edward that only dressed like a wealthy family,

Bella and Rosa dressed casually in jeans, t-shirts or blouses and gym shoes or cowboy boots at times and when they were younger their parents didn't have much money either.

Angie received more complements than she had expected. But the complement she cherished the most was from Shelly. Angie wanted to impress her more than anyone. "I think I finally impressed you Shelly. Almost more than anything I wanted to impress you."

"Why would you care so much about what I would think Angie?" She didn't understand.

"Because for as long as I can remember you looked elegant and I never took the time to learn how to dress and make myself up to be elegant myself. And I have always secretly admired you."

"You admired me? Why? I always kind of admired you because you are so pretty without dressing up. You are so pretty in jeans and a t-shirt and I need to work hard to look pretty."

"Really? You are to kind Shelly. I think you would be pretty in just about anything. I do not know why you think you would not be. I have seen you without makeup and without a fancy dress, and you are very beautiful as well."

"Angie, you can always make me feel good, you are always so upbeat. Well, you always make everyone feel good. Maybe we should try to hang out more and maybe you would rub off on me. Because I am beginning to feel like I was not that beautiful after seeing you like this. You really are so beautiful it is bringing tears in my eyes, I have never had that happen. I do not know why, I just want to hug you cuz." Shelly reached out and hugged Angie. (The cousins always called each other "cuz")

"You really think I am that beautiful?"

"Are you kidding me? You could be on the cover of Seventeen Magazine just as you are now, and they would sell millions of copies."

"I never thought of myself like that."

Angie hugged her back. This was one of those hugs that you see wealthy people do where they gently put their hands on each other's waists and they lightly touch cheeks. Lilly noticed and gave Lizzy a nudge and said, "Look Elizabeth, look at that!" Then she poked at her mother and said the same. All three of them watched and smiled. They hadn't seen Shelly and Angie ever hug like that.

Elizabeth said, "If I knew all it would take to bring them this close was to have Angelina wear a dress I would have insisted she dress like this more often. Maybe this will begin a new trend."

Kristina said to Elizabeth, "Do you think it is possible that Angelina will love the reactions enough to dress like this more often? I have to say again, Angelina is so beautiful! You are blessed Elizabeth." She looked at Lillian and said, "Oh, I do not mean to take anything from Shelly, she is always very beautiful Lillian. I cannot believe this. I would never have thought Shelly would have a response like this to anything Angelina wore. Our families have been blessed with exceedingly beautiful women."

Bella and Rosa told Angie, "We love how you look. This gown transformed you into a princess, cuz."

"You really think so? I kind of feel like a princess and it is a new feeling for me."

Angie walked with Shelly to Kristina, Elizabeth and Lillian and Aunt Lillian turned and said, "Since your mother refuses, Angelina, tell me about your new boyfriend and his car. And where is he?"

Maria said, "I have a feeling it is not a boyfriend." Lillian and Kristina gave her a look of disbelief.

Angie looked a little confused and asked, "Why do you think I have a boyfriend Aunt Lillian?"

Well is it not who owns the pink car?"

"Nooo! I was going to wait until later so Eddy would be more comfortable and would not be so jealous."

"Of a boyfriend?"

"No, because it is my birthday present from mother and father."

"Your birthday present?" Lilly turned to Lizzy and asked, "Really? You bought her a car? That car? I do not believe it."

Maria had a strong intuitive feeling the car was a birthday gift and smiled.

"We had been looking for this car since the beginning of the year. It was a difficult car to find and in that color almost impossible. Evidently it was not a popular color but we knew it is Angelina's favorite color."

"Her favorite color is pink? I did not know that." Lilly said.

"Pink is not her favorite color Lillian, this is her favorite color for this car. Her favorite color is still blue."

"I understand. I can certainly understand why. After seeing that car in pink I cannot imagine it looking quite as extraordinary in any other color."

"We felt the same. And you know Angelina built a model of this car and painted it pink so we already understood. Come, I will show it to you. I still cannot believe that she has done such an exceptional job building these. You are not going to believe she built these. I had not really looked at these until recently and I was completely astonished."

"Elizabeth, do you mind if I come as well?" Maria asked.

"Of course not Maria, you should see these as well." Lizzy took Lilly and Maria to Angie's bedroom to show them.

"I would not believe these if I did not see them! Angelina had mentioned that she built model cars but I never really thought about it." Maria said.

Lilly saw all of the cars Angie built and was really taken back. "She built all of these? This is incredible! Look at the detail, I am so impressed Lizzy. Is there anything Angelina does not excel in?"

"I do not have the faintest Lilly. It just appears that if she decides to do something she does it exceptionally well. You know Dominic has been telling me that she is learning auto repair so well and she is pestering him to send her to get some kind of certification when she graduates. He said she would be the first female mechanic in Tucson to obtain this."

"Really? Can you imagine that? She is likely the only female mechanic in Tucson, and to obtain this certification? That would make me proud as well. You know I never understood why she wants to repair cars but for her to be the first I would encourage her Lizzy."

Maria said, "That is wonderful Elizabeth! Angelina is a very talented woman."

"We are planning to send her as soon as she graduates. I do not know how to feel about it however Lilly. We believe she will finish this year with a 4.0 grade average again, and Dominic has told me she is doing well at the shop, she had built these model cars, and then today I almost did not recognize her when she finished dressing."

"Just before we came in here Rosa told me Angelina looks like a princess and I agree." Maria said.

"I do not know how to feel Lizzy but I feel like hugging you." Lilly reached and pulled Lizzy to her. "All of our kids are doing so well but I just cannot get over Angelina. She is not doing what we both expected but I could not see her doing anything else now."

"We should return to the party, everyone is going to wonder where we went. The only thing I worry about is that she has not made any friends at school. She said that it is because she is too involved with studying. But sometimes I think she is missing out on a part of life." Lizzy said as they walked back to the party.

Angie's Cousin Eddy kind of looked shocked and said to Angie, "You have a Barracuda?"

"Not just any Barracuda, Edward, a HEMI Cuda."

This was the first time Angie ever saw Eddy speechless. He just stood there with his mouth open. He wasn't so much into cars but he definitely knew what a HEMI Cuda was.

"Catching flies Edward?" Eddy gave her a dirty look, but asked if she could show him the car. She said absolutely and announced that she would show her new car to anyone interested. Everyone went outside to take a look. Lilly thought this had to be the nicest car her sister's family ever had.

Rosa looked at the car and said to Angie, "Cuz, this car is so cool! I cannot wait to get a ride."

Eddy asked Angie, "This car is stick shift. You can drive stick shift?"

"Of course Edward, I learned a few years ago from father."

Lizzy asked, "A few years ago? How?"

Dominic replied, "She learned at the shop. She has been moving cars in and out for a while now."

"Neither of you told me about that."

"At first I was afraid, then after a while it did not seem important any longer Mother. I probably should have told you."

"I see, it is not a problem."

"Angelina?" Eddy asked, "Would it be alright if I sat in it?"

"Go ahead Edward." Eddy got in and sat back. He still couldn't believe this was Angie's car. He was imagining that he was driving it although he didn't know how to drive yet. He still had a little under a year before he could even get his permit. But his smile told Angie that he liked it.

Grandfather Joseph asked Dominic, "This car looks almost new Dominic. Where did you find it?"

"We bought it from a collector in California a few weeks ago and Jack arranged for it to be shipped here."

"It looks like you did well Dominic. You make me proud." Joseph then glanced to see if Kristina could have heard him.

"Thank you Joseph. That means quite a bit, sir."

Eddy was jealous for sure but also shocked. He didn't understand how his Aunt Elizabeth and Uncle Dominic could possibly afford a car like the Cuda. His mother and father talked often about how poor his Uncle Dominic and Aunt Elizabeth were. Eddy grew up with money and always felt a little uneasy visiting them. And now Angie had a cool muscle car and they lived in this big house. He just didn't understand. Why was he feeling jealous of poor people? In a way he was feeling like Angie and her family were more like his family than he had believed.

Bella and Rosa felt happy for Angie. They never felt jealous of anything Angie had. Maria had taught them the same values as Dominic taught Angie.

Everyone returned from looking at Angie's new car and gathered in the Arizona Room. During this time everyone was involved talking and didn't notice that someone brought in and set up hors d'oeuvres on a table in the room. Dominic had been getting drinks for everyone from the bar in the back of the Arizona Room and the coordinator announced that hors d'oeuvres were served. Nobody noticed that it wasn't Lizzy. This was something different for Lizzy to do in her own house. Lizzy was extremely excited to have servers and a coordinator of her own. It almost felt as if she was still living in her parent's house.

This really impressed Lilly. She went to Lizzy and said, "I am impressed. I did not see you set this up nor do I remember seeing anything here when we returned."

"That is because we contracted a caterer for the party with servers included."

"Elizabeth, I am very impressed. Frankly, I never thought I would ever see this at your house. I cannot believe Dominic was OK with it."

"Why would you think that? I know you never listened when I tried to tell you and mother about how Dominic was raised. You never seemed to have interest. This is something Dominic has wanted to do almost since we met."

"I do not understand Elizabeth. Why would he want this? He grew up poor. Poor people do not do things like this. Maybe they dream about it but they do not do it."

"Lillian, if you and mother would have listened to me you would understand."

"Well, do not keep me in the dark, sis, wait a moment." Lilly said and she turned and said, "Mother, could you come over here for a moment please?" Both sisters were always very proper with their parents. Lizzy's family never used nick names. "Elizabeth has something to tell us."

Kristina walked over and asked what this was about and Lilly said, "Elizabeth has something to tell us that she claims we never wanted to hear." She said it kind of sarcastically because she did not believe it.

"Well, this sounds interesting." Kristina believed she always took the time to listen to her daughters but it never dawned on her that she would not have listened to something Lizzy had to say.

"Well Mother, we were just talking about the caterer, coordinator and servers that we contracted for today."

"What are you talking about? You have a caterer? For today?"

"Yes, we do mother."

But before she could say anything else her mother interrupted, "Really? I do not believe it!"

"Mother, today we have Angelina's birthday completely catered along with a coordinator and servers. I thought you would be impressed. What you and Lillian never wanted to listen to is that this has been our plan since before Dominic and I married. You and Lillian always dismissed me when I tried to tell you about Dominic's past. However, I tried to keep this from bothering me. I always knew that one day the both of you would listen. This may just be that day."

"I never dismissed anything with you." Kristina said in disbelief.

Just then Joseph, Lizzy and Lilly's father turned, walked over and said, "Dear, I witnessed this a few times if I remember correctly. This was one thing you never wanted to hear. You always changed the subject and had never heard Elizabeth out."

"I did?" Kristina replied looking surprised. "I am so sorry Elizabeth. I thought I always listened to both you and Lillian. Please tell me now what you tried to say. I am listening now."

Lizzy was a little shocked that her father said what he did because with things such as this he always remained silent and would leave it to Kristina. But Lizzy didn't know that her father had known about this since the first day he met Dominic.

This was not a typical response with her family. It took a minute for Lizzy to compose herself and say what she had wanted to say for some time. "Mother, Lillian," she paused for a minute, "you both have always made me feel as though I married poorly by continually putting Dominic down. You always said he was poor and insinuated that I would not be happy because of this."

"Elizabeth," her mother said, "I would never say anything like that." And Lilly agreed.

But Joseph made a kind of clearing his throat sound with an expression that said, "Really Sweetheart?" Joseph himself had been waiting for this moment for over18 years.

Kristina looked at Joseph at first with slight annoyance. Then she thought for a minute and replied to Lizzy, "OK, yes, I admit, I dismissed you. Somehow, thinking about this, I feel like I did not want to hear what you wanted to say. I am so sorry honey. It really never dawned on me that what you had to say was important." Then she looked like she was thinking very hard, "I mean, I, I, cannot believe I just said that. I always believed I was there for the both of you. I am really sorry Elizabeth. Now thinking about it I may have consciously dismissed you." Kristina was getting tears in her eyes. She was very disappointed in herself.

Lilly had tears in her eyes. When she thought about this she felt disappointed in herself as well. She never realized she had been doing this to her sister as she usually followed her mother's lead and never thought about it. She felt somewhat selfish. This was really affecting her because she didn't believe she could do this to her sister. She always thought that they were open about everything and didn't keep secrets. "I am very sorry as well Elizabeth. Please tell us what you tried to tell us all of this time."

Lizzy continued, "Well, as I just began to say, you never let me forget that Dominic was poor. You constantly reminded me of this. I felt that you were treating him like he was an outcast and even though I tried to put it out of my head it still did bother me."

Lizzy went on, "Yes, you could say Dominic was poor when we met, but he was not always poor. He and Maria grew up in an environment very much the same as we did. Dominic's father was killed in an automobile accident when he was 14 years old. His father was a partner at a large Law firm downtown. They lived in the Catalina Foothills on Camino Real not far from our house. Afterwards, his mother worked herself to death trying to provide for Dominic and Maria. She had to sell their house and she used the money from that to buy a small house on Yavapai close to Amphitheater High School, the same house we lived in until recently. She had never worked and had no experience so she could not find a well-paying job. I know the both of you were puzzled at why Dominic had such good manners and always acted like a gentleman. His mother continued to teach Maria and Dominic how to be a lady and gentleman until the day she died. With the exception of the first time you met Dominic you never commented on how articulate he is or how every time we visited he was a perfect gentleman. You were so stuck on saying that he was poor that I do not think you ever saw any of these things. Then when Dominic was 17 his mother died from pancreatic Cancer. That left Dominic and Maria alone and in the position of being placed in foster care. Dominic was able to keep he and Maria together in that most difficult time. He turned 18 a few weeks later and found a lawyer to help him legally become Maria's Guardian. Dominic then found a job and supported them both and worked very hard to get Maria enrolled at the University of Arizona. He assisted her and found grants to cover most of the costs of the University. He did amazing things for an 18 year old. This was only possible because of his parent's upbringing and teachings. I am not certain that Lillian and I could have done this had we been in his position."

"He has been working hard and looking forward to the time he could live and provide for Angelina and me in the same manner as his parents provided for him before they passed. This is why I fell in love with him the minute we first met. He is so well mannered, proper and he is such a gentleman. I always knew that someday he would impress you and you would finally see what I have seen in him from the moment we met."

Both Kristina and Lilly had tears in their eyes. They felt so sad that Dominic's father and mother had passed when he and Maria were so young, how Dominic and Maria had to change their whole life and that neither of them would listen to Elizabeth. They also felt as if they had been very pompous and they felt like they owed Dominic and Elizabeth an apology, actually much more than an apology.

Lilly reached out and hugged Lizzy while trying to hold back the tears. "I feel so terrible. Will you ever be able to forgive me for how insensitive I have been?" The tears were running down her cheeks.

Lizzy had tears in her eyes as well. "There is no need for forgiveness. You are my sister and I love you. I do not hold anything against anyone."

Just then Kristina pulled Lizzy from Lilly and hugged her. "I would never have believed that I could be so insensitive about anything with either of my daughters. I am so sorry honey. I promise I will take Dominic aside before we leave tonight and apologize properly for how I treated him all of these years."

"You do not need to mother, Dominic already understands."

"I very much want and need to, Elizabeth."

By now everyone was noticing the three of them standing together teary eyed. Maria walked over and said, "What happened? Did we miss something?"

"Ahh, No, nothing." Lilly said.

"You need to have some of these hors d'oeuvres, they are amazing!" Maria said.

Kristina went over to Joseph and asked, "Did you know about Dominic's family and his terrible loss? I got the feeling you did from you verbal nudges."

"Do you want the truth sweetheart?"

"I do not know, do I want to hear the truth?"

"Well, now that Elizabeth has told you the story I can tell you what I knew. Let's move to another room so we can have each other's attention." And they walked to another room. "I made a gentleman's promise and I could not break it. I promised that I would not talk about this until Elizabeth was able to tell you the story." Joseph began, "Remember the night when we first met Dominic?"

"Yes, I remember it like it was yesterday. However, I do not know why I remember it so clearly."

"Do you remember that I sat and talked with Dominic for some time before he left?"

Kristina was beginning to wonder if she did remember that night so clearly. She thought that Joseph and Dominic just had a quick friendly talk to get to know each other. "You knew since then? And you never told me? I cannot believe you kept this from me all these years. How could you?"

"Please let me finish Kristina. There is much more than you think and I made a promise to Dominic not to tell anyone until Elizabeth was able to tell you first."

"OK, I am listening. I think I am in for another shock tonight, please continue."

"We had just met Dominic and something about him puzzled me. You know how I usually know when someone is lying? Well, I felt something but it was not the usual way I feel when someone lies to me. This was different and immediately I knew I needed to talk to him that night. Do you remember you asked me how I felt about Dominic shortly after we met him?"

"Yes, and you said you liked him."

"Yes, I liked him at that moment, he said, 'Good Evening Sir, It is an honor.' Something about him, I felt pure sincerity. I had never met a young man that gave me that feeling. So before he left I made a point to talk to him alone. At first I believe he was scared to death but the fear only lasted a short time. I asked him how he met Elizabeth and he told me the story of her car breaking down and then Elizabeth bringing it back the next day for service. He then said something that shocked me, yes I was shocked. He said that he would never lie to me because he thought he was falling in love with Elizabeth already but he did not understand how that could be possible. Then, he told me about how she met him for coffee that night after work. And how she grabbed his face and kissed him."

"She did what?" Kristina said very cross.

"Calm down honey. Everything turned out fine, well better than fine as you can see. And Yes Elizabeth did that. Dominic told me that Elizabeth told him she was so afraid that if they did not kiss, they would not see each other again so she kissed him. I told him that I really admired his honesty and confessed that if I were in the same situation I do not think I could have told her father. We continued to talk and I got to the proverbial question of "What is it you do for a living Dominic?" He told me that he would tell me but he had a story to tell me first about his family but asked if I could keep it a secret. He was set on this because if he and Elizabeth eventually married he would want Elizabeth to tell you, not him. He pleaded with me to keep it a secret. So I reached out for his hand and told him, "One gentleman to another I swear I will keep this secret until the time comes that Elizabeth tells our family. So we shook on it. So you can understand why I never said anything?"

"Yes I can. And that is one thing I have always admired about you is your ability to keep a promise."

"He told me about his father and how he was a lawyer downtown and that he was killed in an automobile accident. I then told him that now I knew why his name sounded familiar. I did some business with that office and I believe I met his father, Dino, once. So Dominic continued and told me that they had to sell their house and move into a much lesser house and explained how his mother had no experience so she ended up with a clerk job at Seinfeld's Department Store. He told me the address of the house that he had lived in and I drove past the house the next day. There was a man trimming some bushes at the entrance of the driveway and I stopped and asked him if he knew anything about the people that used to live there. He told me that all he knew was that the father had died and they had to sell. So I knew Dominic was being truthful. It is walking distance from our house. He went on to tell me how hard she worked to keep them in food and cloths and that she passed away only 3 years later from pancreatic cancer. This left Dominic and Maria orphans. He explained how he immediately went to the office where his father worked and talked with the only lawyer he remembered and pleaded for his help to keep them together and how he wanted Maria to be able to go to college. Then he explained that he was able to get guardianship of Maria and he began to work full time the day after he graduated high school. All this time I was thinking what this kid did was more than amazing. So then he told me he was just an auto mechanic and he had hoped that sometime in the future he would be able to open his own shop.

I sat there dumbfounded. I asked him how old we was and he told me 19 years old. I just sat there and tried to absorb all of what I just heard. I told him his secret was safe and that he was a real gentleman and amazing kid for handling all of this so well. I told him he was always welcome at our house and that I wanted him to feel comfortable here. And that night is when I began to believe in fate."

"He told you all that? On the same night we met him?"

"Yes, but there is more."

"More? After all of that?"

"Well that night I decided that if he and Elizabeth were to marry, I actually think somehow I already knew they would, that I would do whatever it took to help him obtain his wish. So when Dominic was ready to open his shop, I gave them the money that they required. I knew I had to do this behind you back, and I am sorry, but I knew you would never agree unless you knew his story."

"I do not know what to say. Now I know why you always tried to push me to bless them when they got married. I could be angry at you for giving them money behind my back but now I cannot, I completely agree with what you did. But, but," Kristina couldn't get any more out because she was crying again.

"But what sweetheart?"

"But now I feel absolutely terrible for saying everything over the years to Elizabeth, and I do not think I have been all that nice to Dominic. It was so terrible of me." Kristina continued to cry. "How could I have been so heartless to my own daughter? I was so crass, so obtuse?"

Joseph took her in his arms and hugged her tight. "I am sure the both of them will understand sweetheart. I always knew this day would come. I just did not expect it on Angelina's birthday."

Kristina tried to compose herself. She told Joseph that she was going to go to the bathroom to clean and freshen up and she would be back as quick as she could.

Joseph said OK, although he never expected what Kristina would do when she returned from freshening up.

Kristina came back, smiled at Joseph and they went back to the party. They walked into the room where everyone was and Kristina said out loud, "Could everyone please gather here because I have something to say." Everyone gathered together and she cleared her throat. "Everyone, I would like all of you to hear what I have to say to Elizabeth and Dominic."

Kristina heard most everyone whispering saying, "What is this about?

"I am certain all of you know that I have not been exactly ecstatic about Elizabeth and Dominic being together. I have been obtuse to Dominic and have been treating Elizabeth, my own daughter, with contempt when I knew she had something to tell me. I just learned something tonight that has made me feel ashamed for acting this way to them both since they met. Elizabeth and Dominic, I want you to know that I am truly sorry for treating Dominic like he is unworthy to be your husband. And Elizabeth, I am truly sorry for constantly telling you that you made a mistake by marring Dominic. And Maria, I believe I have not treated you and your family as well as I should have either. I am so, so sorry and I want to do what I can to make it up to each of you. And I know this even affected Angelina as well. So this is for all of you."

Elizabeth couldn't believe her mother said this in front of everyone. She stood there in disbelief. Her mother never liked to admit she was wrong about anything. In fact, she was shocked. So she grabbed Dominic and Angelina's hands and went to her mother and they all hugged her and told her thank you and that they loved her. Kristina was feeling like she didn't deserve this.

Everyone else in the room clapped. After this, the tension in the room seemed to fade. Usually any time Kristina, Elizabeth and Dominic were together everyone else felt that tension. Now this feeling was gone. And some noticed that Kristina looked relieved—possibly even happier. They could see it in her expression.

At this point the whole tone of Angie's party changed. Everyone felt as though the underlying stress that everyone felt at family gatherings was gone. The whole atmosphere was more relaxed and everyone seemed much more jovial.

Soon it was dinner time and the server announced that dinner was served. Everyone moved to the dining room and all were impressed at the table settings. Along with contracting the caterers they rented very elegant place settings and serving dishes and utensils. They were fine china and silver. The table had an ornate linen tablecloth. There were two elaborate silver candelabras on the table which held five candles each lighting the table. The room lights were dimmed giving the ambiance of a table only lighted by candles. They had fine linen napkins that were trimmed with lace and elaborate crystal goblets at each place setting.

As everyone was sitting Joseph said, "Elizabeth, I believe you have outdone even Kristina. The table is perfect and if this meal is half as good as the aroma, we are in for a wonderful treat. Angelina, please wait to sit." He walked around to Angelina's chair, pulled it out for her, placed the napkin on her lap when she sat down and helped to move her chair into place. "Angelina," Joseph began, "I want to help to make your 18th birthday something to remember. Today has been an extraordinary event for you and for the whole family. I love you Angelina."

"Thank you Grandfather, I love you as well."

The meal began with a toast to Angelina from Dominic. The servers filled the adult's goblets with Chianti and the kid's goblets with cola. Dominic stood and raised his goblet, "Would everyone please join me in a toast to Angelina," Everyone raised their goblets. "Angelina, it is your 18th birthday and it brings joy to my heart, I watched you grow from your birth and you have become a beautiful woman. I could not be more proud. I believe if you follow your dreams and continue to strive for the best you will achieve all that you seek in life. I love you sweetheart." And he tipped his goblet to drink. Everyone clapped.

Angie was getting tears in her eyes. She looked around the table at everyone and said, "Thank you father, I love you too! If I may, I would like to say grace."

"Please do." Lizzy said.

Angie bowed her head and folded her hands as everyone did, "Heavenly Father, Thank you for this opportunity for my family to be together and share in this celebration. Thank you for our health and our love. Thank you for the feast we are about to partake in and may it nourish our bodies. Thank you for your love, caring and direction throughout our lives and bless us and everyone in the world. Amen"

At the finish of Grace, one of the servers turned on some background music. It was chamber music from the Baroque period. There was music from Bach; Handel; Vivaldi; Telemann; and others.

At this point the servers began serving the salad. It had iceberg and romaine lettuce with sliced cucumber and tomatoes, shredded carrots and cheddar cheese and croutons with Italian dressing. The next course was a small cup of minestrone soup. Then the main course was served which was blackened roast beef. Along with this there were garlic mashed potatoes, garlic parmesan green beans and fresh baked rolls with butter.

As everyone was eating Angie's grandfather asked, "Angelina, if you do not mind, I would like to hear what you plan to do after graduating high school."

Everyone turned to Angie, she took a sip of wine and put the goblet down, "Grandfather, what I would very much like would be to learn everything about running fathers business and take it over when he eventually retires."

Dominic had a surprised expression. He had never considered this. He hadn't thought of what Angie might do after high school yet.

Angie's grandfather sat for a moment and replied, "You would not want to go to college first?"

"Grandfather, I have put much thought into this. There is not an automotive technology program at the University of Arizona and nothing offered at any other school, which is what I would have chosen. And at this point I feel as though I am on the path of learning from studying and practical experience to excel in this field already. And I plan to study and obtain certifications from a new program that is offered here in Tucson now. It is called ASE, Automotive Service Excellence. What this shows is that the person performing the repairs is certified to know how to properly repair your car. And I want to be the first woman certified in Tucson. I look at this as a method of adding to the business for the future."

"Well, it sounds as though you have put much thought into this, Angelina. Have you discussed this with you father?"

"Not as of yet grandfather, but I am certain that now I will be."

Different discussions went on throughout dinner. When everyone was finished, it was time for the cake. The servers bought a small table and then the cake and set it on the table. It was a beautifully decorated sheet cake. It said, "Happy 18th Birthday Angelina" written in butter cream frosting. There were candles on it and they were ready to light them. Lizzy told them to go and light them. Angie stood and went to the cake and everyone else gathered around. They began singing "Happy Birthday" and afterwards one of her cousins said "Make a wish Angelina!"

Angie thought for a few seconds and blew out the candles as pictures were taken. Then everyone sat down for cake. The cake was two layers and filled with strawberries and cream. Everyone loved it.

Afterwards everyone gathered in the Arizona room so Angie could open her gifts. She received cloths; a few crime/suspense novels (these were her favorite) and Shelly gave her something she couldn't believe. It was a 1963 Nova gasser car model, very much like her father's car. She couldn't believe it! Shelly usually gave her cloths but this was almost a shock because Angie thought Shelly didn't really approve of her liking cars. Angie stood up and went to Shelly and gave her a big hug and told her, "Thank you so much Shelly. I cannot believe you would give me something like this."

"Well mother said that she had a feeling that you were going to try to impress me somehow so I thought about what I could do to impress you. And the model popped in my mind. But I think you made the greater impression cuz! I never would have believed you would dress like this."

Angie said, "I do not know, the way I see it your gift made a huge impression on me. It shows me that you acknowledge what I like."

"I do not want to argue but I feel the same Angelina. Before today I would never have believed you would dress like this for anything. I think I was shocked more than surprised. I still think you should be on the cover of Seventeen Magazine."

Angie got around to everyone to say thank you. Then she told Lizzy that she wanted to say something to everyone. Lizzy asked what it was about. Angie just repeated that she wanted to say something to everyone. Lizzy then said it was fine. Lizzy announced, "Angelina would like to address everyone. Please gather around."

Angie went and stood on one of the stairs leading to the Arizona room so she was high enough to see everyone. "I want to thank every one of you for celebrating my 18th birthday with me. And I want to thank all of you for always being there when I needed to talk, and I believe over the years I have talked to each of you many times. I love you all and I feel honored that you are my family." Everyone clapped.

Later that night Kristina got Elizabeth and Dominic alone. She had more to say to them. "I know that Joseph gave you the money to open the shop. Even yesterday I would have been furious but now that I know what happened to Dominic and Maria's parents and how they suffered from the loss and what Dominic did to keep them together, I fully approve of what Joseph did. And Dominic, I have seen how dedicated you are to Elizabeth and Angelina and how hard you have worked to make your business a success. And at times I wanted to give you praise but my obstinateness stopped me. I want you both to know that I feel like a huge weight has been lifted from my back. I meant it with all of my heart that I want to make it up to you. I want you both to know that both Joseph and I are here for you always."

"You do not need to do anything Mrs. Hall. I fully understand and I am sure Elizabeth feels the same." Dominic told Kristina.

"Dominic, would you please address me as mother from now on? I want you to know that you are as much a part of our family as Elizabeth. And Elizabeth, if I do not have an opportunity get to speak with Maria before she, Enzo and their children leave, would you please let her know that she and her family are also just as welcome here. I feel like Scrooge after the visits from the ghosts. And part of me is sad because I missed all of those years getting to know Dominic and Maria's family."

"Mother, are you alright?" Elizabeth asked. She couldn't believe she was hearing this from her mother.

"Yes dear. I have not been for some time, but now I am remarkably alright."

"I cannot believe this. Almost from the time I met Dominic you have shunned him and I just kept putting it out of my head. I never realized how much this did actually affect me mother. And for Lillian, she has always been very much like you. But I could never hold this against either of you. I love you both too much." Elizabeth told her mother.

Kristina just stood there teary-eyed. Dominic said, "Just like everything I have experienced with your family, mother, "mother," that actually feels good to say and it feels like it is somehow filling a void I have had since my mother died, God Bless her sole, I have felt that this day was coming for a while. You would think I would have been able to recognize these feelings and be prepared by now. It has been quite some time since the first time I felt as I do now and there have been many other times I have felt this way since. It is the same feeling as I had that day in June 1955 when a young woman in an Eldorado came into my life. I have said this before and will likely say it again; I believe we are all blessed because we have found each other."

Chapter 4

Dino Tucci was born in 1914. His mother was very sick during the pregnancy and they had been told that the baby may not make it. His parents prayed and did everything that doctors recommended in the hopes that the baby would survive. This was her third pregnancy and losing two babies had already taken a toll on her. The time came and the baby delivered with a mid-wife and survived, they named him Dino. For the most part the Dino was just fine. But it didn't take long before his parents noticed that Dino seemed to be stiff—as in his ability to move his arms and legs like a normal child. They learned that Dino had Cerebral Palsy but only a mild form. As he grew they only saw that he had difficulty because of stiff muscles and a slight limp. Otherwise he looked to be normal. They had some trouble with other kids teasing him but this didn't seem to affect Dino very much.

As Dino grew it could be seen that he continued to have stiffness in his body and the slight limp remained but that was all. No other symptoms ever developed. Dino's parents were happy that he would be able to live a mostly normal life. But because of this Dino couldn't play hard with other kids or get involved in sports in school. But he was very smart. He did well in all of his academic schooling and ended up going to college and graduating with a degree in Law from The University of Arizona. During school Dino met the love of his life, Carolina. They married in 1934 while they were both in college. They lived with Carolina's mother after they got married since they didn't have much money with both of them going to school full time. Dino had no issues with his studies and did complete the curriculum 1 semester early.

Then on May 1, 1936 Dominic was born. Carolina's mother was thrilled! She had wanted a grandchild more than anything and had been worried that Carolina wouldn't have any children. Carolina had been a twin but her sister died at childbirth so she ended up being an only child. And with the problems Carolina's mother had with childbearing she worried.

Dino was then was hired by a large law firm in downtown Tucson. And about 1 year later on April 21, 1937, Maria was born. Carolina's mother felt blessed to have two grandchildren now. Dino and Carolina found it very difficult to take care of two babies while Carolina was still in school full time. Carolina told her mother that she was just going to leave school so she could take care of her children, but her mother would not allow it. She insisted that Carolina continue and graduate. No one in her family had had the opportunity to go to college and she desperately wanted Carolina to be the first. So Carolina's mother did what she could to help until graduation. Carolina graduated with a Bachelor of Science degree in Home Economics.

Dino worked hard and moved up through the ranks quickly. Within a few years he was a partner. And also during this time he and Carolina had been associating with many of the rich around the city. From this they quickly learned the mannerisms that the rich have. Carolina became friends with a few of the ladies and they taught her how to be a proper lady. Dino had no problem picking up the manners and language of the rich. Soon they both fit in as if they had lived that type of life since birth.

Then early in 1941 Dino and Carolina had saved enough to buy a house so they began looking and found one that they loved. It was one of the first houses that John Murphey built. They were not the first owners but the house was only a few years old so to them it was new. The address was 5276 N. Camino Real, north east of River Rd. and Campbell Ave. It was a big house with 5 bedrooms and 3 bathrooms. They lived there with their son and daughter until the tragedy in 1950.

Chapter 5

In June of 1950 shortly after the kids were out of school for the summer, two Police officers knocked on Carolina's door and notified her that Dino had been killed in an auto accident. She went into shock. It was fortunate that Dominic and Maria were there. They were shocked as well but they did not pass out like their mother. One of the officers helped Dominic carry his mother to the couch and lay her down. They were very professional and told Dominic and Maria that they were sorry and gave them information as to where they could go to see the body and information to find a family counselor if the needed one and then promptly left. Maria was crying as Dominic went and got a cold compress to put on their mothers forehead. He was in shock but was more worried about his mother. After a few minutes Carolina came to and when she saw Dominic and Maria, she knew it was real. The thoughts running through Carolina's mind were frantic. "What are we going to do now? How will we live? What do I need to do now? What about a funeral? I do not know what to do?" and she thought more. She took comfort that Dominic and Maria were there giving her what support they could but they were only 14 and 13 years old. She was panicked. She usually confronted her problems head on but Dino was always there to support her. She never expected her husband to be gone so young. She never even thought about it. She counted on him to do so many things for the family as well as provide for them. She wasn't really coherent when Maria started talking to her. She looked like she was staring into nothingness.

Maria was saying through tears, "Mother, Mother, Mother can you hear me? Mother," Maria shook her a little, "Mother, we need you, Mother?"

Dominic also was concerned. He stood there looking at Carolina with sad tears in his eyes.

Carolina finally realized Maria was trying to talk to her. "Maria sweetheart, I am so sorry."

"It is not your fault." Maria replied. "It is not your fault. What are we going to do Mother?"

Carolina began to compose herself. Inside she knew that she was a strong woman but this was a complete shock. And now she is faced with a myriad of things to do.

Throughout her grieving she will need to plan the funeral. Then figure out how they will live without Dino's income.

They had Mass for Dino at St. Augustine Cathedral on Stone. Everyone from the lawyer's office attended along with many prominent people from the Tucson area that they knew. Carolina tried to thank everyone for coming but had a very difficult time talking through her tears. However, one of the lawyers that Dino worked with impressed on her. This was Mr. Clarence Humboldt. He made a point to tell Carolina that if she needed any legal help for anything to please call him and she would not need to pay him. Mr. Humboldt told Carolina that he felt he owed it to Dino since Dino had helped him through some very difficult cases and he was never able to properly thank him or pay him back. He left her his card and told her helping her was the least he could do. Carolina thanked him and said that she may call him.

Dino was buried in Holy Hope Cemetery on Oracle Rd. Carolina was fortunate that they had some savings to cover the costs.

Carolina determined that in order for them to be able to live they will need to sell their house in the Foothills and buy a small cheaper house in the city. Maybe they will have enough to buy a cheap car to get around, like a 1939 or 1940 Chevy or Ford she thought. Then she will get a job. But Carolina had no idea what she would be qualified to do. She had a Bachelor Degree in Home Economics and never worked. She had no idea what she could do, so she asked everyone she knew and searched through the newspaper every day. She finally found a job listing at Steinfeld's, a large department store on Stone and Pennington.

Carolina filled out the job application at the store and she was told to please wait. In about a half an hour she was called to speak to someone from the personnel department and that person called in the store manager. The store manager talked to her and found out she was the wife of the lawyer that was killed in the big auto accident recently and that she had 2 kids, 13 and 14 years old. He brought her to Women's Clothing, the department with the job opening. He found the department supervisor and she discussed the job with Carolina. They hired her on the spot. She thanked the store manager and the department supervisor very politely and was told that she would begin the following Monday.

Carolina cleaned up the house with the help of Dominic and Maria. It was difficult for her because she had so many wonderful memories there. She didn't want to sell the house but there was no way she could afford to pay for it and raise her kids. She looked for and found a realtor to represent selling the house as well as for the one they needed to buy. The realtor told her that she would have no problem selling the house. It was in a very desirable location and the housing market was booming.

While the house was on the market Carolina took Dominic and Maria and went house hunting. Since they didn't have a car (it was destroyed in the accident that killed Dino) now they needed to take a cab to the neighborhood where they were looking. They looked at a few houses and were repulsed somewhat. They found the houses kind of cheap looking, rundown and small, nothing like the one they were currently living in. But they didn't have much of a choice. They found one at 315 E. Yavapai Rd. It wasn't great like the house they had to sell but it would do. It was a 3 bedroom 2 bath house with two places to park off of the street covered by the roof. Dominic and Maria would continue to have their own rooms. The house was small and not what they were used to but the asking price was good and it is within close proximity to Amphitheater High School. (Less than 2 blocks) Carolina called the realtor and told him she wanted to make an offer on this house.

Everything worked out and they sold the old house and bought the new house. She paid the house in full and they ended up with money remaining after the deal so Carolina went to a car dealer to look for a decent used car, something big enough for them but not too expensive. She found a 1948 Chevy Fleetmaster sedan 4 door for $700 that was in good shape. It ran well and it was a pretty good price, so she bought it.

Now they have a house and a car and some money remaining from the original house sale. Carolina put this in the bank in a savings account. They had moved the furniture that they could from the old house, sold what was remaining and moved into the new house. She began the job at Steinfelds and had been working there for a month already. Things were looking somewhat better now. Now Dominic and Maria could walk to school instead of riding the bus and she had a straight drive south on Stone to her job at Steinfeld's.

Since Carolina has some extra time now that Dino was no longer around she found herself thinking about him. She was feeling lonely and began to cry. Maria walked into the room and saw her mother crying. She knew why she was crying and went to her and hugged her and cried along with her. Maria asked, "Why did this happen to us mother? It is not fair. Why did father have to die?"

"I do not know, sweetie, I do not know."

Dominic heard the crying, (this was a small house) so he went over to his mother and sister. "I wish I knew what to say. I feel lost too." He and Maria would be consoling their mother for quite some time as she had a difficulty recovering from the trauma of her husband passing.

Maria would continue going to Prince Middle School for 8th grade and Dominic would be a freshman at Amphitheater High School now in September of 1950.

Chapter 6

It was 1953 and Carolina continued worrying that Dominic and Maria wouldn't be able to go to college and she knew this was necessary for them to be able to have the means to live well like they did before Dino died. This was only a setback she thought. Somehow she would figure out how to put both of them through college. Both Dominic and Maria had always done extremely well in school so she knew they would be able to get accepted, she just needed to figure out how to pay for it.

But still Carolina worried. She didn't have much left from the sale of their house as it wasn't easy to have two teenagers and a house to support, and only on her salary from Steinfeld's. As frugal as she was, she couldn't keep from continuing to draw money from the savings account but she didn't have a choice. Some nights she worried herself to sleep. She worried about paying bills and keeping food on the table. She worried about possible car trouble and keeping up the house, how she still missed Dino. She tried to keep from letting these worries get to her kids because she felt that this wasn't baggage that teenagers should have.

But Dominic and Maria knew something was bothering her. They would try to ask her why she wasn't as cheerful as she used to be. They both missed that. But felt that this was all because she missed their father and didn't make much money. They both liked how she had told them the story about how she and Dino met and about their wedding. And they both missed their father as much as their mother did. There were times that she would be telling them a story about something before they were born and she couldn't keep tears from rolling down her cheeks. But they didn't know what they could do to help her to feel better. So they always told her how much they loved her, and it seemed like it helped a little.

The first week of March1953, Carolina began to feel a strong pain in her abdomen. At first she thought it is gas or maybe she is getting an ulcer from all of the worrying she has done in the past few years. She had felt this same pain quite a bit lately but not as intense. She didn't tell Dominic and Maria however as she didn't want to burden them. It had been very difficult for her working full time and trying to raise and teach her kids the same manners and etiquette that she was taught. Since Dino died she felt as though she was killing herself taking care of her kids, working and trying to bring them up as a Lady and a Gentleman. This was how she was raised and how she and Dino were raising Dominic and Maria. Just because she was alone now and struggling didn't mean she couldn't continue to teach them these things. She was very determined and she always knew that both of them would eventually do very well and live the same kind of life she did.

It wasn't long before Carolina felt too sick to prepare food and do her regular chores. It was the beginning of April 1953 when Dominic came home and found Maria next to their mother in her bed. Carolina was feeling so sick that she couldn't finish preparing the night's dinner. When he saw Maria's tears he knew something was wrong. His mother was very weak and she didn't look very well. Dominic told Maria that they needed to take her to the emergency room. They were both worried now as they never had seen their mother sick like this. She was a strong woman and had never been sick.

Dominic went and started the car and then helped his mother into the passenger seat. Maria got in the back seat and they drove to St. Mary's Hospital because it was the only emergency room that he knew of. He pulled up and Maria got out and ran into the Emergency Room to get help. She screamed that her mother needed help so they rushed out a wheel chair and helped Dominic move their mother out of the car and into the wheelchair.

As soon as Dominic and Maria were inside the nurse began asking for information about their mother. Carolina told them her name and they could see she was in poor condition as she struggled just with her name. The nurse asked Dominic and Maria many questions about what happened. Maria told the nurse that she came home from school and found her mother on the kitchen floor bent over and holding her stomach. She said that she helped her to get to her bed and that's when her brother came home. Then they left for the emergency room.

They rushed Carolina away to a patient bay and told Dominic and Maria that they could go to the waiting room until they knew more about their mother. Dominic and Maria sat down and waited. Maria was still crying but she managed to tell Dominic that she felt in her stomach that it was bad. Maria always seemed to know what would happen. Dominic didn't understand how. Dominic tried to calm her down with no avail. He sat next to her and put his arm around her. All they could do now was wait.

Dominic and Maria had been sitting there for hours when a Sister came to talk to them. (St. Mary's Hospital was a Catholic Hospital and it was originally opened by the Seven Sisters of St. Joseph of the Carondelet and at this time it was still run by the Catholic Church, however, this changed in 2016 and is now corporately owned) She introduced herself as Sister Ellyn. She asked, "Are you Maria and Dominic?"

Dominic replied, "Yes, Ma'am."

"Will the two of you please come with me to a room where we can talk privately?"

"Yes, Ma'am." Dominic replied.

The Sister led them to a small room with a table and chairs and asked them to sit down as she closed the door.

Then Sister Ellyn began to ask questions about their mother and family history. "Where is your father?"

Dominic said, "Our father was killed in a car accident 3 years ago, ma'am."

"I'm so sorry, that must have been difficult for all of you. Do you know much about your mother's family, such as any diseases or aliments that may have run in her family?"

"There is nothing that we know of Ma'am. Why? What is wrong with our mother?" Dominic asked.

"They don't know yet, they are running tests. There are many things that can cause abdominal pain. But based on observations by the doctors, I won't lie to you, I feel as though you need to know this, they are suspecting pancreatic cancer."

After hearing that Maria began crying. Dominic was trying to be strong but tears were forming and he began to shake. Maria looked at Dominic and forced out through her crying, "What are we going to do Dom? We do not have anyone else."

"I do not know Maria. I do not know."

Sister Ellyn was very concerned. She asked them how old they were. Dominic said, "I am 17 and she is 16, Ma.." He tried to say Ma'am but couldn't get it out. At this point he began to cry.

"Dears, they aren't positive yet, but I don't want to give you false hope. We have a program to help kids that lose their parents. I will get you the contact information right now." She got up and excused herself and left.

Maria grabbed a hold of Dominic and hugged him hard crying. "What are we going to do? What happens to us now? Everyone knows that that kind of cancer is really dreadful. Oh Mother." She continued crying on Dominic.

Dominic was probably more upset than when he heard that his father had died. His mother was everything to them. He started thinking about this. Dominic always could clear his head to think through a problem in an emergency regardless of what is happening. He instantly thought of a plan. He told Maria, "I need to talk to that lawyer friend of father's. I think he can help us. And I will get a job."

"You graduate in less than a month. You are going to quit now, after everything mother taught us?"

"I did not say that, I can get a part time job at the gas station that Jack's father owns. Then when I graduate I can work full time." Jack is Dominic's best friend from school since the beginning of middle school. His father owns a gas station on Stone and 5th Street and they do repairs on cars. Dominic was hoping that Jack's father would give him a job. "But I need to talk to father's friend. It might work. My birthday is next week and I will be 18 then. It might work."

"What might work Dom?"

"I am going to go and see father's friend and plead with him to get guardianship of you. We have a house, a car all paid for. Then we can care for mother and I will make the money now, I think."

"You would do that for mother and me? Really?"

"You are my family and you are my life, I love you and mother. I have to do this. What other choice do I have?"

Just then Sister Ellyn knocked on the door then came in, closed the door and sat down. Dominic stood up as a courtesy. "You may sit Dominic. We have a few programs that may be able to help you and Maria, Dominic. You don't really have any way to pay for you mothers hospital costs do you?"

"I did not even think about that Ma'am. But we do not have much money and our mother works for Steinfeld's. I do not think she will be working there anymore now. So I do not know how we could pay for this, Ma'am." Dominic told Sister Ellyn.

"I think the hospital will be able to work something out for this. I have to say Dominic, it is refreshing to see a young boy that is so polite and proper, that is not very common and I respect you for that."

"Our mother practically beat it into our heads that we be polite and proper to everyone, Ma'am. Is there any news about our mother?"

"No, nothing yet. The sisters here have a program to help people in your position. Since both of you are not yet 18 years old you cannot live on your own. So if the worst happens we need to be prepared. So I can get you in touch with Sister Grace. She will help you in the event of the worst. In the meantime, we will all pray for the two of you and your mother."

"Thank you Sister," Dominic began, "If we cannot live on our own what will happen to us?"

"If the worst happens, Sister Grace will work to find foster care for each of you."

"But I will be 18 in a week Ma'am. Does that not mean anything?"

"Oh, I didn't know that Dominic. Then we will only need to place Maria in foster care. Will you have a place to live Dominic?"

"Yes Ma'am. Our house is paid for so I will live there. Why could Maria not live there with me then?"

"Well dear, you are not her legal guardian. And as far as I know a sibling cannot be a guardian of another sibling."

Hearing this hurt Dominic. He was sure that Maria was worried that they would be split-up; he was already feeling the loss of not only his mother but his sister as well.

"Sister, when can we see our Mother?" Maria asked.

"We can go and see her now." Sister Ellyn brought them to their mother and let them go in and see her.

Maria ran to her mother's bedside in tears. "Mother,"

Carolina turned and looked drugged up. "Hi sweetie." She said sounding like she was half asleep.

Maria started to say mother again but couldn't get it out so she just bent over to hug her. Carolina reached around with one arm to hug her back.

Dominic was standing next to Maria. He couldn't hold back the tears this time. She didn't look very well. He thought she looked worse than when they brought her to the emergency room earlier. He had a gut feeling that she did have cancer even though the doctors didn't know yet.

"Where is Dom? Carolina asked.

"I am right here mother. We will be here every minute we can."

"I am sorry, I am so sorry for this. I did not want to do this to you."

Dominic told her, "Do not feel sorry, mother. It is not your fault."

They stayed until the Sister said they needed to leave. They went home and tried to sleep. Tomorrow he will need to go to the office at school and after school he will need to go to Prince Middle school office to tell them what is happening. He was sure that his mother couldn't go to the schools.

Their mother was diagnosed with pancreatic cancer and they started her on Doxorubicin to try to slow the growth. But since it was in such an advanced state it didn't help. She passed away a week later in front of Dominic and Maria. They were both crying.

"Maria, let's go find the chapel. I think that is the only place we can be alone for a while."

"OK Dom, I want to pray for her."

They walked into the chapel at St. Mary's and went to the front pew. They were the only ones there, although it didn't matter. They knelt down there and tried to pray but their tears made it to difficult.

The Hospital Chaplin walked in and saw Dominic and Maria kneeling at the front pew, he could hear crying so he knew they were hurting. He was wondering if they were the children of the lady that just passed away.

He walked to them and asked why they were there and if there was something he could help them with.

Dominic cleared his throat and wiped his face, "Our mother just passed away, she was all we had, Father, now we are all alone."

"My son, you are never truly alone. You always will have our heavenly father with you. And you have each other."

"But they want to split us up because we are not adults yet. That would destroy us." Dominic told the Father.

"I'm sorry but I cannot do anything about that my son. But we can pray together. This may help you feel better. May I ask your names?

"I am Dominic and this is my sister Maria, Father."

"It is good to meet you two." The Father knelt down. He began by crossing himself, "In the name of the Father, and of the Son, and of the Holy Spirit." Dominic and Maria followed along with him.

"Heavenly Father, We pray to you to give Dominic and Maria courage to endure and understand that their beloved mother is in Heaven with you. Give them strength to continue their lives as your devoted children. Please show them the way as they are feeling lost and alone need your guidance. Give them comfort and direction that they may see that their lives are only just beginning. Heavenly Father please show them your love and guide them.

Our Father, Who art in heaven,
hallowed be Thy name.
Thy kingdom come,

Thy will be done
on earth, as it is in heaven.
Give us this day our daily bread,
and forgive us our trespasses,
as we forgive those who trespass
against us,
and lead us not into temptation,
but deliver us from evil.
AMEN"

The Chaplin then crossed himself as he said, "In the name of the Father, and of the Son, and of the Holy Spirit. My children please go in peace."

Dominic was able to thank the Father and he took Maria's hand, they stood and left. They both then went to St. Augustine Cathedral to talk to the father that held Mass when their father died to find out if he would do the same for their mother.

The Father told Dominic and Maria that he would hold Mass for their mother and he just needed to know the date. He also offered them help to contact everyone that they wanted to invite and help them plan the funeral. He also gave them the contact information for Holy Hope Cemetery

They had Mass for their mother at St. Augustine Cathedral on Stone the following Saturday. Most everyone from the lawyer's office attended along with many prominent people from the Tucson area that their parents knew just as with Dino's funeral. Dominic and Maria tried to thank everyone for coming but had a very difficult time talking. Maria was crying and Dominic had a lump in his throat from forcing himself not to cry. The same lawyer that offered help to their mother came up to them and said he was so sorry that Carolina passed away. Again this was Mr. Clarence Humboldt. He told Dominic that he could give them any legal help for any accounts or their taxes. He gave Dominic his card like he did with Carolina when Dino passed away. Dominic thanked him and said that he would keep him in mind.

Carolina was buried in Holy Hope Cemetery on Oracle Rd. next to Dino. They paid with some money their mother had left them before she died. Now they didn't have much left and they were not certain what they would do about that.

Dominic and Maria went home and both cried. After a while Dominic thought it would be good to call the schools and tell them they would not be there Monday. He walked to a pay phone near the high school. He explained that their mother passed away and they needed to see a lawyer to tie up loose ends.

Since Dominic and Maria were now in a position where they were about to be separated, Dominic thought that he needed to see Mr. Clarence Humboldt. He did offer his help although he didn't know if he would be able to help keep them together. Dominic looked for the card that Mr. Humboldt gave him at the funeral and decided to go and talk to him. Maria asked Dominic what they would do even with a lawyer's help and Dominic reminded her that he can work part time until he graduates and full time after. But he needed to find out if he could get guardianship of her. Maria was afraid they would get split up anyway. She didn't think it would be possible and as upset as she was she couldn't think about anything else.

On Monday morning Dominic drove downtown to the office where his father had worked. He hoped Mr. Humboldt would see him. He would have called first but they didn't have a phone. He found a place to park and walked to the front of the building and went in the main entrance. He walked up to the receptionist and said, "Excuse me Ma'am, would it be possible for me to see Mr. Clarence Humboldt?"

"I can ring his office, who shall I say is calling on him?" the receptionist asked.

"My name is Dominic Tucci. My father, Dino Tucci worked and partnered with Mr. Humboldt before he passed away."

"Oooh, I remember your father. We were all shocked and saddened when he passed away. I was so sad for your family. I'll ring him now." It had only been 2 days since their mother's funeral and he did offer help so he shouldn't be surprised to see Dominic. The receptionist turned and told Dominic, "Mr. Humboldt will see you right away. Please go down this hallway and it is the third door on the right." She said as she directed Dominic to the hallway.

"Thank you, Ma'am." Dominic was very nervous because he had never been in a lawyer's office. But he needed help for himself and Maria so he was willing to do whatever was necessary. He walked to the door, opened it and entered. It was a small waiting area with what he thought was either a secretary of paralegal.

As Dominic turned from closing the door behind him the secretary said, "Hello sir, you must be Mr. Tucci's son Dominic?"

"Yes Ma'am."

"Mr. Humboldt said I should send you right in." she said pointing to the door on the right side of the desk.

"Thank you very much, Ma'am."

She said, "You're welcome."

Dominic knocked on the door and heard, "Come in Dominic."

Dominic opened the door, walked through and closed the door.

"I am so sorry about your mother, son. She was one of the sweetest and most dedicated lady's I've ever met." He looked closer at Dominic, "Wow it's amazing! You look just like you father! I don't know why I didn't see the resemblance at the funeral. So what can I do for you Dominic?"

Dominic was shaking and didn't know what to say.

"Sit down and relax. There's nothing to be afraid of here. What is it that I can help you with son? You know, you father and I worked together for a long time. He was a good partner and friend."

Dominic dug down and got some courage and said, "Thank you sir. Mr. Humboldt, I am 17 years old and my sister is 16. I will be 18 next week and I graduate in a few weeks. Now that both of our parents have passed away and there are no other relatives the Sister at St. Mary's Hospital told me that Maria will be placed in foster care within a week. We are all we have now. I do not know what to do. It may sound odd but I feel like I am being punished. First my father is killed, then my mother passes away from cancer and now they want to take my sister, sir. Is it possible for me to obtain guardianship or something for her? I have already found a job and start part time next Monday and will be full time right after I graduate. Our house and car are paid for as well so I should be able to make enough to support us."

Mr. Humboldt sat back in his chair looking at Dominic. "You really think that you can provide for you and your sister? You will be taking on a big job, son."

"Yes sir, Mr. Humboldt. Maria is very dedicated to her school work and gets very good grades. We had been taking care of my mother before she passed away. I graduate from High School in a few weeks and as I said earlier, I begin a part time job Monday which will be full time as soon as I graduate. Maria has one year of high school remaining and shortly before she graduates she will be 18 years old. Oh, and she has also been applying for grants for the University of Arizona. I want very much for her to be able to go to college, sir. And I fear that if she is placed into foster care it will cause her so much trauma that she may not even complete high School. And I will feel lost without her around. We just lost our loving mother and I cannot bear to think about losing Maria as well, sir."

"I'm impressed, son. I almost feel like I am talking to your father. You have thought through this situation well. Although I don't think that it would be easy for you. But it does sound like you care for your sister very much. This is something I would expect after knowing your father. This is the right thing to do. So I will help you as a favor to your father. Your father helped get me out with some very difficult cases and I never was able to properly thank him or return the favors. He was a good man and I can see he was a good father as well."

"Thank you so much Mr. Humboldt. Oh, I almost forgot. Do we need to get our house and car put in our names? Both are paid for. What do I need to do, sir?"

"The house and car will be just filing some paperwork and won't be a problem. But this will be a unique case as I am not aware of a brother ever applying for guardianship for a sibling. But don't worry, we will succeed. You will need to prepare to sit with me and a Judge and you will need to tell the judge the same things that you told me. However, when this is scheduled I will coach you on how to state everything. Do you own a suit and tie Dominic?"

"I have a pair of dress pants a dress shirt, a tie and a nice suit coat sir."

"That will be fine. I will file the papers right away to temporarily block any move to place Maria into foster care. Then I will prepare the papers for guardianship. The judge may want another adult to commit to assist if you have any difficulties during this guardianship. Is there anyone that you could ask, Dominic?"

"Sir, we have no family besides ourselves and I do not believe my mother kept in touch with anyone she knew after my father died. I cannot think of anyone." Dominic said with a worried look. "I cannot lose my sister sir." Tears formed in his eyes. He tried to hold them back but could not. He was so worried that they would be separated that he began to shake again. "If I need someone I do not know what I could do, sir"

"We will figure something out if the question comes up. In the meantime, go home and relax. I will get in touch with you in a few days. Do you have a telephone Dominic?"

"No sir. We could not afford one and I do not think I will be making enough at my new job to afford one either. Is this going to be a problem, sir?"

"Oh no, don't worry. Many people in Tucson don't have phones. Here fill out this basic information form for me. It asks for your names and your address and such. Put you and your sister's full legal names and your address. That's all I need right now. I will get in touch with you to discuss specifics in a few days. Now go home and relax, son. I can see this was very difficult for you. But don't worry, I will take care of everything. It was very good to meet you Dominic."

"Likewise sir. And thank you again sir."

"You know Dominic you are just what I would have expected of Dino's son. Very polite, proper and well spoken, not what most would expect from a 17 year old."

"Thank you sir." Dominic said as he waited for Mr. Humboldt to stand. He then stood up shook Mr. Humboldt's hand and said, "I cannot thank you enough. Maria will be very happy to hear this." He turned and left.

Mr. Humboldt smiled and thought that maybe he should have gotten married and had children. He liked Dominic very much.

Mr. Humboldt was able to get guardianship granted without too much difficulty. And since Dominic turned 18 by the time everything was signed and filed he didn't need to have another adult for supervision.

After graduation, Dominic was able to work full time as a mechanic at Jack's father's gas station. The summer went by without too many problems although it was difficult for Dominic to learn about paying the utilities and then he had to save some money for property taxes. Mr. Humboldt schooled him on how to prepare to pay the property taxes and how to file income taxes and offered to help them when the time came. Maria began senior year and graduated high school. Dominic learned everything and anything he could from Jack and his father. He learned quickly and learned some tuning tricks from Jacks father that Jack hadn't picked up.

Maria was able to get grants for school with Dominic's help and went to U of A and majored Sociology. She and Dominic continued to live in the house that their mother bought after their father died. Dominic worked hard. He wanted to open his own shop someday because he knew he could do much better. He kept in contact with Mr. Clarence Humboldt because he had helped Dominic and Maria more than he could have expected.

Chapter 7

Joseph Hall worked any job he could find. He always had trouble finding work with having a birth defect. This caused a limp from the day he began walking as a small child. It wasn't bad from his point of view because he could still function fine he thought. But at that time most people were afraid of hiring someone with a disability like this. This kept him out of WWII as well. He tried to enlist to fight for his country but was turned down. Besides having the disability he also had two kids already 2 & 3 YO. He helped any way he could: he collected metal, paper, rubber and anything else that was needed. He eventually got odd jobs from people that were impressed by what he was doing to support the war. Eventually he got a steady job working at a newspaper.

He and Kristina had some money that he had inherited when his father died and they had that tucked it away in the bank. And they saved as much money as they could with the thought that they would need it one day. This ended up being their savior when Joseph met John Murphey. John came into the newspaper agency looking to place an ad for investors to finance his dream to develop the 7000 acres of land in the Foothills that he bought from the government shortly before the depression.

Joseph met John Murphey when he was learning to do type-setting. This was 1935 and recovery from the depression was beginning. Joseph overheard Mr. Murphey talking about his ad and asked him if he could talk to him sometime outside of work. He told Mr. Murphey he thought he may know someone that would be interested in investing in his development. Mr. Murphey, of course, agreed as he didn't want to lose a prospect. So they agreed to meet right after he got off of work.

John Murphey met with Joseph just as he agreed. Joseph told him that it was he that wanted to invest. Mr. Murphey thought it was a joke and started laughing and said, "How much could someone like you have to invest? I need serious investors, son" and turned to walk away.

Joseph stopped him and said, "Sir, I am not joking. I have $1000, some of which I inherited from my father when he passed away and I have been saving every penny I could since I started working." (In 1935 $1000 was a lot of money—about $20,000 in 2022 money)

"Well Joseph that is a lot of money for someone like you. Are you sure you would want to risk it with me, son?"

"I have been saving because I always knew that one day I would have the right opportunity come and I believe this is it, sir. I have this gut feeling that this is what I need to do, sir"

"Do you have a wife, son?"

"Yes sir. And I have two little girls, 2 & 3."

"What will your wife think of you giving me all of your money?"

"I am not sure, sir. But I would like to tell her about this and afterwards I would ask if you would come and explain like you did to my boss."

"I can do that son."

So they made plans for Mr. Murphey to visit Joseph and his family the next day after work. Joseph knew this was the right thing to do and he rushed home to tell Kristina.

Kristina was not so sure about giving someone all of their money. This was a fortune to them and she thought it would be there for an emergency or maybe to buy a house. Joseph assured her that this is what he had been thinking about since he got his inheritance. Kristina didn't know. Joseph told her that this fellow, Mr. John Murphey was going to meet them there after work tomorrow and he would explain his plan and show them some drawings of the types of houses he will be building. She agreed with some apprehension.

Mr. Murphey showed Joseph and Kristina drawings and assured Kristina that this would be a legal agreement prepared by an attorney.

Mr. Murphey picked them up on Saturday afternoon and drove them to the area at River Rd. and Campbell Ave. At this time the streets were dirt roads so it was dusty. He explained that Josias Joesler was his architect and he had been busy working on drawings for a few houses. He walked with them and showed them a couple of the architect's drawings of the houses. He pointed out stakes in the ground showing where the first few houses will be and the size of the lots. Kristina thought they were beautiful and thought that maybe someday they could live in a house like these.

Kristina still was reluctant but agreed. This was a lot of money to her. She worried that this Mr. Murphey would take the money and disappear. But she signed the contracts and agreed to the terms. As each house was sold they would receive a portion of the profits. He only needed a bit more to begin but he was certain that he would find someone to invest this as well.

Mr. Murphey found other investors for the project. Now he had sufficient funds to begin. It took about 7 months from the day that Joseph and Kristina gave him their money when the first house was built. And the second house was already under construction.

The first house sold almost immediately. The second house sold just as fast. Mr. Murphey visited Joseph and Kristina to bring them their first check. He explained how the first two houses had sold as soon as they listed them. Joseph asked him how much more they could make if they put the proceeds back into the project. Mr. Murphey was hoping he would ask because using all of the proceeds would allow him to build more houses faster.

Joseph told Mr. Murphey to put their profits back into the project for now. This was a very good decision because this was the beginning of Joseph and Kristine building their wealth. After a short time Joseph began investing in the stock market. He found that he was good at it. It didn't take long for him to make the kind of money it would take to buy one of John Murphy's houses.

In 1940 they were able to buy one of the houses that Mr. Murphey built. This was 4801 n. La Lomita. It was a 5 bedroom 5 bath Spanish Colonial house.

Chapter 8

On Tuesday June 7, 1955 Dominic's life changed again. Dominic woke and remembered the dream he had had. He needed to tell Maria about it because it was unlike any other dream he had in the past. He went to Maria's room, knocked lightly because he didn't want to wake her if she was sleeping.

"Dom?"

"Yes Maria. Could we talk for a minute please?"

"You may come in." Dom opened the door and went in. Maria was sitting on her bed studying as usual. "You know I will always have time for you Dom. What is it?" She could see that something was bothering him.

"Well, last night I had a confusing dream. It was all dense fog and I was just there. Then I heard this voice but it was in my head."

"A voice in your head?"

"Yes, in my head. It was a calming voice and it said, 'Dominic, you are a good man and you have a good heart. You have cared for Maria and helped her through your mother's death. You worked hard to keep the two of you together during a difficult time. You will be rewarded when you least expect it.' That was it. It has been bothering me since I woke."

"What do you think it means Dom? Who do you think was talking?"

"What first came to mind I find difficult to believe. But I cannot think of anything else." Dom said shaking his head back and forth as if saying "No"

"What was you first thought? I think I know but I need to hear you say it."

Dom thought for a minute then said, "I thought it was God. But it could not be. Why would he talk to me? I am not anything special."

"You are special to me Dom. You gave me hope when I had lost it. That alone makes you special. You kept us together and you made certain I got registered and began college and you have supported the both of us. Who else has or would have done that? And do you not think God talks to people when they are at a low point with themselves? He is always watching over us all."

"But the whole time I have been depressed and struggling to keep myself going. I do not see myself as special. If I was special I would be happy."

Maria thought for a minute and then said, "Maybe you will be getting a reward somehow for everything you have done and to cheer you up. That is what I think Dom. And you deserve it."

Dominic thought about what Maria said for a few minutes. "Well, OK. You are always so optimistic Maria. I love you. You always can make me feel better when I am down, thanks."

Dominic got ready and left for work. "Just another day," Dominic thought, "Ho Hum." He began working on a tune up on a customers' car. As he was removing the ignition wires for replacement the first one came out of the spark plug boot. Then the next one did the same then a third. He thought, "It is going to be another one of those days where everything goes wrong, great."

Jack looked at Dominic and asked, "Bad day already buddy?"

"Yes, I guess." Dominic was feeling down today, and on top of that, he kept thinking about the dream and just thought it was his subconscious thoughts.

Later in the morning Dominic saw a car limp into the gas station and stop. "Does not need gas, did not pull up to the pumps." He thought. So he headed out to see what the problem is. "Good morning, Ma'am, my name is Dominic how can I help you?" Even though he was feeling down he would never show it to the customers. He saw that it was a beautiful young woman in a Cadillac Eldorado Convertible.

She was in tears. She struggled to say, "I am supposed to meet my Mother and sister for lunch in a few minutes and my car is dying. I do not know what to do, my father always handles these things. I am sorry, where are my manners, good morning sir, my name is Elizabeth."

"Well Miss Elizabeth, let me take a look and see what I can do." Dominic opened the hood to take a look. The engine had a definite miss and it turned out to be something simple. "Well Miss Elizabeth, could you please shut off the car?"

"Yes sir." Elizabeth said and proceeded to shut the car off.

Dominic reached over and removed an ignition wire that was shorting to the frame of the car. "Here is the problem Ma'am. You have a shorting ignition wire. I will have you going in a minute." Dominic ran into the shop and grabbed a new generic ignition wire and ran back out. He reached over and installed it. "Miss Elizabeth, please start your car."

She started it and it is running fine now. "Thank you so much Mr. Dominic." She had a big smile on her face. "How much do I owe you?"

"This is on me Miss Elizabeth. Your big smile is payment enough, Ma'am. You really need to get a tune up and service. I would be very happy to do this for you if you bring it back when you have some time. It was very nice to make your acquaintance Miss Elizabeth. I hope to see you soon. Please drive safely now."

Elizabeth smiled and said, "I will Mr. Dominic. It was very nice meeting you as well and thank you again." And she drove off.

Dominic watched her drive away and thought that she was so sweet and then he smiled and walked back into the shop. But all day the thought of he and Elizabeth getting married kept going through his head. He kept thinking that this was his ego day dreaming. But he couldn't get over her beauty. He was feeling that she was the most beautiful woman he had ever seen. But he kept telling himself that he needed to stop this. But his mind kept going back to it. Elizabeth was petite with long light straight light blonde hair, beautiful blue eyes and china like skin. Dominic thought to himself, "I need to stop this, it is going to drive me crazy. And besides, she is so out of my league, I will probably never see her again anyway." But no matter what he thought he couldn't get Elizabeth out of his head.

Dominic went home that night and had to tell Maria. "Maybe she can talk some sense into me," he thought.

When he got home Maria was preparing dinner. She said, "Hi Dom, how was your day. You were feeling kind of down this morning."

Dominic went over to her, gave her his usual hug and told her about this woman that came in how he cannot get her out of his head. Maria told him, "Maybe she is the reward you talked about this morning."

"Oh, c'mon Maria. She is so out of my league it would never happen. She came in with a new Cadillac Eldorado."

"You never know Dom. Crazier things have happened."

"Well, maybe but not to me." They ended the talk and Dominic went to take a shower and change, the whole time still thinking about Elizabeth. "I have to get her out of my head. I only met her for a short time, how could I be so hung up on her already. She's so wealthy; I could never compete with that." He thought.

They ate dinner and just like every night he complemented Maria on her cooking ability. It didn't matter what she made, he loved it. But Italian was their heritage and she excelled in Italian food. He cleaned up as usual and Maria went back to studying. Dominic sat down to read the newspaper. Even that wouldn't distract him. He was beginning to think something was wrong with him. This was serious he thought. Time passed slowly because of this and he found himself wishing it would get late enough to go to bed. Finally he went to bed but had trouble getting to sleep because he kept thinking about this woman. Eventually he fell asleep.

The following morning he felt good and didn't even remember thinking about the girl from yesterday. He told Maria good bye and left for work. The day was going pretty well and he really felt good for once.

Then Dominic happened to look out the window and saw the Cadillac parked and then saw Elizabeth get out. Then she walked in. Dominic came into the lobby, smiled and said, "Well hello, Miss Elizabeth. How are you today, Ma'am?"

"I am doing well Mr. Dominic, thank you for asking. I brought my car back for the tune up and service you suggested, and I wanted to thank you again for what you did yesterday."

"That is great! Ma'am and you are very welcome for yesterday. I was happy to help. We will get it in right away. Do you have someone picking you up or are you going to wait, Ma'am?"

"I will be waiting if that is alright."

"That will be just fine Miss Elizabeth. Would you like a cup of coffee while you wait?"

"If you have some I would love one."

"We have a small stove in the office and make coffee all day. It helps us stay awake when we are here late. Miss Elizabeth."

Dominic said and walked into the office and got a clean cup and poured some coffee. He brought it out to Elizabeth. "Would you like cream and sugar, Ma'am?"

"Black is just fine. And please call me Lizzy, Mr. Dominic."

"OK, Miss Lizzy."

"Please, just Lizzy. No need to be so formal."

"Alright, Lizzy. As you wish."

"You surprise me Mr. Dominic, I never would have expected someone so polite working in an auto repair shop."

"Well Lizzy, my mother taught my sister and me to always be polite. It makes people more comfortable she always said. And it shows respect for the person you are speaking with as well as it gives you self-respect. That is how a Lady and a Gentleman speak. She always told us. And I would never disrespect my mothers' wishes."

"I still do not think you sound like a mechanic Mr. Dominic."

"Thank you Lizzy, I will take that as a compliment. Please just call me Dominic. If you will excuse me, I need to get to your car. If you need anything, just ask. I will be in the shop."

"I will just be sitting here waiting for you Dominic."

Dominic went into the shop and asked Jack if he would drive Elizabeth's car into the shop. He also asked Jack to help so they could finish quickly. He didn't want to keep the lady waiting longer than necessary.

After about an hour Dominic came back to the waiting area to check on Lizzy. "Ma'am, we are almost finished with your car."

"Please just call me Lizzy, Dominic. No need to be so formal."

"Please excuse my habit, Lizzy, we are almost finished with your car."

"Dominic, do you have a few minutes to talk?"

"Of course, I would be happy to."

Elizabeth began, "You are a very well-spoken man, and attractive, if I am not being too forward Dominic."

"No Ma'am, you are not being too forward and I would then need to complement you as well. You are a very beautiful woman Lizzy." He was a little uncomfortable complementing someone like this but he really liked her and he felt an unusual attraction even though he knew that she was rich and out of his league. Dominic could see that she wanted to ask him something but was a little shy. So he thought he would break the ice and try to make whatever it was easier. "What can I do for you Lizzy, please ask?"

"Well, I do not know how to ask this and I do not want you to think less of me for doing so. I have never asked this of a man, and my mother would likely disown me if she were to hear this, but...."

Dominic could see that she was very nervous. He wished there was something he could do to make her feel more comfortable. The attraction was becoming stronger. He was both intrigued and confused, so he pulled up a chair and sat down.

"Well, um, ah, I sound ridiculous. I am nervous. I came back as soon as I could because you made such a big impression on me with you gentleman like actions. You do not strike me as an automobile mechanic. Automobile mechanics are gruff and not well spoken, you are charming. I like you and would very much like if we could meet for coffee, possibly after you finish work tonight, if you do not already have plans."

Dominic was almost speechless. How could he turn her down? She was so beautiful and sweet unlike anyone he has ever met. "I would be honored to have coffee with you Lizzy. And please do not feel like you are too forward. You do not need to worry, I will not tell your mother, your secret is safe with me Madam." He said jokingly. He was actually shocked because this is what went through his head when she stopped yesterday, he just never thought it could happen.

"Dominic you have made me very happy" Elizabeth blushed. "Ooh, Did I say that? Now I feel I have embarrassed myself."

"Please do not feel embarrassed Lizzy. However, your blushing brings out the blue in your eyes and you have beautiful eyes." Dominic said hoping he wasn't pushing his luck.

"You are making me blush more Dominic. But thank you."

"You are very welcome. I normally finish here around 7 PM. If my boss was here I could ask if I could leave a little sooner but he is not."

Just then Jack came and said, "Dominic, the car is finished and I pulled it outside. Here are the keys."

"Thanks Jack. Let's settle your bill then we can decide about tonight."

They both got up and walked over to the counter and Dominic totaled the bill. Lizzy looked and said, "Is that the whole bill? My father told me it would be much more."

"This is the whole bill. We believe in fair prices and good work."

Lizzy paid him and said, "How about I stop here at 7:00 and pick you up Dominic?"

"Well, that will be fine. Do I need to be worried?"

"Do not worry, I probably will not kidnap you – but you never know." Lizzy said. She smiled, winked and said, "See you later alligator."

As she walked away he replied, "After while crocodile."

She smiled and proceeded out the door, got into her car and drove away.

Dominic smiled and thought that he was one of the luckiest guys ever. He walked back into the shop and Jack said, "Beautiful lady isn't she Dominic, and it looks like she is sweet on you, lucky you." Jack chuckled and teasing said, "oooooh somebody has a girlfriend"

"OK Jack, enough."

Later that evening, Jack finished cleaning up and left for the day. Dominic washed up and put on a clean shirt and pants. He usually kept at least a clean shirt in case he gets spilled on or tore something. It was the best he had to prepare to meet Lizzy.

At 7 PM Dominic was locking the door as Lizzy pulled up. He turned to meet her and Lizzy said, "Get in, right on time. I like when people are prompt." The day was a warm spring day with a cool breeze and clear sky so Lizzy had the top down on the Cadillac.

Dominic reached out and opened the door and got into the car and closed the door. "Good evening Lizzy, how are you tonight?"

"I am doing well tonight Dominic, thank you. There is a café across from JC Penney. How does that sound? It's the Pioneer Hotel Café."

"That will be fine." He was a little nervous. He never was picked up by a girl before or anyone for that matter. He didn't know how to act. Lizzy parked and was about to get out of the car and Dominic said, "Wait please. I want to make this proper." He got out and walked around the car and opened the door for her and offered his hand to help her out. Lizzy was dressed all in white. She had a long pleated shirt and a blouse with lace on the sleeves and she had a white ribbon in her hair.

"Thank you Dominic."

Dominic took her hand in his and made sure to walk on the curb side of the sidewalk as his mother taught him. He then reached and opened the café door and let her in first then followed her through the door. This was more of what Dominic's mother had taught him. She used to say, "A gentleman always walks on the outside of the sidewalk to keep the lady safe."

"Good Evening Miss Elizabeth. How are you this fine evening? Oh, I see you have a friend with you tonight."

"I am doing very well David, thank you."

Dominic said, "Good evening sir."

He brought them to a table, pulled out the chair for Lizzy, she sat, and he pushed the chair in, and left them with menus.

Dominic waited for Elizabeth to be completely seated before he sat down. He ordered coffee for the both of them.

"See, these are the little things that you impress upon me. You are unusual Dominic. And you speak very well, just as though you grew up wealthy."

"I have a back story I could tell you that would help you to understand. But first I would like to ask you some questions if I may?"

"I am eager to hear your story Dominic. Please ask."

"Would I be out of line to ask your age Lizzy? I just want to know I am not with someone underage and with your beauty I do not believe I could guess accurately."

"No it would not Dominic. But I think you are trying to sweep me off of my feet with that comment. If you are it's working. I am 18 and I just graduated from River Road High School. Did you think I was under age Dominic?"

"I do not know what I thought, and no I am not trying to sweep you off of your feet. I am just stating fact. I truly believe you are very beautiful Lizzy."

"Well thank you Dominic."

A waitress brought the coffee to them along with cream and sugar and set them down. Dominic said, "Thank you Miss."

"Lizzy, you come here often I presume?"

"Yes, I was in route here to meet my mother and sister yesterday when my car had trouble. We were meeting for lunch, you see."

"Do you have lunch with your mother and sister often?"

"Usually twice each week, it has begun to be a sort of tradition."

"Do you have other siblings, another sister or a brother?"

"I just have my younger sister."

"And your father?"

"Yes, I have a father. He is at home working."

"At home working? May I ask what his profession would be?"

"Yes you may. He is an investor, mostly in real estate here in Tucson, but he also invests in the stock market."

"Do you have a boyfriend? I want to know if I am competing with someone for your company."

"Well, I may have a boyfriend but it is not official." Lizzy said teasingly.

Dominic felt his heart fall into his stomach. "Oh" He didn't know how to comment on that.

Evidently he looked crushed because right away Elizabeth said, "I am talking about you silly. So to answer you, no, I do not have or ever had a boyfriend. My mother does not believe in girls dating before graduation from high school."

"What a relief. I do not want to have to compete for you company, I want to be your company." Then Dominic thought about what he just said. "Ah, I did not mean to say that. I thought I just thought it and it just came out. Now I am embarrassed." He was blushing. He never blushed before because he never cared about what anyone thought of him until now.

"You are so cute."

Dominic continued to ask questions. He wanted to get to know her. "Do you plan on going to college?"

"I do not know Dominic, maybe not. My mother did and she never worked. As long as I remember I have wanted children and I do not know how someone could work and raise children properly."

"What do you do in your free time?"

"I do many things. I want to know about you too Dominic."

"It sounds as though you have a close family. You are blessed to have a close family, Lizzy."

"Why do you think I have a close family Dominic?"

"I sense it in the way you speak of them. I do not perceive any ill feelings. You sound very sincere."

"You are very observant Dominic. And I would think you would have a close family as well."

"My sister and I are very close."

"And you parents?"

Dominic became a little teary eyed and said, "They have both passed."

"Oh, I am so sorry Dominic, I did not know. But I can sense that you loved them and miss them." Elizabeth said in a sympathetic tone and reached across the table, took Dominic's hand and lightly squeezed it. "I feel your pain honey."

"Thank you Lizzy, I have never been with anyone that I could feel comfortable enough with to share anything about myself. I find it interesting that I feel so at ease around you. Thank you."

"You are very welcome Dominic. I feel at ease around you as well. There is something about you that draws me to you. I cannot believe I am going to say this but I felt this way yesterday when my car broke down. After I left I knew that if I did not come back today it would have been the biggest mistake in my life. I do not know why. It was the strangest feeling."

Dominic sat for a minute and contemplated. "Since you have been so honest, I will be as well. I had that feeling yesterday but I tried to push it away. To be honest, I could not stop thinking about you last night Lizzy, I felt that you were far out of my league and it must just be a fantasy. I do not know how to feel right now." He sipped his coffee. They sat in silence for a minute or two.

Dominic broke the ice and said, "Do you live near here Lizzy?"

Elizabeth had been in a slight daze but responded, "No, I live in the Catalina Foothills. And you Dominic?"

"I live with my sister in the house my mother bought when my father died. It is not much." Dominic was feeling a little uncomfortable now because it is beginning to occur to him the class difference between them.

"It is home to you and that is what really matters the most, is it not? Are you feeling uncomfortable because I come from a wealthy family? I am sensing that you are uneasy."

"I believe so, somewhat. Things change but not always for the better."

"I do not understand Dominic. What things? What are you talking about?"

"I am sorry; I did not mean to bring this down. I guess I am just feeling sorry for myself."

Elizabeth looked at Dominic and said, "How could you feel sorry for yourself? You have a good job and you are sitting and talking with a highly desirable beautiful young woman, well that is what my mother keeps saying about me, and one that is fully enjoying your company. And, my mother would scold me if she ever heard me say this, but I do not care that you are not wealthy. I care that I have such a strong attraction to you. To me that means everything."

"Really? Are you just saying that to raise my spirits?"

"No I am not. I would not be here unless I chose to be here. My mother always tells me that I am too strong minded for a woman and I should keep my mouth shut but I do not usually."

"Alright. I was just thinking how much different my life would have been if my parents had not passed away. Then I would not feel this way." He thought that he already killed the moment so it doesn't matter anymore.

Elizabeth thought for a minute than said, "Why would your life have been so much different? You would still be the same person and that is what matters. It is what you hold in your heart. And from what I know of you so far, you have a big heart."

Dominic was thinking he should just shut his mouth and change the subject but if she still likes him after his story maybe they were supposed to meet. "Well, I am not usually emotional with other people. I have a difficult time trusting most people with my feelings. However, somehow deep inside I feel I can trust you. This is so unlike me, I feel as though I am on new ground here. Well," he hesitated and swallowed, "I did not think it was appropriate to tell you this because I just met you. But somehow I feel like I need to tell you about my family history."

"Go ahead Dominic, I am listening." Elizabeth said as she reached out to take his hand again.

"Well, you know the big law firm downtown near Seinfeld's?"

"Yes I do."

Dominic just realized how beautiful her face was. He had not really looked that closely at her face up until now. "My father was a partner there. We lived in a very nice house in the Foothills near River Road and Campbell. I had a very happy childhood. And I know my mother and father really loved each other. To me at the time it was almost like a storybook. Then one day when I was 14 we got a knock at the door. My mother opened it and it was the police. My sister, Maria and I, saw the look on the officer's faces and we knew something was wrong. It turned out my father was killed in an auto accident shortly before they came." Dominic tried to keep the tears from coming but he couldn't.

"Oh Dominic, I do not know how to tell you how sad this makes me feel."

Dominic thought he could see tears forming in her eyes. "I am not finished yet."

"There's more? Elizabeth was looking very sad and concerned.

"We ended up needing to sell the house and most of our things and we moved into the house that Maria and I now live in. My mother never worked but now she needed to get a job to support us. She ended up getting a job at Seinfeld's as a clerk. But about 3 years later she got sick. We took her to St. Mary's emergency and found out she had stage 4 Pancreatic cancer. She passed away a week later." Dominic was almost fully crying now.

Elizabeth stood up and walked around the table and hugged Dominic. "Oh my! I cannot even imagine how you and Maria must have felt. I am so sorry. You poor dear." Elizabeth just stood there and hugged him. Then she thought for a minute. "That means you were only 17. Did they not want to put the both of you into foster care?"

"The sisters at St. Mary's started the process immediately. But I thought fast and remembered one of the lawyers that my father worked with and I went to see him. He helped me obtain guardianship of Maria so we would not get separated. This was about a week before my 18th birthday and graduation. When I graduated I got a job. Maria was able to get some grants and she just began school at U of A. That brings things to now." Dominic told her.

"I cannot believe how well you managed this situation Dominic. You are amazing! Now I understand why you are such a gentleman. Your mother did a superb job raising you. I would very much love to meet Maria sometime." She went back and sat down again.

Dominic waived to the waitress to get a refill on his coffee. Elizabeth didn't want any more but thanked the waitress.

As Dominic drank some coffee Elizabeth looked at Dominic and said, "Dominic, My parents are having a small get together on Saturday night. It would make me very happy if you would come. It would mean everything to me. I have never had any-one and it would fulfill my dream to bring someone that I care for with me to one of their gatherings. I always feel so alone at these. Would you please come?"

Dominic put his cup down and looked at Elizabeth. She was so beautiful, and so sweet. He felt like he could fall in love with her that instant. He had never felt this way with anyone. He never even felt so close to anyone either. So without even a thought he said, "Of course I will. But what do I wear? Is this a formal type of thing?"

"Dominic, you have made me very happy. It will not be very formal. If you have a dress shirt and dress pants it would be more than enough."

Dominic sat to let this all sink in. Then he asked, "Where is your house? What is your address? How will I find it?"

Lizzy pulled a pen out of her purse and wrote the address and directions on a piece of paper she also found in her purse. "Here is my address and directions. I will begin from Campbell because I do not know where you would be coming from." She handed the paper to Dominic.

Dominic looked at it and read, 4801 N. La Lomita; take Campbell to River Rd. and turn right; (west) Take River Rd. to Camino Real and turn left; this is right after El Corral Restaurant; drive about ¼ mile then bear right onto La Lomita, drive about ½ mile and it is on the left and there are big rocks on each side of the drive. You cannot see the house from the road but it is about 200 feet from the road on a hill.

"It is not too difficult to find. There are only a few houses around there. It is getting late so I will take you back to your shop now."

"I know about where this is. It not far from the house where I lived before my father died. It was on Camino Real."

"Really! So we were neighbors! I wish I knew you then."

"Alright." Dominic stood and walked over to help her out of the chair.

"You are a perfect gentleman Dominic." Elizabeth said. And as they walked towards the front the café, the host said, "Should I put this on you tab Miss Elizabeth?"

"Yes thank you David."

As they walked out Dominic said to Lizzy, "I was supposed to pay for that."

"I know Dominic. But we were in my world tonight so I just put it on the tab. Do not worry, it will be paid for. I do not want you to even think anything of it. You gave me coffee at you shop so I gave you coffee at…well, let us just say I wanted to return the favor."

"OK, for this time." He held the door of the café open and followed her out. Again he walked on the outside of the sidewalk. Lizzy reached for his hand and took it in hers. When they got to her car he opened the door for Lizzy and helped her in.

"Thank you Dominic."

"It is always my pleasure." It was only a few minutes to the shop from the café.

Elizabeth pulled up to the front door. Dominic turned and said, "It was wonderful tonight. I enjoyed every minute."

"I enjoyed it as well Dominic."

Dominic wished her good night and Elizabeth did something again that her mother would likely be very angry about. She said, "Dominic?"

Dominic turned and said, "Yes?"

Elizabeth leaned over and grabbed his face with both hands and kissed him. Dominic could not help but kiss her back. "I am sorry, I was afraid I would not get to kiss you. I hope I am not scaring you off by being too forward Dominic." She had a concerned look.

"No, you are not scaring me off Elizabeth. I actually think it is kind of sweet." He got out of the car and said, "Until Saturday night—Oh, you didn't say what time I should be there."

"Around 7:30 would be perfect." She blew him a kiss and drove away.

Dominic unlocked the door and went in to get his things, locked the door, walked to the car and drove home. As he drove he thought about tonight with Elizabeth. He couldn't believe they just met yesterday. He had to tell Maria about it as soon as he got home. Maybe she could help him understand how he could have such strong feelings for someone he just met. He pulled in the parking spot, shut the car off and went into the house.

Maria was sitting on the couch studying. She looked up and said, "Really busy at the shop today, Dom?"

"Hello Maria. Well no, not really. Can you spare some time from studying?"

Maria marked her page, closed the book and got up and said, "You know I will always have time for you big brother." She went to Dominic and hugged him and told him that she had been a little worried. "You never come home so late."

"Let's sit down. It is kind of a long story and maybe you can help me understand."

Maria had a teasing smile and said, "This is about the girl you met yesterday is it not?" But she was certain this was it.

"How did you know?" Dominic was shocked that she knew.

"I really did not but it was the first thing that just popped into my head. "So it is about her?"

"Yes."

"Well tell me everything; I want to know all of the details." Maria said excitedly.

Dominic told her about meeting her yesterday and what happened today. He told her how easy it was to talk to her, how he told her all about what happened to their father and mother and how he got teary eyed.

Maria sat and listened intently waiting for him to finish before she said anything. "You got teary eyed? You?"

"Yes, yes. And I felt afraid that she would reject me then."

"But she did not, did she?"

"No, she did not, how do you know this?"

"It shows that you do not know women very well. What you did was close the deal with your tears."

"How is that?"

"Silly, you did something that most women wish their boyfriend or husband, would do." Maria told him. "You made yourself vulnerable. And you did it the first time you met. Do you like her Dom?"

"Are you kidding me? How could I not like her? She's beautiful, very forward, sweet and very sure of herself. And her eyes..."

"What about her eyes?"

"I could look at them for the rest of my life and never get tired."

"Do you think she likes you too?"

"Well, I have not told you what else she did." Dom said with some hesitation. He didn't know what Maria would think of Elizabeth after he told her. He really trusted Maria's advice but he was a little afraid she would think poorly of Elizabeth for kissing him like she did.

"OK, what did she do? C'mon, don't leave me hanging. It's like stopping a movie just before the climax. C'mon Dom. You're going to make me wait all night?" Maria was acting like she was waiting for that kiss in a love story but she didn't want to wait.

"OK, OK. First she invited me to some kind of gathering at her parent's house on Saturday night. I could not tell her no. I felt as though I needed to go. No, I wanted to go even though her parents are very wealthy and live in the Foothills where all of those huge houses are very close to where we used to live." Dominic explained. "And...."

"And what? You're making me crazy. What, What?"

"Fine. I just hope you still think I should see her again after I tell you." Dom was really worried that Maria would think she was some kind of floozy or something.

"C'mon Dom you are going to make me angry if you do not tell me." Maria was almost insisting. This made Dominic feel even more hesitant.

"When she dropped me back at my car before I could get out she grabbed my face with both hands and kissed me right on the mouth. She said she was afraid we would not kiss."

"Tell me you kissed her back. You had to, did you?"

"Well yes I did. I could not help myself. Then she asked me if she was scaring me by doing that. And I told her I thought it was sweet. I cannot believe I said that."

Maria had a big smile when she told Dominic, "Oh Dominic, I always thought that you would not even date because of me. I am so happy for you. I have a good feeling about her. You have not told me her name."

"Her name is Elizabeth but wants me to call her Lizzy. And why would I not even date because of you? What do you mean?"

"Well, you are always worried about how I am doing and if I need help with school, if anyone is bothering me. You seem to be always preoccupied with making certain I am OK. I did not think you were thinking about yourself. Big Bother. Tell me more about Elizabeth. I already like her. She knows what she wants."

"She has a sister and they live with their mother and father. They are very formal when they speak and they only use full names, not nicknames. Her father is an investor."

"What does she look like? I know she has blue eyes."

"She is about the same physique as you and has beautiful long light blonde hair and china like skin, and her voice is soft even though she is so forward. Oh, and when the tears came she got up and put her arms around me and held me, then she told me how she could not even imagine how it felt to loose both parents. I felt like it was a dream. It felt so good when she held me. I do not know how to describe it exactly."

"Dom, I am so happy for you. I have worried since Mother died that you would be alone. I mean I would be here, I mean alone without someone special. You are such a good man. You have done so much for me. You deserve to have this."

"Maria, I never knew you felt like that. But I could not have survived without you after mother died. I could not afford to lose you to a foster home; you know how close we have always been. I felt that if they took you away it would rip my heart out."

"I know Dom. You have such a good heart. Mother and father would be proud."

"I think we helped each other Maria. You have a good heart as well. And if mother and father would be proud of me they would be proud of you as well."

The rest of the week was uneventful. Dominic went to work and Maria went to school.

Chapter 9

When Saturday arrived Dominic woke up nervous about going to Lizzy's house and meeting her parents. But he had another dream that confused him.

He was already apprehensive about the gathering at Lizzy's house. He was worried about the same things most anyone would be worried about in his situation. He had never dated so he wasn't certain how to act and he would be going to the house of wealthy people and wasn't sure he would be able to fit in. And he hadn't seen or talked to Elizabeth since the day they went for coffee and he wondered if she still wanted him to go.

Maria overheard Dominic mumbling these things and poked her head in his room and asked, "You are not getting cold feet are you Dom?"

"No, it's just my thoughts. I am going for sure."

"Just wondering. My intuition is usually correct you know you have no choice but to go."

"Yes Maria, I know. Don't worry I am going. This is all new to me. I do not know how to act."

"Just be yourself, you did just fine when you went for coffee with Elizabeth."

"Yes, but her mother, father and sister will be there and who knows who else."

Maria looked at Dominic and said, "You will be fine, just wait and see. I know you better than anybody and I know you will be OK."

"If you say so. OK, I will be OK."

The day passed and soon it was time for Dominic to leave. He grabbed the directions that Elizabeth wrote and told Maria he was leaving. Since he knew about where Elizabeth's house was he gave himself about ½ hour. He pulled out the piece of paper that Elizabeth wrote the directions on and noticed she had drawn a little heart at the bottom. He wondered why he didn't notice it when he first looked at it, but it made him smile. Then he realized he wasn't as nervous anymore.

The drive was uneventful. And on the way he saw a flower shop so he stopped to buy a single red rose. He hoped that her parents would approve of the gesture. As he drove he felt like driving past the house he grew up in but didn't want to be late, especially since Lizzy specifically stated when she picked him up for coffee how she liked punctuality. He wasn't going to be late under any circumstances.

He turned onto Camino Real and he looked at the odometer and made a mental note. Lizzy said about ¼ mile. After ¼ mile he hadn't seen La Lomita yet. The first thought was that he passed it but he knew he had not. Just then he saw the street and turned to the right onto La Lomita. Then he noted the odometer again. It was beginning to get dark but he could still see fine. He looked around and saw that there weren't any houses that he could see. 'Her house is in an area just like where he grew up," he thought. Then he came to a driveway with large rocks on both sides on the left side of the street so he turned. It was quite long but then he saw a house. There were 6 or 7 other cars parked near the house so he pulled in next to them.

When he got out of his car he noticed his Chevy looked like a piece of junk. He was still driving the 1948 Chevy his mother bought after his father died. The other cars were Cadillac's and one Lincoln. This made him a little uncomfortable but he tried to shrug it off. He followed the brick walk to the front door and saw that there was a door bell button so he pushed it. He heard a series of chimes something like a grandfather clock Westminster chime. He stood there holding the rose.

Then someone unlocked the door and opened it. It was Lizzy. She smiled big and said, "Dominic, you came! I was afraid you would not." Then she saw the single red rose. "Is that for me?"

"Good evening Elizabeth. This is for you."

Before he could finish Lizzy said, "You are so sweet. I never received flowers from anyone." and took the rose and hugged him hard with both arms.

He thought she looked like a child getting her first ice cream cone, almost giddy. Dominic smiled.

"Please come in Dominic. I told my mother and sister all about you. They cannot wait to meet you."

Dominic said as he walked in, "I hope I meet your mother and sister's expectations."

"You will, you will. They were impressed when I told them what a gentleman you are. Do not be nervous, Dominic, just be yourself. Let me introduce you to my mother."

She walked him into a large room and up to a very elegant lady. "Mother, I would like to present Dominic Tucci."

Kristina looked at Dominic and said, "Hello Dominic, I am Kristina Hall, Elizabeth's mother." And she held her hand out.

Dominic took her hand firmly but not tight and said, "Madam, Good evening. I am honored to meet you.

Kristina smiled and said, "likewise Dominic. Please call me Mrs. Kristina."

Dominic replied, "Yes Ma'am, Mrs. Kristina. And I hope you do not think this out of line, but I have to say that I can see where Elizabeth's beauty came from, Ma'am."

"Are you flirting with me Dominic?" Kristina looked at Elizabeth with a big smile and said, "He is charming, my dear." She returned to look at Dominic.

"No Ma'am, I would never do that. That would be rude."

"I am not serious Dominic, I am just teasing you a little. Thank you for the complement. You are charming." Kristina excused herself and said, "Please excuse me." And she turned to attend to her other guests.

"Come, let's find my sister." She still was acting almost giddy. "You really impressed my mother Dominic and she is not easy to impress. There she is." And she almost pulled Dominic to follow behind her. "Excuse me Lillian, this is Dominic, the one I told you about."

"Dominic, I am Lillian, Elizabeth's younger sister." And raised he hand.

Dominic took her hand the same as with Kristina and said, "Good evening Ma'am, It is a pleasure to meet you. And if I am not too being too forward, you're just as elegant as Elizabeth."

"Where did you find him Lizzy. He is so sweet and proper, just like out an old movie, and so handsome." Lizzy said smiling.

Dominic blushed.

"Did you introduce him to mother?"

"Yes, just now Lilly."

"What did she say?"

"Well, she told him to call her Mrs. Kristina. And she never says that. I think she approves."

"I never heard her say that either. Maybe you are lucky then. Dominic, don't mind us we are just having some girl talk. Have you met our father yet Dominic?"

"No Ma'am."

"You can cut the Ma'am thing. We don't need that. As you can see we use nick names---but never with our parents. He-He." Lilly said.

Just then, Dominic heard from behind him, "Elizabeth, you're not going to introduce your friend to me? What, I do not count anymore?" Joseph, Lizzy and Lilly's father said.

"Oh, father, do not tease. He just arrived. Father, this is Dominic Tucci, Dominic this is.."

That was all he let her say. "Elizabeth's father." And he held out his hand.

Dominic reached and gave him a strong handshake while looking at him directly and said, "Good Evening, Sir. It is an honor."

"Likewise, son. You can call me Mr. Hall son. It is nice to meet you. I need to get back to my guest's now but I hope we can talk a little before you leave."

"I would like that Sir." Dominic said feeling like he was put on the spot.

Joseph thought that he really needed to make a point to talk to Dominic before he left. He was feeling something about him but couldn't put his finger on it.

"Your family is very nice Lizzy. They are somewhat frightening but I like them. They remind me of my parents. God rest their soles."

"Your parent's both passed away? I am so sorry Dominic." Lilly said.

"Yes, Ma'am both of them."

"Call me Lilly, Dominic, well except when our parents can hear, then it is Lillian."

"As you wish, Lilly"

"Lizzy, show him around, make certain he gets something to drink. And get him some of the hors d'oeuvres, you do not want him to starve, do you?"

"I will, I will. Give me a few minutes. I had to introduce him to Mother and father and you first."

"Do not fuss ladies. I will not starve." Dominic said trying to make light in the moment.

"C'mon Dominic, come, I show you around."

As they began to walk away Lizzy's mother called to her as she was walking towards them, "Elizabeth. Could I see you for a moment?"

"Yes mother." Lizzy turned to Dominic, "Just wait here. I will be back before you know it." And she walked over to her mother.

"Come over here Elizabeth." Kristina pulled Lizzy aside. "Is he for real or is he just putting on a show?"

"Mother, I told you this is how Dominic is. That is what drew me to him. I never met anyone so polite and proper. Your friends are not even like that."

"Well, Elizabeth, if that is true you need to hold on to him. He is a gem, and very sweet. Someone with manners like his I would not have believed existed in this day and age. So far, I approve. Did your father meet him yet?"

"Yes, a few minutes ago."

"How did he react?"

"Just like usual. Except Father told him he would like to talk a little before he leaves. I do not know if that is good or bad mother." Lizzy was a little apprehensive.

"Oh, do not worry, your father is not going to do anything." Kristina said. Well, she didn't think he would.

"If you say so mother. I need to get back to Dominic. He has been standing there alone."

"Go right ahead, dear."

Lizzy went back to Dominic. "She says she approves of you."

"I hope that is a good thing."

"It's a wonderful thing Dominic. Come, I will show you around." Lizzy showed Dominic a good part of the house, but of course, not any of the bed rooms. That would not be proper she thought. Then she took Dominic outside to show him the pool and horses.

As they walked into the stable Dominic exclaimed, "You have horses?"

"Yes. Do you ride?"

"Well, my mother brought Maria and me a few times to learn just before my father died, so not really."

"Oh, it is easy. I will teach you." Lizzy walked with Dominic over to a bench and the sat down. She looked at Dominic as if asking for something.

Dominic took it as she wanted to kiss. So he leaned over to kiss her and she put her arms around him. They kissed for quite a while. Lizzy stopped and looked at Dominic kind of seriously, "I know this is way too soon, but I feel like I am falling in love with you already." She then looked very concerned, "Please tell me this will not drive you away. I am just saying what I am feeling deep in my heart, but I would die if I lost you. As I said before, my mother always says I should keep my mouth shut, but something about you makes me feel safe and protected."

Her serous look turned into what Dominic thought was a scared look. "Do not be afraid Lizzy. You just said what I was thinking and am feeling in my heart as well. I do not understand what is going on or why our feelings are so strong in such a short time. I just did not get to say it yet. You make me feel the same way Lizzy. I do not know if it is good or not but I love the feeling. I feel like I am falling in love with you as well. This is not supposed to happen like this in real life."

She looked at Dominic and her eyes teared up. She hugged him and said, "I feel so lucky and blessed Dominic. Do you believe in fate?"

"I do, but I do not understand it."

"I believe we were meant to meet the other day. I think my car had trouble so I would meet you. You know if anyone would have asked me a week ago if I was happy I would have said yes without hesitation. But a week ago I did not yet understand what genuine authentic and pure happiness was. I feel as if us meeting was our destiny!"

Dominic and Elizabeth got married in January 1956 about 6 months after they met. And by that time Elizabeth's mother and sister were against it. They felt that Elizabeth was rushing into marriage with someone poor and would suffer because of it. Elizabeth did not agree and remains very happy.

Chapter 10

In 1964 Dominic and Joseph began discussing the plans and needs for Dominic's new auto shop. They went over the numbers and Joseph told Dominic that there are multiple ways he can go on this. Joseph could co-sign for a business loan; Joseph could lend Dominic the money. Joseph told Dominic that if he lends him the money it would be at no interest. He said it would be hard enough without adding interest which would add thousands to the loan.

This discussion went on for about a week working out the details. Joseph spent some time with Josias Joesler, the architect that works for John Murphy and had a building layout drawn up for the building Dominic would like. He liked a building that used to be a Studebaker Dealership that had gone out of business at 847 N. Stone. They brought this to the City of Tucson for approval and applied for permits. Joseph told Kristina that he is helping Dominic figure out the financial end so he doesn't get in over his head. Since Joseph has had years of experience handling money it was a good choice. He didn't however tell her what he had decided to do. He also did not tell Dominic what he had decided to do either.

Joseph had a contract drawn up by his lawyer to cover everything necessary. He then brought it to Dominic to go through the details. Both he and Dominic signed it. Dominic believed this was a loan and there was explanation on how it is to be paid back.

Joseph really liked and trusted Dominic and knew he will put in every ounce of effort into this endeavor. And since this is also for Elizabeth and would only make his granddaughter, Angelina, have a better life, he decided that the best thing would be to give Dominic the money as a gift, although he didn't want to tell Dominic yet.

Joseph and Dominic went to the bank to set up the account and transfer the money to the account. Then they went to the listing agent and made a deal for renting the building with an option to purchase after 5 years. Now they had the building secured they went to the city of Tucson to pick up permits and business license. Tucson already had the business plan and the details for modifications to the building so it was simple to get at this point. Next they went to a sign maker to get signage made for the Business. He needed a sign for the front of the building, an Opening Soon and a Grand Opening sign made. Afterwards they met with the contractor that they chose (actually Joseph chose him) to begin the construction inside the building and for all of the added equipment. This included the installation of the lifts, the air compressor and distribution lines.

Then Dominic went to find a pick-up truck to use for the business. He found a used 1960 Chevy C10 for a good price and bought it.

When all of the walls and partitions were complete Dominic brought Lizzy and Angie there to begin painting, assembling shelving and cabinets. Jack showed up as well to help. He already knew that he will be working for Dominic and wanted to be a part of getting ready to open.

Jack's dad had just closed his gas station/garage and retired. Jack had been telling his regular customers and many of his new customers about Dominic's new Garage that would be just down the street. He is hoping that Dominic would have customers as soon as he opens.

Soon they were ready to open. They had planned food and drinks for opening day and an open house to show everyone his new shop and store. They planned this for 11:00 AM on Friday September 4, 1964. So Dominic, Elizabeth and Angelina (she was 7 years old) went to the new shop on opening morning to help prepare for the opening. Jack and Sofia arrived with his father, Donato, and they helped as well. Jack brought his charcoal grill, filled it with charcoal and lit it. About 11 AM Jack started cooking hamburgers and hotdogs. People started to arrive and because there were so many they needed to direct cars to park in the back. Many drag racers came, just to see what the new business was about. Lillian and Carl came with the kids as did Enzo and Maria and their kids. Joseph and Kristina were there as well. Maria was so proud of Dominic. He finally was able to open his own shop and she told him again that their mother and father would be so proud.

They gave away all of the hamburgers and hotdogs during the afternoon and by the end of the day they considered the grand opening a big success. A few people scheduled tune up's and oil changes for their cars and there were many of the regular customers from Jack's dad's gas station/garage. They came and talked to Dominic and Jack, familiar faces to them. Quite a few were happy that they would have the same guys working on their cars as before.

Jack's father, Donato Ramirez, took Dominic aside to congratulate him on his new shop and to thank him for hiring Jack. Dominic said, "Thank you Mr. Ramirez. I would not have been able to open this shop if it was not for you saving Maria and me by hiring me to work at your station. I also need to thank you for teaching me and showing me all of your tricks and shortcuts, especially for modifying distributors and carbs. And I made a promise to you that I would hire Jack when I opened my shop and I never break a promise. There were times that you were like a father to me during those early years. And

Jack, he is my best friend and he is also like a brother to me. Both of you have done more for me that I could have asked and I thank you. You are a good man Mr. Ramirez. And, I want you to know that if you need anything to please ask me and I will do whatever it takes."

"Mr. Ramirez, you have gained my trust, admiration and loyalty over the years. You accomplished things that still amaze me. You lost your wife and emigrated when Jack was young and opened your gas station in a new country. You learned English and worked hard to build a large customer base. You took time with me to teach me things that would have taken me years to learn otherwise. I cannot thank you enough sir."

"Dominic, you are a good man too." Donato said. "And I wish you the best."

After it was all over and everyone was cleaning up, Joseph took Dominic aside to talk to him. This is when he told Dominic that he decided to make the loan a gift. He did not want it paid back. He said it was a gift for him, Elizabeth and Angelina as well as an investment in his family. He did remind Dominic that he cannot say anything to Kristina about it because she would be very angry. Joseph reminded Dominic that Kristina continues to think that Elizabeth shouldn't have married him. But he didn't need to worry about it because sooner or later Elizabeth will be able to tell Kristina and Lillian his story and they will finally understand what a good man he is.

Dominic was surprised. He asked if he could at least tell Elizabeth. Joseph said that was fine but to tell her that she cannot talk to Kristina and Lillian about it until they hear his story. Dominic agreed, again with a gentleman's handshake. Later he would have some very good news to tell Elizabeth.

When Dominic, Elizabeth and Angelina got home they all sat together and talked. Dominic reinforced the reality that the first few years were going to be a struggle because it is a new business. He figured he would be working some long hours but in time he felt that would let up. Since they all had a hamburger and hot dog late in the afternoon they weren't very hungry. Elizabeth just made some small sandwiches. They sat together on the living room floor, Elizabeth sitting in front of Dominic leaning on his chest and Angelina sitting on Elizabeth's lap leaning on her.

After they got Angelina in bed Dominic told Elizabeth that he needed to tell her about something. She asked him if there was a problem and he assured her there was not. They went back into the living room and sat on the couch. "It's about the new shop is it not?" Elizabeth asked Dominic.

"Yes, Elizabeth, but I am sure it is not what you think." Dominic told her. "Your father pulled me aside just before he and your mother left." Elizabeth looked worried. "Calm down honey. First, he made me promise to remind you that you cannot discuss this with your mother or sister until you have the opportunity to first tell them my story. So it could be a long time."

"OK, I promise Dominic you already know I will not say anything." Elizabeth said. She was still worried.

"Your father pulled me aside to tell me that he changed his mind about the loan. He said that it is now a gift and he does not want us to pay it back. He said for him it is in investment in our family and a gift to all of us. He said he does not want to see us struggling and he wants Angelina to live in a better situation."

"He said that? My father is wonderful is he not? I know he really likes you Dom and wishes he could show it but my mother and sister still will not hear me out. Sometimes I feel sad when I think about it. And I know my mother hurts you with her attitude and hurts me as well but I feel inside that at some point they will finally listen and find out what a good man you are Dom." Elizabeth said. "I love you so much and still want to thank you again for asking me to marry you. You are my life."

"Elizabeth, I love you so much! As you said in June 1955 we were destined to be together. I cannot even imagine where my life would be if we did not meet that afternoon. I still struggle to make sense of all of that. But we may never really know what happened to us that first afternoon. But it was the highlight of my life. And Angelina, I do not even know how to say this, but she is my miracle. I almost cannot believe how blessed we are." Dominic told her.

They hugged and kissed and went to bed.

The following Monday Dominic went to the shop and it was officially open. Jack came in and they decided to arrange the store with the performance parts that Dominic ordered while they were preparing to open. It didn't take long for the first customer to come in. One of the regulars from Jack's dad's gas station/garage came and wanted to be the first to get work done. He wanted a complete tune up and service.

Dominic took out the first work order form from the package, #1000. He had been able to get these from the printer in time for opening day. Jack took care of this Job while Dominic showed the customer around. This was the only customer of the day. But as the days went by they had more customers. By the end of the month they were already at the point of needing to schedule cars for the next day. After a couple of months Dominic was scheduling work a week ahead. They were getting pretty busy already.

Then Dominic got the first performance job. A guy came in with a 1962 Pontiac Catalina 421 Super Duty, a rare car even in 1964. He wanted Hedman Headers and mufflers installed and he wanted the distributer re-curved and the carbs. re-jetted, adjusted for the headers. Dominic needed to order the headers so he got a deposit and told the customer he would schedule the work as soon as the headers arrived. The headers came in about 2 weeks later and Dominic called the customer and scheduled the installation for a week after that.

The job turned out to be not as difficult as he had expected. He then made adjustments to the distributor curve in stages. This is a tedious job without a distributor machine. Already this was on Dominic's wish list. Then he moved to the carbs. These are AFB's and tricky to modify but he had learned about AFB's from Jack's father. Jack's father had lots of little tricks for repairs and performance modifications. Dominic learned all of them.

The shop was becoming so busy that he and Jack were falling behind, even though they were working late into the night. Dominic already had Maria helping with paperwork because he just couldn't get it completed himself with the workload. Dominic decided it was time to hire at least 1 new mechanic. Dominic placed an ad in the Tucson Citizen for a mechanic the last week of June 1965. Fortunately there was quite a bit of interest and Dominic ended up hiring two mechanics. This freed up Dominic to take care of all of the paperwork and accounting. Maria's help was only a temporary agreement so now Dominic could handle it himself.

Dominic hired the 2 mechanics in July 1965. They were Johnny and Scott. They had 10 and 12 years of experience so they could begin working immediately. They began working alongside of Jack and quickly proved themselves capable of handling any work. Business continued to grow. They did everything from brakes and tune ups to engine replacements; headers; intake manifolds, performance camshafts, installation of performance heads; ring and pinion swaps; etc. By 1971 Dominic was ready to hire an additional mechanic so in September 1971 he hired Hector. Then he hired Miguel in May 1972 and Eric in September 1972.

The business was beginning to become too large for Dominic to run alone so he made Jack the service manager. He had a huge amount of performance work on muscle cars. He was too busy to begin rebuilding automatic transmissions so he had an agreement with a local transmission shop. He would remove and replace but send the transmissions to this shop. This shop also built performance transmissions so Dominic had performance transmissions he could advertise. He could do everything from a stock rebuild to a full race manual shift automatic.

Dominic also partnered with a tire shop so he wouldn't need to stock tires. He usually had a few of the specialty tires at the shop but he couldn't stock enough to cover everything. The tire shop also carried custom wheels as well so he could order a set for a customer and have then delivered and install then at the shop.

He was also doing some exhaust work. Initially he began with just replacing stock exhaust systems. Then he progressed to connecting headers to the original exhaust on customer cars. Then he began building complete exhaust systems. For these he used lengths of straight pipes and 90 and 45 deg. bends. He cut and welded these together and used whatever mufflers the customers wanted. He also added factory side pipes to a few Corvette's.

Chapter 11

Angie left home early partly because she hadn't driven to the school at 6:30 AM yet. The first period began at 7:30 but she wanted time to find her way and get to the office to pick up her official schedule and get settled into her locker. It took her about 15 minutes to get to Canyon Del Oro High School.

Angie had a full schedule from 7:30 AM to 4:00 PM. Most students during senior year only had a few classes. Angie wanted to learn everything she could to get a well-rounded education because there were limited offerings for college in Tucson. And no colleges in Tucson had an Automotive Technology curriculum which is what she wanted. Because of this she would need to learn everything from her father and the guys at the shop. She was also reading about a relatively new automotive certification that began in Tucson in 1972. This was called ASE or Automotive Service Excellence.

Angie arrived at Canyon Del Oro about a quarter to seven, parked and found her way to the office. No one was in the office yet so she had to wait. The sign on the door said that the office opened at 7 AM. As she waited a couple teachers walked past and asked her if she needed help. She told them that today was her first day at this school and she needed to pick up a class schedule and locker assignment. Each told her the office opened at 7 AM. She said, "Thank you" to each and continued waiting. Shortly before 7 AM a lady walked up to the door and unlocked it. She asked Angie if she was waiting for the office to open and she said, "Yes Ma'am. Today is my first day at this school and I need to get my class schedule and locker assignment. Is this something you are able to attain for me?"

"Of course, I'm Miss Cardenas the school secretary. Students normally pick up their schedules a week before School begins. Why didn't you pick it up then?"

"My family just moved into the district and I am transferring from Amphitheater High School. My mother took care of the details but they did not have a schedule at that time. I know she did register me for a full day of classes."

Miss Cardenas was looking through a file cabinet drawer while Angie was talking. "Here it is, Angelina Tucci, right?"

"Yes Ma'am. And the locker assignment Ma'am?"

"It is listed on the schedule, dear. And here is the combination. Just follow the hallway to your right and it should be close to the end."

"Thank you, Ma'am." She left the office and went to look for her locker. She knew that she would need to find out what books and supplies that would be required for each class from each teacher. Then she would need to find out where she needed to go to pick up the books. And she figured that she would need to do this right after school. As Angie was looking for her locker, she heard someone behind her.

"Angelina, Angelina Tucci? Angie turned to find Mrs. Abbot, her physics teacher from Amphitheater.

"Mrs. Abbot? Hello Ma'am, I did not expect to see you here."

"I didn't expect to see you either, Angelina. I finally was able to get a transfer to Canyon Del Oro. I have been trying for the last few years."

"My parents just bought a house in this district and I transferred as well. Today is my first day. What are you teaching here?"

"The same subject, physics."

"I have physics III this semester." Angie looked at her schedule and saw the teacher was ABT which was the same as it had been at Amphitheater. "You are my physics teacher! I cannot believe it!"

"Since I am the only physics teacher that would be correct. And I believe this will be an interesting semester. You challenged me quite a bit last semester. I liked that, no student has ever done that."

"Maybe I should not say but you are my favorite teacher because you challenged me as well. You were the only teacher at Amphitheater that did that. I have the expectation that the teachers here will do the same."

"I believe they will Angelina. Good luck this year. I need to get to my classroom now."

"Thank you Mrs. Abbot. I will see you shortly Ma'am." She realized that Physics was her first class of the day.

Her first day went well. No problems with any other students and at least after the first day she had a strong feeling that all of the teachers would be good. This was quite a difference from Amphitheater. At Amphitheater she knew immediately which teachers would be a problem. But she would find out in time if she would have any problems. Angie figured that just as the students, the teachers would be on their best behavior.

After a few weeks, Angie found that everything was just as she expected. She liked all of her teachers and Mrs. Abbot in particular. She had already had a few short debates with her in class and felt that she learned quite a bit. At this point Angie was feeling like this would be the best year of high school.

As usual, there are always bullies and it is no different at CDO. At Amphitheater Angie tolerated everybody and didn't have any problems with anyone outside of teasing. But CDO is a little different. With more wealthy families in the district there was more focus in sports and thus, more jocks that think they are owed everything, the usual type, arrogant and obnoxious.

It didn't take long for the jocks to notice Angie. She is new to CDO and is a very beautiful girl, is very smart and drives a Panther Pink HEMI Cuda. Because of this she stood out compared to everyone else there. They could already see that she brownnoses Mrs. Abbot, the Physics teacher. However, Angie doesn't "brownnose" Mrs. Abbot, but the way they saw it, she did. The jocks thought they had multiple reasons to break her and they laughed with each other about it. They had a new conquest now and as is typical for jocks, they were all talking amongst each other about how they were going to have sex her and who would be the first. And Mike, the schools star quarterback already was jealous of her because of the CUDA. Mike told all of his jock friends that no girl has ever turned him down. This is because if they turn him down he just forces himself on them. And because of him there are a few girls that are outcasts in the school because Mike forced himself on them, in other words, he raped them, but since he is the star quarterback and his father is the Tucson City Manager, everyone turns their heads. Now he wants Angie.

First he was nice and asked her out like a normal guy. Angie politely turned him down and told him she doesn't have time in her life right now for relationships. Mike continued trying over the next week and Angie replied politely about the same each time. So the next week he decided to try something different.

Mike kind of cornered Angie and started to ask if she would give him a ride in her "Fine Machine" hoping to get her to take him for a ride and then he would have his chance. But again Angie politely turned him down. Now Mike was getting angry. He told his best friends, Paul and Jim, that no one turns Mike down and gets away with it. Paul and Jim edged him on which really built his ego. Mike told them that at the end of the day he was going to get her to go out with him, whatever it takes.

They saw Angie at her locker after last period and Mike decided this was it. The three of them walked up to Angie and Mike said, "Hi Angela."

She turned to him and told him, "My name is Angelina not Angela."

"OK, Angelina." Mike said in a smart ass tone, "We're going for a ride and you're not saying No." Mike grabbed her purse and gave it to Jim.

Angie said in an irritated manner, "Mike, I have tried to be nice and polite but evidently you do not understand that. Now please give me my purse back."

Mike said, "No, you are going to take me for a ride like it or not. Mike doesn't accept No from any girl. And you are going to do it or you might get hurt."

Angie was now getting annoyed. Just then, they heard this voice telling them to give the purse back. Mike starts to say, "Fuck you, assh..." as he turned and saw that it was Derek. Mike and most everyone were afraid of Derek because he is 6'4" tall and appears to be solid muscle. Mike was 5' 10" tall so Derek towered over him. Mike changed his attitude and said, "Derek, ah, we were just joking around with Angelina." and handed Angie her purse back and the three of them left.

Derek said to Angie, "I can't stand guys like Mike and his cronies. You OK Angie?"

Angie knew Derek from her Physics class. "I am fine Derek, thank you."

Derek said, "You know, when I was in grade school I was very short and I constantly got picked on. I promised myself if I ever got big enough I would try to make sure this never happened to anyone. You just don't deserve this kind of thing, especially being new to this school. And no, I'm not hitting on you."

"Well Derek, I did not think you were hitting me. I would be flattered but the reality is that I do not have time for guys. Besides studying, I train twice a week, I work at my father's shop and I also go with him drag racing so I do not really have time for anyone, sorry."

"Wow, a girl into cars. That's so cool! It does sound like you're quite busy Angie, but I am really not interested in dating either because I need to care of my mother when I'm not at school. She is very sick and we have no one else. Just scream if you ever have trouble with those guys. I know they are afraid of me."

"You could easily be someone's hero Derek. Thanks though. I need to leave now. See you in physics class." She left.

Angie went out to her car, put her books, folders and purse in, got in and closed the door. Before she could do anything else Mike grabbed the passenger door handle and got in. "I told you were going to give me a ride," and laughed sinisterly. He figured now he had her and he's going to have sex with her tonight.

Sherri was leaving school at this time and saw Mike get in Angie's car and thought, "God! That bastard is going to rape Angie."

"Angie mumbled to herself, "Really? Again? What an asshole!" Now she was angry because this is going to use some of her study time. Very sarcastically Angie said, "So you want a ride, do you? Fine!" Angie reached behind her seat and grabbed her helmet. She put it on and fastened her seat belt tight. She started the Cuda, backed out of the parking spot and started driving.

Mike asked, "What's with the helmet?"

"It is standard safety equipment, Mike. I always wear it when I race." Angie said sarcastically to Mike.

"What do ya mean when you race?" Mike asked with a little fear in the tone.

Angie didn't say anything. She just drove to Oracle and turned left. Then she stopped.

"Why are you stopping in the middle of the street?" Mike barely got that out when he heard the HEMI engine rev high and Angie dumped the clutch.

The tires spun and smoked and they were plastered into the seats. Angie banged second, then third. The whole time Mike was screaming for his life. He never was in a car like this. He continued screaming. Then Angie power spun the car around onto the other side of Oracle, she straightened out the car and stopped. "You had enough of a ride yet Mike?" Angie said again sarcastically.

Mike said, "Wha..."

Angie did it again only this time she banged 4th and the speedometer was pegged. The HEMI was screaming. She could heard Mike crying. She slowed down and turned back onto Calle Concordia and pulled up in front of the school. "Now get out of my car asshole!"

Mike was shocked at the language as he never heard Angie even say darn much less swear like this. His eyes were red, he had a pounding headache and he thought he shit his pants. He opened the door and started to get out and Angie raised her right leg and pushed him out with her foot. He fell out onto the ground and Angie sped away spewing dirt and sand all over him. Mike just sat there in shock. Paul and Jim ran over and said, "What the hell happened, Mike?"

"She's a crazy bitch, she's insane."

"What do you mean?" Paul asked Mike.

Mike just got up and said, "Fuck that bitch. I'm out of here."

Then Jim saw the back of Mike's pants and asked, "Did you shit your pants Mike?"

Mike just said, "Fuck you." and walked away. He never was humiliated like this before. He was already trying to think of a way to get back at Angie. He was talking to himself, "Nobody does this to Mike, the star quarterback, nobody." Mikes arrogance shows by referring to himself in the first person.

The next day in school some of the kids were talking, laughing and looking at Angie. She thought to herself, "Go ahead, think that is going to bother me?" She was thinking they were laughing at her. She was feeling very self-conscious and down because of what Mike pushed her to do. But they were actually looking at her and laughing at Mike, thinking Angie had the guts to finally put that asshole in his place.

Then she saw Mike walking around the corner. One of the cheerleaders said out loud, "Do you need diapers, Mike? I could bring you some of my baby brother's diapers from home." She and the other cheerleaders were all laughing.

Another girl that Angie thought was Sherri from her Physics class came to her and said, "Wow nobody ever stood up to Mike before. You're a kind of hero now Angie."

Angie just said, "He got what he deserved." And she walked away. The most of the day Angie was kind of angry because she never had to do anything remotely like that to anyone before and kept thinking, "He caused me to become angry. I dislike becoming angry, I become irrational." She was finely able to shake it off and finished the day the same as usual.

Then on Friday, a few days later, Mike, Paul and Jim cornered her again. Mike grabbed Angie's arm and slammed her against the lockers and said, "Bitch, now you are going to get what you deserve. Nobody turns Mike down or humiliates him so now I'm going to cut that pretty face of yours." Then he pulled out a switchblade and it clicked open. He raised the knife and Angie just reacted. She used a Palm Heel punch to his nose and BAM! She broke Mike's nose. He never saw it coming. The knife went flying and Mike fell back on the floor holding his nose bleeding all over. He sounded like he was crying. Paul and Jim ran away and just left him.

Just then Mrs. Abbot came out of the classroom across the hall and started to ask what all of the commotion was. She was shocked when she saw Mike on the floor bleeding. She looked at Angie and asked, "Are you OK Angelina?"

"I am just fine Mrs. Abbot." She had contempt in her tone.

Mrs. Abbot said, "Angelina, would you please go and get Mr. Luis and bring back the nurse as well?"

"Yes Ma'am" She turned and jogged to the principal's office. She saw Mr. Luis and called to him to catch his attention. "Mr. Luis, Mike pulled a knife on me and said he was going to cut my face. And I believe I broke his nose, sir." Mr. Luis started to smile and giggle and caught himself.

"Go get the nurse please, Angie. Where is he?"

"He is on the floor in front of my locker, sir."

Angie got the nurse and the two of them went back to where it happened. Mr. Luis was already there and had the knife in his hand and he looked very angry. The nurse went and started to help Mike.

Mr. Luis asked Angie, "What exactly happened."

"Mr. Luis, Mike, Paul and Jim kind of ambushed me and threw me against the lockers. Then Mike said he was going to get back at me for humiliating him by turning him down for a date and he was going to cut my pretty face. Then he pulled out that knife. Paul and Jim were here cheering him on. I just reacted."

Mr. Luis looked at Mike and said to Mrs. Abbot, "Would you please go and see if you can find Paul and Jim Mrs. Abbot? They should be at practice about now. Then bring them to my office."

"Yes, I will Mr. Luis." Mrs. Abbot said and walked away.

The nurse had the bleeding mostly stopped, she had Mike hold a cloth on his nose and hold his head back. Mr. Luis looked at Mike and said, "Get up Mike. Don't you know knives of any kind are not allowed in school? And to pull one on a fellow student is just cowardly. Now come with me to my office." He looked at Angie and said, "Could you please come too Angie?"

Angie replied, "Yes sir." And she walked with Mr. Luis, the nurse and Mike. She was thinking that she was in big trouble for fighting in school. She was afraid, shaking and her legs felt like jelly.

When they got to Mr. Luis' office Mrs. Abbot was already there with Paul and Jim. "I want you guys in my office NOW! He looked at Angie and Mrs. Abbot and asked them to please wait for now and he would call them if he needed them, then went into his office and closed the door.

Mrs. Abbot asked Angie again if she was alright. "I am fine Mrs. Abbot. You know I have been training for this kind of situation for 11 years now and I never thought I would actually need to use it. And now I fear that I will at least be reproved." Mrs. Abbot could see that Angie was shaking.

Mrs. Abbot looked at Angie and said, "Try and calm down Angelina, I doubt you are in trouble. You just defended yourself. What do you mean by training for a situation like this?" She had no idea what Angie could be talking about.

"Mrs. Abbot, I have been in Martial Arts Training learning a modified combination of Aikido; Taekwondo and Karate since I was 7 years old and I have earned the ranking of 3rd Dan black belt. This has taught me wisdom; confidence and self-control. Because of this I was able to stay calm. Otherwise I may have either not reacted in time or I may have lost my temper and continued after I neutralized Mike and severely hurt him."

Mrs. Abbot looked at Angie up and down and said, "Really? My lord! I would never have guessed. It's good for you that you had this training or you may not be alright now." She thought for a minute and said, "Oh, this is probably why you are so confident, more so that any high school student I have ever taught."

Just then the office door opened and the 3 boys walked out. They didn't look very happy. Mr. Luis said, "Paul and Jim admitted what they had done without any issue. Paul and Jim are suspended for a week which means they won't be playing in any game for a while. And for Mike, I called the police and they are going to visit him and decide if they will charge him. Mike is now been expelled. His father won't be very happy. Angie, are you sure you are alright?"

Mrs. Abbot answered, "She is Mr. Luis, and she has been in training for self-defense for 11 years!"

"Really? That's great!" But I hope you will never need to use it again in this school, Angie."

"Mr. Luis, I already feel bad that I had to use it at all. The training teaches us to only use it as a last resort and only for self-defense. I viewed this as the only way to keep from being hurt."

"Well, Angie, I'm glad you feel this way. You may go now."

Angie replied, "Thank you sir." and left.

Angie had been sure she would be in trouble for fighting in school but was relieved that she wasn't. She walked to her car. She was just about to put the key in to unlock the door and she heard, "You fucking Bitch you fucked up my chances of getting a football scholarship. Now I'm going to kill you, I got nothing to lose now." He started to run at Angie and she dropped her books and got into her stance.

Just as he was close enough she hit him with a reverse 360 degree roundhouse kick on the side of his head and with one move he was out. She just left him there laying on the ground and went home.

When Angie got home she told both parents what happened. Her mother was horrified. Her father asked her if she was OK and if she needed him to go see Mr. Luis. She told him that he didn't and that everything at school is fine.

Later, Angie's father asked her, "You really knocked that kid out with one roundhouse?"

"Yes father I did. And that was not a strong kick. If I did it full force I could have severely injured or killed him. My Sensei said that this kick can generate as much as 2000 pounds of force."

"Wow, I did not realize that what you were learning was so lethal. Well, I am glad you are OK. Oh, Did you hear about the inmate that escaped from the state prison today?"

"No, father, I have not."

"I'm elated you have this ability as I will not need to be concerned. The news stated that this guy murdered 3 people while robbing them and he did it just for fun. I trust they catch him soon."

"Do you believe he would remain in Tucson? I believe he would want to get away as quickly as possible."

"You are probably right."

The next day, Saturday, Angie went to the shop with her father as usual. When she walked in the guys there looked at her kind of odd. She asked, "What's up guys?"

"We heard what happened yesterday. We're all glad that you are OK, Angie."

"It was nothing, guys. Not to worry."

"Oooh, look who has a big head." Angie overheard.

"C'mon guys, stop teasing." They all had a tight camaraderie between them.

Chapter 12

Sunday late afternoon Angie went with her mother to the grocery store. The day was a picture perfect day, sunny without clouds with a constant breeze. Angie was wearing her standard t-shirt, jeans and gym shoes and her mother had a white pleated sundress and flats. They were out on a leisurely afternoon to pick up a few things; they paid and left the store. They had put the bags in the trunk and closed it when someone behind them said, "Give me you purses and no one will get hurt." He had a Bowie knife in one hand.

Lizzy screamed. "Do as he asks honey." as she handed him her purse.

Angie said, "Not again?" She was irritated that today would be ruined by another jerk, just like at school.

The guy said, "shut the hell up and give me your purse, bitch."

"You are the guy that just broke out of prison are you not?"

"So what, gimme you fucking purse." He repeated. "I'll cut you."

Lizzy exclaimed, "Angie what are you waiting for?"

Angie got into her stance and the guy swung his knife. Angie used a forward roundhouse kick and the knife went flying out of his hand. Angie's mother was stunned. Other people began to watch.

"You're going to pay bitch" the guy said as he started to pull out a gun. Angie just reacted. She thought about all she was taught and did a 360 degree reverse roundhouse but not like she did on Mike. This time she put almost all of her strength into the kick. She hit the guy on the side of the head, his head twisted in a strange way and he went down like a sack of potatoes. When he fell his head hit the curb so hard that it sounded like dropping a watermelon on the pavement, a kind of a hollow cracking sound. Angie kicked his gun away.

Lizzy was in shock. She couldn't believe what she just saw. Did her daughter just kill this guy with a kick she thought?

Angie screamed, "Someone please call the police."

Everybody stood around just looking. Angie was holding her mother. Her mother was shaking from shock. It was almost dark now and you could hear the sirens from the police cars coming. Headlights flashed as multiple police cars screeched to a halt. In a few seconds there were police everywhere. One went and picked up the knife and gun. Another went over to the man lying on the ground and felt if he had a pulse. There was no pulse. He turned the guy's head and gasped, "This is the guy we have been looking for that just broke out of State!" A couple of other police officers came over and looked and one pulled out his picture.

"It's definitely him." He said. "He looked up at Angie and her mom and asked, "You did this?" in disbelief. "What happened?" Angie continued holding her mother. She explained what happened in detail. How he tried to stab her, how she kicked the knife out of his hand and then threatened them and pulled the gun.

"Sir, it was an automatic response to fatal danger."

"What was an automatic response Ma'am?"

"I used a 360 degree reverse roundhouse, sir, just as I was taught."

"What's a 360 degree reverse roundhouse? How were you taught to defend yourself from someone with a gun? I don't understand?"

Angie was coming down off of all the adrenalin and starting to feel weak. Her legs were feeling limp and started fall. One of the other officers caught her and helped sit her on the curb. "Ma'am?" he said. "He called out, "Does anyone have some water or something?"

A guy from the store brought out a cold bottle of Coke. "How about this?"

"Ma'am, try drinking some of this." He held up the bottle.

Angie took it and took a big couple of gulps. "Thank you sir. I feel strange."

The officer said, "You're in shock ma'am. Just relax, take your time."

After a few minutes Angie said, "I believe I am fine now officer."

The officer said, "If you feel alright, could you answer the question please?"

"Yes of course, A 360 degree reverse roundhouse is a kind of kick I learned training in the Martial arts. I have been training in a modified combination of Aikido, Taekwondo and Karate, officer. I have been training since I was 7 years old. Reaction time is part of the training along with instantly identifying a threat and reacting. All I thought was, 'You are not going to hurt my mother and I and you not taking my car!' and when I saw him pulling out the gun I reacted officer."

"And that's how you killed him? With a kick? Boy, I never want to make you angry. This your car?" he pointed to the Cuda?

"Yes, it is officer."

"I can see why you wouldn't want anyone to take it. It is beautiful. I never saw a pink car before though."

The guy from the store brought another Coke for Angie's mother and handed it to her.

"Thank you so much sir." Lizzy said.

The guy said, "You're welcome Ma'am."

While they were talking the coroner came and took the body away. Other officers were taking statements from the onlookers and people were beginning to leave. All this time Angie and her mother hadn't noticed the reporters. Then they saw the people with cameras and lights. They were talking to the police and some of the bystanders. Then they saw Angie and her mother with the officer. They rushed over and flashed the lights and were asking questions.

"Can you tell us what you did here today Miss? Angie and her mother looked away and ignored them. "Miss, did you know this was the escaped prisoner? How did you defend yourself from this attacker? Are you still in school? What school do you go to? For the record, what is you name. Miss? The reporter asked.

The officer told them to move away. He asked if Angie and her mother would come with them to the station to make an official statement. He said he would take them in his police car to get them away from the reporters. Angie and her mother agreed and the officer helped both of them stand up and led them around the crowd to his police car. The officer told them that when they were finished he would have someone bring them back to their car.

After Angie and her mother made their statement another officer drove them back to their car. Again, he asked if they were OK. They assured him that they were. They thanked him, got out of the car went to the Cuda and went home.

Dominic was waiting in front of the house when they arrived. He ran to the Cuda when they stopped. "My god, are you both alright? I was getting worried and turned on the news. I almost lost it when I saw your car and they said a young girl killed the escaped inmate. I thought the worst. Thank God you are both alright." He was hugging them both, grabbed the grocery bags and walked them into the house and locked the door. They went into the Arizona room, sat down and talked.

They talked for quite a while and Angie and her mother were feeling better.

Monday morning Dominic called CDO to explain what had happened the previous night. They had already known. They told him that Angie could stay home until she felt ready to come back. They were very sympathetic. Dominic thanked them and hung up. He told Angie and Lizzy that the school said that Angie can come back when she is ready.

By Tuesday night, Angie felt she stayed home long enough. She said to her father, "Father, I desire to go back to school. And I am getting somewhat worried that I will fall behind in my classes. So I would like to return to school tomorrow." Tomorrow was Wednesday.

"Are you certain you are ready Angie?"

"Yes father, I already feel as though I have been home too long.

Chapter 13

Angie went to school Wednesday morning just like any other day. She never thought about the implications from what happened. When she arrived Mr. Luis met her and brought her to his office. He wanted to tell her what to expect from everyone. "First I wanted to tell you that if you have any problems with anyone or anything that the school staff and I are here to give you any support. You counselor said she will be available all day if you need to talk."

"Thank you Mr. Luis, but I do not understand all of the concern. I am fine and have already made peace with myself through meditation. My head is clear and I am ready to continue school, sir."

Mr. Luis sat for a moment. "Angelina, I don't think you have considered how everyone else in the school is feeling."

"Why would everyone feel different? They were not involved in this." Angie said feeling slightly concerned.

"Angelina, I want you to understand how serious this is. Monday, it got so, how should I describe it, out of hand. What happened made a huge impact on everyone. Some students were afraid. So I called for everyone to go to the auditorium. I explained to everyone that you were just defending yourself and no one needs to be afraid."

"What were they afraid of? Sir."

"Well, to be frank, they are afraid of you Angelina."

"Afraid of me? Why? I just defended myself. Why would that make anyone fear me?"

"Well, I don't think what happened would have been much of a problem but there was the incident with you and Mike. Because it happened in the school some of the parents were worried that their kids were in danger from you."

"Why would parents think that I would be a danger to their kids? All I have done was to defend myself. I was not the aggressor. If Mike would have ended up cutting me or beating me would they fear him? I think not." Angie was beginning to get irritated. "I just wanted to come here to learn. I devote more time and effort into my school work that likely every other student at this school. My expectation was that this school would be different. I had been so thrilled about going to this school because it is highly rated and because the teachers are listed as exceptional. I did not treat anyone poorly; I did not start any trouble with anyone. I even went out of my way to turn down Mike's advances politely so as to not cause him to perceive that he was failing. I indicated that it had absolutely nothing to do with him, that I study, work for my father, train twice each week and go along with my father drag racing and I simply do not have time for anyone now. I went so far as to tell him that he appeared to be a nice enough guy. I do not understand what made him so angry at me. And everyone is afraid of me because of that?"

"Angelina, I believe everything you say is true. I wish I could have a school full of students like you. You are the kind of student that makes teachers feel like they actually make a difference. But what is happening here is because of ignorance. It really has nothing to do with you. It's about them Angelina. You are very well spoken and confident and most of the students don't understand this, so they look at you as being different. I only brought you here because I want you to be prepared in the event anyone causes you trouble. I am going to be around the school along with many of the teachers watching. Nothing will happen if I can help it Angelina. This school and everything that happens in these walls and on the grounds is my responsibility and I don't want anyone to feel afraid, especially you Angelina. So please go to class and try to think of everything as usual. And please come and see me if anyone gives you any trouble, this means teachers as well. I want you to know that every day I look forward to seeing you here, it makes me feel that there are still good students. Do you understand Angelina?"

"Yes sir, Mr. Luis. I appreciate what you have said. Thank you." She got up and said, "Have a good day, sir." She picked up her books and left for her first class which fortunately was Physics. She was looking forward to seeing Mrs. Abbot, even if she didn't have an opportunity talk to her today.

Angie walked to Mrs. Abbot's class, took a deep breath and walked in. Mrs. Abbot turned and said, "Angelina, I glad to see that you're back at school."

"Thank you Mrs. Abbot." She felt like everyone was staring at her, like they were drilling holes in the back of her head. She sat down thinking that she should never have chosen a front seat. She tried to ignore it but that didn't help much. She tried to concentrate on the class but she kept feeling like all eyes were on her. She found that she was sweating and thought, "Why is this affecting me this much?"

When class ended Angie got up still feeling like everyone was staring. Mrs. Abbot said, "Angelina, could you stay behind for a minute, please?"

"Of course, Mrs. Abbot."

Once everyone had left the room Mrs. Abbot went to Angie and said, "Angelina, I just wanted to welcome you back and tell you that I am truly sorry for what happened. If you need anything, anything at all, please come and ask me."

"Thank you, Ma'am"

"Oh, and Angelina, I also wanted to tell you that most of the students are looking at you as a hero now, for what happened with Mike and how you handled the incident with the convict. You managed to give them hope, something that is very difficult to give anyone in high school. I think Mr. Luis is just a little paranoid. Mike's father came and talked, well, more like screamed at Mr. Luis the next day and he was furious because of the expulsion. But believe it or not Mr. Luis held his ground and told Mike's father that just because Mike was a star quarterback, all of the rules apply to him just like everyone else. I just thought you would like to hear that, Angelina."

"Thank you Mrs. Abbot, I feel much better, Ma'am. And it is very credible hearing this from you, Ma'am." Angie turned around and went to her next class.

One thing that helped Angie's position was that Bella had heard about Angie's encounters with Mike, and she knew about the incident with the convict from the news and from her mother, Aunt Maria, so she did quite a bit to tone down the incident. This is part of why so many kids weren't afraid of Angie. Unlike Angie, Bella is fairly popular and has many friends in school. She is one that kids flock to. She is sweet and very sociable so she used her position with the kids to explain that Angie was a victim here. She explained that Mike was the one everyone should be afraid of. She told everyone that she had overheard some cheerleaders discussing that Mike may have raped some girls there. A few said that they had heard that too. Many of the kids began to feel bad that they had been afraid of Angie.

Throughout the day Angie was quite surprised because many of kids said "Hi" to her with big smiles. Usually no one would say anything to her. Then after school as she was walking to her car, she heard someone calling her. "Angie, Hey Angie, wait up." It was Sherri from Physics. Angie stopped and waited for her. "Angie, I have been trying to talk to you all day."

"Why, what is it that you want, Sherri?" She sounded harsh, maybe a little bitter.

"Hey, don't be angry. I just wanted to tell you that you are my hero."

"Hero, hero? Why? I am not a hero, I am merely a student comparable to everyone else her."

"No, you are definitely not comparable to everyone else Angie. You are like a role model now, at least for me. Maybe you don't know but lots of kids say the same thing. I'm sure you don't know everything about Mike. He is evil and a creep, I wanted to tell you. There are 3 of us who look up to you now, me, Janet and Kathy. You might not know them. Well," Sherri hesitated, "Um, I don't like to talk about this. It's difficult and embarrassing for me, it makes me feel sick but, but since you stood up to Mike I feel somehow that I can trust you, I guess I will. Um, ah, it's hard to tell anyone this." She sounded upset.

"What? What is so difficult to say?" Angie had no idea what she was talking about but would be disgusted when she finally heard what Sherri had to tell her.

"The three of us were all raped by Mike."

"What!"

"He raped us and he got away with it because he's a jock." Sherri began to cry. "He forced each of us into his car and drove somewhere secluded then threatened us with his knife and raped us." Sherri said trying to stop crying. "And we were all virgins."

Angie could clearly see that Sherri was very upset.

Sherri was talking through her tears, "When we first heard that he tried to do it to you we thought he got away with it again. But you did what all of us wished we could do."

"Did you not tell anyone at the time?"

"Yea, our parents went to Mr. Luis and we told the police. Nobody did anything. Mike's dad is the Tucson City manager so I guess everyone is afraid of him. So now everyone at school says we made it up because we didn't want to admit we wanted to have sex with him. That's not true." Sherri was crying again. "So we are like outcasts, no one talks to us anymore so we are all alone here."

"Sherri," Angie's tone and demeanor changed completely. She said softly, "I understand why you are so upset. My mother says it is good to let out your feelings and that we should never tell anyone that they should not be feeling something. You need to feel your feelings with someone that will listen and give you support" She put her books and things down on the ground and took Sherri in her arms and hugged her, Just as her mother always did. "It will be alright, I will not let that creep, or anyone else for that matter, do that to any of you. Now I will be watching Sherri. This is not right."

"Really? You would do that for us?"

"I never break a promise Sherri."

"What you did stopped Mike. That's why you are our hero." She had stopped crying and pulled a tissue out of her purse and blotted her eyes.

"I just did what I had to. He threatened me so I reacted. That does not make me a hero."

"Well, heroes usually don't think they are heroes. That's what my dad always says. And now I believe him. We want to invite you to sit with us at lunch. Nobody ever sits with us because of what Mike did to us, but we would love it if you would, and you are always sitting alone and that makes me sad." Sherri explained. "We would finally have someone to be friends with at school. I also heard that you are very busy. They told me that you study all the time and work for your dad and, go drag racing? Really?"

"Well, yes. I do all of that and I also train in the Martial Arts. And after I graduate I am going to start racing my car."

"You're going to race yourself? Wow, I never heard of a girl racing. That's so cool! Maybe we could come and watch when you do it sometime."

Angie saw the excitement in her eyes. "Well, possibly. I will come and sit with you tomorrow at lunch, OK? I never really made any friends because I have been too busy with everything else in my life and I have never cared for anyone in school enough so it seemed pointless. But maybe it is time."

"Great! We'll be waiting Angie." Sherri said and walked back towards Janet and Kathy.

Angie got into her car, started it and drove home.

The next day at school Angie felt a little better. She didn't feel like everyone was staring at her. She smiled back when anyone smiled at her. She started to notice that they all weren't laughing at her or making fun of her but she actually felt that they were saying good things about her. At lunch she went to sit with Sherri, Janet and Kathy. Right away Sherri became excited and said, "Hi Angie, this is Janet and this is Kathy."

Janet said, "It's nice to meet you Angie."

And Kathy said, "Yea, nice to finally meet you."

Angie said, "I am pleased to meet you as well." and sat down. She felt a little self-conscious because making friends was a new thing for her.

Relax Angie, "We aren't going to bite." Kathy said. "We have wanted to ask you to sit with us almost since school started, but we were afraid."

"You were afraid of me?"

Before any of them could answer, another girl that Angie didn't know stopped at the table briefly and said, "Hi Angie."

Angie looked a little surprised and replied, "Hello."

"It looks like you are becoming pretty popular Angie. Well, you are different than other kids. We heard you liked cars and worked at an auto repair place so we didn't know how to ask.

And you don't seem to talk to anyone much but the teachers. So we didn't know what to do." Janet said.

"I am not different; I am just a student like everyone else."

"Not really, you're so smart and so confident. We admire that." Kathy said. "And we are outcasts because of what Mike did to us. Nobody talks to us, it's like we have a disease or something."

"Sherri spoke of it yesterday. I found it very saddening and distressing, and what Mike did must have been emotionally painful for each of you. But it must be very difficult to know others will not talk to you because someone raped you. That is very disturbing."

"See, you speak differently than everyone too, you use different words. I wish I could do that. Why do you choose not to talk to other kids? Don't you like anyone?" Sherri asked.

"No, I am just in a position where I do not have time to spend outside of school. And no one had shown interest or spoke to me. It has been my choice not to talk or associate with others. I perceived it as pointless."

"Pointless? Why can't you have friends just at school? There are lots of kids that do that. Don't you think that you are missing out?" Janet asked.

"When I was going to school at Amphitheater no one talked to me and those that had anything to say would say I was stuck up, pretentious and conceded. They did not approve on my caring about my studies and earning straight A's. They teased me and called me names so I did not associate with anyone. Then when my father started taking me to the drag strip, I was so hyped-up. Immediately I wanted to race myself once I came of age. Then he told me that if I kept my grades high he would purchase a car for me. So I have been studying every minute I can to keep my grades high. And when my father opened his shop I wanted to learn everything I could, and it paid off. My mother and father bought me the Cuda for my 18th birthday a couple months ago. So I do not believe that I am missing out on anything."

"They bought you that car? They must be rich! I wish my parents would by me a car." Sherri said. "I just have an old junky car that used to be my mothers."

"Us too! We don't even have cars." Janet and Kathy said. "Where do you live Angie?"

"I live in the Foothills on Christie Drive north of Ina. How about you?"

"You guys must be rich, the houses there are huge and I heard that they are all over a half a million dollars. I live in Casas Adobes right near Ina and La Canada." Sherri said. "And Janet and Karen live close to me."

"I do not believe my house is worth that much. I have an Aunt and Uncle that live in Casas Adobes. They live near Oracle and Ina. My mother's family is wealthy; their house may be worth that much. They have a house that makes mine look small and they have horses."

"Horses? Oh I love horses. Do you ride Angie?" Janet asked.

"Yes, I learned when I was a child. But although my grandparents are wealthy I grew up kind of poor."

"Really, I can't imagine what you consider poor then." Kathy asked.

"I grew up in a little house on Yavapai a couple of blocks from Amphitheater High School. We did not have much. My father drove an old 1948 Chevy up until he opened the shop. Then he had a very old Chevy pick-up truck then and when he bought his race car he bought a newer pick-up truck which is still only a 1968. We moved into this house on Christie over the summer from that small house. My father opened up his shop in, I believe, in 1964 but they have told me that they struggled to pay the bills until a few years ago."

"Wow, I would have thought you were rich all of your life. You act like rich people. You don't talk like regular kids. You walk and move different; you have a kind of elegance and grace to you. Then you have the Cuda." Janet said.

"Since my mother grew up wealthy, she taught me how to walk, move and speak properly. My grandmother, my father's mother also taught my father and my aunt the same things. My mother always told me that my life would change in the future and I needed to know how to be proper, courteous and how to be a lady."

"We can tell. Your manners are perfect and the way you speak, like "Mother and Father" not "mom and dad," and you are always so proper. You use Ma'am and Sir; please and thank you to everybody. I wish my parents taught me that. It's so elegant, or umm, refined, you do act like a lady. You even walk differently like Janet just said." Kathy said.

"My mother and father taught me that it shows your respect for yourself and others."

"I never thought of it that way. I always thought being polite like that was to show you are superior or something. What your mom and dad said sounds more reasonable. I like that. Maybe I could learn something from you Angie." Sherri said.

"Do any of you know a freshman by the name of Bella Bertini?"

"Yea, she is in one of our classes, why?" Janet asked.

"She is my cousin, my aunt's daughter."

"Really?" Kathy said. "She acts and speaks a lot like you too. Wow!"

Janet asked, "Has your family always lived in Tucson?"

"My mother's family has been in Tucson at least since the late 1800's. I have been told that I have a relative that taught in Amphitheater School district between 1896 and 1899. Her name was Mrs. F. Hall. I do not know anything other than that. And I only know that my father's family has lived here since about 1900. And you?"

Janet said, "I only know about my great grandparents lived here but that's it.

Karen said, "I only know about my grandparents. My Mom and Dad never talked about anything before them."

"I don't know anything about my grandparents. I was adopted just after I was born. My Mom and Dad told me that my real mom died in childbirth so I don't know anything. But I consider my mom and dad as my real parents since I never knew anything else and I think they are great parents." Sherri said.

"What is it about your parents that makes you say that Sherri?" Karen asked. "I never heard you say that before."

"Well, I can always go to them if I have a problem. They always will listen and they don't make me feel shameful or silly for asking. And they have never even slapped me. I hear that so many kids can't talk to their parents."

Angie said, "That is wonderful Sherri. It saddens me to think that so few have supportive parents."

"Angie? I think the way you speak makes me feel good, I wish I could speak like you, you sound so soothing sometimes. "Sherri said.

"Thank you Sherri, that is a very nice complement, I am delighted that I affect you so positively.

Just then the bell rang and lunch was over. Angie stood and said, "I enjoyed this quite a bit, thank you for inviting me. Now if you would please excuse me, I need to get to my next class."

The girls said "OK, will you sit with us again tomorrow?"

"Of course I will ladies." Angie answered and she left for class. As she walked away another girl said hi to her, Angie thought it was a nice change.

The girls looked at each other and said, "Ladies? We have never been called that." They continued talking and decided that they really like Angie.

As Angie walked to her next class another girl walked up to her and said, "Hi Angie, I'm Gina. A bunch of us have been watching you and at first we thought you were kind of odd. You kept to yourself and we thought you were just shy or something. But after this week you really surprised us."

Angie kept walking and replied, "Who are those you refer to as, "WE,"

"Oh, just me and my friends." Gina said. "We want to get to know you. You are really nice Angie."

Angie thought, The kids here have such poor grammar, not much different than Amphitheater. "I have a very busy schedule which leaves me limited time to make friends."

"So busy you don't have time for friends? What could you possible do with all of your time?" Gina asked.

"I study every day to keep up my grades; I train twice a week; I work at my father's shop on Saturday's and usually on Sunday's I go with my father drag racing. So I have little time for much else."

"Wow, I never knew anyone that does so much. What kind of shop does your dad have?" Gina asked.

"It is an auto repair and performance shop."

"So you do like paperwork or something then"

"No, I do repairs on customer cars. His shop is Dom's Automotive and Performance Center on Stone and 2nd street."

"You don't really work on the cars?

"Yes I do, Gina. I need to get to class now. We can talk further, possibly just after school. I could spare some time then if you like."

"OK, cool. I'll meet you after school then."

When she left her last class, Angie gathered everything she needed to study and walked towards the Cuda. Since she never really had any friends from school she wasn't thinking about meeting Gina. As she walked she heard, "Angie, wait."

It was Gina. She thought to herself, "Oh, I forgot I said I would meet her." and felt a little embarrassed. "Gina, I was just going to put my books in my car."

Gina said, "OK," she caught up to Angie. "Where's your car?

"Right over there." Angie pointed to the Cuda as they were walking towards it.

"That's yours? Cool! I was wondering who owned it. Wow! A pink car, I like the color. You're so lucky."

"Thank you Gina." Angie said. She opened the door and put her books on the front seat, closed and locked the door.

"Come with me, you can meet my friends. C'mon." Gina motioned to a few other girls. They started walking towards them. They met at the edge of the parking lot. "Hey guys, this is Angie, the one everyone was afraid of. See she's just like everyone else. Angie, this is Denise and this is Paula."

"I recognize her from the news report." Denise said.

Angie was a little apprehensive with Gina saying, "she was the one everyone was afraid of." She felt like she was put on the spot. "Hello Denise and Paula. I'm pleased to make your acquaintance."

"Weird," Denise said.

"Why is it weird?" Gina asked.

"She talks funny. No offence Angie." Denise said.

"I am not offended. I speak in the manor that I raised."

See? Who says that?" Denise said.

Paula said, "Denise, that wasn't very nice. You are just meeting her, have some respect." She looked at Angie, "It's nice to meet you too. Don't mind Denise, she can be annoying sometimes." She looked at Gina, then back at Angie, "I wasn't afraid of you. I don't know why anyone was. To me, that was stupid to think that. I figured you were just reserved and that's why you didn't talk to anyone much."

"Well Paula, that was nice to hear. I am not reserved; I have just chosen not to associate with anyone. I don't have time for any relationships."

"I can respect that Angie. But that doesn't mean you can't say "HI" or not have any contact with other kids when you're at school." Paula said.

"That's true. I have been learning that from Sherri recently. I never made any friends in school because it did not make sense to put in the effort. At Amphitheater they mostly said I was stuck up. But Sherri has shown me that I have been missing out by not making friends."

Denise said, "You talk to Sherri? And those two weirdoes she hangs around with?"

"Why would you say that about Sherri, Janet and Kathy? They are kids with feelings just like anyone else." Angie asked Denise.

"Well, it's that whole 'we were raped' thing. Why can't they just admit that they wanted it?" Denise said.

"Really? That is what you think? Maybe if it was you that was raped you would have a different perspective. Rape is a serious crime and a violent aggression on someone. That is very insensitive of you Denise." Angie said with some anger.

"If it was true why didn't anybody do anything about it then?" Denise said.

"Think about it Denise, the star quarterback rapes a few girls and his father is the Tucson city manager. Do you not think that his father would do anything to cover it up? And look at Mike, he looks at all girls with contempt and he believes women are worthless. It is likely his father feels the same, that is likely where he learned that." Angie replied.

"Well, um, I don't know, maybe. I just thought"

Angie cut her off. "You just thought, Really? What If someone started making accusations about you around school? Something bad such as," Angie thought for a minute, "If someone began telling everyone that you are having a sexual relationship with you father. How would you feel? I do not believe you would like that much, would you?"

"I don't have sex with my father! Why would you say that? That's sick!" Denise said.

"Caught!" Gina said. "See Denise, just saying that between us made you angry and I bet you got a little scared didn't you?"

"Well, yea, but why would anyone say that about me?" Denise said.

Paula snickered a little and said, "That was the point of what Angie said. You were already getting defensive and this was just hypothetical talking between us. How would you feel if kids passed that around school and then no one would talk to you anymore? And you know it isn't true. Could you imagine that?" Paula's expression changed. "Oh, um, that's what we have been doing to Sherri, Kathy and Janet, isn't it? That isn't very nice. It's pretty bad, I see that now."

"I, thought, I thought,---no, I didn't think, I am a real jerk aren't I." Denise was visually upset. "I'm sorry Angie. I didn't mean to do that to Sherri and her friends. I mean, um, ah, I'm just going to shut up."

"You're going to shut up? That would be something to see." Paula joked.

Gina was laughing. "Yea I wouldn't bet on you not talking for very long Denise."

"Oh that's what you think?" Denise said.

"That had to be, what, maybe 30 seconds?" Angie joked. "We can continue this another time. I have to get home, I have training tonight. It was very nice to meet all of you."

"You have to go so soon?" Paula asked.

"Yes I need to begin my homework and I will be at the Dojo for about two hours. Then I need to finish my homework."

"What's a Dojo?" Gina asked.

"A Dojo is where you learn and practice Martial Arts and also learn to meditate."

"Wow! How long have you been doing this Angie?" Paula asked.

"It has been about 11 years now."

"Do you, like, go to tournaments?" Paula asked.

"No, I learned this for self-defense and for discipline."

"Oh, so that's why you were able to defend yourself against Mike. That's so cool! So, they have ways to, um, like measure how good you are, right? Kind of like you see in movies about belt colors or something? Paula asked.

"All martial Arts have methods of measuring your progress and the levels you reach."

"Then where are you? What do they call where you are? After 11 years you have to be pretty high up, right?" Paula asked.

"The level that I have achieved is called 3rd Dan black belt. The easiest method of explanation is what they commonly use on movies where they say someone is a 3rd degree black belt."

"Wow! You must be really good. I really never knew that someone could actually get something like that. I thought it was just movie stuff." Paula said.

"I need to go ladies, I wish I had more time to talk, but I have a full schedule tonight."

Well, see you later Angie, I liked talking." Paula said. Gina and Denise said "see ya later."

Angie turned and walked to her car.

Gina said, "See I told you that you don't need to be afraid of her. She's nice."

"Yah, she's nice but she talks funny. Ladies? Who says that? It makes me feel like she is acting better than us." Denise said.

Paula said, "Angie says that. And I don't think she does it to do that Denise."

"No, I overheard Sherri talking about that and she said that Angie's parents say it shows you and the people you talk to respect. I'm not sure what that means though. Besides, she did say she learned it from her family and I don't think she means any disrespect." Gina said.

"I feel bad now for picking on Sherri, Janet and Karen" Paula said.

"I don't know, I feel bad too. I don't know what to do now. I am just going to go home. See you tomorrow." Denise said. She walked away feeling like crying. She wasn't exactly sure why though. When she got home she ran to her room and cried.

Paula and Gina said bye to each other and went home. Paula was feeling pretty down. She was thinking about what Angie said. By the time she got home she had tears in her eyes. She quickly said hi to her mother and went to her room and cried.

Gina was walking home and she was going over what Angie said in her head. She was so involved she walked into the street without looking and a car blew the horn and the guy in the car called her an idiot. She was thinking, "Have we been that nasty to those girls? I guess I wouldn't like to be treated like that." She couldn't get it out of her head all night. Although Gina didn't cry about it she felt embarrassed and very down. She didn't say much to anyone at home all night.

Angie has been making friends at school for the first time. She wasn't exactly certain how to have friends, she never thought about it before this. She thought to herself that is was kind of nice.

After some time Sherry, Janet and Kathy told Angie that after becoming friends with her they are finding that everyone else has been treating them a little better. Sherry told Angie that she doesn't feel like as much of an outcast anymore and she had Angie to thank for it.

Angie didn't understand how she could make such a difference. She still didn't understand why so many looked at her like a hero just because she stood up to Mike and then humiliated him with the ride in her car and then she broke his nose defending herself. When she thought about taking Mike for a ride she started chuckling. She was thinking that she can't believe she did that, but at the time he really angered her.

Chapter 14

Someone began vandalizing Angie's car. She came out of school one day and found that she had a flat tire. Angie thought, "Great, a flat." She was a little upset because now she had to change the tire. So she put her books in her car and grabbed her work gloves from the glove box then she opened the trunk and got out the jack, spare tire and the inflator bottle. She put on the emergency brake then put the bumper jack in the base then in the slot in the bumper and began to jack up the car. Before the tire was off of the ground she used the tire iron and loosened the lug nuts. Then she finished jacking until the tire was off of the pavement. She removed the lug nuts and removed the flat and replaced it with the space saver spare put on the lug nuts and snugged them. Then she screwed the inflator bottle onto the valve stem and the tire started to expand. When the tire was full she unscrewed the can and began lowering the car. At this point one of the jocks came over and offered to help. She told him, "No thank you I am fine," as she finished lowering the car. She grabbed the lug wrench and tightened the lug nuts. Then she put the jack and flat tire in the trunk and closed it. She put the inflator can in the car and put the gloves back in the glove box. She got into the car, started it and drove straight to her father's shop.

When she got to the shop she pulled in the back lot and went to tell her father what happened. "Father, I had a flat when I got out of school, so I changed it and drove here."

"I will have Hector look at it, do not worry." He went into the shop and said to Hector, "Hector, could you please bring Angie's car in here and check out the flat tire in the trunk. See what it needs to be repaired."

"OK Mr. Dominic." Hector said. Angie walked over and gave Hector the keys. He went out and drove the Cuda into the shop and onto a lift. He pulled the flat out of the trunk then raised the car. He filled the tire with air and put it into the water tank to find the leak. He didn't see any bubbles. Then he felt all over the outside of the tire and didn't find anything in the tire. He went up front to tell Dominic. "Mr. Dominic, I can't find anything wrong with the tire, nothing."

"Nothing? Then how did it get flat?"

"Don't know. It is holding air fine and there isn't a screw or nail or anything in it."

"Well, then could you put it back on the car and put the spare back in the trunk please?

"Ok Mr. Dominic."

"I will need to order another inflator bottle. Did you see anyone near your car today Angie?"

"No father, why?"

"Well, there is nothing wrong with the tire. It looks as though someone intentionally let the air out. Do you think that jock guy came to mess with your car?"

"I have no idea. That business happened over a month ago. Would you not expect if Mike was going to do something he would have done it sooner?"

"Well, possibly. But who else would have done this? The only way the tire would go flat is if there was something that pierced it or someone let out the air."

"I cannot think of anyone. But I will try to watch and I will mention it to Mr. Luis."

"That would be wise, Angie. The tire is back on and the spare is in the trunk still filled in case you need it again. Just go home and do not worry about it for now."

"Alright father, thank you." Angie gave him a hug and went into the shop, thanked Hector then got into the Cuda and went home.

Chapter 15

Mikes dad, Leonard Conrad, is the Tucson City Manager. He has been fixing things so Mike wouldn't get into trouble when he does something such as threaten a girl with a knife. He has put pressure on the school principal and police Chief to keep Mike from charges of rape against the three girls he raped. Now he wants Mike back in school and all allegations dropped. He has been working with his lawyer to figure out how to do this. But he received some bad news when he found out who Angelina Tucci is. She is the granddaughter of Joseph Hall, someone that has brought the city huge amounts of money. He may not be able to do anything for Mike this time he thought. Mike is really angering and embarrassing him this time.

When he got home, he called Mike to talk to him. "Mike, you really did it this time. Why are you such a fuck up? Come here." He demanded. He grabbed Mike and started slapping him. Although it isn't just slaps, it is actually hard slaps to the side of his face back and forth. Usually, it leaves marks. Mike's dad has been slapping him and beating him for years. He says it is the only way to get Mike to listen. He routinely beats Mike for just about anything he does wrong, such as not getting passing grades or messing up in a football game. He has used his belt and a wooden paddle. He told Mike he doesn't tolerate lying down on the job and then told him that he needed to beat it into him. Sometimes he would slap Mike in the head to the point of giving him a bad headache. Mike has felt at times like he would pass out, but he doesn't ever fight back, even now when he is in High School. He is afraid of his father.

A few times his mother has brought him to the emergency room from her husband's beatings. She always told the doctors and nurses that his injuries are from playing football. This is how they got around being asked about abuse.

Mike's father is not the only one that beats Mike. His mother does her share of beating him as well. She has a big wooden spoon that she used when dying fabric that she uses on him. She's hit him on the back of his legs, his butt, his back, she's hit his arms a few times and a couple of times she broke her spoon over his head. That made her so angry she wanted to punch him in the face, for "breaking her spoon." She has replaced it many times.

Besides beating, Mike is verbally abused. Both parents belittle him in front of other people and his friends; they call him a worthless waste of a human being. His dad calls him a looser and when he is really angry, he calls him a human size piece of shit. Mike doesn't remember his parents ever giving him a complement or telling him that they loved him, or even giving him a hug.

And along with this his father constantly berates his mother, mostly when he is angry or drunk. He tells her she is worthless and that she is only there for his pleasure. That's all she is good for now, he says, since she let that kid rape her years ago. She deserved it.

With all of this abuse Mike developed some very bad habits interacting with others. When he was a little kid he would climb trees and if he saw a bird nest he would break the eggs. He has trapped squirrels and rabbits and tortured them to death. He secretly began worshiping Satan around 8th grade and pledged his allegiance. It's a wonder he has been able to stay in school and stay on the football team.

Mr. Conrad has always been a dirty politician. Throughout his career he has done whatever he needed to get ahead and he could care less about who would get hurt. Even though Mike calls him dad, he is his stepdad. Shortly after Mr. Conrad married Mike's mother, she got pregnant from being raped and beaten by a young kid. Mr. Conrad never considered Mike his kid and hated it when Mike called him dad. Sometimes when he is beating Mike he thinks about this and beats him even more.

"You know who you messed with, you human piece of shit? This Angelina is the granddaughter of Joseph Hall. He brings in millions of dollars to the city. You really fucked up, and you're embarrassing me again." He is slapping Mike. Then he took off his belt and started beating him on his back. And when Mike tried to move away he hit him on the back of his neck.

"Stop, you've been doing this since I was a little kid, I'm not a kid anymore." Mike was beginning to fight back, at least verbally.

His dad told him, "I am still bigger than you and you live under my roof. Keep this attitude up and you will really get a beating. I should just kick your sorry ass out of here, Mike. All you do is embarrass me, dam it, go to your dam room." He kicked him in the butt as he left. Leonard isn't really bigger than Mike but since he has been telling Mike this since he was a little kid Mike believes it.

Just then Mike's mom walked in, "What did he do this time, Len?"

"The little prick attacked and threatened to cut the grand-daughter of Joseph Hall, that's what he did. I am so pissed off at him."

"Who is Joseph Hall?"

"He brings in millions of dollars' worth of business into the city. I don't know if I can fix this one. It is possible he will get jail time for this. What an embarrassment."

"Little bastard."

"He is you know." He gave her a spiteful glare. He always reminds her how she let that kid rape her almost 18 years ago and how he feels about it. Of course, that's what he thinks, that she let the kid rape her even though she got beaten and cut up. "I should have divorced you and kicked you ass out when you got pregnant from that asshole kid. Mike isn't even mine." Len said as he slapped his wife across the face with the back of his hand. He left to go get a drink.

Mike's mom sat down in the kitchen and cried and mumbled, "Bastard." Then she thought that she should have left him after she was raped but she had nowhere to go. Shortly after it happened she decided to just live with the abuse from Len. She has endured verbal and physical abuse almost daily. After years of this she began taking it out on Mike. As Mike got older she beat him more and harder, she never thought about what she was doing and never realized that the abuse that she and Len did to Mike had very negative effects. She didn't know that Mike found relief in worshiping Satan.

Since Mike found Satan he felt he was more able to live with the abuse. He prayed that one day his mom and dad would suffer horrible deaths. For years he thought of elaborate scenarios on how they could die and ways they could get maimed. And, as the years past these got more and more realistic in his mind. In time he found that he could care less about them. He stopped thinking of them as parents and just thought of them as some people that sooner or later would die horribly. Mike was psychotic and this just fed it. And watching his dad beat his mom, berate her and tell her she was just for his pleasure is what drove him to rape Sherri, Janet and Karen. To him they were just toys.

Chapter 16

A few days later Angie was at school and told Sherri about the flat. Right away Sherri said she thought it was Mike. She told Angie, "I think he won't stop and it will just get worse." Janet and Kathy agreed.

Janet said, "I think you're going to have a lot of trouble from Mike because now he's mad and will do anything to have sex with you. But I really hope I'm wrong"

At the end of the day Angie was walking to the Cuda with Sherri and saw her tires were slashed. Well, two of them were.

"Oh Angie, I don't even know what to say! My god."

Angie became teary eyed and ran back into the school to call her father. Hector answered the phone, "Hello, Dominic's Automotive and Performance Center."

"Hector, please call my father, Thank you sir." She manages to get out without crying but she sounded very upset.

Hector poked his head in the office and said, "Mr. Dominic, it's Angie and she sounds very upset."

Dominic went and took the phone, "Thank you Hector. Hello, Angie? What is wrong honey?"

"Someone slashed my tires..." Angie was now sobbing.

"Oh Angie, I am sorry. I am going to leave now with the trailer. I will be there as fast as I can. It will be alright, I will be there soon."

"Thank you father."

Angie grabbed a tissue from her purse and wiped her eyes and tried to compose herself. Sherri was still there and she hugged Angie, "It will be OK Angie, you'll see. Your dad, um, father is coming and he will take care of everything like he always does." Sherri was trying to speak like Angie.

"I know, and thank you Sherri. I am grateful that you remained with me."

"That's what friends are for. You know, well, I don't know if this is going to sound right but I'm glad that you cried, you are always so strong and it makes me feel so much better to know that you can cry too. It shows you have a soft side."

"I understand what you are saying Sherri, thank you, you are very sweet. I Now understand what I had been missing after all. I value having you as my friend Sherri."

It wasn't long when Angie's father showed up and backed up to the Cuda. Angie told Sherri, "I need to go now, thank you so much for staying here with me. I will talk to you tomorrow." Then Angie went over to help load the Cuda on the trailer.

"Do not worry honey; I will get this repaired right away. How are you handling this?"

Angie was wiping her eyes, "I feel relieved now that you are here father."

"Do you think it was that Mike guy"

"That is what my friends think."

"You made friends? That's wonderful Angie! I am so proud of you."

"Proud of me because I made friends?"

"Yes. You never made friends before and that's tremendous!"

"Why do you say it is tremendous, father?"

"It gives you someone your age that you can talk to about anything, someone you can confide in and that can give you support that you cannot get from your mother and me."

"I always confide in both of you for all of my issues and you have always helped and supported me. How can friends do any more than that?"

"Well Angie, there comes a time when you need other perspectives in your life. Your Mother and I can only give you our love, support and direction based on what we learned from our lives. And we grew up during a different period, one that was surrounded by many different things than you have now. So there are times when we likely do not quite understand how you feel. It is not that we do not want to, it is that we cannot because we did not experience life as you have. So we have a different point of view. Friends can give you the kind of support that we are not able to. Do you understand Angie?"

"I think I understand father. Even when you do not know how to respond to me I still appreciate you and mother's support. It still helps me and I do not want to lose that."

"You know we will always be here and you also have your grandparents and your Aunt Maria and Aunt Lilly that you will always be there to talk to you."

"Yes father, I know. I have talked to each of them before and I know they are all here for me as well. I just never thought about friends because at Amphitheater there was not anyone that I could be friends with. But at CDO I am finding that overall the kids think differently. They do not speak very well or have good manners but they think differently. Maybe it is because the majority of them come from families that are middle and upper middle class instead of lower class as with Amphitheater. I do not mean to sound intolerant father, but I just could not get along with them. They always said that I was stuck up and snobby so I could not connect with anyone."

"Angie, you are very intelligent and I can see that you can easily identify differences. And it is your choice with whom you decide to interact. I do not believe it is intolerant to choose one person over another based on comfort. People generally feel more comfortable with people in their class, which is just being human. Everyone has a method for doing what they do and there are some distinct differences. You need to decide to whom you do or do not befriend. There is not anything wrong with that."

"When your mother and I met I had had some issues related to this. I originally looked at your mother as being upper class and wealthy, and thought she was way out of my class. I had been looking at myself as poor lower class. But your mother saw through that and only saw that I articulated my speech and that I was a gentleman. She did not see that I was poor. She saw that I had to have been raised in an upper class family and just had a low time in my life. She could not believe that I was a mechanic but did not speak and carry myself as a typical mechanic. This is the same thing you are recognizing Angie. It is not good or bad. It is what you are comfortable with and what you expect of others."

"I think I understand father. Then you approve of my choice of going to CDO?"

"Angie, it is not so much that I approve your choice as that you approve of your choice. You need to live with your decision more than your mother and I. We would support you either way. We have had the opinion that you have been more in the position to make this decision that we were. If you would like an answer, yes we both approve. We trusted that you would make the decision that was correct for you."

"Father, you and mother are so insightful. It gives me something to strive for."

They arrived at the Discount Tire store on Kolb and went in to pick up tires for the Cuda. This is the store that Dominic used for the shop so he just had them put them on his bill. Dominic had all of the equipment to change and balance tires at the shop so he was just picking them up. Dominic only bought 2 tires to replace the slashed tires since the Cuda only had just over 4000 miles and they had the same tires that were already on the Cuda. He brought them out and put them in the bed of the pickup. Dominic and Angie got into the pickup and drove back to the shop.

When they arrived at the shop, Dominic backed the trailer with the Cuda in close to a lift. Miguel asked, "Angie, someone slashed your tires? Man that sucks."

Hector looked as they pushed the Cuda off of the trailer and went to help. "If I saw who did this I would make sure he never did it again. Or I would tell my cousin and he and his boys would take care of it."

"Hector, I appreciate that you care so much for Angie and her car but I do not want anyone "taking care" of whoever did this. This is why we have police. If we find this person we will turn him in, OK?"

"Yes Mr. Dominic. This just makes me mad." Hector said.

"Thank you for the thought Hector, I really appreciate how you guys have my back. You guys are commendable, but I agree with my father, whoever it is, we need to turn him in."

"OK Senorita Angie." Hector said. Hector was teasing Angie a little. The guys in the shop always referred to Angie as just "Angie."

They got the Cuda up and the two wheels off and the tires changed and balanced in a short time. The guys liked doing things for Angie as she is so sweet and nice to them. Besides, she is the boss's daughter. They also respected Angie because she knows her stuff around cars. They put the wheels with the new tires on the rear since those usually are worn first on muscle cars.

The tires were changed and Angie went home. She needed to study and do her homework and entirely too much time had already been wasted with the slashed tires.

When she arrived at home she went into the house and said, "Hello mother."

"Are you alright Honey? Your father called and told me what happened."

"No mother. Not really, some girls at school are positive it was Mike. They believe he will not stop. Why is this happening Mother, I did not do anything to him." Angie was broken up.

"Honey, everything will be fine. You will see."

"How do you know?"

"Well, I really do not know, honey. I feel that it will be fine but I do not know what else to tell you. I am afraid as well."

Chapter 17

Leonard Conrad learned that Mike has been stalking Angelina and vandalizing her car. When he got home he went to Mike's room and began to beat him again. Leonard told Mike as he began slapping him with his belt, "Slashing her tires Mike? Stop this petty shit or you will end up in jail. My lawyer came to me today with an idea that might get you off but you need to stop this shit now." When he felt that he beat Mike enough he left to get a drink.

Mike half stumbled down the stairs to get something to eat and his mother started on him. "You stupid son of a bitch, you never listen. You're going to make it so your dad won't be able to get you off if you keep it up. You're a real stupid asshole. I should have aborted you, you bastard. All you are is trouble." Mike ran out the door and his mom screamed, "Where the hell are you going?" He didn't answer and slammed the door as he went out.

The next day Leonard Conrad talked to his lawyer and his lawyer explained his idea. He said, "I think I can put a case together showing that Angelina pulled the knife on Mike. And when he tried to get it away from her she broke his nose. Then she looked for him and knocked him out. You know that Karate stuff can be lethal. We can portray her as a lethal weapon and that she is a danger to herself and everyone else." Leonard thought for a second and smiled, "Get started then. Great job!"

Leonard's lawyer began putting the case together. He filed the papers and the clerk of the court signed and affixed the court seal. At that point Leonard's attorney could get the papers served. Leonard wanted them served directly to Angie and he wanted them served to her while she was in school just because he wanted to upset her as much as possible for getting his son expelled.

A few days later he had the court papers served directly to Angie. Leonard wanted a sheriff's deputy to serve them and he wanted the papers served when Angie was in class. Leonard's attorney dropped of the papers at the Sheriff's office with instructions to deliver them when Angie was in class. The Sheriff didn't like Leonard or his attorney but he had no choice than to deliver them. He called Deputy Moody told him to make certain to get there late enough to have the office call Angie at the end of the day. The least he could do is spare her the embarrassment of getting papers served in class in front of everyone.

Deputy Moody left and drove to CDO. He parked and walked towards the office. He went into the office and said, "Good Afternoon Ma'am, I am here to serve court papers to Angelina Tucci and I want to be as discrete as possible. Could you call her to the office and ask her to bring her things please? I'm sure she will be very upset and I want to spare her the embarrassment from doing this in front of her classmates."

Miss Cardenas, the secretary, asked, "What is this about?"

Deputy Moody said, "All I can legally say is that I have papers to serve Angelina Tucci. But I can say I don't like being forced to do it this way, Ma'am."

"I can send someone to fetch her right away Deputy." Miss Cardenas said.

"Thank you Ma'am." He replied. And he said to himself quiet enough so he didn't think she could here, "That bastard."

"Excuse me, I didn't get that sir." Miss Cardenas replied.

"Oh, I'm sorry, I meant to think that not say it Ma'am. I'm sorry if I offended you." Deputy Moody said.

"Oh, I didn't understand so I am not offended." Miss Cardenas said.

"I'll just wait over there alright Ma'am?" Deputy Moody said. He walked to a chair and sat down.

"That will be fine sir." Miss Cardenas went and told Dean Campbell, the Dean of Girls, "There is a Deputy here to serve Angelina Tucci some kind of papers and he said he didn't want to do it in her class in front of everyone. Angelina is in Composition, Mrs. White's class."

Dean Campbell could see the worry in her expression and replied, "Yes, I will go now." She got up and walked through the office. She walked up to the Deputy and said, "Good afternoon sir, I am Dean Campbell. How can I help you?"

The deputy stood up and said, "Good afternoon ma'am, I have papers to serve to Angelina Tucci. I did not want to upset the whole class so I came to the office. I hoped we could keep this as discrete as possible to spare Angelina embarrassment."

Dean Campbell replied, "I agree, that would be much better sir. I will go and retrieve Angelina now." She thought about what this could possibly be because Angie couldn't possibly be in trouble, she is the most courteous and astute and sweet student she has ever had. She told herself to stop thinking like this because she did not want to alarm anyone. She knocked on the door and Mrs. White turned and came to the door.

Mrs. White opened the door slightly and Dean Campbell said, "I need Angie to gather her things and come with me now Mrs. White."

"Is there a problem?"

"I Hope not. Thank you, Mrs. White." Dean Campbell said.

Mrs. White turned and said, "Angie, could you gather you things and step out of the class room please?"

"Yes Ma'am." Angie said. She gathered her things and walked to the door. She was wondering what this was about. She went into the hallway and Dean Campbell waited for Mrs. White to close the door. "What is this about Ma'am?"

"I'm not quite certain Angie. I was just asked to bring you to the office."

"Ok." She was now somewhat frightened and she got more stressed as she got closer to the office.

As they walked into the office Angie saw the Sheriff's Deputy and immediately thought the worst. She thought, "Someone must have been killed or died." and her eyes began to get teary.

The deputy stood and walked up to Angie and pulled out the envelope. He said, "Angelina Tucci, this is a summons to appear in court Ma'am." He handed it to her and held up the paper and said, "Please sign here."

She took the envelope and signed. When she finished the deputy said, "I'm sorry I had to do this Angie. But I was told I may lose my job if I refused. This is why I wanted you to come to the office. They wanted me to go to your classroom to do this in front of your classmates, but I wanted to spare you the embarrassment."

Angie recognized the deputy because her father knew him but she didn't really know him well. She said her usual, "Thank you sir. I appreciate your thoughtfulness." But she knew something was wrong.

Deputy Moody promptly turned and left. Angie stood there wondering if she should open it there or wait until she got home.

Dean Campbell could see her distressed state and told her, "Angie, maybe you should wait until you get home to open it. I have no idea what it is but whatever it is I know you will be upset and you would be better driving beforehand."

Angie just stood there looking at the envelope. She felt as if she was frozen in place. After a few minutes Dean Campbell said, "Angie, Angie," She reached out and touched her shoulder. "Angie?"

Angie kind of snapped out of it. "Um what? W-What? Who? Uh," She then realized where she was and who was standing in front of her. "Oh, I am so sorry Ma'am. I—I never responded so poorly to anyone. I am very sorry for my actions Ma'am." She looked like she was going to cry.

"Angelina, please don't cry. Everything will be alright. Do you want me to call you mother or father to pick you up?" She waited and didn't get a reply. She never saw Angie like this. Angie is always so strong and confident. She was actually shocked. She reached and took Angie's shoulder and guided her to a chair. "Angie, please sit down. I going to call your father to come and pick you up. I couldn't let you try to drive in this condition." She went and picked up the closest phone and realized she didn't know Angie's father's phone number. She whispered to Miss Cardenas, "Could you please get me Mr. Tucci's work phone number?"

Miss Cardenas fumbled through student information cards and found it. She handed it to Dean Campbell. The dean dialed the number to Angie's father's shop. She heard, "Hello, Dominic's Automotive and Performance Center, How can I help you?" She thought, "Good it's her father. "Hello Mr. Tucci? This is Dean Campbell from Canyon Del Oro High School. Would it be possible for you to come to the school office now?" she asked. She wasn't sure what to say as she didn't want to alarm him.

"Yes Ma'am, Is there something wrong with Angie?" Dominic sounded concerned.

"Angie isn't feeling well and I didn't think she should drive. I don't think it is anything serious."

"I will leave now Dean Campbell. I will be there as soon as I can. Thank you ma'am."

Dean Campbell replied, "Thank you Mr. Tucci." And she hung up. She went over to Angie and asked her if she wanted some water.

Angie was still frozen and staring at the envelope. She didn't answer. Dominic arrived in about 25 minutes and rushed to the office. He came through the door and began to say, "Good afternoon, I am Mr. T.." just then he saw Angie sitting there staring at a big envelope. "Angie, what is wrong honey?" He looked at the envelope and it looked like a summons. "What is this?" Angie looked at her father teary eyed and handed it to him.

"A sheriff's deputy came today to give me this. I am too frightened to open it." She told him in a shaky voice. She was shaking quite a bit.

Dominic turned and looked at Dean Campbell, but before he could say anything she said, "I don't know what this is about Mr. Tucci. The Sheriff's deputy said he couldn't say anything legally. So I was very concerned. I didn't want Angie to drive in this state."

"Thank you Dean Campbell. That was very thoughtful."

Then Miss Cardenas said, "Sir, the deputy was angry that they made him serve these here at school. I overheard him say, Please excuse my saying this sir, 'That Bastard' I'm sorry for saying that but I thought you needed to hear what he said."

"Thank you Ma'am, and do not worry it is OK. What you told me may be important." He turned back to Angie, "Come Angie, let's get you home. I will ask Uncle Jack to come and get your car and bring it to the house." He turned to the dean and secretary, "Thank you both very much." He picked up Angie's books and folders and guided Angie to the door and to his truck. He got her into the seat and buckled her seat belt and walked around, got in and drove home.

When they got home he opened the door and Lizzy was near and said, "Hello Angie how was school today?" she walked around the corner and saw Dominic helping Angie to the couch. "What happed, is she alright?"

Dominic turned and said, "Basically. Not long ago a sheriff's deputy went to the school and served Angie with court papers."

"Court papers? Court papers? What could that possibly be for Dominic?"

"I do not really know sweetheart. But judging by what they told me at school I would bet it is something from that Mike kid's lawyer. I cannot think of anything else. Angie, sit down here please. Sweetheart, could you please get a glass of water for her?"

"Of course." Lizzy turned, went to the kitchen and got a glass of water and brought it back and gave it to Angie. Angie took it and drank most of it in one gulp. "Take it easy Angie"

Dominic sat down next to Angie and Lizzy sat on her other side. "Let's open this and find out what it is." He opened the envelope and pulled the papers out. "Just as I thought, it is something about that Mike kid....What? What? This is crazy, I cannot believe this." Dominic said loudly.

"What is it Dom?" Lizzy asked.

"They are saying that Angie attacked Mike with a knife and threatened him and when he took it away Angie broke his nose. Then she followed him and kicked and knocked him out. They say Angie is a danger to herself and the public and should be institutionalized."

Angie screamed and cried, "Oh my god, I do not want to go to jail oh god!" and began to cry hysterically. "What am I going to do, oh god."

Lizzy reached out and held Angie and told her, "It will be alright, you will see. I do not like seeing you like this Angie, It makes me very sad." Lizzy hugged her in an attempt to calm her as Angie was shaking unlike she had ever seen.

Dominic immediately said, "I need to talk to Mr. Humboldt about this. This is insane. How can they do this? Maybe he is still in the office. I am going to call him now." He stood up and went to their bedroom and called Mr. Humboldt.

"Hello, Mr. Humboldt?"

"Oh Dominic, how nice to talk to you, what can I do for you?"

Dominic told him about the court papers, how they delivered them and what they said.

"This sounds like Leonard Conrad for sure Dominic. This is something only he would do. Oh, Leonard Conrad is the city manager and between you and me, he is a complete asshole. Excuse my French Dominic. And he is Mike Conrad's father. Mike Conrad is the boy that attacked Angie, the one whose nose Angie broke. Don't worry about it too much until I can see just what they claim. How is Angie taking this Dominic?"

"Well, if I said not well I would be lying."

"Try to calm her down. It's a shame this jerk did this to her. Can you and Angie come to my office tomorrow so we can go over this and formulate a plan?"

"Of course, whatever you like. We will be there sir, what time?"

"Is 9 AM alright"

"That will be fine. We will be there sir."

"Then go take care of that sweet daughter of yours. She doesn't deserve this. We will talk tomorrow."

Dominic went back to where Angie and Lizzy were sitting. "Mr. Humboldt would like Angie and me to go to his office tomorrow so he can read the papers and formulate a plan. Angie, when you feel calm enough, could you make a list of everyone that you are aware of that has seen Mike harass someone or had Mike harass them? I want to do everything we can to be prepared."

Angie was sniffling and wiping her eyes with a tissue and said with a crackling voice, "Yes father."

The next morning Dominic and Angie went to Mr. Humboldt's office. They sat down in front of his desk. "Good Morning Dominic and Angie. Make yourself comfortable as we may be here for a while. Let me read these papers and see what we are up against." He took the envelope from Dominic. He was shaking his head back and forth as he read them. "Hmmm, I see what he is trying to do but I don't believe he has anything that will back up his story." He pulled out a pad of paper. "Angie, do you know of anyone that has been harassed by Mike and/or anyone that has witnessed Mike harassing anyone?"

Angie pulled out a folded piece of paper from her purse, unfolded it and said as she gave it to Mr. Humboldt, "Mr. Humboldt, I made up this list last night."

"Wow! This is some list Angie, this is perfect. Let's see, of course you had a few instances, who is Derek?"

"Derek is just someone in my Physics class and he just happened to show up one of the times Mike grabbed my purse and was harassing me. He is maybe 6' 4" tall and very muscular and Mike is afraid of him. Mike immediately gave me my purse back and said he was just joking and quickly walked away."

"Oh, this is something, Mike raped 3 girls and his dad threatened the principal and the police chief so they wouldn't investigate. Interesting, do you think they would be willing to testify Angie?"

"Possibly, I will need to ask them but from what they told me already they would love to see Mike pay for that. They told me that they were all virgins and were so upset about it that they missed school for a week."

"Who are Jim and Paul?"

They are Mike's friends. They were with Mike each time he harassed me. I thought maybe because one of the incidents got them suspended it would be possible that they may be willing to testify."

"Who is Mrs. Abbot?"

"Mrs. Abbot is my Physics teacher. She was my Physics 1 & 2 teacher last year at Amphitheater. She transferred to CDO this year and I have her for Physics 3 & 4 this year. Since she knows me quite well and was there just after I broke Mike's nose. I thought she might be someone that could vouch for me."

How about Mr. Luis? He is the principal I see. Maybe we can get him to testify that Leonard Conrad harassed him to drop the investigation on Mike for the rapes. I'll talk to the police chief and see if he would be willing to testify. If we can get all of these there is no way they can prove what they say. So I will contact each one of these people and if everyone or even most agree we will have a very good defense."

"I will talk to Sherri, Janet, Kathy and Derek tomorrow at school and find out if they are willing to testify."

"That would be very good Angie." Mr. Humboldt said. Here are some of my cards. Feel free to give one to each of them. I will contact the school and talk to Mr. Luis and Mrs. Abbot tomorrow. And I will find Jim and Paul and talk to them as well. Angie, could you call me tomorrow when you find out about the girls and Derek?"

"Absolutely, sir."

"We should be in good shape then. I think I have everything necessary to get started. So go home and relax. I don't think you need to worry."

"OK sir," Dominic stood up and reached out to shake Mr. Humboldt's hand. "And thank you for everything sir."

Angie also said, "Thank you sir, after discussing this with you I feel somewhat relieved."

"It is always my pleasure to see you Angie." Dominic and Angie turned and left.

On the way home they talked about the law suit and Dominic found Angie did not appear upset now. He felt good about that. When they arrived home they went into the house and told Lizzy about the discussion with Mr. Humboldt and she was relieved as well.

The next day Angie went to school and at first everything was like always. Then Sherri told Angie, "Pretty much everyone knows that the police were here yesterday afternoon for something related to you Angie. Everyone is shocked. I'm worried."

"Sherri there is nothing to worry about yet. I need to talk to you, Janet and Kathy about this. I think you will be surprised for what this is about. I will see all of you at lunch, alright?"

"OK Angie, I'll tell Janet and Kathy that you need to talk to us then. See you at lunch." Sherri said and they both went to their classes.

Lunch time came and Angie sat with Sherri, Janet and Kathy. They were anxious to find out what Angie wanted to talk about and what had happened two days ago with her and the police. They all said Hi and Sherri asked, "Angie, so what happened the other day with the police? We have all been wondering."

Kathy said, "And some of the kids said you left with your father because you were too upset to drive. What happened?"

Angie sat back and took a big breath and exhaled, "It amazes me how fast rumors get around. Well, Dean Campbell came to my Composition class and brought me to the office. There was a Sheriff's deputy waiting there for me to serve court papers from Mike's father. He is saying that I attacked Mike and when he took the knife from me I broke his nose. Then I followed him and knocked him out. He says I am a danger myself and to the public. Can you believe that?"

Sherri said, "But that's not what happened! It was Mike!"
Kathy said, "How can they do that!"
Janet said, "What's going to happen to you Angie?"

"I sat with my father and his attorney a good part of the day yesterday. He told us that we need to find anyone that has had trouble with Mike to show that Mike is the danger. I hope you are not upset with me, I told my attorney that you three were raped by Mike and he said that if you would agree to testify that this happened it would be one of the largest things that would implicate Mike. Would any of you do this?"

Sherri said, "I would do anything to get that bastard. He took my virginity and that destroyed my dream of losing it to my true love. I will testify without any hesitation."

Karen said, "I would like to but I would be scared. Would I need to sit on that chair next to the judge and then have attorneys ask me questions? I don't know if I could do that."

Janet said, "I'm scared. I want to help you Angie, you are the only friend I have had since Mike did that. I don't know if I could stand some sleazy lawyer asking questions trying to make it look like it was my fault."

"I understand your fear. If Mike would win I could end up in jail or in a psych institution and he would get away again. I really need you, all of you and I would not ask," Angie started crying, "if—if my life was not depending on it." Angie had her hands over her eyes. "I am sorry, I did not want to cry. I did not want to use this as leverage to get you to do this. I am so embarrassed."

Right away Sherri stood and hugged Angie. Karen was sitting next to her and reached out to rub her back.

Janet had tears in her eyes as well. "Angie, I'll do it, I promise. I want that bastard to pay."

Angie looked up at Janet and asked, "You would do this for me, really?"

"You're my friend Angie, I don't like to see you hurt. I am going to do it for you and for the three of us." Janet said.

Karen reached for Angie's hand and took it in both hands, "I will do it too Angie. I am going to be scared but I will do it. I was just thinking about myself but you really need us now."

"All of you will? I cannot believe it. I was afraid to even ask. You are definitely good friends." Angie said through her tears.

Karen asked, "You were afraid to ask us? You?" Angie looked at her. She looked small and vulnerable. "You are so strong Angie. You are like a role model to us, I think we all would do anything for you."

Angie was calming down. She wiped the last tears from her eyes. "You are all very laudable. I cannot believe I have such wonderful friends!"

Sherri asked, "Laudable?"

"I am sorry, you are praiseworthy or great. When I am emotional I do not think about what I am saying, sorry."

"You don't need to be sorry Angie. We understand." Janet said.

"And maybe we will learn some of the words you use too." Karen said.

"My attorney would like me to talk to Derek today and he will talk to Mr. Lewis and Mrs. Abbot as well. Derek happened to walk up the first time Mike harassed me and chased them away. But I do not know if Mr. Lewis would testify. My attorney said he would like to get Mr. Lewis to tell the court what Mikes father said to him to keep quiet when Mike raped you. Oh, and he said he would talk to Jim and Paul."

"Wow, your Attorney is smart Angie. I heard Jim quit sports and doesn't talk to Mike anymore since he got suspended. But I don't know about Paul." Karen said.

"Thank you for standing with me. I really appreciate it and I value it greatly." Angie told them. "I almost forgot, here are business cards from my attorney. He said I should give them to each of you so you will know who he is when he calls." She handed each one a card.

"OK Angie Sherri said. Will we see you later?"

Angie said, "I have Martial Arts training tonight so I will be kind of rushed after school. I need the workout to help calm me."

"OK, see you" Sherri said.

By the end of the week Mr. Humboldt had spoken to all of the people on Angie's list. He was very happy that Sherri, Janet and Karen were going to testify. He thought these would be the most useful. Derek said he would be happy to do anything he could to help Angie because he thought she was the nicest girl he ever met. Jim agreed and said that he quit sports and he wants nothing to do with "that freak." (this is how he referred to Mike now) Paul just told Mr. Humboldt to "go fuck off" but Mr. Lewis agreed along with Mrs. Abbot to testify. The police chief didn't want to put his position in jeopardy or tarnish the department and declined.

Mr. Humboldt thought he had a very good case against Mike so he thought he would call Leonard Conrad's attorney to see if he could get them to back down. He found out it was a worthless call, Leonard Conrad's attorney said it would be "a cold day in hell before he would back down and get that menace Angelina away from her potential victims."

Chapter 18

Weeks went by and nothing happened. Things at school were just fine, but every day when Angie walked to the Cuda she expected to find something done to it. But nothing happened. Soon it is Thanksgiving week. Angie's father decided to go racing the Sunday after Thanksgiving and asked Angie if she wanted to make a few runs in the Cuda. Angie said, "Really? Of course!" She had been looking forward to this since the first time he brought her to the track. At the shop Dominic prepped his car and they looked over Angie's Cuda and all it needed was a driveshaft loop. He had Angie bring the Cuda into the shop the Saturday before Thanksgiving and he showed her how to put one on her car. Then he showed her what the safety inspectors will look for. They finished and went home. Angie worked at the shop Monday, Tuesday.

Thanksgiving was Angie's favorite holiday and they always celebrated at her grandmother and grandfathers house, although Angie wanted to do something different this year similar to what she had done for her birthday. A few days before Angie asked, "Mother, I want to wear something like I did at my birthday, not so flashy but something nice. And I would like if you would assist me.

"Of course Angie. I would love to assist you. We could look through all of my gowns and dresses and you may choose one. And then we will go and buy some nice heals to go along. Heals would make up the difference in our height," Lizzy was slightly taller than Angie. "They would be your first. How does that sound?"

"That sounds wonderful mother. I adored the responses I received at my party very much. Especially when Shelly said I could be on the cover of Seventeen Magazine."

"You did not tell me she said that."

"I guess I had not thought of it since then. But I felt like a princess and I loved that feeling. And since then I have been thinking that I would love to dress in that manor for our family celebrations. Everyone treated me very differently."

"Angie, I always dreamed that you would tell me something such as this. I do not think you have any idea how I have dreamed to have a daughter that would at least sometimes want to dress up and be feminine." Lizzy had tears in her eyes.

"Mother, I did not know you felt like this. If I knew I would have done this sooner."

"I did not want to force you honey, I wanted you to want to do it. Otherwise it would not be genuine."

"Oh mother." Angie went and hugger her mother. They both were teary eyed. "You would not have been forcing me I would have done it because I love you. And since you do so much for me I would have wanted to just so you would be happy."

They looked through Lizzy's dresses and gowns and picked out one that was bone color satin with lace around the scoop neckline and lace sleeves. It was full length in back but was cut to show the calf in front. Angie loved how it looked and felt. "This is so beautiful mother! I do not remember seeing you wear it."

"I do not believe I have yet Angie."

"You have not worn it? And you would let me wear it?"

"Of course, why not? I think it looks better on you. We just need to get you some shoes with about 4" heal and it will be perfect!"

"Mother, you are so sweet. When will we look for shoes?"

"We can go whenever you have time you have such a busy schedule. But if we go on Wednesday we could both get our nails done if you like."

"Oh, I would love that mother! And will you help with my makeup?"

"Absolutely. You really do not need much, you are so beautiful without makeup. We will just do enough to bring out your features."

"Oh thank you so much mother!"

Lizzy couldn't believe how excited Angie was about getting dressed up like this. She would never have expected this before Angie's birthday. And evidently she hadn't picked up how much Angie loved wearing the gown on her birthday. For the first time Lizzy felt that she really had a daughter and not a tomboy.

Angie went to work on Monday and Tuesday because Dominic was swapping a bigger engine in the pick-up and she wanted to see how it is done. She learned how to put front disc brakes in place of the drum brakes about a year ago. All that was left was the engine. Dominic didn't like that the truck only had a 396 big block and he felt that he needed more pulling power to pull the Nova and trailer. He came across a 1969 427 L71 engine which was 435 HP with 3- 2bbl carbs. This would give the truck an additional 110 HP over the 325 HP that the 396 had. The truck already had a Turbo 400 transmission so he was just doing the engine. He also added headers and some tuning. Since the truck already had a big block it was a matter of just pulling the 396 and replacing it with the 427. There were minor things he had to modify such as the throttle linkage and air conditioning brackets and he needed to connect the headers to the exhaust system. He would be adding custom exhaust at a later date. This went quickly and they were finished Tuesday afternoon. It took a little longer do to the truck due to having factory A/C but everything went back together well. Angie was able to see how easy it was to swap like engines. And of course the guys in the shop all loved performance modifications so they all pitched in.

Angie didn't go to the shop on Wednesday. She told her father she had something to do with her mother. She got up and showered and was about to put on jeans and a sweater. Lizzy told her it would be better if she wore the gown so they could choose shoes that not only matched but were the correct height so the gown would not touch the floor. So Angie put on the gown and Lizzy picked one for herself, although she chose one that was less flashy so everyone would notice Angie again.

When they walked into the shoe store everyone turned to look at Angie. She didn't notice as she was too busy keeping the back hem from touching the floor. They looked at many shoes and Angie focused on one pair. They were bone colored Swede with ankle straps and had a 4" high heal.

They went to sit down and Angie heard someone say "Angie? Is that you?" Angie turned and it was Paula from school.

"Well, hello Paula." She turned to her mother and said, "Mother may I present Paula, from school."

Lizzy said, "I am very pleased to meet you Miss Paula."

Paula was a little surprised at the introduction. She just had expected Hello or Hi. She didn't know how to respond so she said, "Ah, it is nice to meet you too, Mrs. Tucci." She hoped she answered alright.

"It is nice to know that Angelina has nice friends."

"I almost didn't recognize you Angie, or should I be calling you Angelina? Is that what everyone calls you? I'm sorry, I didn't know. And seeing you in a gown Angie doesn't sound right."

"Angie is fine. We are buying shoes to go along with this gown."

"It is a beautiful gown Angie and you look amazing in it. I just wanted to say hi, I'm here with my mom, she just bought some shoes. See you at school, have a great Thanksgiving!"

"It was nice to see you Paula, and I hope you have a great Thanksgiving as well!"

"Have you made more friends Angie?"

"I just met her a few weeks ago along with 2 of her friends. I really do not know her yet, mother."

"She seems like a nice girl, I could see she tried to be polite. That was nice gesture."

"Yes, but as I said I just met her and do not know much about her. We just spoke in the hallway between classes and then after school for a few minutes."

They sat down and the salesman brought a pair for Angie to try. They fit perfectly and the gown hung off of the floor about an inch. Angie had a little trouble walking at first. She had never worn high heeled shoes so this was a new experience. They bought the shoes and went back home. Angie wanted to change before getting her nails done. She was worried that something could get spilled on the gown.

Angie put on her usual jeans and a sweater and her favorite cowboy boots. Lizzy put on a pleated mid length dress and she wore a sweater. It was the day before Thanksgiving and it was chilly. Then they went to get their nails done. Angie had her nails in a light beige color that looked close to the bone color of the gown and Lizzy got her standard French manicure.

That night when Lizzy had laid down, she told Dominic about how Angie wanted to dress in a gown for tomorrow. She explained what Angie was going to wear and that they went and bought high heeled shoes for her. Then she told him that they both got a manicure. Dominic was very surprised. He didn't know how much Angie enjoyed dressing for her party.

He told Lizzy that he couldn't wait to see her when she was ready tomorrow and that everyone will be shocked again.

On Thanksgiving Day Angie helped her mother prepare and package the vegetable dish, the Jell-O mold and biscuits that Lizzy prepared to bring to her grandparents' house. Dominic asked if they needed any help, as usual, but they said they did not. Then they went to get dressed. Lizzy helped Angie with her makeup. She used just a small amount of powder, a slight brush of blush, dark eyeliner and some light eye shadow. She finished with mascara.

They each put on their gowns and shoes and Angie brushed her hair. Her straight hair always looked beautiful and along with the makeup she was stunning! They walked out to the master bathroom and Dominic again was stunned! There were two absolutely beautiful women standing in front of him. Dominic said, "You both are absolutely stunning! And Angie, if I was a casual friend I would not recognize you. If you ever went to the shop dressed like this I would need to beat the guys away with a bat!"

"Thank you Dom,"

"Father, I can see it in your eyes. Your complements mean so much."

Dominic already put the dishes that Lizzy and Angie prepared in the car so they all just needed to get into the car and leave. They drove to Lizzy's parent's house and when they parked Dominic reminisced a bit. "I remember the very first time I parked right here in this spot. I was afraid but something pushed me to the door. I remember the feeling like it was yesterday." He gave Lizzy a hug and told her how beautiful she was. They walked to the door.

Evidently someone was watching for them because as soon as they got to the door it opened. They were surprised by someone they didn't know. "Welcome and please come in. Please let me take these from you and bring them to the kitchen." The lady said. "Please join everyone, they have been expecting you. This way." She led them into the solarium.

Everyone else had already arrived and Kristina said, "I see you met Alana, she is a server today." She paused for a few seconds, "Oh my lord, Angelina, you have managed to astound me a second time! You are enchanting my dear!'

Just as at Angie's birthday party, Kristina saw her first and her reaction drew the attention of everyone. Shelly smiled and walked up to Angie and hugged her and said, "Angelina you look so beautiful. I cannot believe you did it again!"

"Thank you Shelly, I think it was what you said to me at my birthday party that made me want to dress like this today."

"What I said? You did this for me?"

"I would not say I did it for just for you but you inspired me. Your reaction, and of course everyone else as well, made me feel like a princess and that is what I always thought that you were when we were kids. I would say I wanted to do this for me and because how I effected everyone, especially you, Cuz."

"I cannot believe I inspired you. But you do look amazing, Oh, I love your shoes, where did you get them?"

"We bought them at the shoe store on Stone near Steinfelds."

Lilly walked up to Angie, "Angelina, I am speechless! I could not believe it on your birthday and now, I do not know what to say. You give the appearance of a completely different person. Your," She thought for a few seconds, "Your presence has been transformed. Everything, you are walking gracefully just as your mother and I do, if I keep this up I am going to get tears in my eyes. You do not know how much your mother and I have longed for you to dress like this. Oh Angelina." She reached out and hugged Angie.

Maria told Angie that she looked very beautiful.

When Angie talked to her grandmother the response was very much the same. Angie still couldn't believe the difference in her family from just dressing differently. She was also amazed, just as she was at her birthday celebration. How could she make such a difference from just what she was wearing she wondered. But she loved how everyone looked at her and how it appeared that everyone treated her differently as well; at least that was her perception.

Angie always loves to get together with the whole family but she was thinking that now just because she dressed like all of the other women in the family she may love it even more. And like always, the turkey and stuffing and everything else was so good she ate far too much. But it is only one time a year so she didn't worry about it. And every year they take a picture of the whole family and this year would be the first where she dressed differently so it may be a year she would hold special significance. She has learned that how you dress can make an impact on everyone else. There are 3 generations of the family in the Thanksgiving picture and Angie's mother, aunts and grandmother hope that one of the kids will get married and have kids so they can take a picture with 4 generations.

As usual, the family discussed going to see the Nutcracker. They go every year and afterwards Grandfather Hall takes the family out to the Palomino Restaurant for dinner.

Denise, Gina and Paula got together on the Saturday after Thanksgiving. They talked about their Thanksgiving dinners. Gina complained about her weird family. Then Paula remembered that she saw Angie on Wednesday.

"I forgot to tell you, I saw Angie at the shoe store Wednesday afternoon and I met her mother. Remember how we said Angie talks different? Well so does her mother."

"She talks like Angie too?" Denise asked.

"I didn't recognize her at first."

"What do you mean you didn't recognize her? How could you not recognize her?" Gina asked.

"She wasn't dressed like we see her, she and her mother were wearing gowns, and very expensive ones. But then I saw her face and I knew it was her. So I said Hi. And Angie turned and said Hello Paula, then she turned to her mother and said something like, 'Mother, may I present Paula from school.' And her mother said something like "I am pleased to meet you Miss Paula." I didn't know how to answer. I stood there for a minute and I think I said, 'It's nice to meet you too Mrs. Tucci."

Denise said, "Really? So they talk like that all the time I guess."

Gina asked, "Did they sound like they were talking down to you?"

"No, her mother was very nice. It just surprised me what she said. But you should have seen Angie in that gown. I was amazed. She looked like a different person, and so beautiful."

"Wow," Denise said. "I would have liked to see Angie dressed up. I wonder what she was dressed up for?"

"Maybe for Thanksgiving." Gina joked.

Paula said, "Maybe. After meeting her mother she looked so elegant, and she walks like someone in an old movie, kind of, I guess graceful. So maybe they do dress like that for Thanksgiving. I know we were thinking that they talk like that to make themselves look better than everyone else, but I don't think so. They both were very nice. You know, like Angie is all the time."

Gina said, "Well maybe Sherri was right and they do it for respect. I don't exactly know how it shows respect though."

Paula said, "Maybe by being proper and polite you are respecting everyone around you. It sure made me feel good and I didn't have that shy feeling in my stomach like I always get when I meet someone new. So maybe it is showing respect."

Gina said, "Maybe, but I don't know if I could do that all the time. It's probably easy for Angie because that is all she knows. I don't know. But thinking about it, didn't you guys feel comfortable talking to her that day? I feel like she made me feel, I don't know, like you said Paula. I guess I didn't feel awkward like I do meeting new people. You think talking like that did that?"

Denise said, "Maybe, I never talked to anybody that talks like her so I don't know."

"I feel like we could be friends. There is something about her, I don't know, doesn't she seem like she has a lot of confidence?" Paula asked.

"Maybe that's it. It can't be that simple. Someone is confident and speaks proper and is polite? Denise asked.

"Maybe," Paula said.

Chapter 19

Len, Mike's dad, came home and told Mike, "I spoke with my attorney today and he told me that he spoke to that Angelina girl's attorney and he doesn't think we can go forward. Their attorney has the 3 bitches you raped, the principal, Mrs. Abbot, Derek and even Jim lined up to testify against you. So you're probably through, Mike. You finally did something I can't get you out of, you stupid shit. This is an embarrassment to me and my office and the City of Tucson."

Len hasn't noticed that Mike has been acting more and more psychotic every day. Not that he cares anyway. He just doesn't want to be embarrassed by Mike again. Mike has been talking to himself very loud and ignoring everything his dad tells him. He has a demented smile lately. His dad and mom hadn't noticed because they don't look at him in his eyes, even when they are screaming at him. Mike thought for a minute. "I can take care of this no problem. If Angie isn't there the rest will be too afraid to testify. She is why they are all against me."

"Stay the hell away from her, Mike. You're going to make things much worse." Len said.

"No I won't and you can't stop me. I'm going to take care of it once and for all and there is nothing you can do about it." Mike said as he ran out of the house.

Len was very angry and thought about calling the Police Chief to pick Mike up but then thought that could turn into a nightmare for him, especially if the news picks up on it. "Bad idea" he thought.

Chapter 20

On Saturday evening Dominic, Jack and Angie went to the shop to load the Nova on the trailer and gather the tools and extra parts together. Angie was very excited, almost like the first time she saw her father race his car. She almost couldn't hold it in. Soon everything was ready and they left for the night. Dominic had filled the Cuda with racing fuel on Saturday afternoon before he closed the shop then he adjusted the tune. Dominic thought to himself that the Cuda is going to run extremely well. He has been coaching Angie for the past week on how to stage and get ready for the lights to drop.

Mike talked to a few kids from school that will still talk to him and found out where Angie lived and also that she is supposed to race the Cuda on Sunday. He had this plan to sabotage the brakes so she can't stop at the end of the track. He thought to himself that he is so smart. It will be perfect, no one will suspect and that bitch will die in front of everyone; there will be no way to pin it on me. Then everyone else will be too afraid to testify. Mike laughed to himself and thought that he was such a genius. He looked through his dad's tools and found a file and decided to wait until very late Saturday night. On Saturday night he went to Angie's house and saw the Cuda. He thought, "Stupid bitch doesn't put it in the garage, good for me, bad for her." He was laughing.

Mike ended up waiting in the bushes in front of Angie's house for the lights go out. Then he quietly made his way to the Cuda. He shimmied underneath and found the brake lines. He carefully filed them around the diameter as much as he could until he saw a touch of brake fluid leaking. Not enough to empty the system, just enough to make the lines wet. He thought," when she hits the brakes hard at the end of the track the pressure will burst the lines and she will have no brakes, then she is going to crash and die!" He laughed. He got out from under the car and went home. Len wasn't there but his mother screamed, "Where the hell have you been? Don't you walk away from me!" But he ignored her and went to bed.

Sunday morning Dominic and Angie met Jack at the shop and they left for the track. Dominic drove the truck with Jack and the trailer and Angie drove the Cuda following him. When they got to the track they found a place in the pits and unloaded the Nova. They filled out the tech cards with the necessary information, and got in line to go through the Technical Inspection. Technical Inspection verifies that the cars do not have any issues that could cause trouble or could be dangerous when they race. They also verify that a driveshaft loop in place. Dominic drove the Nova first, and they found no issues. Then one of the inspectors said, "OK bring up the Cuda." He took the tech card from Angie, "A 70 Cuda, oh a HEMI Cuda, Nice!"

Angie drove the Cuda up and they began the inspection. They walked around the car, verified that a driveshaft loop was in place. But when they stuck the mirror under the car they saw something wet. "Wait a minute," the inspector said. "Hey bring over the jack. He jacked up the car so he could see better. This isn't good. You have some leaks in you brake lines Miss. (Although they didn't know it was done on purpose) This has to be repaired before you can race."

Dominic said, "What? Are you certain?" and he got down and looked and sure enough the lines were wet. That is odd, last Saturday they looked fine. OK she cannot race today, thanks." He said to the tech inspector.

Angie was crushed. She couldn't believe it. She and her father looked at everything and there was nothing wrong anywhere. So Angie drove the Cuda back over next to the truck and got out. She looked sad. Dominic and Jack talked and decided that they're not going to race. They didn't want to make Angie feel worse. They put the Nova back on the trailer and packed up to go home. Dominic told Angie, "I cannot let you drive the Cuda with leaking brake lines, so I going to bring the Nova back to the shop and then come back for you and the Cuda. Jack, would you please stay with Angie until I get back?"

Jack said, "Sure, then we can watch some racing while you are gone."

"OK, I will be back in about an hour and a half." Dominic said.

Jack said to Angie, "Angie, let's go sit in the stands while we wait. We can at least watch some racing."

"OK Uncle Jack. But I am still disappointed."

"I know you are. And I am as well. I was looking forward to see you race for the first time."

They walked over to the stands and found a place to sit. Angie didn't notice Mike sitting near them.

"What the hell? Why isn't she getting ready to race?" Mike said to himself. He was very angry now. He walked down from the stands to see if he could find out what was going on. Mike walked over to technical inspection and asked, "What's going on with the girl and that pink Cuda? I came just to see her. I go to school with her and I was hoping to see her run."

"We found leaks in the brake lines so she can't race until they make repairs." The Technical inspection guy told Mike.

"Oh, what a bummer, she must be upset. Well thanks." Mike was trying to act like a concerned friend and walked away.

When he thought he was far enough he said, "Dam it! Now what? I have to think of something else. She was supposed to crash and that would be simple." He was very angry. He walked to his car and sped out and back home.

Mike drove like a mad man going home, he was so angry he didn't care. He couldn't think about anything else but Angie. Dammed Technical inspection, it would have been great. "Now what, think, what can I do." Mike thought.

Dominic backed the trailer into the shop and unloaded the Nova, blocked the tires and put the cover on it. Then he pulled out onto the street, closed and locked the overhead door and drove back to the track. The whole way he thought about what could have caused the lines to leak. He knew they checked the lines the week before. They must have missed something but how could he miss something like this?

He pulled into the track and drove over to the Cuda. Jack and Angie saw him and walked back from the stands. Dominic asked Jack, "Jack, could you pull the Cuda onto the trailer please?" He thought Angie might have a problem if the lines broke while pulling up onto the trailer. Jack slowly started to drive up the ramps and onto the trailer. He pushed the brake pedal and it went right to the floor so he used the emergency brake to stop.

Jack got out of the car and said to Dominic, "Dominic, the brakes just failed and the pedal went to the floor. Angie was so lucky this did not happen on the drive to the track." They got the Cuda tied down and they all squeezed into the pickup with Angie in the middle.

They had no issues during the drive home. Jack got out of the truck and opened the overhead door so Dominic could back in. Dominic backed the trailer as close to a lift as he could so they wouldn't need to push the Cuda too far. They pushed the Cuda onto the lift, then Dominic pulled the pickup out, parked in the back and disconnected the trailer. When he went back in Jack told him that he was going to go home and spend the rest of the day with Sofia and left. Angie said, "Thank you Uncle Jack." And she gave him a hug.

"It's always a pleasure Angie." Jack replied as he left.

"Well let's get this up in the air and see what happened." They got down on their knees and positioned the ends of the lift under the frame members of the Cuda then lifted it. Dominic looked at the wet part of the brake lines and it appeared as though someone used a file on them. But then thought maybe they were tooling marks from manufacturing. So he measured the lengths and went to the stock room to see if he had the right length replacements.

Dominic has always taught Angie to always do a clean job on anything she does and this also means bending the line exactly like the one you take off and cutting it to length and re-flaring the ends. He found that he only had one piece long enough so he called his friend Bob that owns an auto parts store to ask if he could get another piece of line today. The store is closed on Sunday's so he would need to go meet him there. And when Dominic said it was for Angie's Cuda, Bob told Dominic, "How could I turn down something for Angie, she is such a sweet and polite girl I would do anything for her."

"Thanks Bob, Angie will be happy to hear this. I can be there in about 45 minutes, is that alright Bob." Dominic said.

"No problem, see you soon then." Bob replied.

Dominic brought the brake line he had in stock back to where Angie was and told her that they only had one piece of brake line. So he said, "Angie I am going to go to meet Bob at his store to get another piece of brake line. It is going to take about one and a half hours. Will you be alright here alone or would you care to go along?"

"I need to practice making these double flares so I will remain here father. It is going to take some practice to master these flares, they are a little tricky. I will be fine father. I am using the couple of pieces of old brake line from the trash to practice."

"Alright, I will be back before you know it." He walked through and closed the overhead door, locked it and left. He didn't think to check the back door to see if it was locked even though all of the employees always park in back. This was Sunday so he never even thought to check and he didn't notice that Jack left that way.

Mike got home and skidded to a stop in the driveway. He got out and slammed the car door. As he walked into the house he was talking to himself out loud. "Fucking bitch was supposed to die today, dam it. I need to figure out how to kill her some other way. Maybe they went to her dads shop to fix the car." He thought. "Yea that could work, he, he." He said out loud. "I'll fuck that bitch then burn her and the place down. That will cover it up. With her gone no one will testify they'll all be afraid. Then I get off free! This is even better. I'll have some fun with her first. I knew I would get a chance with her."

Just then Mike's mom walked in the room. "What are you screaming about? You're going to kill someone and burn the place down? What the hell is this about?

"Nothing you can do about it. Yea, I'm going to fuck that bitch and burn her dad's shop down to cover it up. So what?" He sounded very psychotic, as though it was going to be the best time of his life.

His mother saw Mike's eyes for the first time and was stunned. But she was too angry to think much about it, "You're going too far, why can't you listen to your dad? He said keep the hell away from her you little punk. Shit, I'm calling him right now maybe he can beat some sense into you."

She walked towards the phone and just before she picked up the receiver, Mike screamed, "You're not calling anyone bitch, and he isn't my fucking dad." He grabbed her by the neck and through her onto the floor. She screamed from fear and pain. "I've had enough of you bitch. You never stuck up for me for anything." He straddled her stomach.

"What the hell are you doing?" She screamed. "Get off of me you bastard!"

He grabbed her neck and squeezed. He had an insane crazy looking smile as he did this. Then as he squeezed her neck he started banging her head on the floor as well. 'Fuck you, bitch. All you do is scream, now shut the fuck up." He screamed as he is choked her and banged her head on the floor.

His mom's eyes were wide open and bulging. She was trying to pull his hands off of her neck. She was kicking then started to beat his sides then scratched his face with her nails but nothing made him stop. Her kicking and scratching started to slow down then her arms and legs fell limp. Mike kept squeezing and banging her head and he finally realized she was dead. "You got what your deserved you bitch. You finally shut up." Mike stood up and looked at her lifeless body lying there. For a minute he thought that he should stab her to make sure she was dead. He thought how in movies the bad guy always got up again after you thought he was dead. "That's just movies, this is real." So he gave her body a good hard kick to the side, "Bitch." He said and kicked her again much harder. "She's dead."

As he was standing there looking at his mother's lifeless body Mike remembered that his dad kept a gun in his desk drawer so he turned and ran upstairs to get it. The drawer was locked. He looked around for something to use to pry it open. He started emptying the other desk drawers and he found a screwdriver. "Yea, just what I need." He said out loud as he pried and broke the front of the drawer open. He grabbed the gun and opened it, "It's a 45 revolver and full of bullets, perfect!" He took the gun and ran to his car. He put the gun on the seat next to him.

He passed Jim's house as he was driving to Angie's fathers shop and saw him outside. He skidded to a stop, backed up and called out, "Hey asshole come here for a minute."

Jim reluctantly walked over to Mike's car.

"I heard you're ratting on me, asshole."

"You look crazy Mike." Jim said. And he saw the revolver on the seat.

"Don't go anywhere Jim. When I finish with Angie I am coming back for you, and I'm going to kill you too, Fucker." And he sped off.

Jim was shocked and ran into his house and tried calling Mike's house hoping to get Mike's dad. No one answered. So he decided to go check out Angie's dad's garage thinking maybe Mike was going there. He got into his car and left. But he thought that he should drive past Mike's house first hoping Mike's dad would be there. As he pulled up he saw Mike's dad getting out of his car. He slammed on the brakes and called out, "Mr. Conrad, you've got to come, Mike is going to do something bad. He has a gun. I think he wants to kill Angie."

"Park your car Jim, I'll drive."

Jim parked and ran to Mr. Conrad's car, got in and Mr. Conrad sped off. "What did Mike say Jim?"

"He said something like, don't go anywhere. When I finish with Angie I'm coming back for you, and I'm going to kill you too."

"What is going on with that kid, has he lost his mind?"

"Mr. Conrad, Mike looked like he is crazy and psychotic, like a demon."

While they are on their way, Mike parked down the block so no one would see him. He grabbed the gun and tucked it in his belt on the small of his back and ran to the back door because the overhead door was closed. He grabbed the knob and turned it slowly. Mike thought, "Perfect, it's not locked. He slowly opened it and saw Angie at a bench with her back to the door and it didn't look like anyone else is there. Mike was giddy had to work to keep from laughing out loud. He thought to himself, "I'm finally going to get this bitch. She deserves this. No one humiliates Mike and gets him thrown out of school like she did and gets away with it." He entered through the door and ran towards Angie. Angie thought that she heard something and turned around to see just as Mike swung and hit her in the cheek. Then he hit two or three more times in the side of the head until she was knocked out. He grabbed her as she was falling and laid her on the floor.

Mike looked around for something to tie her up with and found some bungee cords. "This will be good," He then pulled off Angie's shoes, jeans and t-shirt so now she just had panties and a bra on. Mike was laughing. He laid her back down on the floor and wrapped one bungee cord around one ankle and stretched it to a bench leg and tied it around the leg. Then he did the same with the other ankle only he tied this one to the bench next to the first. This held her legs apart. Then he pulled her arms over her head and wrapped her wrists together with another bungee cord and stretched it to the support on a lift. The bungee cords were stretched tight. Mike said to himself, "She won't be able to do anything now and I can fuck her with no struggle." Angie was still out cold but now he wanted her awake. He kicked her in the right side ribs, "Wake up Bitch" and she didn't move. Then he kicked her again harder, "Wake up bitch." Mike screamed. "Wake up, I want you awake when I fuck you!" Angie began to come to and saw Mike and realized that she is tied down and almost naked. She went to scream but when she breathed in her ribs on the right side hurt severely, so much that it kept her from taking a deep breath. Angie was now panicking.

"Why are you doin dis, Mik?" Angie blurted out. Her jaw and the side of her face hurt and made it difficult for her to speak. She could already feel swelling around her eye.

"Because you're a fucking bitch and you mine now."

She tried to talk him out of it but all she could come up with was, "You on't get away wit dis. Eweryone will know. It's so ovious. I wnow you are not a bad guy, aksually you are kond of nice. If I was not so buusy I wald have gone out wit you. Goin to Afphiteter tere was no one wike you tere so I jut begam to fill my tim. I always wanded to go owt wit a goy wike you." But humoring him didn't work.

Mike got down over her with one knee on each side of her hips, "Shut up bitch." Mike told her and slapped her hard across the cheek. Then he noticed that Angie had a gold cross on a chain around her neck. He can't stand looking at it because he was worshiping Satin. It reminded him of his Catholic upbringing and he hated that. He grabbed it and said, "You don't need this now," and pulled it off of her and through it across the shop.

Angie screamed, "NOO, wat was my ganmoters!" Mike looked at her and screamed, "Shut the hell up" and slapped her so hard across her cheek that her vision blurred for a few seconds. Then he grabbed her head and slammed it onto the floor.

Angie's head was pounding, her lip was cut and swollen, the whole side of her face was swollen and the pain from her cheek was almost unbearable. Angie was crying and frightened almost to the point of being paralyzed. But something inside of her began building up. Anger. This anger was helping her to focus and it covered up some of the fear.

Mike looked at her and said, "Now I'm going to fuck the shit out of you and mess you up anyway I want. I want to hurt you like you hurt me. Maybe I can find something huge to really tear you up when I'm done," He looked around and saw a big pipe, one that they use at the shop when they have very stubborn bolts to loosen. Maybe I'll use that pipe. You're going to die anyway so I can do anything and I am going to enjoy hurting you." He laughed out loud. "Then I'm going to dump gas on you and all around this place and burn you alive and the whole place will go. I can't wait to see you burn. You were supposed to die earlier from failed brakes in front of everyone but the dam tech guys fucked that up. I worked so hard filing your brake lines last night."

Angie continued to plead with Mike but he just ignored her. She wished she would have gone with her father now. Mike started to unbuckle his belt.

Angie saw more than anger in Mike's eyes. It looked as though he had lost his mind. He looked insanely crazy with lust. His eyes looked to Angie like a demon was behind them. She continued to fight. She pulled her hands and struggled to get free to no avail. Mike is just laughing like he was crazy mad. Just when she began to feel like it was hopeless and was about to give up......

Mr. Connor pulled up and Jim saw the door open and jumped out of the car before it was completely stopped. He ran in and saw Mike getting ready to rape Angie, and it looked like she was tied down.

Jim screamed at Mike as he was running towards him. "What the hell are you doing Mike?" Mike looked up, jumped to his feet and re-buckled his belt. Jim took a swing at Mike but missed and Mike punched him in the side. Jim punched back and hit Mike in the jaw. Mike swung back and hit Jim in the stomach and then a left and right in the head then again then again and Jim fell back onto the floor. Mike looked at him for a few seconds and kicked him hard in the side multiple times then once in the head.

"This is perfect. Now I can blame Jim for burning the place down. ha ha ha." Mike said out loud. He turned back to Angie and said, "Things are looking up. Without you everyone will be afraid to testify and they will find you guilty of everything." Mike tells Angie. "And I get off Scott free!"

Angie said, "It wull nevor wok Mike Tey will see dat Jim coun't burn me amd hinself before the bulding."

"Oh really? Looks like it's working to me." Mike said. "Soon you will be dead anyway bitch." He knelt down and tried to kiss her. Angie turned her head. He grabbed her head by her cheeks and turned her head back, the pain was unbearable. Then he kissed her and bit her lip bad enough to split the skin. She did all she could to resist.

Angie screamed as loud and she could, "Hewp, hewp sonone hewp mae pease!" But her ribs hurt and she couldn't get a good enough breath to be very loud. The screaming was hurting her throat.

Mike said, "No one can hear you, we're all alone now, just you and me sweetheart! Now we are going to have some real fun." He straddled her and started to open his pants again.

"No! Mik, ou can't do dis. Mik!" Angie screamed. "Noooo!

Just then Mike's dad came in and screamed "Michael." He looked up. "What the hell do you think you are doing?"

"I'm fixing it so she can't testify and having lots of fun doing it. Everyone else will be too scared now. With her gone nobody can hurt me."

Mr. Connor was walking towards Mike. "I already asked the lady at the house next store to call the police. It's over Mike. Now get off of her."

"The fuck it's over old man."

"Mike its over. Now get off of that poor girl or I will pull you off."

Mike stood up and stepped away from Angie. "No, you're not going to spoil my fun, No one is! So get the fuck out of here."

"You are breaking you're mother's heart, Mike."

"Not possible. I took care of that bitch before I left. Just go home and see." He laughed.

"You did what?"

"I took care of the bitch. I had enough of her screaming at me so I strangled her." Mike said as if just making a statement. "She's dead."

"You killed her?" Mr. Conrad was shocked. "You killed your mother?"

"What part of strangled and dead don't you understand old man? Yea, I killed the bitch. Go look for yourself." Mike was getting pissed again.

"You son of a bitch." Mr. Conrad said as he went to grab Mike.

Mike grabbed the 45 from the back of his pants. "Stop there or I will kill you too."

Mr. Conrad stopped. "No you won't, Mike. You're just a punk. I should have thrown you and your mother out long ago. Now you're going to jail. I have had enough of you. Now give me the gun!" He lunged forward and Mike shot him in the forehead. Mr. Conrad had a blank stare and fell backwards onto the floor.

While Mike was arguing with his dad and looking away from her, Angie prayed for the strength to break free and pulled as hard as she could and was able to grab the hook on the bungee cord tied around her wrists with a couple of fingers from one hand. The pain was excruciating but she was fighting for her life. She pulled on the hook with all of her strength and got it unhooked. The bungee sprang back and bounced off of the lift. She sat up and unhooked the bungee cords on her feet. Then she jumped up. Adrenalin was pumping through her veins and she was focused solely on Mike. It was like she had tunnel vision, she saw nothing besides Mike. She was now in survival mode.

Mike turned around to get back to his fun and was greeted by a forward roundhouse to his right hand and the gun flew out of his hand and across the floor.

Mike immediately swung at Angie's face but in one fluid move she expertly pushed his arm away and used an Aikido move where you grab the wrist and bend your other arm and you pull the wrist and thrust you other arm into the elbow. This broke Mike's arm. She followed with 4 straight fast punches to his face which broke his nose again.

Dominic pulled over to let the police go by, then an ambulance and fire truck. He was only a few blocks away from the shop and he was wondering what was going on. Then he realized that they turned and stopped next to the shop. "Oh my god, Angie!" He floored it and the tires squealed and smoked (the truck now had a 427 in it) and screeched to a halt in front to the shop. He jumped out and ran into the shop through the front door.

Mike stepped back a few steps back and screamed, "You broke my fucking arm you bitch! You're gona fucking die" Mike looked at Angie. His face was twisted and demonic. He screamed, "Ahhhhh" and lunged forward.

Neither of them heard the sirens from the police cars. They screeched to a stop and the first cop through the door saw Angie doing a 360 degree reverse roundhouse to Mike's head. He saw her spin around and her foot hitting the side of Mike's head, he saw Mike's sweat spray off of his face and Mike went down falling almost limp.

Angie turned and stepped over to Jim and knelt down, "Jin, Jin, are you alwite? Jin." She lightly taped his cheek.

Mike was dazed but not knocked out. He shook his head, pushed himself up with his good arm and reached and grabbed the gun. Sergeant Hernandez rushed towards Mike seeing him grab the gun. Mike was raising the gun towards Angie and Sergeant Hernandez pulled his gun.

"Put the gun down!" Sergeant Hernandez screamed. Mike turned and fired at Sergeant Hernandez and it grazed his right forearm. Sergeant Hernandez immediately shot back and it hit Mike in the chest. Mike looked surprised then fell back limp.

Sergeant Hernandez ran up and kicked the gun away from Mike just as Lieutenant Edwards came running in. He had his gun drawn. He ran up to Sergeant Hernandez, "You're hit Sergeant!"

"It just grazed my arm. It's not bad."

"Go get that taken care of by the paramedics Sergeant."

Angie heard the gunshots but didn't look. She was worried about Jim. She saw Jim open his eyes. It looked as if his nose was broken and had two black eyes and maybe cracked ribs. She helped him up. He was breathing and wheezing very hard and gasping like he couldn't breathe. She thought maybe he had a collapsed lung.

Dominic came running through the door and screamed, "Angie?" He saw Mike shoot at Sergeant Hernandez and then Sergeant Hernandez shoot back and he saw Mike fall back limp. There was someone lying on the floor a few feet from Mike and he appeared dead. Then he saw Sergeant Hernandez run to Mike and kick the gun away, just as Lieutenant Edwards ran in with his gun drawn.

Dominic saw paramedics coming in with equipment. He screamed, "ANGIE! Again and he finally saw Angie helping another guy that looked like he was in bad shape. And it dawned on him she was almost naked and he could see that her face was bloody. "My god, what happened?"

Lieutenant Edwards walked up and said to Dominic, "We don't know yet Dominic we just arrived. We still need to investigate." Lieutenant Edwards is one of Dominic's friends so he wasn't formal.

Angie looked up and saw her father. She helped Jim lean on a bench. She tried to run to Dominic but stumbled and almost fell and caught herself on a bench. Her legs were bruised and it hurt her to stand on her right leg. She limped across the shop and into her father's arms. "Fater." Angie is crying. "Fat.." Dominic held her but she hurt everywhere. She screamed, "Ah-hhh!" as he put his arms around her.

"Angie, sit down." He reached over and grabbed a chair that was next to him. "It's over now. You can relax." She was shivering quite a bit. One of the officers brought a blanket and helped Angie put it around her. She was shivering because she had almost no cloths on and was in shock. Dominic put his arms around her and she screamed, "AAHHH" again. Shocked, Dominic realized she was hurt far worse than it appeared and he didn't know where to touch her. He didn't know what was over but he needed to console Angie.

A paramedic came over to Angie. "Hello Ma'am, I'm here to treat your wounds, OK? And I have a few questions as well."

Angie replied, "Yas, you muay, Mah'om." Her throat was sore from all of the screaming she did and her swollen lips and whole side of her face and sore jaw made it difficult for her to speak. Her voice sounded gravelly and weak and the words were slurred. "Is sumone hwelpin Jin?" Her voice was shaky because she was shivering so much.

"The boy that was beaten as well? Yes, I think they are putting him in the ambulance now. They think he had a collapsed lung and maybe some other internal injuries." The paramedic gave Angie an ice pack to put on the side of her face and began cleaning the cuts on Angie's face and lips. "Ma'am, I need to ask you some personal questions. We can go some-where alone if you like."

Angie struggled but said, "Yoou muay osk me anoy qestions, Mah'om. Dis is muy fater ant I want him to her what I sauy." Dominic had difficulty understanding her.

"OK, Ma'am. Did the perpetrator penetrate you in any way?" The paramedic asked.

"No Mah'om. Hue dudn't get tat far tanks to Jim and Mike's fater." Angie started to cry again.

Dominic looked shocked. He thought, "Someone tried to rape her?"

"Are you sure Ma'am? Take your time. If he did I will need to take samples, do you understand, Ma'am?"

Angie tried to stop crying. She sniffled and tried to clear her throat but it hurt. "Yas I undustand. Aund no, he did not pemetwate me. And she began crying again.

"Are those ligature marks Ma'am" the paramedic asked while looking at Angie's wrists then her ankles.

"Yas Ma'am."

Dominic was shocked, "You were tied up?"

"Yas Fater."

"What did he use Ma'am?" The paramedic asked.

"Bunge cowds, Mah'om."

The paramedic carefully cleaned the ligature marks on her wrists and ankles. "Ahhh!" Angie screeched. She tried not to make any noise but it just came out.

"I'm very sorry for hurting you, Ma'am. I cleaned the wounds on your face and put a butterfly dressing on your cheek. You need to go to a hospital and get checked for a concussion and you may have some fractured ribs. You will be safe taking some Tylenol now for the pain Ma'am."

"Tank you for yar help, Mah'om" Angie told the paramedic. "And coud you plase tell wuhtenand Ewards tat I have some imhortant infowmaton for hum?"

The paramedic said, "I will Ma'am." Angie knew Lieutenant Edwards because he had been at the shop many times to visit with her father.

Dominic went into his office and grabbed his bottle of Tylenol and went back to Angie and gave her two and a glass of water. She had difficulty drinking the water due to her injuries and some spilled out of the side of her mouth. She wiped it with the edge of the blanket.

Lieutenant Edwards walked over and asked Angie, "The paramedic told me you have some important information for me Angie?"

"Yas sir. I jut rewembered tat Mik told his fater tat he kwlled his moter before he cam her. I tought tis was impordant."

"Yes, that is important Angie. Thank you." Lieutenant Edwards said and he called over another officer and told him, "There may be another homicide at the Conrad house. Could you go over there and investigate then radio me what you find?" The officer said he would and left.

In about twenty minutes the officer called Lieutenant Edwards on the radio and said, "Lieutenant, there is a crime scene here. There is an adult woman and she appears to be deceased. The place is torn up too." The lieutenant told him to please tape off the scene and remain there. The crime scene crew would be there when they finished here.

"Oh Angie, I am so sorry I left." Dominic said.

Angie looked at her father and said, "NO, you coud be deaud too if you wer her. He was afer me. He savotaded my bakes. He wanted me to cwash at da end of my fuirst run; he sauid he was so angwy tat ta technsical inpectiow found it. He was goin to com afer me until he suucceeded. If I was not her he may hav come to our hous."

"You are right Angie, but it is very difficult to be a parent and find your child hurt."

Dominic looked up and saw news people. He had been too busy with Angie and the paramedic to notice them. "Angie, I need to call your mother. The news is here and she is probably watching right now. She's going to be in hysterics."

"Go call moter, I will be fiin." It hurt for her to speak; her lips and the whole side of her face and jaw was swollen and sore.

Chapter 21

Lizzy, Angie's mother was at home preparing baked manicotti for dinner and was talking to Lilly on the phone. She thought Dominic and Angie were racing so she was taking her time. She had the television on in the background. She heard a special news report come on but wasn't really paying attention. Lilly all of a sudden screamed, "Lizzy, Look at the TV now!"

Lizzy didn't understand the agitated tone and turned and saw the reporter.

He said, "We have a developing situation here at Dom's Automotive and Performance Center 847 N. Stone Avenue. Information is sketchy at this point but we know two people were shot and killed here this afternoon, and there are 2 others that were badly beaten."

In the background was the shop and there were police cars, an ambulance and a fire truck there. Police were all around.

The news man walked up to one officer and asked, *"Officer, can you give us any information about this situation?"*

The officer replied, *"We don't have much yet at this point but I can tell you two individuals have been shot and presumed dead, and there are 2 additional individuals that have taken a serious beating."*

Lizzy was shocked. She said to her sister, "My God, Dominic, Angelina," Is all she could get out. She dropped the phone and sat town. She was in shock. The thought of Dominic or Angelina shot and killed was almost more than she could take. She was shaking and began feeling feint. Her mouth was dry, her heart was beating like it was going to come out of her chest.

Lilly was still on the phone screaming, "Lizzy, Lizzy, are you there? Lizzy." She didn't know if she fainted or if something else happened.

After the reporter described the situation further he walked into the shop and asked another officer, *"Officer, can you give us an update on the situation?*

The officer then replied, "There are two fatalities, one of which was shot by police and is presumed to be the suspect. We have just been notified that there is another fatality connected to this at another address. And there are two individuals that have also been beaten. One high school aged boy and one high school aged girl. I cannot release the names at this time. That is all I have."

The reporter asked, "Could I get your name for out records officer?"

"Lieutenant Edwards"

"Thank you officer." The reporter said. "We will give you update as information becomes available. This is Brian Atkins for KGUN NEWS."

Then Lizzy saw video from inside of the shop and she thought she saw two people lying on the floor and someone that could be Angie in the background but it appeared that the person was wearing a white bikini. "But why would someone be wearing a bikini at the shop," she thought. Then she saw another person that could have been Dominic. At this point she was hysterical. "A high school aged girl" she exclaimed. Lizzy didn't know what to do and just sat there stunned and shaking. She didn't realize she had been crying until she felt her tears drip on her hands. She reached for a tissue.

Sherri, Janet and Karen were together hanging out on Sunday at Sherri's house and the TV was on in the background.

Sherri kind of jerked like she was just shocked and said, "I feel strange, like something bad happened. This is so weird." Then Sherri heard, *"We have a developing situation here at Dom's Automotive and Performance Center 847 N. Stone Avenue."*

Sherri said alarmingly, "Isn't that Angie's dad's place?"

Janet and Karen looked at the TV and Janet said, "I think so." When they saw the story they were horrified. But then they heard that a high school age boy and one high school aged girl were badly beaten and the suspect was dead, shot by police Sherri immediately knew it was Mike. And they knew that the girl had to be Angie even though the news didn't say. Sherri said, "It's Angie!" And they were so glad that she was OK, well, that she survived. Angie had been their only friend since Mike raped them. Now they were worried how badly she was hurt, if she was really OK. They too were now panicked.

Janet looked at Sherri and said, how do you know that?"

"I don't know, it is so weird, I just feel it." Sherri replied.

Gina, Paula and Denise were hanging out at Gina's house on Sunday. They were lazing around complaining that they had to go back to school tomorrow already when Gina's mom went to change the channel on the TV. Just before she changed it they heard, *"We have a developing situation here at Dom's Automotive and Performance Center 847 N. Stone Avenue."*

Gina's mom said, "All there is on the news as violence lately," and reached to change the channel.

Gina screamed, "Mom! Leave it on, my God!" She jumped off of the chair she was sitting on so fast it tipped over and ran to the TV. This shocked Paula and Denise. She said, "oh my God!" and covered her mouth. "Oh my God!" And she sounded like she started to cry.

Gina's mom asked, "What's the problem Gina? It's just more violence, what's the big deal?"

Gina said through tears, "Mom, remember I told you about my new friend? The one that does Martial Arts stuff? This is her father's shop.....Oh No! Three people are dead and two were beaten?"

Denise said, "What are you talking about?"

Paula went to the TV and said, "What about Angie's dad's shop?"

Gina said, "Look!"

Paula looked and heard the news man and got upset too. "Oh my God!"

Denise came to the TV and asked, "What this was about."

Paula said, "Who is dead? Who got beaten up? They're not saying. Is Angie there?" She asked Gina.

"How would I know, you're seeing what I am." Gina replied.

"Isn't that Angie's Dad's shop?" Denise said casually not understanding what was going on.

Gina looked at Denise and said, "Denise, don't you hear? Three people are dead and two are beaten, and their not saying who."

"What? Who is dead and beaten?" Denise sounded a little stunned.

"We don't know Denise. But this is Angie's dad's shop. What? A high school girl and boy are beaten? Oh my god, it's probably Angie! What other high school aged girl would be there?" Paula said.

Denise now understood and was shocked. They didn't say anyone's names or show anyone. And the special report ended. The three of them looked at each other in complete shock. Gina's mom asked, "You're saying your new friend got all beat up? What happened?"

Gina said, "We don't know, they didn't say much." She thought for a minute and said to Paula and Denise, "It has to be something to do with Mike, I know it. That bastard!"

Paula and Denise agreed. They sat on the floor with tears in their eyes. Paula said, "Maybe they will say something in school tomorrow."

Denise said, "I hope she is OK. Maybe it isn't bad."

"I thought you didn't like her that much Denise," Gina said.

"I didn't at first. But she made a big impression on me. That thing she said about me having a relationship with my dad, no one ever did anything like that to me before and it made me understand what we were doing to Sherri, Janet and Karen. I cried all night. She made me think. I don't do that much."

"No you don't think much, do you?" Gina teased.

"Wait, that's not what I meant. You twisted it." Denise said.

"Come on Denise, you know I'm kidding." Gina said.

"Oh, OK, but what about Angie?" Denise asked. Denise is kind of an air head type. But that's what Gina liked about her. Gina thought it always made her feel smarter. Paula kind of felt a little sorry for her but liked her anyway.

"I guess we need to wait for tomorrow and maybe the school will say something about it. I hope so." Paula said.

"I wish we didn't have to wait." Denise said.

"I don't know what else we can do. We don't know where she lives and if it is her I don't think anyone would be home." Gina said.

The three of them talked about this all afternoon and then Paula and Denise went home.

Dominic went into the office to call Lizzy. She was hysterical but somewhat relieved when she heard Dominic. The news didn't say much other than three people were dead, two at the shop, one somewhere else and a high school aged boy and girl were beaten. Dominic told Lizzy what he knew which wasn't much but at least he could tell her that Angie was basically fine. He also asked her if she could bring some cloths for

Angie. He didn't tell her that Angie was almost naked; he just said her cloths had been soiled.

Lizzy was still shaking and told Dominic, "I will gather some cloths and come forthwith." Then she hung up the phone. She missed putting the receiver on the hook twice before she finally got it. She had to call her mother, Lilly and Maria to tell them that Angie and Dominic were OK first. She couldn't just leave them hanging. She picked up the receiver again and dropped it. She couldn't handle the phone because she was shaking so much. At first she couldn't push the correct buttons. She kept trying and finally she dialed Lilly. "Hello Lilly, Dominic is fine but he did not say much about Angie except that she needed cloths. I need to get cloths and bring them there. Could you please call mother and Maria? I am shaking so much that I cannot push the buttons."

"Of course Lizzy. Is there something I can do to help?"

"Right now I do not know I just have to get cloths to Angie. I will call you later when I know more." She was still shaking.

"OK Lizzy but you know we are all here for you." She could hear that Lizzy was very upset and her voice was shaky. Her voice was sounding very distressed.

"I know, I need to go." And she hung up the phone. Lizzy didn't realize she didn't say goodbye or tell her she loved her like always. Then she gathered cloths and shoes for Angie. She brought a bra and panties as well as a pair of jeans, a t-shirt and sweater as she didn't know what Angie needed. She got into her car and drove to the shop. She was finding it difficult to drive because she was so upset. Lizzy was worried. What happened? She thought, 'Why does Angie need cloths? Did something get spilled on her? Was she the high school aged girl the reporter mentioned?" She couldn't think straight.

Lilly called her mother then Maria. Her mother didn't know anything happened because she didn't have the TV on. But she was now worried and shaky. Lilly told her that she was going to call Maria next. Her mother suggested they get together at Lilly's house so they could be updated together.

Lilly hung up the phone and it immediately rang. She picked it up and it was Maria. She sounded frantic. "Maria, Maria, Maria!" Lizzy said trying to get her to stop talking she could tell her what she knew.

Maria had felt uneasy. She felt something bad happened at the shop but did not know details. She saw someone shot and someone tied up and beaten in her head but it was vague. "Maria kept talking frantically, "Lilly, I have been trying to get a hold of Lizzy and the phone was busy and now she is not picking up. I called the shop too and no one picked up either. I do not know what to do." She finally stopped for long enough for Lilly to talk.

"Maria, I just talked to Lizzy. Please calm down a little so I can tell you what she said." Lilly said.

"Alright." Maria said.

Lilly explained, "I just talked to Lizzy and she said that Dominic is fine. She did not know much about Angie except that she needed cloths and she was going to bring cloths to the shop for her. I do not know anything else. Lizzy said she would call as soon as she knew more. So all we can do is wait."

"Should we go there? I mean to the shop?"

Lilly said, "If you saw this on the news you saw all of the police and everyone else involved. I do not think they would let us even get close right now. If you would like you can come over here, when Lizzy calls you would get updated right away. I think my mother will be coming as well."

"Thank you Lilly, I will. Then we can all be together when she calls. I will be leaving shortly." Maria didn't see the news but was just as worried and shocked as Lilly and her mother. She was afraid to say it was a vision.

Lieutenant Edwards walked over to Angie and asked, "Where is your father Angie?"

"He wemt to cal my moter."

"We are ready to interview you now Angie but I want you father present. And we will need to get pictures of all of your injuries. We have a female officer that will take them."

"OK sir." Then asked, "Sir, is it posable to move to ta bweak room, I am fweezing out her in the chop. Tere is also a table and chawirs where we cun all sit." Angie was still difficult to understand because half of her face and her lips were swollen.

"Sure, I want to get you as comfortable as we can Angie."

Angie stood and limped into the break room. It was obvious that she was in great pain. Lieutenant Edwards went to get Sergeant Hernandez and Inspector James. Then he asked Sergeant Hernandez how his arm was and Sergeant Hernandez said it was fine. Then he asked if he would go and get Officer George. Officer George was taking pictures of the scene.

As Dominic hung up the phone he saw Angie limping to the break room so he went in to join her and sat down. "Fater, evewyone is cooming in hewe to intervew mea. I awsked him becase I was cold in the chop. Oh, and tey hav a female officer heer to tak pitures of my ejuries." In a few minutes Officer George came with the camera and told Lieutenant Edwards that she would be taking the pictures now. She continued into the break room and closed the door. "I want my fater her, mah'om.

"Hello Angelina, I am Officer George and I will be taking pictures to document your injuries."

"I unwerstand Mah'om."

"I will begin with a picture of the front of your full body then the rear full body. Then I will take close ups of your face and the back of your head; each arm front and rear; your upper and lower torso front and rear; your legs front and rear and your wrists and ankles front and rear. I will try to take these without asking you to move around much so I cause you as little pain as possible. Do you understand Angelina?"

"Yes Mah'om."

"OK then, please remove the blanket." Angie took off the blanket and stood facing her. She took the front full body picture, then the rear full body picture. Then she told Angie that she could close her eyes so she doesn't get blinded by the flash. Then she took the close up of Angie's face then the back of her head. Officer George looked at the pictures and said, "I'll need to take a close-up picture of each side of your face as well. I can't see those in the pictures." Then she took a picture of each side of her face. She took one of her front upper torso, of course with her bra on, then of her stomach area. She moved to the back and did the same. She took the pictures of the front and rear of each arm and decided to take close ups of her wrists so the ligature marks from the bungee cords were clear. She took the front and rear pictures of her legs and also took close ups of her ankles to get the ligature marks as well. "Angelina, you can put the blanket on and sit down while I look at the pictures to see if I need any others." She looked at each picture closely. These were Polaroid pictures so they develop almost immediately. She was satisfied with them and said to Angie, "Thank you Angelina, these all look fine. Thank you for your cooperation."

"Yor wellcom Mah'om, tank you." And Officer George gathered the pictures and the camera, opened the door and told Lieutenant Edwards that she was finished and left.

At that time everyone that would be present for the interview walked into the break room and sat down. Dominic got water for everyone and sat down. Lieutenant Edwards looked at Angie and said, "Angie, we need these pictures for evidence. I wasn't sure if you understood that."

"I uwnderstwand sir. I hav wead enough crime dwama books to know standard pwolice pwocedures."

"Are you sure you are alright to do this now Angie?" Lieutenant Edwards asked.

"Yas sar." Even though it hurt to talk she was determined to do this. She hurt everywhere and was very tired now that the adrenalin was wearing off. She didn't want to have to do this another time. She felt like just crawling into her bed and going to sleep.

Lieutenant Edwards began by introducing everyone. He turned on a small tape recorder and said, "Today is December 1st 1974 and we are here to interview and take a statement from Angelina Tucci about this incident. To my right are Inspector James, then Sergeant Hernandez, Angelina Tucci and her father, Dominic Tucci the owner of this establishment. We will begin with a description of the scene. We arrived and found the perpetrator, Michael Conrad, reaching for a gun and Sergeant Hernandez ran in and screamed for him to drop it. Michael shot at Sergeant Hernandez grazing his right arm and he returned fire striking Michael in the chest. I entered and immediately secured the scene and determined that there was no additional threat. I didn't know who the surviving victims were at that time but identified two individuals, one young female assisting a young male, that both appeared severely injured. The female appeared to only have a bra and panties. I also identified a middle aged adult male with a bullet hole in his forehead to whom appeared deceased lying on the floor. I checked for a pulse and determined that the individual had none. At that point, Dominic Tucci came running in and identified the young female victim as his daughter, Angelina. She attempted to run to him but had issue due to significant injuries. Angelina limped to Dominic and fell into his arms. At that point the paramedics and fire department arrived. A fire Department Captain pronounced the adult male along with Michael Conrad deceasd. I called the paramedics and asked them to bring some blankets. I gave one to the female victim.

An officer assisted her wrapping herself with the blanket. One paramedic went to assess the young male. At this time the crime scene investigation team arrived. A paramedic came over to examine Angelina and provided first aid. When the Paramedic finished she informed me that Angelina had important information for me. I walked to her and she informed me that Michael Conrad said he strangled his mother to death. I sent an officer to the Conrad house and was informed of another crime scene and Mrs. Conrad appeared deceased. Officer George took a series of photos of Angelina's injuries. Afterwards we came into this break room to interview and take a statement from Angelina."

"Angelina, do you feel strong enough to describe what happened here today?" Lieutenant Edwards asked.

"I myt nout be verry cleear or understndable with my spech but I wull try, sir." "Tobay, I was gooing to rache my Cuda for the furst time. My fater and I inspeected the Cuda thooroughly last Suderdy noght and foud no isses. Dis morrming when I went throough tehnicul inspetion they foud leks in the brak lines wohich meaant thut I coud not rac. My fater puut his rac caw omto the twailer amd took it bach here to the shop dhen came bach to the twrack and picked up the Cuda, mysulf and my Uuncle Jawck. We cam bac her to the shap amd my uuncle dib not come in and juust went home. My fater amd I unwoaded the Cuda and wolled it onto a wift. Them he dwrove his truc aroound the bac amd discommeced the twrailer and parwked in the yard. Aferwards he came bac ino the shap. We waised the Cuda and begam to wook at the braake wines, fownd the weaks and remooved the damagd wines. We puut dhem on the benwch and saw wat appeawed to be cut maks wher the weaks were. I am sworry I am noot tawking wewl but miy jaww hurts."

"You are doing just fine Angie." Lieutenant Edwards said.

My fader went over to his stawc amd fouwnd dhat he onwly haud one brak wime of the corrwect size, so he callwed his fwiend dhat owns a parts stor, and made awangements to pick up amother bwrak wine. I was at the bench fwoughout dis. I took owt the dowble farring tool and was fwamiliawizing myself wit it and my fater bwought a few short piecees of owld bwrak wime to teach me how to mak dowble flawes. He told me dhat he needed to get awother wine from his fwiend's store and it woould tak about am hower and a half. He asted me if I waned ta goo awong but I decided ta stay and pwactice making dowble fwares. My faher weft and I went bac to pwacticin. Some pont ater dhat I hoard someting and turned awound and saw Mik an instamt befor his fist hit da side of my fac. He wepeatedwy punched me untiw I was unconschious. Da next ting I wemember I was wying on the fwoor wit my jeans and T-shert wemoved with my amkles tied to bench wegs and my wists tied togeter and stwapped to part of a wift. He had used bunggee cowds. This was wen I fiwst felt my wibs hort. Maybe he kicwked me, I do not know. Fwom what I rimember, he told me dhat he cut my bwake wines becawse he wamted to see me cwash and die in front of everyome at the twack and that he was wery angwy dhat the tecwnical inspectows said I cowld not wase. He had dhis insane cwazy wook in his eyes. I hav never been so fwightened. He told me he was going to waape me and den do whaever else he wanted amd he suggesed impawing me wif a pipe. Dhen he told me he was going to pow gassoline aw over me and burn me to dewth and he was going to emjoy waching me die. And aterword he was going to bwrn the shap to cower it up. He said somehing dhat I did not understand and gwabbed my cwoss, wipped it off and trew it acwoss the shop. Dhat cwoss is so deaw to me I scweamed something like dhat's mine and he swapped me acwoss the fac so hawd dhat my viseon blurred and I almost passed owt."

Angie got teary-eyed and said, "Fater, you hawe to find my cwoss. You just hawe to." Tears were running down her face.

"I will find it Angie." Dominic said.

Angie composed herself as best as she could and continued, "I kwept trwing to talk him out of doing dhis and he kwept swapping my fac and tewing me to shut up. A few times he gwabbed my head and swammed it onto da flor. I scweamed help so many times dhat my twroat is now swore I was vewy tewified and felt helpwess and was about to give up amd just wet him do what he wanted. Dhat's whe Jin came wunning in. He twied to stop Mik and booff he amd Mik fought. Mik ended up beatin him untwl he was unconschious. Mik came back to me and twold me dhat he cowld bwame this all om Jim now and he would burn wit the shop as wewl. Den Mik's fater cam in. Dhey began awguing and dhat gav me dhe oppertunity to bweak fwee, so I pulled my arms with ewery bit of stwength I had and was able to weach the hook on the bunge cowd wit my fingers amd unhooked it. I sat up and umtied my ankles. I tink adwenalin was pumping because I was not feewing amy pain. I jumped up and I heard the gum go off and Mik's fater fewl. I got into my stonce and Mik turned awound. He had a shocked wook for a few seconds. Den he began to waise the gum and I kicked it owt of his hand. The gum flew away. Mik dhen took a swing at me and I bwocked it and wsed a move to bweak his arm. At dhis point the onwy ting I saw was Mik and the danger he posed. I wsed some stwaight punches and hit him im the fac tree or 4 times, maybe more. I tink I bwoke his nose again and he was stummed for a minute. Dhen he got dhat cwazy lwok again and lwnged at me and I used ta weverse 360 degwee woundhowse but I put evewyting I had in it even more dhan with the convict. I tink dhat's why I am wimping. I tink I hwrt my weg. Mik went down and da only ting I fought of dhen was Jin. He saved my wife. I went over to him and twied to get him to come to and I tink dhat's wen Sergeant Hewnandez came wunning in. When I hewped Jin up I heawd a few addifional gum shots. I tuwned and saw Sergeant Hewnandez stwanding over Mik. Dhen I saw fater and twied to run to him but I cowld not. I did not wealize how sewious my injuwies were, so I wimped. Dhat is all I wemember, sir." And Angie looked as though she was going to pass out. Her father handed her a bottle of water and she drank most of it at one time.

Lieutenant Edwards said, "Angie that is quite a story. If Sergeant Hernandez didn't see you kick Mike I don't know if I would have believed it. You explained what happened extremely well for someone that just had such a traumatic experience. You are one lucky girl. This could have ended much worse." He looked at Inspector James and he shook his head and said that they were finished.

Lizzy arrived at that point and found a place to park in front of the shop. The fire truck and ambulance had already gone and all that was left were police cars, a couple of cars she didn't recognize and Dominic's pickup with the driver's door open. She parked, got out, closed the door on Dominic's pick-up and walked around to the overhead door into the shop. An officer stopped her and said that this was a crime scene. She told him that she knew and she told him who she was and that she had cloths for Angie. The officer told her to wait there. He walked to the break room and told the inspector that Mrs. Tucci was here with cloths for Angie. He told him to let her in.

As Lizzy waited she saw people documenting things and taking pictures. She saw what looked like a blood puddle in the middle of the floor. There was an outline of two bodies in what appeared to be chalk. Another officer came over and told Lizzy that everyone was in the break room. Lizzy thanked him and went to the break room. She was still shaking and now her legs felt like jelly again.

Dominic stood up and went to meet Lizzy at the door. He didn't want her to see Angie until she was dressed. He thought at least the cloths would cover all of the bruises on her body. He said, "Lizzy I know you are worried and concerned about Angie but please let me give these to her and let her get dressed before you see her. It will be less of a shock if she has her clothes on."

"Why, does she not have anything on?" That was all Lizzy could get out without crying.

"Sweetheart, please wait here for a minute. Once she has the cloths she will go into the bathroom to put them on. Then you can come in and sit down. But I want to warn you, she got serious beating so be prepared." Dominic said in a soft voice. He was trying to calm her. He went and gave Angie the bag of cloths and she went to the bathroom to change. Dominic took Lizzy's hand and brought her into the room and pulled a chair out for her and she sat down. Lizzy felt just as terrible as she looked. She was still shaking.

Lieutenant Edwards looked at Lizzy and said, "Elisabeth, Angie was very lucky, this could have been much worse. Just remember that when you see her. Angie is a very brave and resourceful woman. She thought fast and neutralized the perpetrator long enough for us to take over."

Nothing could have prepared Lizzy for the sight of Angie. When she came out of the bathroom Lizzy gasped and in a loud voice said, "Oh, My Lord, Angelina!" Lizzy had one hand over her mouth and immediately began to cry. "My baby, what did he do to you, my God." She was almost unrecognizable due to the abrasions; swelling; bleeding; messed up hair and black eyes.

Angie looked terrible, she had two black eyes; her nose was black and blue and still dripping blood; one cheek had the butterfly bandage covering a big abrasion and was very swollen up into her eye which was partly shut; her lips were swollen and had been bleeding and the whole side of her face and neck was bruised. Her hands and arms were also scraped and bruised, there were visible ligature marks from the bungee cords on her wrists and her hair was all full of dirt and a was a mess. This was all that Lizzy saw since Angie now was dressed. She didn't see the bruises and scrapes on her chest; the bruising on the right side of her ribs; the scrapes and abrasions and the dirt from the shop floor on her back; the bruising on her legs and feet and the ligature marks on her ankles. She also had a big bump on the back of her head. Since Angie just came out of the bathroom and only took a few steps to the chair. She sat down very slow due to the pain. Lizzy didn't notice that Angie was limping. Lizzy got up and ran around the table to take Angie in her arms but she was afraid to touch her because of all of her wounds. Her hands and arms were shaking. She just sat down in the chair next to Angie and took her hand. Dominic gave her some water.

"I am sowy moter, I am so sowy dhis happened." She was in tears again. She knew how much it upset her mother and she was feeling terrible that her mother had to see her like this. Her speech was still slurred and sounded strange because of her sore throat and the swelling.

Through her tears Lizzy said, "Honey, this is not your fault."

"I jwst did not wamt you to see me wike dis, I kmow how much dhis is upsewing you, moter." She was feeling very tired and sore now that the adrenalin had worn off and everything with the police was finished.

The Inspector James then said, "We have everything we need from you, Angie. Can I call you if I have any more questions?"

"Wes, sir, I will be awailable for anyting you need, sir. Dhank you for all you hawe done, I mean dhis to everyone hewe and the pawamedics as wewl. I would wike to tank the pawamedic that tweated me as well. She was wery pwrofessional and tweated me with wespect."

Lieutenant Edwards looked at Dominic and said, "Dominic, I've known you for maybe 6 or 7 years now and it still amazes me how polite your family is, even during something serious as this."

Dominic said, "Thank you sir."

"Oh, and get Angie checked out for a concussion. And she said the right side of her chest hurt so maybe she has some cracked ribs. They should be finished in back soon and you can have your shop back."

"Thank you again, sir." Dominic replied and raised his hand to shake. Lieutenant Edwards shook hands with Dominic and turned and walked out.

Dominic looked at Lizzy and said, "Lizzy, could you please bring Angie to the emergency room to get checked out? I will stay here until they finish and meet you there afterwards."

"I will take her Dom." She stood up and they kissed and they squeezed each other's hands. "We will be at St. Mary's Emergency."

"Are you ok to walk Angie?" Lizzy asked.

Angie stood up, "wes moter, I wiw just be a bit swow." She limped around the table with her mother. She hugged her father very lightly as she passed. "I wove you fater."

"I love you too sweetheart. See you soon."

Lizzy stood and Angie put her right hand on her shoulder to help her walk. Angie limped to the car, visibly in pain, and Lizzy helped Angie get in. At that time they saw vans for KVOA; KGUN and KOLD. Fortunately Lizzy parked in front of the shop so they were able to leave through the front door without the news stations seeing them. Then they drove to St. Mary's. They walked into the Emergency Room and a nurse saw Angie and rushed over with a wheelchair. "My lord, what happened to you?" the nurse asked as she helped Angie to sit.

Lizzy answered, "She is from the incident that was just on the news." She looked and saw a television and it was still on the news. "It is still on the news."

The nurse looked and saw it. "Oh, you're the poor girl that got beaten up. I'm so sorry."

Angie answered, "Tank you, Mah'om."

"Let's get you into a bay and checked out then." The nurse said. She pushed Angie into one of the bays and went to get some paperwork. She went to give it to Angie.

Lizzy said, "I am her mother, I can fill most of it out so Angie only needs to fill out what is necessary." She wanted to spare Angie any work that she could.

The nurse took out a gown and asked Angie to put it on and that she could sit or lay on the gurney if she would like. She also grabbed a blanket and put it on the gurney. She pulled the curtain so Angie had some privacy.

Angie got up and Lizzy helped her change into the gown then she sat on the bed. As Lizzy helped her she was able to see all of her other injuries. She helped her put the blanket around her. "I am so sorry Angie. Do not worry honey, your father and I will take care of everything."

"I know, I kin always depewd on you and fater. I hope tere is not awything sewious moter."

"We will know soon enough honey." She reached out and carefully took Angie's hand. "Honey, it looks like you hurt everywhere."

"It is not tat bad, like the officer said, it could hawe bem mwch woorse. I woder how Jin is doing. He weally took a bweating."

"Who is Jim?"

Jin was one of Mik's fwiends until dhat incicent in school. Jin came into da chop to stop Mik jwst as he was abowt to wape me. He saved my wife. You do not know what took place today, moter. I wilw tew you ewerything when we finish here and get home, Awright? It is a wong stowy."

"I can wait, honey."

Just then the doctor said, "Angie, is it alright for me to come in?"

"Yass or you mae."

"Hello Angelina and Mrs. Tucci." The Doctor took the paperwork from Lizzy and looked through it. "Let's take a look." The doctor did a thorough examination on Angie. He checked the bumps on her head and then her neck. Then he checked her ribs. He gently pressed her ribs on both sides and when he got to the right side and Angie said, "Ahhh! Dat hwrts." The doctor looked at her arms and legs.

When he finished he said, "You were very lucky. It looks like you have a few fractured ribs and possibly a mild concussion. I am going to order some chest x-rays to be certain. Someone will come to bring you to x-ray. Oh, and I think you may want to know that the police kept the news far enough away from you that no one could recognize you. I saw the reports. It seems to me that is a good thing. It was nice to meet you Angelina."

Angie said to Lizzy, "Dhat wilw not wast wong. Dhey wull find owt who I am and wikely hawass us for infowmation."

"Do not think about it honey, you have more than enough to cope with. Your father and I will do our best to keep them away from you."

Someone came and wheeled the gurney that Angie was on to x-ray. They told Lizzy that she can wait there and it would take about 45 minutes.

Lizzy asked a nurse if there was a pay phone nearby and she brought her over to one. She called Lilly and explained what she knew. She said she would call her later after they are home.

When they brought Angie back, Lizzy saw that Angie had fallen asleep. The nurse told Lizzy that the doctor would be in to go over the results shortly. Lizzy pulled the blanket over Angie.

In about 30 minutes the doctor came back with the x-rays in his hand. Lizzy woke Angie so she could hear what the doctor had to say. The doctor said to Angie and her mother, "Angie, you have a strained hamstring; 4 fractured ribs and likely a concussion. You can see the fractured ribs here." He pointed it out to them on the x-rays and it clearly showed the fractured ribs. "Since you have a concussion I can't prescribe anything for pain so you should only take Tylenol. Other pain relievers are NSAIDs which can increase the risk of bleeding and the narcotics can't be used because of the concussion. And because of the pulled hamstring I want you to use crutches. These will keep the weight off of your leg so your hamstring can heal." He continued, "A nurse will come with after care instructions and paperwork to bring to your regular doctor. You will need to see your doctor as soon as possible so you should make an appointment right away."

Dominic arrived at the emergency room and a nurse took him to the bay where Angie and Lizzy were. They were happy to see him. Lizzy explained that Angie had a strained hamstring, 4 fractured ribs and a possible concussion. The nurse with after care instructions came and explained what Angie needed to do. "You will mostly need bed rest and no lifting and definitely no training or lifting until your doctor gives her a release. And you need to use these crutches until your regular doctor tells you that you don't need them." She repeated, "lots of rest and liquids and it is imperative that she uses a cold pack or ice packs on her leg until the swelling is reduced. Most likely two to three days but it would be wise to call your doctor. Swelling will make recovery much longer and the possibility of re-injury much greater." The nurse said.

Finely they were able to go home. Lizzy helped Angie get dressed and it took some time. Everything hurt. When she was finished Lizzy helped Angie off of the Gurnee and into the wheel chair. She pushed her out of the room but before they left Angie wanted to find out if they brought Jim here and if he was alright. So she stopped one of the nurses and asked, "Mah'om, did tey bwing anwyone else hewe from dhe incident"

The nurse said, "I think there was a boy but I don't know what his status is."

Angie said, "Tank yow Ma'am." Angie rode with her mother and slept all the way home. Dominic followed. When they pulled in front of the house Dominic got out of his truck and came over to help Angie out of the car and into the house. Angie wanted to lie down in the Arizona room so she could tell her mother everything that happened.

Lizzy got Angie her pillow and a blanket. She also brought her a glass of water and two Tylenol. Angie took them and laid back and Lizzy put the blanket over her. Angie said she wanted to tell her about today but fell asleep almost before she finished the sentence. Lizzy watched her for a few minutes and thought how delicate life is and how quickly your life can change. She thought how fortunate she and Dominic were that Angie survived. As Lizzy stood there she thought she needed to pray and give thanks for keeping Angie away from death.

Lizzy, sat down and prayed. She thanked God for watching over Angie and protecting her from death. She thanked him for everything that they had and forgiveness for thinking such bad things of Mike. Then she finished with Amen.

Lizzy stood and checked Angie and then went to find Dominic. She found him outside sitting in a patio chair looking at the mountains. She walked around and saw that he was crying. She sat down on his lap across his legs and put her arms around his neck and hugged him.

"This was all my fault. I did not lock the door when I left. Angie is badly injured because of me. I will never be able to forgive myself." Dominic said and continued to cry. "I got one of the two most important people in my life hurt and almost killed."

Lizzy looked at him and said, "Sweetheart, it is not any fault of yours. If you had locked the door Mike would have continued trying to hurt Angie and possibly succeeded in killing her. If you locked the door it just would have prolonged it. So it is not any fault of yours." She talked in a soothing voice to him just as they always talked to Angie when she was upset. And it made him feel better. Dominic put his arms around Lizzy, thanked her and told her that he loved her. They sat there for some time just enjoying the closeness and view of the mountains.

Chapter 22

The next morning, Monday, Lieutenant Edwards called and talked to KGUN; KVOA and KOLD news first thing in the morning. He gave them the information that they asked for including the information about the murder of Mrs. Conrad. The news was mostly interested in the Conrad's because Leonard Conrad was the Tucson city manager. They didn't even ask much about Angie besides how she was doing. When he hung up with the last station he gave Dominic a call.

"Hello Dominic, this is Lieutenant Edwards, how is Angie doing?" he asked.

"Well, about as good as you could expect. She is in significantly more pain today and because of the concussion she can only take Tylenol. Thank you for asking sir."

"And I also wanted to tell you that the TV news wasn't at all interested in Angie or the other boy Jim. All they wanted was information about the Conrad's so I don't think you will need to worry about any harassment from them."

"That is good news Lieutenant. Thank you so much for calling to let us know. I am sure this will make Angie and Lizzy feel much better, sir."

"I am always happy to help Dominic. Good bye."

Dominic went to tell Lizzy the good news. It gave her a huge relief. She said she would tell Angie when she woke. She asked him, "Are you going into the shop today Dom?"

"Yes, I did call all of the guys to tell them we would be closed today but will re-open tomorrow. I need to clean up. But mostly because I promised Angie I would find her cross necklace."

"Her cross? You need to find it? How did it get lost?" Lizzy was visibly upset as Angie was the 5th generation of Tucci's to wear it.

"Evidently when Mike was attacking Angie he was angered by the sight of it and pulled it from her neck and threw it somewhere in the shop. So I need to find it. I think Angie was more upset from this than what Mike did her."

"I can understand that. She has a very deep attachment to it. I think she would be heartbroken if you could not find it. So please do you best Dom."

"I am just going to find it if I have to disassemble the whole shop. I know how much it means to her. I will be back later honey. Call me if you need anything, OK?"

"You know I will dear." Lizzy said and they hugged and kissed. And he left.

Dominic went to the shop and began to clean up. There was a mostly dried puddle of blood on the floor and spots around the area where Mike and Jim fought and some additionally where Angie was tied up on the floor. He got out the mop and floor detergent and mixed it in the bucket. Then he mopped up the blood. He changed the water 3 or 4 times before he was able to remove the stain from Mike's father. Then he mixed another bucket of water with bleach and mopped the whole area again. He put the mop and bucket away and began looking for the cross. He crawled all over the floor looking using a flashlight and didn't see it. Then he looked around the benches and tool boxes and even pulled them out. He looked around the lifts. He looked around the walls and couldn't find it. He was beginning to worry that he wouldn't find it and he didn't want to tell Angie it was lost. The phone rang and it was

Lizzy. She asked how he was doing and he told her he hadn't found it yet, and how worried he was that he may not find it. She could hear the disappointment in his voice and told him that she felt very strongly that he would find it somewhere. He told her that he appreciated her confidence but he didn't want to disappoint her and Angie. They said "I love you" and hung up. He went back to looking. After a few more hours of looking he was getting very worried because he couldn't find it when he heard knocking at the side door. He went to see who it was and it was Sergeant Hernandez.

"Hello Dominic. I saw your truck and thought that I would stop. I have something I found on the floor yesterday and thought I have seen it on Angie in the past." He reached in his pocket and handed Dominic the cross. "There were so many people here and didn't want anyone to take it. I didn't have an opportunity to see you before you left."

Dominic was shocked. "I have been looking for this for hours. This is very important to Angie. She is the 5th generation of Tucci's to wear it. How can I thank you sir?" Dominic had tears in his eyes.

"Your reaction was more than I need sir. And you know, Angie's reputation at the station is miraculous after yesterday. You would think she saved everyone there. So it was the least I could do for her."

"Well thank you again sir, you have made my day. Now I can actually show my face in my house again."

"It was my pleasure. Have a good day Dominic." Sergeant Hernandez turned to leave.

"Oh, how is your arm Sergeant? Lieutenant Edwards mentioned you had been shot."

"The bullet just grazed my arm. But I'll live."

"That's good to hear. You are a good man sir."

"Thank you Dominic. It was good to see you again. And take care of that daughter of yours. Have a good day." Sergeant Hernandez said as he left.

Dominic closed the door and was still in disbelief. Now he could lock up and go home. He put the last things away including the flashlight he was using. He washed up and locked the door as he left. He smiled all the way home. Angie was going to be ecstatic!

When Dominic got home he went into the house and Lizzy happened to be near the door and she came and hugged him. When she saw his face she knew he found the cross. "Is Angie awake?"

I believe she is I just brought her some chicken soup." Lizzy wouldn't miss Angie's reaction for anything.

Dominic knocked on her door and he heard, "You muy com in."

He opened the door and he and Lizzy went in. "How are you feeling Angie?"

"I balive a widdle bedder. I stull hwrt all over." The swelling on her cheek was somewhat less so she sounded better. She really didn't feel much better but she didn't want them to feel bad.

"Well, I have something to cheer you up."

"Wearry, whut do you hav fahder?" Angie smiled and looked better than when they came in.

"Close your eyes and hold out you hand, please."

She did and he put the cross and chain in her hand. "You fouwd dit! You fouwd dit. I con not bewieve it!" She reached out to hug him. He leaned over her and she started to hug him tight but it hurt and she moaned so she stopped. "Sorrwy I con not hug you fowd dit fahder. You maude me so hoppy."

"Well, let me tell you how I found it." He pulled up a chair and Lizzy sat on the edge of the bed. Angie sat there lying against her pillow with her eyes wide open, well her left eye was wide open. "I had looked everywhere, I moved the benches and the tool boxes, battery charger, the compressor, the cabinets, I crawled around the lifts, looked around and under the Nova and I could not find it. I was feeling very apprehensive. Then someone knocked on the door. It was Sergeant Hernandez. He told me he picked this up yesterday because he remembered seeing you wearing it and he did not want anyone to steal it. He said he did not get a chance to see me before I left so he came today hoping I was there."

"Reawy! I con not balive it! We are so bwessed fahder. Whun I feel well wenough I wunt to go to dhe stashion and tank him personawy, ok?"

Lizzy said, "Of course you may honey. I would not expect anything less from you. You have such a kind heart. Maybe in a few days we can go. We will let you rest now." Lizzy bent over and kissed Angie on a spot on her forehead that wasn't bruised and the both of them left and closed the door. Lizzy and Dominic hugged and kissed. "We are so blessed to have such a sweet and caring daughter."

"I agree." Dominic replied.

Chapter 23

On Tuesday morning Dominic left as usual for the shop. It was only 2 days after the incident on Sunday afternoon. He was hoping this wouldn't hurt business. He knew Johnny, Scott and Eric were not superstitious and Johnny and Scott have been working for him almost since he opened so he knew they would be in. However, he wasn't certain that Miguel and Hector would be. These two guys seemed superstitious and maybe they would have a problem with working where someone was killed. He hoped he was wrong.

Lizzy made breakfast for herself and Angie around 8:30 AM. She decided to put her breakfast on the cart as well and have breakfast with Angie. She thought she would spend some time with Angie now that she had been feeling slightly better. Lizzy knocked on Angie's bedroom door and Angie said, "You may come in mother."

Lizzy opened the door and rolled in the cart. "I thought you may enjoy some company Honey, so I brought my breakfast as well. Is that OK with you?"

Angie's speech was somewhat back to normal because the swelling had gone down a bit so she was much easier to understand. But she continued to feel pain in her jaw when she spoke. Due to this she was speaking slower. "Mother that would be wonderful! I have been feeling lonesome. And when we finish I can finely tell you about what happened Sunday, if you are fine with that Mother?"

"Of Course, you wanted to tell me since we brought you home Sunday." Lizzy had made sunny side up eggs; hash browns; bacon and toast. And they had orange juice with it.

Angie's appetite was beginning to return. Sunday evening she just had some warm milk. It was all she said she could get down. And yesterday she just had toast and a glass of water for breakfast; she had half of a peanut butter and jelly sandwich and a glass of water for lunch; some chicken soup during the afternoon and she only ate part of a chicken thy and a glass of warm milk for dinner. Angie was eating like she used to this morning and Lizzy was very happy to see it.

"How is the pain today? And do you feel well enough for your grandmother; Aunt Lilly and Aunt Maria to visit? They would delight in seeing you."

"The pain has subsided somewhat and I sound somewhat normal now, so certainly they may."

When they finished Lizzy took Angie's plate and silverware and placed it on the cart along with hers, then sat back down.

Angie began with, "Mother, this story is very gruesome so please be prepared. Father found it very distressing, so I wanted to warn you. And so you can understand what I endured I will use to words that Mike used even though they are words we never use and are upsetting to us. Are you OK with this?"

Lizzy thought for a minute and replied, "Yes Honey, please tell the story as it happened. I very much would like you know what you suffered."

"OK mother." She took a breath, "This all began Sunday morning when Father, Uncle Jack and I left for the track.

We arrived at track and found a place in the pits to unload the Nova. We filled out the tech cards with the necessary in-formation, and we just needed to get the Technical Inspection done to verify the cars do not have any issues that would keep us from racing. Father brought the Nova first and it had no issues. Next I brought my Cuda over and when they stuck the mirror under the car they saw something wet. They brought over a jack and lifted the car so they could see what it was. They saw that the brake lines were leaking so they announced that I could not race he car until this has been repaired.

I was very disappointed. Father and I looked at everything and there was nothing wrong anywhere the Saturday afternoon before Thanksgiving. Father and Uncle Jack decided since I could not race we would pack up and go home. Father told me that I could not drive the Cuda with leaking brake lines so he was going to bring the race car back to the shop and then come back for the Cuda. He asked Uncle Jack to stay with me until he returned. He told us that it should not take more than an hour and a half.

Uncle Jack suggested we go sit in the stands while we wait so at least we can watch some racing.

Father returned and Uncle Jack drove the Cuda onto the trailer and the brakes failed. They said I was so lucky this did not happen on the drive to the track. We drove back to the shop and Uncle Jack went home.

Uncle Jack was sweet as usual. Father and I unloaded the Cuda and pushed it onto a lift. Then he went and put the trailer in back and parked the truck. Am I boring you mother?"

"No you are not Angie. Please continue."

"We lifted the Cuda and saw the leaking brake lines and Father said that the damage was very strange, almost as if it someone had cut them intentionally but then he thought that maybe it was just marks from manufacturing. We removed the lines and put them on a bench. Father measured them and went over to the shelves to look for some new lines. He found that he only had one piece long enough so he called his friend Bob that owns an auto parts store to ask if he could get another piece of line today. Since the store is closed on Sunday's he would need to go meet him there. And when father said it was for my Cuda, Bob told father something like he could not turn down something for me, I am such a sweet and polite girl he would do anything for me. Father came back to the bench and told me that he was going to go pick up another line at Bob's store and asked if I wanted to go along. I told him no. He asked me if I would be alright by myself and I told him I would be fine. I wanted to practice making flares on some scrap lines. He told me that he would be back before I knew it. And he left. I did not think anything would happen."

"So I was practicing making double flares and I heard something and turned around and saw Mike an instant before his fist hit my face. He repeated hit me until I was unconscious. The next thing I remember I was laying on the floor with my jeans and T-shirt removed with my ankles tied to different bench legs and my wrists tied together and strapped to part of a lift. He had used bungee cords. This was when I first felt my ribs hurt. Maybe he kicked me, I don't know. From what I remember, he told me that he cut my brake lines because he wanted to see me crash and die in front of everyone at the track. And that he was so angry that the technical inspectors said I could not race. Mike had this insane crazy look in his eyes. I have never been so frightened mother."

Lizzy reached and took her hand in hers.

"He told me he was going to rape me and then do whatever else he wanted and he suggested impaling me with a pipe. Then he told me he was going to pour gas all over me and burn me to death and he was going to enjoy watching me die. And afterword he was going to burn the shop to cover it up. He said something that I did not understand; it sounded demonic, and grabbed my cross, ripped it off and threw it across the shop. Since that cross is so dear to me I screamed something like that is mine and he slapped me across the face so hard that my vision blurred and I almost passed out."

"Oh, my lord, Angie." Lizzy said.

"I kept trying to talk him out of doing this and he kept slapping my face and telling me 'shut up bitch.' A few times he grabbed my head and slammed it onto the floor. I screamed help so many times that my throat was sore. I was so frightened and I was about to give up and just let him do what he wanted when Jim came running in. He tried to stop Mike and Mike beat him until he was unconscious. Mike came back to me and told me that he could blame this all on Jim and he would burn with the shop as well. Mike was getting ready to rape me and Mike's father came in. Then they began arguing and that gave me the opportunity to break free. I pulled my arms with every bit of strength I had and was able to reach the hook on the bungee cord with one of my fingers and unhooked it. That bungee unwrapped from my wrists and I sat up and untied my ankles. Adrenalin was pumping because I wasn't feeling any pain. I jumped up and I heard the gun go off and Mike's father fell. I got into my stance and Mike turned around. He had a shocked look for a few seconds. Then he began to raise the gun and I kicked it out of his hand. The gun flew away. Mike then took a swing at me and I blocked it to the side and used a move to break his arm. At this point the only thing I saw was Mike and the danger he posed. I used some straight punches and hit him in the face 3 or 4 times, maybe more. I think I broke his nose again and he was stunned for a minute. Then he got that crazy look again and lunged at me and I used the reverse 360 degree roundhouse, like I used on the escaped convict, but I put everything I had in it even more than with the convict. I think that was when I hurt my leg. Mike went down and the only thing I thought of then was Jim. He saved my life. I went over to him and tried to get him to come to and I think that is when Sergeant Hernandez and Lieutenant Edwards came in. When I helped Jim up I heard a few additional gun shots. I turned and saw Sergeant Hernandez standing over Mike. Then I saw father and tried to run to him but I almost fell because I did not realize how serious my injuries were. So I limped to him. That is when the news showed up. And this very nice, respectful paramedic came over to help me. She cleaned up all of my wounds and put the dressing on my cheek. Father realized the news was there and said he had to call you. When he returned, a female officer went into the break room with me and took pictures of all of my injuries. All I did for that was just stand for her. Afterwards everyone went into the break room for my interview. I think that is all of it mother."

Lizzy sat there with tears in her eyes. She had no idea it had been that bad. She couldn't comprehend being told that someone was going to pour gas on you and burn you to death. She couldn't believe after all that Angie was able to jump up and kick that guy. "I have no idea how to respond to that. It was a nightmare! No, worse than a nightmare. Oh Angie, I love you so much. I do not know what I would have done if you had not survived. I can't believe after all of that you were able to kick him." She stood and went to hug Angie. Angie reached out and said for her to be careful because she still hurt everywhere.

"I will ask again, are you feeling well enough for your grandmother, Aunt Lilly and Aunt Maria to visit you"

"Yes mother. I understand that they are all just as worried as you and they need to see me."

"Alright dear. I will go and call them now. We usually all meet for lunch today so I will make something for everyone while we wait. When they arrive I can bring in a few folding chairs and we can eat together. I do not want to get you out of bed." Lizzy called everyone and they decided to visit at the time they usually meet for lunch. Lizzy also told them that she would have something for everyone to eat.

Lizzy went to the kitchen and made some sandwiches with French bread, fresh cold cuts and fresh provolone. She lightly spread some mayonnaise on the bread and added some romaine lettuce. Then she cut the sandwiches into small pieces that would be easier to handle. But mostly she felt it would be much easier for Angie to eat. She made enough iced tea for everyone. She put everything out on a serving cart along with small plates, the iced tea and glasses. Then she folded some dark red paper napkins into a kind of flower shape and put one on each plate. It looked very nice she thought.

Lizzy then went to a storage closet and pulled out 4 folding chairs and brought them to Angie's room. These weren't the cheap metal type you see everywhere. These chairs were made from oak and had the seat and seat backs covered with padded leather. She set them folded against the wall next to the door in the hallway. She went back and got the serving cart and wheeled it next to the chairs in the hallway.

It took Lizzy about an hour to prepare everything and the doorbell rang. She went to answer and it was her mother and sister and as they walked in, Maria pulled up. She parked, got out and met everyone at the door. Everyone hugged. Lizzy closed the door and led them to Angie's room.

"We are all so worried about Angelina." Lilly said. Everyone agreed.

When they got to Angie's room they saw the cart with everything Lizzy made up Kristina said, "Plain sandwiches would have been sufficient. And how did you fold the napkins like that? They look wonderful!"

"Thank you mother, but this was not much trouble. I wanted to make something nice for us all. Now I do not want to alarm you, prepare yourselves, Angie's injuries very dreadful and shocking." She knocked on the door.

"You may enter mother." But her grandmother and aunts were already shocked that her voice sounded different.

Lizzy opened the door and they all went in. They were all aghast. As much as they tried not to be, they all had tears in their eyes. "OH, Angelina! My lord!" Kristina said. She couldn't think of anything else to say.

Lillian just stood there with her hand over her mouth. Maria said, "Angelina, I am so, so sorry. How do you feel?" Then right away she said, "No, do not answer that. It's obvious you do not feel well. I do not know why I said that."

"It's not that bad." "I am improving every day." She wasn't very convincing.

"Besides all of the bruises and scrapes, what other injuries do you have?" Kristina asked.

"I have a mild concussion, a bruised hamstring in my right leg and 4 fractured ribs. But other than that I am fine." Angie said trying to make light of the situation.

"Oh, only that? Angelina, we know this is serious. You have no need to minimize this, honey." Kristina said.

"I am not trying to minimize it, Grandmother; I just thought it might make everyone possibly smile. You all look so morose. Please do not feel so gloomy. It may have been much worse. I could have been killed. I will be fine, I just need to heal."

"You could have been killed? I do not know what we would have done if that happened. I think we need to hear about this. Angelina, I want to know what really happened before I leave. I do not know if I would be able to sleep tonight otherwise." Kristina said to Angie.

Lizzy began bringing in the chairs and opened them. Then she pushed in the serving cart. "All right, we can sit down and talk. Feel free to help yourselves." She picked up a plate and put two of the cut up sandwiches on a plate and handed it to Angie. "Here honey."

"Thank you mother. May I have some iced tea please?" Lizzy poured some in a glass and handed it to her. "Thank you Mother."

They all sat and talked while they ate. They asked Angie if she would describe what happened. Lilly wasn't certain she wanted to hear the story. She doesn't like gruesome details in any story, especially from her niece. But she listened anyway. And they were very alarmed when she told them she needed to use crutches to keep her weight off her leg. Now they all realized how serious her injuries were.

They were all horrified at what happened and amazed at what Angie did to defend herself. Maria tried to make light of the situation and said, "If I ever need to go into a bad neighborhood would you be my bodyguard Angie?" They all laughed but saw that it hurt Angie to laugh. She was smiling however. And that made everyone feel better.

They stayed for about an hour and then excused themselves so Angie could rest. Angie said as they were leaving her room, "Thank you for coming everyone. You cheered me up. And I love all of you so much."`

They all smiled somewhat teary eyed and told her they loved her as well. They said that they wanted to hug her but didn't want to hurt her. She understood.

Chapter 24

Lizzy had been able to schedule an appointment for Angie with their doctor for first thing Wednesday morning. Angie got up and was going to take a shower but Lizzy wouldn't let her. She was fearful that Angie would put weight on her leg and fall and since they hadn't seen their doctor yet she wasn't certain that Angie should get wet. She was fearful that it may cause an infection. So Lizzy gave her another sponge bath.

She helped Angie dress because Angie's pain was making it difficult for her to raise her arms much and bend her back. Her ribs were very sore and it was difficult for her to lift her right leg because of the strained hamstring. She needed to get used to using the crutches as well. Angie struggled with the crutches and found them very cumbersome to use. Lizzy chose loose sweat pants and a loose long sleeve sweat shirt for Angie. It was a cool breezy day with the usual full sun. Then she put Angie's slippers on her. They were loose fit and would be easier for her than shoes. And, of course, she wore her cross necklace. Angie told her Mother, "Mother you have such good fashion sense. The sweat pants and sweatshirt are both gray and match!" Lizzy chuckled. It was good to see Angie's sense of humor return.

In contrast, Lizzy dressed elegantly as usual and was wearing an off white glittery long sleeve blouse that had a tie around the waist and light pink long pleated skirt with beige hose and beige low heeled shoes. She also wore a short pearl necklace and matching bracelet.

They were the first patients in the office. The doctor examined all of her injuries including her ribs and the hamstring in her right leg. "I want you to continue to use the crutches for now, Angie. I want you to discontinue the cold compresses and you will begin to use an ACE bandage around your leg at the point where you have pain. I want you to take it off for about 10 minutes every few hours. You need to do this for the next 2-3 days. Then I want you to begin seeing a physical therapist to help you keep from re-damaging the hamstring. It is very important to follow these instructions. This is especially important for you Angie since you train with martial arts. It is critical to keep from re-injuring the hamstring. The physical therapist will be able to show you exactly how to exercise the muscle. I would also expect your Sensei to know what to do as well. You need to keep your leg elevated until the physical therapist tells you can stop. I would also expect it would be wise to visit your Sensei as soon as possible so he can work out a plan with your physical therapist. Do you understand Angie?"

"Yes sir, I understand. And thank you for your help sir."

Lizzy asked, "How long should we keep her out of school doctor?"

"I will leave it up to your physical therapist to determine. And the nurse will give you a referral for the physical therapist. Then I want to see you next Wednesday to check on all of your injuries. Please schedule this before you leave."

"Thank you so much doctor." Lizzy said.

Before they left the office the nurse gave them some information about strained hamstrings and the referral for the physical therapist. So they left the office and went directly to the therapist's office.

The physical therapist set up daily visits for the next two weeks and told Angie that he will continually evaluate her progress and based on her progress he will determine when she could return to school.

Lizzy and Angie left the office and visited Angie's Sensei to discuss the treatment and so he could understand why Angie hasn't gone there this week. He understood and would be working with the physical therapist throughout the treatment. They thanked him for his help and understanding and left.

Their next stop was Canyon Del Oro High School. They needed to give them an update on Angie's condition and make arrangements for her to get her homework. As with everyone else, they were completely shocked at Angie's condition. Angie came in on crutches with Lizzy and her face was still swollen and scraped up and her black eyes were very visible. They happened to see Mrs. Abbot as they were in the office. Mrs. Abbot saw Angie and began to cry. She couldn't believe what had happened and was so shocked with how Angie looked. This made Angie sad as well because she really cared about Mrs. Abbot and didn't want her to cry. Angie assured Mrs. Abbot that she would fully recover and be back to her class before she knew it. Mrs. Abbot told her that she was so sweet for caring so much. But she needed to get to her next class and said bye to Angie and Lizzy.

Angie had already been upset because she had missed 3 days already and was concerned that it would affect her grades. The school assured them it would not. So they arraigned to have Angie's homework ready in the office at the end of each day. And also gave them a list of phone numbers of her teachers and the time she could call them if she needed additional help. Lizzy told them that she would come and pick it up.

After they left CDO Angie asked, "Mother, could we please go to St. Mary's so I could visit Jim? I would very much like to thank him for saving my life."

"How do you know he is still at St. Mary's?"

"I do not know but he was hurt much worse that I so I am assuming he is still there."

Alright, we will go and find out." So she drove to St. Mary's and Lizzy dropped Angie at the main entrance and went and parked.

Angie struggled to get through the lobby doors at St. Mary's but managed. She waited for her mother. Her mother came in and they walked to the information desk. Angie said, "Good afternoon Ma'am, I wish to find out if I may visit James Parker, he was brought here on Sunday in an ambulance. He was beaten excessively, more so than myself."

"You were the female student they spoke about on the news?" The receptionist asked. "Oh, my dear, are you OK?"

"Yes Ma'am. I am improving daily Ma'am but have a long way before I will be completely recovered."

"I'm so sorry dear. Let me look here and see what his status is. Ah, yes. He is in Acute Care. I will need to find out if he is accepting any visitors. You may sit down while I check." The receptionist called the Acute Care unit. Angie and Lizzy sat down.

A few minutes later the receptionist went over and told Angie, "He is accepting visitors so you may go back. Just go past the elevators and turn right then follow the hallway as it turns to the left past the double doors and the first right with double doors is Acute care. You may ask any nurse there and they will take you to the bed that James is in."

"Thank you Ma'am."

Lizzy said, "Angie I will wait here in the waiting room while you visit with Jim."

"Thank you mother." Angie followed the directions and hobbled on her crutches to the nurse's desk and asked the first nurse that she saw. "Good Afternoon, Ma'am. I am looking for James Parker."

"Follow me hun." The nurse said. Angie followed her into a bed area that was enclosed with curtains and she said, "Here he is Ma'am."

"Thank you Ma'am." She walked up to the curtain and said, "Hello, Jim? This is Angie."

"Angie? You can come in." Jim replied. Jim was in a bed with bandages on his face and was lying on his back, Angie assumed the lady with him was his mother.

He didn't look well but he turned his head and kind of smiled and said "Angie! I never expected you to visit, or anyone else for that matter. I have been such a jerk to everyone."

"Well, Jim, that is sad to hear. I came here because you saved my life and I needed to and thank you. You know that makes you a hero. A week ago I would not have said that but Sherri told me that I was a hero for standing up to Mike and I did not believe it then. But after being in the situation Sunday where I was about to give up, you came running in. You showing up when you did gave me hope I needed. And Mike's father coming in when he did gave me the time I needed to break free. If you did not come when you did I do not think I would have even tried."

"I didn't do anything anyone else wouldn't have done Angie. That doesn't make me a hero." Jim said. "And I got the shit kicked out of me so I didn't even get to help you."

"But you showing up made me think that I had a chance. That is what you did. I was severely beaten as well Jim, but without you I would likely be dead now."

"I don't feel like a hero. I feel beat up and I'm stuck here in the hospital now."

"Is this your mother, Jim?"

"Yea, it's my mom."

Angie turned to his mother and said, "Hello Ma'am, It is nice to meet you."

"Nice to meet you too. You were the girl there on Sunday?"

"Yes, Ma'am."

"You don't look to good, and you are on crutches. I'm so sorry."

"Yes, Ma'am, I did suffer some serious injuries."

"And your wrists," she started to get tears in her eyes, "your wrists, what happened to you? I feel so bad just seeing them. Jim hasn't said anything about what happened yet."

Angie stood there for a few moments and said, "If you really want to know I will explain what happened. It is gruesome. And I do not know who emerged worse Jim or I. Evidently, he had some severe injuries or he would not still be here, but I also have some emotional injuries as well that are making it difficult for me to sleep well, Ma'am."

"I would like to know it you would tell me. Jim doesn't want to. Besides what you see, he has broken ribs, a concussion, a broken nose; he had a collapsed lung; a bruised spleen and he was peeing blood. They needed to do emergency surgery on his spleen because of that but at least they didn't need to remove it. And they have been giving him blood due to the internal bleeding."

"Well, I have 4 fractured ribs and I bruised my hamstring muscles in my leg, oh, and I also had a concussion."

"Oh dear, how did you do that to your leg?"

Jim said, "Mom, remember I told you about the martial arts girl? This is her. From what one of the officers told me she almost completely took out Mike, even though he acted crazy drugged up."

"You? You're the martial arts expert? I never would have guessed. Maybe a model but martial arts?" Jim's mom said.

"Ma'am, I would not say I am an expert. I am a third degree black belt and that is not expert. But yes I am her. I have had many people tell me I am very beautiful lately. But I never looked at myself like that. I have learned many things about myself in the past few days as well. I was called a hero, which

I did not believe just as Jim does not believe now. At my birthday party just before school began this year, I got dressed up and did makeup and had my nails done and my cousin told me I should be on the cover of Seventeen Magazine. That was another thing I did not believe. So I should say you thank you Ma'am for the complement."

"Dear, you are very beautiful. That was what Jim told me when he was suspended from school. He said something like, 'this martial arts girl that is sooo beautiful broke Mike's nose so fast.' Or something on the way of that." She said to Angie.

Angie turned to Jim and asked, "You really said I was so beautiful Jim?"

Jim was blushing, "Yea, I said that and even though you are messed up you still are beautiful. You're the most beautiful girl in school. That's why Mike went after you in the first place."

Now Angie was blushing. She still didn't consider herself beautiful, much less very beautiful, even after all of the complements from her family at her birthday party and Thanksgiving. She always thought she looked alright. "Now I am blushing." And she was trying to cover her face and keep from falling with her crutches at the same time.

During this exchange between Jim and Angie, Jim's mother pulled a chair in from outside of the curtain. "Sit down Angie. You are making me feel bad standing there with you crutches."

Angie struggled but sat down. "Thank you Ma'am. As for what happened, evidently Mike got seriously crazy after he was expelled so he wanted to take it out on me. He tried sabotaging my car. He told me that he wanted to see me crash and die at the drag strip but the safety inspection guys identified it and I could not race."

"You race at the drag strip? Really?" Jim's mother asked.

"It was going to be the first time, Ma'am. But Mike spoiled it. He told me he was very angry because he could not watch me die. So I believe he followed me to my father's shop and when my father left to pick up a part he snuck in. He ran up behind me and punched me in the head repeatedly until I passed out. Then he took off my cloths and tied me up on the floor. He started to tell me he was going to rape me and whatever else he decided and slapped me around. I think he kicked me in my side and that is what fractured my ribs. He said afterwards he was going to pour gasoline on me and watch me burn to death and Jim came running in. I do not know how he knew but when he came in he got into a fight with Mike and I thought that maybe I had a chance to get free somehow. But Mike ended up beating poor Jim until he passed out. Right then Mike's father came in and he argued with Mike and tried to stop him. That was when I pulled with everything I had in me and was able to get my hands out of the bungee cords he used and then I untied my feet. I heard a gun go off and when I jumped up I saw Mike's father lying on the floor. I got into my stance and when Mike turned I immediately kicked the gun out of his hand. This invigorated and angered him and he tried to punch me and I broke his arm with an Aikido move. Then he rushed at me I kicked him with every ounce of energy I had and he went down. I presume that was when I hurt my leg. I went to Jim to try to help him as I did not see what had happened to him. I thought possibly Mike killed him as well. The police arrived when my back was turned and there was some shooting and Mike was dead." Angie told her. "This was the condensed version as I did not think you would need the fine details."

Jim's mother was sitting there absolutely shocked. Finally she said, "My god Jim, you never stood up for anyone before. I am so proud. And Angie, I can't believe you went through all of that and you are already telling me the story a few days later. I would still be a basket case. You are am amazing woman. I am so glad you survived. And thank you for telling me this. Now I understand why Jim was hurt so bad. My dear, your parents must be proud. If someone else told me this story I would think you would be this big strong tomboy type. But you are so sweet and beautiful. I don't know what to say."

"Thank you Ma'am. And I need to say Jim," she turned towards Jim, "you saved my life and I am very grateful. Just as I was told about myself, you are a hero Jim whether you believe it or not." Angie struggled to stand up and walked over to Jim and carefully leaned over and kissed his cheek and said, "If you let the real Jim out, not the follower Jim, I would like being friends if it is OK with you."

Jim was shocked because of the kiss and also because Angie said she would be friends with him. He stuttered and finally got out, I'll try my best to be the real Jim. I would like being you friend Angie, very much. You have inspired me to be a better person. Thank you Angie."

"You are very welcome Jim. I need to get back to my mother now. She is sitting in the lobby likely wondering what happened to me. It was very nice meeting you Mrs. Parker and it makes me feel much better seeing that you will recover Jim."

"Angie," Would you mind if I met your mother?"

"No Ma'am. I am sure my mother would be delighted to meet you as well."

"I will walk with you then, Angie." As they walked towards the waiting room she continued, "You speak differently than other students and you are very polite. Those are very good qualities Angie."

"Thank you ma'am." They walked into the waiting room and Angie's mother stood. "Mother, I would like to present Mrs. Parker, Jim's mother."

"I am very pleased to meet you Mrs. Parker." Lizzy reached out with her hand.

Mrs. Parker, not being used to being proper said, "How do you do Mrs. Tucci. I am very pleased to meet you."

"Your son saved my daughter and I am very grateful." Lizzy said.

"Thank you, but as I just heard the story Angie had a big part of ending the situation and she helped Jim afterwards, And I am grateful for that as well. You have an amazing daughter and I am honored to have met her. In the short time they talked today she has made a huge positive impression on my son. His father passed away some 8 years ago and I have struggled to teach him much. But I believe Angie did more in the short time she talked than I have in 8 years and I want to thank you for the time you spent with him Angie." Jim's mother said to both Lizzy and Angie.

"Angie is a very exceptional lady with many talents and she still astonishes me at times. We are very proud of her. It was nice to meet you Mrs. Parker. We have a busy afternoon ahead and with Angie lacking mobility we need to be on our way."

"It was nice to meet you too Mrs. Tucci."

Lizzy and Angie walked away. Angie was beginning to move better with the crutches. She hobbled to where her mother parked and her mother opened the door for her and took her crutches and put them in the back seat. "Were you able to thank Jim properly Angie?"

"Of course mother. He did not expect to see me. I did find out how he was injured however. He has broken ribs, a broken nose; a collapsed lung and they needed to do emergency surgery to repair his spleen Sunday. His mother said that they have been giving blood because of internal bleeding. And he also had a concussion and various scrapes; cuts and was peeing blood. Jim said that he will be there awhile until the internal bleeding stops. He received a much worse beating than I. He was quite nice, which is quite a difference from that day when Mike first pulled his knife on me."

"He isn't around the poor example at the moment."

"That is true mother. He did say that he was not going to be a follower anymore because I inspired him. That would be another first for me mother, inspiring people."

"Angie, you may be surprised at the amount of people you have already inspired. You have a unique method of interacting with others; you do not anger easily and you are incredibly honest and it is very easy to recognize in you."

"I do not see it. I did not inspire Mike very well did I?" Angie said a little sarcastically.

"Angie, do not be so hard on yourself. It is impossible to inspire everyone. One needs to be open to inspiration first and I do not believe Mike was open too much of anything, honey. Remember what I said about learning?"

"Yes mother, I will always be learning. Do you not get tired of learning mother? Do not you ever feel that you have had enough?"

Lizzy thought for a minute, "In time it will be natural and you will search for it, honey. You will find yourself always searching for something. What I become tired of is when I cannot find an answer to what I seek. This makes me very frustrated at times. It is something you will come to know very well. Angie, you are a very intelligent lady and intelligent people are like a giant sponge. You cannot learn enough, you strive for more all of the time."

"Is that what I have to look forward to mother? Getting frustrated that I cannot find the information I am seeking? That does not sound very attractive. I find that this last learning experience is already frustrating. I have not been able to see anything that I have learned from this. All I see is my pain and suffering and becoming behind in school. So I feel sorry for myself. I have not told you yet but every night I cry myself to sleep. I do not want to be learning like this. It makes me feel terrible." She had tears in her eyes. "I have been feeling very sad mother and I do not like feeling sad. All I can think of is my pain both physically and psychologically and I feel bad because I wanted to go to CDO and now people are dead and another in bad shape because I began going to school there." Angie was in tears now.

"Honey, what you are feeling in a normal response to a serious situation. This may begin to disappear in time, but if it does not, we can find someone to help you with this as well. This is something not unlike people feeling guilty when they survive a plane crash. They do not understand why so many died but they lived. I believe they call it survivor syndrome. This is when someone feels like they did something wrong by surviving a traumatic or tragic event when others died. It is possible you are feeling this or PTSD. Either way, your father and I will help you through this. And if necessary we will find someone you can talk to that will help you. You will need to deal with your feelings in a healthy way honey. And do not feel like you are feeling something bad. You feel like you feel and there is not anything wrong with that. And how could you possibly know that two people died because you chose to attend CDO? There is no reason to believe that this scenario would not have played out if you continued at Amphitheater. It is likely that it would still have played out but with different people. And it could be that more people would have died. You would not have been there so Mike would not have had anyone to stop him."

Angie leaned over and hugged her mother. "I never considered that mother. I can see how I was one sided in my thinking. I do not know what to say, you and father are always there for me and it shows me that you care and love me so much." She dried her tears with a tissue.

"Do not ever feel that you cannot come to us Angie, even if it is in the middle of the night."

"But I worry that Father will not get the sleep he needs before he needs to go to work."

"If it is something you need it does not matter. You are always first Honey. You do not know how many nights we were up with you when you were a baby. Some of those nights your father did not sleep at all. But we managed just as we will manage if you need us now."

"Mother,"

"What is it Angie?"

"I hope I can be as supportive as you and father when I have kids."

"Do not worry too much about that dear, you will, I know you will. And there is something else I would like you to know."

"What is it mother?"

"Do you know that I still go to your grandfather and grandmother, sometimes for the same kinds of things?"

"You do? But you are an adult."

"You are never too old to ask for help, never. I know your father does not have his parents to go to so we talk quite a bit and a few times I know he has talked to your grandfather."

"Really? Father? I would not have believed that if I did not hear that from you."

"And because of what happened at your birthday party, I would think he may talk to your grandmother now as well."

"Grandmother?"

"Your grandmother has been very different since your party. You have not seen her since then except for Thanksgiving and Monday afternoon so I am fairly certain you have not seen this, but you will see it as well."

Angie sat and thought for a while, "Thinking about Monday, she was different. She did not show that kind of contempt to Aunt Maria that she had previously. It was in the tone of her voice and how she spoke. I did not notice at the time."

"Do not feel bad that you did not see it then. Remember, you are in quite a bit of pain, physically and psychologically. In that state it is a surprise that you noticed at all. But as I said, you are a very exceptional lady with many talents. You see that you just learned something about yourself. Even though you were suffering terrible pain you did notice subtle differences. Most people would not have noticed any difference."

"Mother, you can always make me feel better. I could not have a more caring mother."

Now Lizzy had teary eyes. "I do not know if I make you feel better, I just point out things that you have not seen yet and help you to understand. But it feels so good to hear you say that. I could say the same of you Angie."

"Where are we going mother?" It was obvious they were not going home.

"You stated that you desire to thank Sergeant Hernandez for returning you cross. It is almost shift change and they said that he would be there at that time."

"Thank you mother for inquiring. I wish to thank him properly, and that would be in person."

"You are learning remarkably well Angie. You will be a very refined lady."

"Thank you mother, you are an exceptional mentor."

They arrived at the police station and parked. Lizzy got out and walked around the car to help Angie. Then Lizzy walked as Angie hobbled to the doors. Lizzy opened the door and Angie entered with Lizzy following. They walked up to the desk and the officer looked up and began to say "Can I help," she paused and she looked horrified. "Oh my, Angie, I, I don't know what to say." They could see her eyes tearing. She knew them because Dominic had been to the station many times to see Lieutenant Edwards, they are friends. "I'm so sorry about what happened. Lieutenant Edwards told me about it. How can I help you?"

Angie asked, "I am here to see Sergeant Hernandez, if he is available."

"I think I saw him returning a few minutes ago. I'll go and see." And she stood up and went to check. A minute or two later she returned with Sergeant Hernandez.

"Hello Mrs. Tucci and Angie. It is good to see you. And Angie you look so much better than you did on Sunday. How are you feeling? I see you have you cross on."

"I am feeling somewhat better, sir. I pain is still quite intense. Thank you for asking sir. I wanted to thank you personally for returning my cross sir. It is my most cherished possession. I am the 5th generation of Tucci's to wear this and I would have been quite distraught if it had been lost. I am extremely grateful that you picked it up and returned it sir. My father told me you were shot in your arm. How is your arm, sir?"

"It was my pleasure Angie. You are one of those rare young people that makes me feel that my job has value. And yes my arm is fine. The bullet just grazed it, I will be OK." Sergeant Hernandez said with a big smile.

"When my father returned with my cross I was so ecstatic I forgot about my pain for a short time. I cannot thank you enough."

"I'm glad I could help. It was nice seeing the two of you." I need to get back to my reports now.

"It was good to see you as well Sergeant Hernandez. Angie said.

"It is always a pleasure." Lizzy said. They turned and left.

They got home and Lizzy helped Angie get out of the car and into the house. They went to Angie's bedroom and Angie went to lie down, she was tired from all of the things she did today. Lizzy helped her raise her leg and asked her if she would like anything. Angie said no. She just wanted to sleep.

Chapter 25

Thursday in school at lunch Sherri, Janet and Karen were talking about Angie and wondering how she was doing. They didn't know her condition as the news barely mentioned her. By the end of lunch break they decided to go and visit her after school, if they could find her house. All that had been announced at school was that Angie is recovering at home. They couldn't find her phone number in the phone book so it must have been unlisted. Then Sherri remembered that Angie told them that she lived on Christie Dr. They looked on a map and found that Christie Dr. is just over a mile long and they knew that there are not many houses in that area. They figured that they could drive there and maybe Angie's pink car would be outside.

Janet said, "Do you think jeans and sweaters are nice enough to visit her?"

Sherri said, "Angie always wears jeans and a sweater or a blouse to school but her jeans are always designer and the sweaters and blouses all looked very expensive. But I think we are fine."

After school they got into Sherri's car and left the school. They took Oracle Rd. south to Magee Rd. and turned left. They followed Magee Rd. slowly because there are two Immaculate Heart Catholic schools on the street. And all the signs say 25 MPH School Zone. They passed the schools and continued until they got to Christie Dr. and turned right. They could only turn right. They followed Christie Drive and Janet and Karen were looking on both sides for Angie's car. There weren't many houses in this area and some are set back far enough that they could not see any cars. There was one house at Magee and Christie Dr. Then they past the first street, E. Calle Elena then they saw two more houses and they could see another street sign coming up then Karen screamed, "This has to be her house. I see her car!"

Sherri said, "Are you sure Karen?"

Janet got very excited and said, "This has to be her house. How many pink Cudas could there be in Tucson?" Sherri turned around at the next street and drove back.

"I see it too!" Sherri said as she stopped her car. They were all excited and started to discuss what they were going to do.

"Should we drive down the driveway? What if it isn't her house?" Sherri said.

"I don't know." Janet said. "Should we?"

Karen said, "We drove out here to see her and now we are afraid to actually go to her house? Common, let's go."

So Sherri reluctantly drove up to the driveway and turned in. She drove very slowly because she was a little afraid. When they got far enough they could see the rear of Angie's car sticking out from behind a garage and they had a much better view. "This is her house! See her car over there?"

Janet said, "Yea, that's her car! We found it! Cool!"

Sherri pulled up and parked. They all got out and walked to the door. "Ring the doorbell Sherri." Karen said.

"You do it." Sherri said.

"OK." She reached and rang the doorbell. They heard multiple bells that sounded real. "Wow, real bells!"

Then they heard someone opening the door. They got scared. "Hello, may I help you ladies?" They thought this must have been Angie's Mom.

"Um, Yea. I mean yes Ma'am. This is Karen and Janet and I am Sherri. We are friends of Angie's from school. We came to see how she is doing. We have been very concerned." Sherri said.

I am very delighted to meet Angie's friends. I am Mrs. Tucci, Angie's mother. Please come in."

"Thank you Ma'am. We are very pleased to meet you Mrs. Tucci." Sherry said as they walked in.

"You may sit down over here and I will see if Angie is awake."

"Thank you Ma'am." Sherri said and they sat down and Lizzy walked away. Wow! I can you believe this house?"

Janet said, "It is so beautiful. I think my house would fit in the entryway here."

Sherri said, "This is the foyer. That's what it's called."

Karen asked, "How do you know that Sherri?"

"I looked it up. I wanted to at least know a few of the right words."

Lizzy walked to Angie's room and lightly knocked on the door. "You may come in mother." She was reading a paperback novel.

"Angie, There are 3 ladies here to visit, Sherri, Karen and Janet. I asked them to wait while I checked to see if you were awake."

"This is a surprise. Would you please bring them here mother?"

"Certainly."

Lizzy returned to the ladies. They thought she walked so eloquently and gracefully. "Ladies, Angie is awake and asked that I bring you to her room. Please follow me."

Janet thought that it seemed like they were in a movie, because of the house and the way Mrs. Tucci walked and spoke. It reminded her of old movies that her mother liked to watch.

They walked through the house and the three girls were awestruck at everything about the house, the size, the décor, none of them had ever been in a house like this. It seemed to them that Angie's room was so far from the door. They came to Angie's room and her mother knocked and announced, "The ladies are here to visit with you Angie."

"You may let them in mother." Lizzy opened the door and let the girls in then closed the door behind them. All three girls were surprised to hear Angie say, "You may let them in."

Sherri walked in first and saw Angie. "Oh my god Angie!" She had her hand over her mouth. "Are you OK?" she was shocked at how she looked that she immediately cried.

Janet and Karen were shocked as well. "Oh Angie!" they said in unison. "How are you? We never expected this." Janet said. "Is there anything we can do?" Karen and Janet had tears in their eyes as well but Sherri couldn't help but cry. She felt so bad for her.

Sherri walked over to Angie and reached and took her hand in hers. She had intended to try to comfort her but she saw the ligature marks on her wrists she cried more. "Oh my God Angie! I feel so sad for you. I am so sorry that, that I am crying. We wanted to cheer you up."

This was the first time Angie had friends visit and she wasn't certain how to act. She was amazed at her sentiments. "It is alright Sherri, your reaction very touching and it shows your true feelings. I am certain that my appearance is very distressing. But seeing your response brings tears to my eyes as well." Her eyes were tearing. She reached for her tissue box and offered tissues to the ladies. "To answer your question, I am as well as could be expected. I am very sore all over. But at least I am speaking fairly normally, now that the swelling has diminished."

"What happened to your speech?" Sherri said in a shocked voice.

"The swelling on my lips and cheeks and my sore jaw made it difficult to speak and I was almost unintelligible.

"Oh Angie I feel so bad for you. And you couldn't speak well. How terrible. All of us saw the news but it didn't really say anything about you. All they cared about was Mike and his dad." Sherri said.

Janet and Karen said they felt the same way.

"How did you find my house? I am certain I did not give you an address."

Karen said, "You told us that you lived on Christie Drive and we looked for it on a map. It isn't a long street so we drove down and looked for your car. And we saw your pink Cuda and knew this was it."

"You are so zealous. I cannot believe it!"

"Zealous? What do you mean?" Sherri asked.

"Please excuse me, this is how I speak at home and around my family. At school I try not to use words everyone would not know. Zealous means enterprising; ambitious or diligent."

"How do you know things like that? Janet asked.

"My whole family speaks in this manner so this is what I learned. A few times at Amphitheater teachers accused me of plagiarizing, oh, please excuse me once more, copying."

"Really? Why?" Karen asked.

"Well, because high school students do not use words in this manner. They called my parents a few times to discuss that. But after discussing this with my parents at school my teachers understood. I think a few did not understand what my parents said."

"I never thought someone could get in trouble from knowing too much. That's weird." Sherri said.

"We miss you at school and at lunch Angie. Do you know when you will be well enough to come back to school?" Karen asked.

"I do not. I have a strained hamstring on my right leg from kicking Mike and he fractured some of my ribs. And I cannot go back until my doctor releases me. I believe it will be awhile. And I am assuming that I will still be continuing to use crutches when I return to school."

"What is a hamstring? And why crutches?" Karen asked.

"A hamstring is a group of muscles in the back of the leg between the hip and knee, and I need to keep weight off of my leg to for the muscles to heal, hence the crutches."

"Angie, it makes me sad to see you like this. What about your school work? How are you going to keep up?" Sherri asked.

"My mother goes to the school every day to drop off my completed homework and pick up school work for the day."

"It must be hard to do schoolwork while you are in bed, and to do everything this way. What if you don't understand something? How do you ask about it?" Sherri said.

"The school gave me the phone numbers of all of my teachers and the times that each of them is available and I have their assurance that the teachers will help me over the phone."

"Look at all of these cars. These are so cool. Where did you get them?" Karen asked as she was looking at all of the model cars displayed around Angie's her room.

"I built them. They are model cars from kits. I believe I built the first one when I was 13."

"Are all of these pictures of your family?" Janet asked.

"Yes, my whole family. And the very old ones are of my great grandparents, and there is one of my father, aunt and my grandparents before they passed away. I never met them but they are very dear to me nonetheless. And this," Angie pulled her cross from under her shirt, "I am the 5th generation of Tucci's to wear this cross. If you look closely at the picture of my grandmother Tucci you can see that she is wearing this cross. And on Sunday Mike ripped it off of me and through it across my father's shop and I thought it was lost. But one of the officers picked it up and gave it back to my father."

"That's so beautiful." Sherri said as she looked at it. "It looks like a cross from the dark ages. I bet you were upset when you thought it was lost, I would be."

"I was very distressed. And when my father came home and returned it to me I was ecstatic! It is a special kind of cross called a Vine Cross. It symbolizes the Christian union with Christ, as related in John 15:1-8. *"Abide in Me, and I in you. As the branch cannot bear fruit of itself, unless it abides in the vine, so neither can you, unless you abide in me. I am the vine, you are the branches. He who abides in me, and I in him, bears much fruit; for apart from Me you can do nothing."* This is paraphrased; I could not memorize the entire verse.

"You couldn't remember the whole verse?" Sherri joked. "How do you remember even that?"

"Many things are easy for me to remember. I have a moderately photographic memory. Some things I remember effortlessly as if I am looking at a printed in a book."

"Wow! I never knew anyone that could do that, that's amazing!" Sherri said, "I wish I could do that, no wonder you are so good in school. And I wish I spoke like you. I love the way you sound and how you use words. You use them so well Angie."

"Thank you Sherri. I appreciate the complement."

"See, I would just say thanks. But you say 'Thank you, I appreciate the complement.' That is so elegant! I am so happy we met. You already made a difference in my life." Sherri said.

"I am delighted I have made such of an impression, Sherri. However, I am not certain what I have done."

Angie, you are one amazing girl. Um, I mean lady. You know, I tried to speak properly to your mother. I think I made a fool of myself." Sherri said.

"Do not think poorly of yourself Sherri, I am certain my mother appreciates what you attempted, and I believe she will be impressed that you tried."

"Really? I hope so. She is so proper and so nice. And she is so elegant and graceful." Sherri said. "We have been talking, maybe you could teach us how to be proper like you are. We think it is so, what's the word, cultured. What you told us about self-respect, I see how it would give you self-respect. It made me feel really good trying to speak like that. If you would we would be very grateful."

"Well, maybe. I do have a book that my mother gave me. It was given to her by my Grandmother. It is called, "American Etiquette and Rules of Politeness" and it was written in the late 1800's. It describes everything you would ever want to know about this subject. It is where the ladies of my family learned how to act proper and polite. Possibly we could look through it and you could learn as well Sherri."

"I would really like that Angie. I think it would be fun."

Karen said, "They have books on this? Wow, I never knew that."

"That's seems so weird. I thought it was just something that was passed down through your family." Janet said.

"It is passed down through families but at some point someone wrote a book on the subject and is good reference for anyone that would like to learn to be proper and courteous."

I am so delighted that you ladies came. In the past I had never had real friends, so this is a new experience for me. But I am feeling very fatigued, so surely you will not feel insulted if I ask you to leave."

"Oh, no, we won't feel insulted. I'm sure I speak for all of us. After seeing how hurt you are I'm surprised you saw us at all." Sherri said.

Angie reached for the intercom button and called her mother, "Mother, could you please show these ladies to the door?"

"Yes dear." They heard over the intercom.

"Thank you for visiting. You have raised my spirits quite a bit."

"You are so welcome, Angie. I love the way you talk." Janet said."

Angie reached for a pad of paper on the nightstand and a pen. She wrote her phone number down and tore the piece off of the pad. "Sherri, this is my phone number. This way you can call before you come to be certain I am available."

"You have your own phone?" Karen asked.

"Yes, it's next to my bed right here." Angie said.

Angie's mother knocked on the door. "You may enter mother."

Her mother opened the door and said, "This way ladies," and gracefully motioned with her hand to follow.

The girls said goodbye to Angie and followed her mother. When they got to the door Sherri said, "It was very nice meeting you Ma'am."

"Likewise ladies. I am delighted that Angie has such warmhearted friends." Lizzy said as she opened the door. "Have a wonderful afternoon, ladies."

"Thank you Ma'am." Sherri replied. They walked to her car.

Lizzy closed the door and went to Angie's room. She knocked on the door. "You may enter mother."

Lizzy went in, "Angie, you never mentioned that you have made friends. That's wonderful, and they are very delightful and polite. It was thoughtful and compassionate of them to visit to see how you are feeling."

"Sherri, she is the one with black hair, told me she tried to speak as I do as a courtesy to you. She said she made a fool of herself. I thought it was admirable."

"Yes, that was my perception as well. It demonstrates that she cares enough to make a good impression Angie. This is a difficult trait to find in someone so she very well may end up as a lifelong friend. That is a wonderful thing!"

"When we met, it was the day after my first confrontation with Mike and it had been a particularly difficult day for me emotionally. Sherri followed me out of school to tell me that I now was a hero because I stood up to Mike. I was very brash and did not believe her. But she was very persistent. She asked me to sit with her and her friends at lunch. And that is when she told me that Mike had raped them and they had been treated like outcasts since. At that point I felt very ashamed. I said that I would sit with them for lunch the next day. I sat with them and we talked quite a bit and we became friends. It feels like everyone in the school has transformed."

"You do understand that it was mostly you that has changed, do you not? You have a different perspective now and the people at school know you somewhat better. They likely now know that besides being courteous, you have good manners, you are astute and you are also unyielding. Those traits can have a very powerful effect on others. Your wish to go to CDO may have been a very good choice for you—with the exception of the confrontations with Mike.

"Mother, you consistently show me how to see things from a different point of view. And that has had a powerful effect on me. I feel that I will learn from you and father indefinitely."

"Learning is never-ending. I am still learning from your grandmother and grandfather, honey, and that will go on after they are no longer with us."

"Forgive me for not understanding, but how will you learn from them after they are no longer with us? I do not under-stand?"

"If you think about it, I believe you will figure it out. I will leave you with that and you can advise me of your answer. Is there anything I can you get for you, honey?"

"A glass of water would be nice mother, if you please. Then I need to get some rest." She replied. Lizzy went and got a glass of water for her and brought it to her. "Thank you mother."

She reached out for a hug. She missed all of the hugs she had with her mother before Sunday. But she knew it was because it was difficult due with her injuries. They hugged but not tight, it did hurt quite a bit. "Ahhh! It still is very sore. I love you mother!" Angie said with tears in her eyes.

"I love you to, dear. I will leave you to rest." Lizzy left the room closing the door softly.

Angie needed to think about what her mother said. It would be running through her mind until she figures it out. She drank some water and laid back. Even though she hurt everywhere, she smiled thinking about how her mother always pushes her to think and figure things out for herself. She pulled the blanket up and fell asleep.

After leaving Angie's house Sherri, Janet and Karen got in the car. As Sherri turned her car around and drove away Karen said, "Can you believe that house? I never was in a house like that."

Janet added, "I can't even imagine living in a house that big. I think I would get lost."

"I think it is beautiful. I dream of living in a house like that. And Angie's mother is so elegant and graceful. It is a little odd but I like it." Sherri said.

"You would want to live like that Sherri?" Karen asked.

"You're kidding right? You wouldn't? To be able to act so proper, as Angie says, like a lady and live in a beautiful house and be rich? Did you see what her mother had on? I bet it is very expensive and it was so beautiful."

Janet said, "I don't know, it is so different I wouldn't know where to start. You don't think it sounds a little conceited? Like they act like that to show that they are better than everyone else?"

"I don't think so." Sherri said. "I think they are just very polite and act better than most people. Didn't it feel good to you to be called ladies? You don't think the way Angie's mother treated us was nicer than you were ever treated before?"

"I guess when you say it like that, maybe. It did feel kind of good." Janet said.

Sherri said, "I read somewhere that the meaning of Lady is someone that is refined, polite, well-spoken, courteous and always tries to make sure everyone as comfortable as possible. Isn't that what Angie's mother did? Doesn't that describe them?"

"Well, I always thought that when they called someone a lady or a gentleman they were stuck up." Janet said.

"I think that's what people think because they don't know any better. Remember that Angie told us that the kids at Amphitheater called her stuck up? Do you think she is stuck up?" Sherri asked.

Janet thought for a few seconds. "No, I don't think she is stuck up. She is sweet and polite."

"So, being a Lady isn't stuck up or her trying to make us feel beneath her?" Sherri said.

"Angie doesn't do that, even though she is rich. And, well, ahh, her mother was the nicest person I think I ever met. I guess you're right, again! You know you're right a lot too." Janet said and giggled.

"She is, isn't she?" Karen said very sarcastically and laughed a little.

"So, what do you guys think about Angie's condition? I was so shocked when I first saw her. I never expected her to be that bad." Sherri said.

"I was shocked too. I can't believe anyone would do something like that to her." Karen said.

"Me neither. I never expected it to be so bad. She took a huge beating." Janet said. "I don't know if I could tell anybody without getting tears in my eyes. And with all that she beat up Mike and broke his arm."

"Mike was such an asshole. I wonder what other injuries she has that we didn't see that were covered with her shirt and the blanket. She said she had 4 fractured ribs too. Did you see her wrists? Those were bad ligature marks. She had to be tied up. It looks like she pulled against it hard." Sherri said.

"Yea, I saw it. It was hard not to stare. I didn't want to be rude. And her lips and the whole side of her face is swollen and cut and scraped. I have tears in my eyes now just thinking about it, I feel so bad for her." Karen said.

"I'm glad that the news didn't go after her. Then everyone would see how bad she looks. And, I feel bad too." Janet said.

"I'm glad that the news didn't go after her too. And you know that some of those jerks at school would be talking all kinds of shit about her. I wish there was something we could do for her. She's the only person that is always nice to us." Sherri said. "Even though we have only known her for such a short time she is already a very good friend. I never knew any-one like her."

"What do we say to anyone that asks us now?" Janet asked. "I don't want to say anything that is going to hurt or make it hard for Angie."

Sherri replied, "I think we should only say something like she is doing better. And if anyone asks for more we can just say that she was hurt and she is getting better. I really don't want to say any more than that. If we start saying everything about her it would just be like the news talked to her. Every-body will be asking questions and making up stuff. She has more than enough to worry about recovering and I don't want to make it worse. We shouldn't tell anyone where she lives either. If Angie wants anyone to know she can tell them."

"You're right. Angie has too much to deal with. And, you know, at least she won't have to go to court now." Janet said.

"Yea, can you imagine how Angie would feel to be in front of everyone in court and have to say what happened again? I'm happy that she doesn't have to." Karen said.

"So we are all in agreement? We only say that she was hurt and she is doing better." Sherri asked.

"Yes, I agree." Janet said.

"Yea, me too." Karen said.

"And if no one asks, we don't offer anything? OK? Because no one knows we visited her today so hopefully no one will ask us." Sherri said.

"Yes!" both Karen and Janet said at the same time.

Sherri was thinking, "I was just thinking, I hope everything heals on her face without any scars. She has such a pretty face. That would be really sad."

"Yea, I didn't even think of that." Janet said.

"Me neither. Karen said. "Oh poor Angie. Why did this have to happen to her? She is so sweet and so nice to everybody. How could Mike do that to her?"

"Well, everyone knows that Mike had a screw loose already. You know, I overheard a couple of cheerleaders talking not long ago and one was saying that his mom and dad would beat him pretty bad all the time. That couldn't be good for anyone." Janet said.

"Man, if he was a little crazy already I could see how getting beaten like that could make him more crazy." Karen said. "I bet we will hear about on the news. He killed his mom and dad so the news is going to keep at this, I think."

Sherri told them, "We need to be careful not to talk about this at school. If someone says something we could just kind of agree or we could just say, 'I don't know' you know like air head girls. Even though everyone is treating us a little better they still don't treat us very well. Angie is the only one. And I don't think she could treat anyone bad, well, unless he's an asshole like Mike."

"I would love to have seen his face when she broke his nose. Can you imagine? The big bad Mike getting his nose broken by a girl? I think I might have laughed!" Janet said and snickered a little.

"I wonder what he thought when after he beat up Angie and then she kicked the shit out of him." Karen said. "I also heard that Mike was worshiping the Devil and torturing small animals, that's sick."

"He was a sick freak." Janet said.

Chapter 26

Monday December 9, 1974

On the following Monday Lizzy took Angie to see a dermatologist. She had been worried that Angie would end up with scars on her face and she couldn't stand to think about that. She wanted to know what could be done about this.

The doctor was a board certified dermatologist and one of his specialties is scar removal. He carefully removed the bandage from Angie's face. He needed to see all of the abrasions to determine what the best treatment would be.

"Angie, these abrasions are not very deep and if you keep them clean, keep them completely covered, and cover them with a light coating of petroleum jelly they will heal with very little scaring. Also do not let them get exposed to the sun and do not pick at any scabs that form. The worst abrasion looks as though it could have some minimal scaring but we won't know positively until the healing process is complete. The other abrasions don't appear as though there will be any scaring but I recommend you treat these all the same."

"I want to see you in 4 weeks. At that time the healing process will be enough to determine if scaring will be visible. If there is scaring there are two treatments that would be possible but which one would be decided when we determine the extent of any scaring. We would use either a chemical peel or dermabrasion. Dermabrasion is normally used for scars that are more visible. We usually use this for acne scaring. But I don't expect any scaring to be this evident so most likely we would use a chemical peel. If you have scaring that requires treatment I would expect that afterwards you will look as though nothing has happened." The doctor told them.

Both Lizzy and Angie told the doctor that they felt much better. Angie was worried that she would have abrasion scars on her cheeks that would be there forever. Now she knew that would not be the case. They made an appointment for January 7.

During the drive home, Angie talked to her mother about what she had left Angie to think about. "Mother, what you said about continued learning, you will still learn from your experiences with grandmother and grandfather after they are no longer with us. This would be due to the changed perspective, is that correct?"

"Yes, Angie. You may learn additionally from change of perspective. When we are involved in the experience we tend to only see things as if we have blinders on. In time you begin to see different perspectives. These are what I call life lessons.

"And along that line of thinking, you will surely learn from the confrontation with Mike. And you may even identify something years from now that you missed now. I know that you are very intelligent and along with high intelligence comes quite a bit of thinking. I know that you always have thoughts running through your mind. You have mentioned this many times. And at times you can't turn it off. You have told me that you awoke during the night many times with answers to questions that you had difficulty with. This is something that will advance you beyond most people. I believe that some of your ideas for the shop came from this part of your psyche along with your problem solving skills."

"Yes, I do wake during the night sometimes with ideas I need to write down so I do not forget, and sometimes because so many thoughts are running through my mind it wakes me up. But mother, how do you know all of this?"

"Angie, I know these things because our whole family shares many of the same traits. And we have discussed these in detail many times. Your intuition is unusually strong just as it is for you father and me. Overall it is very strong in the Tucci and Hall families. There are many things that you may not have recognized or learned how to use that I am sure you possess. For Instance, have you noticed how you usually know when someone tells a lie? Or the times when you felt that something was going to happen?"

"Well, sometimes I feel like I know someone is lying and there have been times that I have felt that unreasonable feeling that something happened before and it could not have. Or I dream during the night and the next day is a repeat of the dream."

"You are realizing some of the most wonderful abilities that God has given us. Such as your Aunt Maria and your father experiencing premonitions, or your grandfathers ability to read someone's character almost as if it was scripted, and when your father and I met the first time, we knew we absolutely had be together. These are all special abilities we all share. Then there is the unique ability that your father and I have to explain things to you in a way that you can understand and drive your thoughts. The unfortunate part is we tend to have pre-conceived ideas that cloud our abilities as well. I have seen all of these in you, Angie. I am certain this is quite a bit for you to understand and process."

Angie looked like she was in deep thought. "I think I understand mother. Maybe I am not just like other kids as I have been telling everyone. This is quite a bit to think about."

"I understand, Angie. I wish I had someone to explain this to me when I was your age. I would have helped me to understand my own feelings and myself to a greater degree. I do not believe I have told you this but when I was your age I had issues with saying what ever came to my mind. If your grandmother had talked to me about these abilities, it may have been easier for me to know when it was a good thing and when it was not."

"Mother, if grandmother and grandfather had these abilities, why did they not explain them to you as you are to me?"

Lizzy thought about this. "That is a very good question. But I believe that the time that I was your age many beliefs were different enough that people did not discuss things such as this. I believe many were afraid that others would think that they were speaking crazy. I believe most kept to themselves and did not feel comfortable discussing with others, even close family. Although I have discussed these with your grandmother and grandfather many times after your father and I married."

"When we told them we wanted to marry only a few months after we met we began discussing these abilities. Your grandfather was very open to this but you grandmother was not. And I believe she did not trust her feelings and instincts. I believe this is why she did not want to hear about your father. I believe she knew this would confirm her inner feelings and she was afraid of these. But when I was finely able to tell her at your birthday her reaction of relief was more than knowing your fathers history, but finally understanding that her inner feelings were authentic."

"You believe grandmother did not believe in her abilities all of those years?"

"I believe in the case of your father and me, yes. Sometimes when you experience these with your close family or close friends you do not want to believe them. And it skews your thoughts."

"That almost sounds unreasonable."

"Angie, many things are unreasonable. We are only human. But if you think about the time period that your grandmother has lived, and how things such as this could have sounded, possibly witchcraft or sorcery, you can see how one could be afraid of these. Remember she would have been your age in the 1930's and society was very different."

"I think I understand mother. It is just difficult to understand the differences then. Thinking that you needed to keep things such as this to yourself had to be troubling and very difficult. I could see that it could affect everything in your life."

"Now do your grandmother's actions sound more reasonable?"

"Yes mother."

Think about the ladies you just befriended. You already have an exceptionally strong connection to one of them, a very uncommon connection."

"Sherri. I feel it mother. There is something about her I do not feel in anyone else."

"You already can see this. This is wonderful. I believe you will build a very strong relationship with her even though each of you has different talents and needs. But you will work together to support each other. You have been blessed with certain abilities and you will search out others with the same." Lizzy said. "I expect that you will realize one day that your interest in martial arts and the particular mix of them that you chose may have been preparing you for the confrontation from last Sunday. Some of this I know because of our shared abilities. I have just had more time to refine them. I also believe that there are some that never figure this out and never use these abilities, and that is sad."

"Mother, are you saying that Sherri may have some of these abilities? This is quite a lot to digest. And I am a little teary eyed, but I am not certain why."

"I have given you some very deep philosophical things to think about Angie so your reaction is understandable. And yes, I believe Sherri does have some of these abilities."

Angie had become very tired from all of this. And now she had quite a lot of thinking to do. When they got home

Angie hobbled (that's how it still appeared when she used the crutches) into the house and to her room. Lizzy set up some pillows for her to keep her leg slightly raised. Angie got into bed and asked her mother to adjust the pillows and asked for a glass of water. Lizzy went and got a glass of water for her and brought it to her. Then she pulled the covers over Angie, and kissed her forehead and she told her she loved her. Angie said, "I love you too mother. And thank you for everything you have done.

"You know I will always be here for you Angie." Lizzy smiled then closed the blinds, turned off the lights and closed the door as she left her room.

As Angie laid there she began contemplating. "I wonder if other people are thinking about these same things right now or am I the only one?" She was very tired but couldn't calm her mind enough to sleep. "My life has become very complicated. I just cannot stop my mind from racing thoughts anymore. I finally finish with one and another takes its place. I feel like this could drive me crazy." She thought about what her mother said and then she went through everything that happened the Sunday before last. One thing she just realized was that when she thought about things that happened in the past she saw them from the outside, almost like she was looking through a window, only she still felt and heard everything that happened. Although these thoughts only included what she experienced, and anything that she had not felt or heard from that time she could not see or feel. She realized that this was how she thought about everything. She wondered why she never picked up on this before. Then she thought, "This is just as Mother said, afterwards you will see things from a different perspective." She was astonished! Now she was kind of wound up and couldn't sleep so she called her mother on the intercom.

"Mother?

"Yes honey, do you need something?"

"Yes mother. I was thinking and I need to talk to you. Do you have some time?"

"Absolutely. I am on my way." There was a knock at her door, "Angie, may I come in?"

"Yes mother, please." And Lizzy opened the door, came in and closed the door behind her.

"What is it that you need Angie?

"Mother, I cannot get to sleep because everything has been running through my head. I had been thinking about what happened that day with Mike and I had a very insightful thought and I need to tell you about it."

Lizzy pulled up the chair from Angie's desk and sat down. "What was your insight?"

"Well, I was thinking about what you said then my mind drifted to a week ago Sunday. I had been thinking how my life was becoming so complicated, then how things running through my head could drive me crazy. Then that Sunday was running through my head and I realized that even though I was watching this play out and I was being attacked, I was watching it happen something like seeing it through a window but more like I was floating there in some way. So it felt like I was watching a movie, well not exactly."

"Really, was it in color as well?"

"Yes mother, how did you know that?"

"Honey, this is something even more involved than out discussion. When you think about something or day dream do you see your thoughts this way as well?"

"Yes mother, always and I just realized that this how I see everything in my head."

"There is a scientific name for this which is Hyperphantasia, which means you see extremely vivid mental imagery. It is something on the way of Photographic Memory. Now there are many that believe in this and many that do not. This again is something I know from experience. I see things in my mind just as you. When I read a book it is like watching a movie in my head."

"Wow! I do that as well!"

"You will find that some people cannot see things like this and it is very difficult for us to understand because it is so natural to us. Not being able to see things like this also has a name and it is called aphantasia and this means they cannot see imagery in their mind.

Hyperphantasia again is something that is very prevalent in our families as well. It appears that you have a strong ability. It took me some time after I met your father before I realized I see things like this. This is what some call seeing something in your mind's eye. But I believe there is much more to it. I have had dreams that are so realistic that when I wake up I think the dream was what happened yesterday. Sometimes it lasts well into the day before I realize it was a dream. This helps you remember many things and helps your creative ability. I look at it as a gift, something we should embrace. There are many other things that you may find that you experience or have experienced. I do not want to get into the possibilities at this point because you have had so much to think about recently."

"Mother, this is both exciting and frightening. When Sunday was running through my mind I began to become very afraid. I wanted it to stop but then I realized that I was seeing this form a different point of view.........Oh, wow. You were just telling me that after I experience something I will look back and see it from a different point of view, and I just experienced that. This is almost overwhelming to think about. She continued, "Now I see why some kids at Amphitheater would give me a strange look when I told them I saw something in my head. I am so elated that you understand, mother. I am so fortunate that I can talk to you about anything. I overheard so many kids at Amphitheater that said they could not talk to their parents about anything. That has to be an awful place to be."

"Well Angie, your intellect is developing quickly. I know the events recently have not been exactly enjoyable but they have helped you grow immensely. Your father and I were concerned that you were changing schools but this is a time that I believe that you made a good choice. The incident that Sunday was horrible but I see that it has helped you grow and the time you have been at CDO I have seen some wonderful changes in you. I could not be more proud of you Honey."

"Thank you mother, that means so much to me." Angie was becoming teary eyed.

"Do you know that you did one thing that made me extremely happy, so much so that I am having some difficulty describing it to you?"

"What is that mother? I am not certain I understand, what did I do?"

"For your birthday and Thanksgiving you dressed in a way I have dreamed of. You were more beautiful that I could ever have imagined. Even though it was just those two times it will be with me forever." Now Lizzy was teary eyed.

"Mother, I never understood how much that would mean to you. But I can tell you, I actually loved it. I could not believe the attention I received and I loved how it felt. It made me feel very feminine as well. Something I never knew I wanted. And, I never thought of myself as beautiful even though many people have told me. But when I looked in the mirror I saw someone looking back that was very beautiful that I did not recognize, I could not believe it was me. At first I took a glance behind me to see who it was then I realized it was me. I will be doing that more often. I just need to learn how to put on makeup like that. I really loved how it looked. Oh, and Shelly said that I was more beautiful than she is. Do you believe that?

"You wanted to impress Shelly and you did, and you are very beautiful Angie. I know you never liked hearing that from me but you should know that I would never lie to you. And maybe now you can see that it is not just my slanted view of you be-cause you are my daughter. And I think that the makeup artist would be willing to teach you." Lizzy got up from the chair and leaned over and hugged Angie. Now they both were teary eyed. "I love you so much Angie."

"I love you too mother. I am really tired mother. Maybe I can sleep now. Thank you for listening."

"I am always here for you Angie, anytime." Lizzy kissed Angie again on her forehead, pushed the chair back to the desk, walked out and closed the door behind her.

Angie laid back and instantly fell asleep.

Chapter 27

A little over a week after the incident with Mike and Angie, Denise, Paula and Gina were walking towards the table where they ate lunch and Denise stopped to talk to Sherri, Janet and Karen. Denise asked if they could sit for a few minutes to talk.

Sherri reluctantly said, "Ah, OK." Somehow she thought Denise looked upset.

Denise said, "I need to tell you that I am so sorry for treating you so bad after what Mike did to you. We met and spoke to Angie, uh, well before this thing happened with her and Mike. Um, she made me realize what I was doing to you. She kind of put me on the spot and I wanted to tell you that I went home and cried all night. I am so sorry. I can't believe I did that to you, I can't believe I was so cold." Denise put her head down and began to cry.

Then Paula looked up at them and said, "I don't know what Angie did but I understand how, umm, I can't remember the word she used but I am embarrassed. I can't look at the three of you without getting tears in my eyes now." Paula's eyes were tearing. "I don't know how to say this or if you will believe me but I'm sorry. We must have made it so hard for you at school. I don't know if I can forgive myself." Paula was trying hard not to cry. "All I can think about now is how you must have suffered and we wouldn't leave you alone."

"C'mon guys, no one died here." Gina said. "I'm sorry too, I know I talked behind you backs about this all the time and I shouldn't have done that. It wasn't a nice thing to do. I'm not good at apologies, I'm sorry. But after talking to Angie I feel really bad. I feel like I hurt you guys. I looked at myself and I didn't like what I saw." Gina started to get tears in her eyes as well. "I never get like this. Does someone have a tissue?"

Sherri, Karen and Janet were looking at each other dumfounded. They couldn't believe what they were hearing. They were shocked. Sherri looked at Karen, then Janet and said, "I don't know what to say. Why do you feel like this now after all of this time?"

"Angie made fun of me, um, not exactly, well sort of, Denise said, "She asked me what I would do if someone started a rumor that I was having an intimate relationship with my father. It scared me. I couldn't believe she said that. Then she told me that this was what we were doing to you guys. I felt terrible. My stomach felt sick and I went home and cried."

Paula said, "This was the day after school that we all met Angie. I was a little afraid because everyone was saying that she was dangerous because of the Karate stuff and Gina brought us to meet her. I really like Angie. In 2 seconds she showed a side of me I didn't like. I cried that night too. I didn't want to go to school the next day I was so embarrassed." She wiper her eyes, "You know, I saw Angie and her mother at the shoe store just before Thanksgiving. They both had beautiful gowns on. Angie was so beautiful almost didn't recognize her. She introduced me to her mother and they were both so nice. Then Mike did the horrible thing to her." Paula began to cry. "I don't even know if she is OK. I don't really know why but the few minutes we talked made me care about her and I feel so bad for her. Poor Angie." Now she was full out crying.

Sherri stood up and went to Paula, put her arm around her and said, "Angie is OK, basically. She is pretty messed up but she will be alright."

Paula looked at Sherri and asked, "How do you know? We don't know if she is in the hospital or if she is even coming back to school."

Sherri looked at Karen and Janet. Then she said, "We were able to see her for a little while. I wasn't going to say anything to anyone because of the whole rumor thing around here. We didn't want to make anything harder for her."

"Really? She's OK? Paula looked up at Sherri and stopped crying.

"Yes, basically. Mike beat her up pretty bad and she hurt her leg pretty bad kicking him." Sherri said.

Gina smiled big and said, "She's OK? That's so great!"

Denise smiled and wiped her tears. "Do you know when she is coming back?"

Janet said, "No, she said she can't come back until her doctor releases her. So we don't know."

"But she is coming back, right?" Denise asked.

"She told us she was. But it might be a while." Karen said.

"Hey, how' bout we get a get well card and we can all sign it then you can give it to her." Paula suggested, she was very excited.

Gina said, "We could get some balloons or something to go with it. Maybe after school we could go and look for something?"

Sherri, Janet and Karen didn't believe what was happening. Besides getting apologies from Gina, Paula and Denise they were being friendly.

"I can go after school," Sherri said.

"I can go too." Janet said.

"Me too." Paula said.

Karen looked a little down and said, "I can't go today. My Mom is picking me up right after school for a dentist appointment."

Denise said, "I have to baby-sit my little brother after school so I can't go either."

"I'm not doing anything after school so I can go too." Gina said.

"If we meet at my car after school we can go from here, OK?" Sherri said.

Everyone said. "OK."

"Pick out a really nice card, OK? And maybe you will see something cute for her too?" Karen said.

"OK, so we meet at Sherri's car after school then?" Gina asked.

Everyone agreed.

After school Sherri, Janet, Paula and Gina met at Sherri's car and they drove to Walgreen's to look for a card. They found one that had a picture of a cartoon puppy that was looking up and had its front paws together and is said, "Get Better, Please" on the front. Then they went to look for something to put with the card. They found a little stuffed puppy with big eyes. They thought it would make Angie laugh. Then they saw a small balloon on a stick that said, "Get Well" and they bought this too.

Sherri dropped Gina, Karen and Paula at their houses and said she would bring everything to school tomorrow.

The next day everyone met at lunch and each wrote something on the card and signed it. Then they discussed how to get the card, stuffed puppy and balloon to Angie. Sherri said she has some big paper bags at home that she could put everything in. And she could drop it off at Angie's house after school. She said she would just give it to her mother and ask her to just tell Angie that this came for her. They all agreed.

After school Sherri dropped Karen and Janet off as usual and went home to get the bag. She brought the card, stuffed puppy and balloon into the house and put it into the bag. Sherri's mom asked her who it was for and Sherri told her it was for their new friend Angie.

"Sherri maybe you should draw something on the bag, you draw so well."

"That's a good idea mom." And she went to her room to get her colored pencils. She drew "Angelina" in large fancy balloon like letters. And under she wrote, "We miss you!" and drew a big heart around the whole thing. Then she put everything inside and folded the top. "How does this look, Mom?" She showed her mother.

"That's very nice, Sherri. Is that for your friend? The one that got beaten up?"

"Yes, mom. We really miss her. It feels like there is a hole now even though we just met her."

"I've had a feeling about that. I feel as if you have a deep connection already Sherri."

"You're right mom, I don't know, there's something. I need to go and drop this off now. I'll be back in not too long."

Sherri got into the car and drove to Angie's house. She hoped her mother was home. She pulled into the driveway and saw Angie's car over by the garage and a Bonneville parked near the door. She figured that it must have been Angie's mother's car. She parked and went to the door and rang the bell. She smiled and thought again, "Real bells"

She heard someone opening the door. "Hello Mrs. Tucci. Some of us from school put this together for Angie. Could you please bring it to her, Ma'am?"

"Well hello, Sherri, correct?"

"Yes Ma'am."

"I would be a pleasure. Angie is fortunate to have such thoughtful friends."

"Thank you very much Ma'am. I hope she is feeling better."

"She is improving I will advise her your sentiments, thank you for asking Sherri"

"Thank you so much, Mrs. Tucci. It was nice to see you again Ma'am. Have a good afternoon."

"You as well Sherri."

Sherri turned and walked back to the car.

Lizzy closed the door and walked to Angie's room. She knocked on the door.

"You may come in mother."

Lizzy opened the door and walked in. "Angie, you had a delivery."

"I did? From whom?"

Lizzy handed it to her. "It is from your friends. Sherri just dropped it off."

"My friends?" Angie looked at the bag and smiled then she opened the bag and took out the balloon, stuffed puppy and card. She was very surprised, she smiled. "Aww, look at this mother!" she showed her mother. It said, "Get Better, Please" and it was a cute puppy with its front paws together.

"That was very sweet of them Angie. What does the card say?"

Angie opened it and read it. "It says 'Hoping for a quick recovery,' and...and..." She got tears in her eyes and her jaw was trembling. Angie sniffled, "Mother, It is from Sherri, Janet, Karen, Gina, Paula and Denise. I cannot believe it. I did not know that they talked to each other. And on the bottom it says, 'You have made a difference in all of us! We miss you!' I.....I..." Her jaw was trembling so much that she couldn't get any more out.

"What are you trying to say honey?"

Angie grabbed a tissue and blew her nose, "Sherri, Karen and Janet did not like Gina, Paula and Denise because of how they treated them since Mike raped them. I do not understand. And I am crying because they did this for me."

Lizzy thought for a moment, "Angie you have real friends now. This is what real friends do. And maybe all of the ladies forgave each other."

"I do not know how to feel. I would not have believed they would forgive each other. They sounded so set."

"Angie, the card says that you made a difference, maybe somehow you interactions with them gave them a different perspective."

"But I have only known Sherri, Karen and Janet for a few weeks and I only talked to the others one time for a few minutes after school. How could I have that much influence from that?"

"What did you talk about that day after school?"

"They talked about Sherri, Karen and Janet and that Mike thing, Denise said something about them wanting sex with Mike but afterwards they were embarrassed so they said it was rape. And she said if it really was rape why did he not get in trouble. I got very cross and told them that rape is a serious aggression. And since his father was the City Manager, I asked if she thought he would be able to keep him out of trouble. I believe I asked her how she would feel if someone started a rumor that she was intimate with her father, and she was stunned. She got defensive and asked why I would say something like that. I replied, "That did not feel good to hear, did it." And I told her that this is what they were doing to Sherri, Karen and Janet. And I think she finally understood what she was doing. She then became apologetic and so did Paula and Gina. That was most of our conversation."

"The example of Denise being intimate with her father was a little brash. But I think you got the point across. What do you think you accomplished from this?"

"I hoped that they would see how they were hurting the other girls. I was very angered by how they were treating them. And......and I showed them a different perspective, did I not?"

"Yes you did. You have done the same thing that your father and I have always done for you Angie. It is possible that because of your little discussion that they may have gone and apologized to the other girls. You may have done more than you think. Maybe this is why they got together and signed the card."

Angie thought about this. "You believe I may have caused them to become friends? Just because of one discussion?"

"It is possible Angie. You may find out that you influence people more than you believed. This was such a nice gesture from all of these ladies. I would believe that they would all have loved to see your reaction when you opened the card. I am confident that they would all be elated."

"It is almost overwhelming to think that I can make such a difference mother. Maybe I should do something. I do not know what but something to show my admiration for what they have done for me. What are your thoughts?"

"What I would suggest that you to think about it for a time."

"Alright mother. This puppy is so cute. Now I getting teary eyed just looking at it."

"It is very cute. You have indeed made some good friends Angie. Is there anything I can get for you?"

"No mother, I am fine, thank you."

"Then I will leave you to rest." Lizzy smiled as she turned to leave.

"I love you mother, thank you."

"You are very welcome and I love you as well." Lizzy closed the door as she left.

Angie laid back and looked at the balloon, the stuffed puppy and re-read the card. It brought tears to her eyes again. "I cannot believe they did this for me. How can I thank them?" As she lay there she thought that she could write each one a short note to tell them how she felt when she opened the card.

Then she could give them to her mother to drop off at school when she drops off and picks up her homework.

Angie called her mother. "Mother, could you come here please?"

"Do you need something Angie?"

"Mother, I would like to write thank you notes for all of the ladies. Do we have envelops that I can use?

"I think I have something you could use. I will be right there Angie."

In a few minutes she knocked on Angie's door. "You may come in Mother."

"Angie, I have these Thank You notes, you can use them if you like."

"Mother, those would be perfect! I was just hoping you had envelops and I could just write notes. These are wonderful! Thank you so much mother. And could I ask you to bring these to the school office when you drop off my homework please?"

"I would be happy to honey. This is just what I thought of when you asked me earlier. I hoped you would choose thank you notes. You are learning well and will be a perfect lady!"

"Thank you mother, I already know what I will write. And it will be one specifically for each lady. I remember you taught me this."

"I will leave you to this then." Lizzy left the room and closed the door.

Angie reached for her note pad to use as a surface to write on and a pen to begin writing. She thought about what to say and first wrote each name down. She didn't want to miss anyone. She began with Sherri because she has felt a special connection with Sherri since the day she chased after her after school,

Sherri,
Thank you for being my friend. You have made
A difference in my life by showing and giving me
something I never knew I needed. It brings tears
to my eyes just from writing this and I want you
to know that I am touched. I love the card, balloon
and puppy that all of you sent me. I feel as though
you will be a very good friend.
Thank You So Much!
Angie

Karen,
Thank you so much for thinking of me. You have
given me a reason to smile and you have touched
me in a way I have not felt in the past and you have
shown me what a real friend is. I have tears in my
eyes as I am writing this. I love the card, balloon
and puppy that all of you sent me.
Thank you So Much!
Angie

Janet,
I am touched that you thought of me while I am
home recovering. You, Sherri and Karen showed
me that I needed friends and what I have missed
without them. The card, balloon and puppy brought
joy to my heart and made me teary eyed. Thank you
for being my friend.
Thank You So Much!
Angie

Gina,
I am delighted that you thought of me while I am
recovering. Even though I have not known you very
long, I feel as if you are becoming a good friend. I
enjoyed the card, balloon and puppy that all of you
Sent me and it brought joy to my heart and tears to
My eyes!
Thank You So Much!
Angie

Paula,
I am grateful that you have become my friend and
it truly touched me to receive the card, balloon
and puppy. Your thought brought tears to my eyes.
I love them. It was nice seeing you at the store shortly
before Thanksgiving. Your courtesy made a good
impression on my mother as well as me and I wanted
to thank you for the effort.
Thank You So Much!
Angie

Denise,
Thank you for your thoughts while I am home
recovering. You brought up my spirits as well as
tears to my eyes. I am sorry for being so brash the
day we met with the example I used with you. But
even though you had angered me I believe we are
becoming good friends. I very much love the card,
balloon and puppy.
Thank You So Much!
Angie

Angie finished the Thank You notes and put them in the envelopes. She carefully wrote each girls name on each envelope. Then she sealed them and called her mother. Her mother knocked on the door. "You may come in mother."

Lizzy entered and saw that Angie had finished writing the thank you notes. "I see you have finished. I will take these to the office with me tomorrow afternoon and make certain that they are delivered to each lady."

"Thank you mother." Angie reached to give her mother a hug. Her pain was not so bad now so she could squeeze a little. She missed being able to do that.

Lizzy smiled and left the room and closed the door.

Angie laid back and thought about how fortunate she was to have finally made friends. She felt as if a void was now filled. She fell asleep.

The following day Lizzy left to bring Angie's homework and the thank you cards to the school. Just as she arrived at the office the final bell rang and the halls filled with students. Just then one of the students came rushing into the office. She went to Miss Cardenas. It was Sherri. "Miss Cardenas, Mrs. Daniels asked me to drop this off."

"Thank you Sherri."

Sherri turned and saw Mrs. Tucci. "Hello Mrs. Tucci, how nice it is to see you. How is Angie feeling?"

"It is very nice to see you as well Sherri. Angie is feeling much better, thank you for asking. I have something for you and the other ladies." She handed Sherri the envelopes. "There is one for each of you. Angie wrote these earlier. I have to say, you have made a wonderful impression on Angie. I was present when she opened the card all of you sent and I am very impressed. Angie got teary eyed then cried when she read it. You ladies are very admirable."

"Really, I am so happy she liked it. I drew what was on the bag. If you will excuse me I would like to get to the other ladies before they leave. It was nice talking Mrs. Tucci." Sherri left. She almost was running. She was excited to give the each of them their envelope and then read hers.

Lizzy smiled and walked up to the desk. "Good Afternoon Miss Cardenas. I have Angie's homework here." She handed it to her.

Miss Cardenas looked surprised. She looked at Mrs. Tucci and said, "What happened to Sherri, I never saw her act so polite."

"Angie happened. It seems that Angie has had some very positive influence on some of the ladies here."

"I'll say. Maybe she will influence more students. I have never seen anything like this."

"It seems that Angie said something to three of the girls that were giving Sherri and her friend's a difficult time and I believe that they have now become friends. At least based on what I saw in the card the 6 of them gave Angie."

"Oh, you mean Gina, Paula and Denise, I know them well. Sherri, Karen and Janet have been complaining that they are being harassed by them."

"Really? Those envelops I just gave Sherri are for each of them. They got together and bought Angie a get well card, a balloon and a cute stuffed puppy toy. From what was in the card I do not believe they have issues anymore."

"I find that hard to believe. Gina, Paula and Denise have been here for discipline related to harassing them many times."

Just then all six girls burst into the office. "You're still here. UM, I mean we are happy you are still here Mrs. Tucci. It's nice to see you." Janet said. "We are so happy Angie liked what we sent to her. She has made such a difference in our lives."

Gina said, "Hello Mrs. Tucci, it is very nice to meet you."

Paula Said, "I very happy to see you again Mrs. Tucci."

Denise said, "Um, I'm happy, uh, to meet you Mrs. Tucci."

Karen said, "it is a pleasure to see you again, Ma'am."

They all voiced their feelings that Angie liked what they sent.

Sherri said, "We were hoping you were still here, Ma'am. We wanted you to know that all of us feel this way. And we really hope Angie recovers sooner than later, we really miss her. Could you please tell her that Ma'am."

"I would be delighted to ladies." Lizzy said.

"Cool!" Gina said.

They were all kind of giddy. "Bye Mrs. Tucci." The all said in unison.

Miss Cardenas sat there with her mouth open. "Am I dreaming? Last week Karen came in here and was so angry because we couldn't do anything to stop the harassment. I wish Dean Campbell was here to see this."

Lizzy smiled, "Angie is an exceptional woman, Miss Cardenas. It seems that she has powerful means of influence. Do you have Angie's homework for today?"

"Oh yes, Ma'am here it is. And thank you Mrs. Tucci."

"It is my pleasure but I do not have any idea what I have done."

"You brought Angie here. I don't believe I have ever seen anything like this before and I have been here for 10 years. It's too bad her influence didn't work on Mike. OH!" she covered her mouth, "I'm so sorry for bringing that up." She was blushing feeling embarrassed now.

"Please do not bother yourself Miss Cardenas. Thank you for Angie's homework." Lizzy said as she left.

When Lizzy returned home she brought Angie's homework to her. She knocked on Angie's door. "You may come in Mother."

Lizzy entered the room and left the homework for Angie. She also said, "Angie, you have indeed made a difference in your friends' lives. I have a short story to tell you from my visit to the office in your school."

"What is this about mother?" Angie wasn't certain what to expect. She wondered if it was not good.

"I walked into the office precisely as the final bell rang and the hallway became crowded with students. And just then Sherri came into the office with something I believe she was asked to deliver to the office from one of her teachers. She gave it to Miss Cardenas and turned and saw me and immediately politely said it was nice to see me again and asked how you were feeling. Sherri is a very sweet girl. I told her that I had envelops for her and the other 5 ladies and her eyes lit up. It was lovely to see. She took them and said she needed to go so she could get them to each lady before they left school and promptly excused herself."

"Miss Cardenas looked shocked and asked, what happened to Sherri? Then she said she never heard her be polite. And I responded that you happened and that you seem to be having quite a bit of influence at school. I could see that she did not really believe me. She responded be saying that maybe you would influence more students here and giggled as if she did not believe me. I continued to tell her that I believe that you influence has made a change in all 6 of the ladies and she said for the most part that she needed to see that to believe it. She said that Karen was recently in the office angry because they could not stop the other 3 ladies from harassing them so she did not think it was possible. I told her about what they did together for you and I do not believe she believed that either. Before I could leave your homework and pick up your new homework all 6 of the ladies burst into the office and said they were happy I had not left yet and told me, after each very politely said hello to me and that it was very nice to meet me, that they were so happy that you loved the gift. They also said that they hoped you recover sooner than later because they missed you so much. And then excused themselves. All of them were acting giddy. And when they left Miss Cardenas sat with her mouth open in shock."

"Mother, you are not just making this up to make me feel good are you?"

"Of course not honey, you know I would not do that. All six ladies acted as if they were best friends! And their sentiments about you were genuine. Angie, your actions have made a positive difference in that school, enough that many others can see. This is something that you should be proud of. Very few people are able to make this much of a difference in such a short time if at all. You have done a wonderful thing Angie! I feel very proud!"

Angie lay there feeling stunned. Her expression was that of disbelief and confusion because she couldn't believe she was able to influence people this easily and she knew that her mother would only tell her the truth. "Mother, I do not know what to say. I do not know how to feel. I do not understand how I could have done this."

"As I have been telling you, you have shown everyone in school that you are confident, intelligent and unyielding, and I would tend to believe many now look up to you now. It is very uncommon for someone in high school to have these traits. Many students will very likely trust what you say and intently listen to you now.

"Mother?"

"What is it Angie?"

"I still do not understand. I did not have any influence with anyone at Amphitheater so why do I now have influence at CDO? It does not make sense."

Lizzy thought for a moment and said, "As I said recently, people need to be open to influence. It is possible that many of the students at CDO have different outlooks on life and therefore are open to different stimuli. You have said that students at CDO are very different than at Amphitheater and it may be this simple. Think about what you said to Denise. If she was a student at Amphitheater last year and the situation had been the same with this same conversation, do you believe you would have had the same outcome?"

Angie thought about this. Then she said, "Thinking about this mother, no, I believe my conversation would have propagated more separation and animosity between us. I am sure it would have had a very negative affect, more towards me than others."

"Do you understand now?"

"Possibly."

"You could possibly equate it to exposure to a group of drug addicts as opposed to scholars. This is a very drastic example but the dynamics would be similar. Does this help you understand?"

"I see now. Thinking about this I see your point. The differences in my case are much more subtle but now I understand. Mother, you always amaze me with your ability to make things clear to me. I believe these talks we have had in recent time have helped me grow. I am now wondering if we would have had these discussions if the incident with Mike did not happen. Could this be following what you have said? That you can learn from past experiences good or bad?"

"You are beginning to understand now Angie. Yes, you can learn from every experience when you reflect on them. Angie you have grown immensely in recent months. Now do you understand what I expressed to you about constant learning and how it will continue?"

"Yes mother. I understand. At times I cannot stop it no matter how much I try. It is very complex thinking about it, but I am beginning to understand the concept of continuing to learn all of my life."

"Remember what your friends expressed today. You have been fortunate to have become friends with each of them."

"I could not forget mother. They have made a difference in my life just as I have with theirs. Thank you mother."

Chapter 28

Lizzy has been bringing Angie to the Physical Therapist every morning and he has been seeing continued improvement. Then on the December 18 the therapist had Angie walk across the room without the crutches. She was not feeling any pain of any kind while walking. Then he took some books from a shelf and asked Angie, "Are these books representative of what you normally carry in school Angie?"

Angie looked at them and said, "If you would add another book or two it would be about correct."

"You carry that much, all the time?"

"Yes usually. This keeps me prepared at all times."

"OK, then I want you to hold these just as you normally do when you are in school then walk across the room again please —but just walk."

Angie took the books and walked across the room again and back. "Your walking looks almost normal. How does your leg feel? Do you feel and pain or pulling?"

"No, not at all. My leg feels normal but the muscles are a little stiff from not using them."

"That's great! You must be doing all of the exercises that I have been suggesting then?"

"Of course. I have done every exercise you gave me to do and always have my mother there in the event I hurt myself. I have done this twice each day, once in the morning and once in the evening."

"Very good. I have some good news for you then."

"What would that be sir?"

"Please don't call me "sir" Angie. As I said before I feel that physical therapy is very personal and adding "sir" takes that away. I really appreciate your courtesy though. Well let's get down to business. Sit down here facing me please." Angie sat down. "You don't feel any pain or soreness Angie?"

"No Si.., sorry. No I did not, just some stiffness."

"Bend your leg up but just from the knee, please." She did that. "With your leg straight do you feel anything?"

"No."

"Now lean back on the chair, keep your knee locked and lift your leg from your hip."

Angie did that. "It pulls a little but it does not hurt. It just feels like I have not been working out for far too long."

"Well Angie, I am going to release you to go back to school, but with stipulations."

"Really! Thank you so much!" Angie said with great excitement.

"I don't want you to do any running or jumping. You don't need to use your crutches anymore. I will write a note for your school and a second for gym teacher. I don't want you to participate in anything in gym class. Remember that you don't want to do anything that will pull the muscle hard. It will also be alright for you to drive as well. The injury was on your right leg so driving won't put strain on it. You told me that your car is stick shift and you use your left leg for the clutch so you will be fine. I still want to see you here on Monday, Wednesday and Fridays until we are sure that the muscle is completely healed. Do you understand this Angie? I will call your Sensei and explain where you are in your recovery so he can work with you as well, but NO kicking and no exercises that stretch the muscle too far." He explained.

"I understand. Then I can return to school tomorrow?" Angie asked excitedly.

"Yes you may."

"Thank you, thank you so much. Finally!"

"I don't think I ever hear anyone your age excited to go back to school, Angie."

"Well, I do not have any interaction with the teachers at home and I also just made friends and I am anxious to see them again."

"Well good for you! I will write the notes for school now. I also want you to follow up with your Doctor as soon as you can. I will call him and tell him about your progress." He went and wrote the notes and brought them back to Angie. "Here are the two notes, one for the school releasing you to go back and the other for your Gym teacher explaining that you are to skip gym class until I release you. Do you have any questions?"

"No. If I think of any, would it be alright to call you?"

"Of course Angie, Good luck."

"Thank you. I will see you then on Friday." Angie said as she left. She took her crutches with her.

She walked out to her mother's car, opened the door and told her the news. She put the crutches on the back seat and sat down in front. She explained what the physical therapist said.

"That is wonderful Angie! You must be very delighted."

"Of course Mother. I find it somewhat strange saying this, but I cannot wait to see my friends!"

"That is something I have not yet heard from you. Would you like me to bring the notes when I drop off your homework this afternoon?"

"That would be wonderful! But I would like it to be a surprise for everyone when I arrive so could you ask them not to tell anyone that I will be there tomorrow please?"

"I will tell them your wishes in the office but they may need to inform your teachers."

"I just do not want any of my friends to know yet, I would like it to be a surprise."

Lizzy did just that and they said that they would only need to inform Angie's gym teacher. When Dominic got home Lizzy told him and he was happy about it as well. He knew how much Angie missed going to school and he knew that she was excited to see her friends again.

The next morning Angie prepared for school and gathered all of her books. She put them in her car. She was also excited to be able to drive the Cuda again. Lizzy made breakfast for all of them. Afterwards, they all hugged Angie left. She started the Cuda and the sound made her smile.

Angie arrived and parked in her assigned place. She was very excited even though you could still see her black eyes, she still had the dressing on her cheek and the ligature marks were still clearly visible. But she was speaking normally now and mostly that was what she had worried about.

Angie picked up her books and purse, closed and locked the car door and walked to the school, slower than she had before the confrontation with Mike because her ribs were sore and leg muscles were stiff. Just as she got to the door she heard, "Angie! Angie!" She turned and saw Gina.

Gina caught up to her and reached out and hugged her. Angie shrieked, almost dropping her books. She said with a grimice, "Careful, my ribs still quite sore."

"Oooh, sorry. I can't believe you are back, I am so happy! How are you feeling? Oou, you have black eyes and your cheek. Oh, Angie I am so sorry." Gina said. Then she glanced down and saw her wrists. "Oh my god! What happened to your wrists?"

"Those are ligature marks from being tied up. I have them on my ankles as well."

"Oh Angie, I had no idea. I feel so bad. You must still hurt all over, huh?"

"Yes, I am still in quite a bit of pain, I need to take Tylenol, it helps somewhat. But they released me because I can walk without pain and crutches. But I am very limited in what I can do."

"I can't believe anyone could have done that to you. If you need any help with anything just ask, I will help you with anything I can. We need to get to class."

They walked into the school and some kids Angie didn't know kind of screamed, "Angie, your back! Look Angie's back!" Most everyone looked and came over and welcomed her back. Most said they were so sorry and felt bad after seeing her injuries.

Angie told everyone, "Thank all of you. We should get to class now, there will be time to talk afterwards." Angie walked to her first class which was Physics.

Mrs. Abbot heard some commotion outside of the room and went to see what it was about. It sounded almost like cheering! As she got to the door Angie came in. "Oh my lord!" she exclaimed. "Angelina, you're back! How wonderful! Ohhh, but you must still be hurting quite a bit!"

"Yes Ma'am, I am still hurting, my ribs primarily but Tylenol gives me some comfort." Angie replied. She went to her seat and it was obvious that her ribs hurt as she sat down slowly and gently. The class went mostly as usual. Angie did notice that many of the students looked at her and appeared sympathetic.

At the end of the class Mrs. Abbot asked Angie to see her before she left. Angie asked, "What is it Ma'am?"

"If you don't mind, I wanted to ask about you ribs. Why do they hurt?"

"No, I do not mind. I have 4 cracked ribs. I am not certain how I got them but as bruised as my side was and still is, I assume Mike kicked me while I was unconscious Ma'am."

"Oh my! I am so sorry, and you were unconscious as well? I feel terrible Angelina. If there is anything I can do to help you, please ask." She looked sincere. "You know, I found it difficult to understand but it seemed that most everyone in the school has been worried about you. Can you believe it? I don't think I have seen so much compassion in my life. I just thought you should know."

"Thank you, Ma'am. I have learned some very valuable life lessons in the past few weeks. So this whole thing has opened my eyes to a world I had no idea existed. And thanks to my mother, I have gained immense self-knowledge. I learned that I have had an astonishing influence on some students here. Somehow I paved the way for Gina, Paula and Denise to apologize to Sherri, Karen and Janet and it seems that they are now friends. And a few weeks ago they hated each other. I am still trying to understand how I accomplished that feat. I am only telling you because I value your opinions immensely Mrs. Abbot."

"I really appreciate that Angelina. I have also missed our little debates. You are a very special lady. And yes I have seen those girls and they do look like good friends now. I couldn't believe it. That's because of you?

"Evidently, when I met Gina, Paula and Denise they made some comments about Sherri, Karen and Janet and it angered me so I came up with a story about Denise and told them how easily someone could make it into a rumor. Denise got very upset and they must have realized what they have been doing. I do not understand how that made such an impact. Well I need to go to my next class, Ma'am."

There were many other students that said hi and welcome back between classes and again students that she did not know. Then at lunch she went to sit with Sherri, Karen and Janet and found Gina, Paula and Denise sitting there already. Even though she knew they had made up she still found it difficult to believe. As she walked up they all got up and went to hug her and to say how happy they are that she is back so soon.

Angie quickly said, "Careful!! My ribs are still very sore."

Angie was becoming overwhelmed. She never had attention like this and she was feeling somewhat embarrassed because she still looked terrible with black eyes, a dressing on her cheek, scrapes on her arms and the ligature marks on her wrists. She didn't feel that she looked presentable. However, if everyone had been as they were before this happened no one would have even noticed. This is what she had expected, but now she felt as though there was a spotlight on her.

She sat down, just as in Physics class, slowly because her ribs hurt. She took a deep breath because that helped the pain. They could all see that she was still in quite a bit of pain. She began to open her lunch and asked, "What motivated this change with all of you? Before I was injured you despised each other."

Gina just said, "We made up. That's all."

Denise said, "It's a lot more that. Remember when we met you after school that day?" Angie shook her head yes. "After what you said to me I went home and cried. I was so embarrassed because of what we did. I just went into my room and cried. My mom tried to get me to stop but I couldn't. I couldn't even tell her what we did to them."

Then Paula said, "It was almost the same with me. I went home and cried too. All I could think was how I would feel if I was in there place and they harassed me like we did to them. I felt so bad and ashamed that I didn't want to go to school the next day." She had tears in her eyes.

Gina said, "Well I didn't cry but I felt bad enough that I didn't say anything to my mom and dad all night. It was all I could think about. I looked at myself and I didn't like what I saw. I saw how cold I was. And I thought about what you said and I realized what we were doing to Sherri, Karen and Janet.

Sherri then spoke. "They came to us at lunch and asked if they could sit for a couple of minutes. I kind of didn't want them to but something inside of me told me to let them. So they sat down and I think Denise talked first and she almost didn't get to say what she wanted before she cried. Then Paula did the same and she cried too. Gina didn't cry but even though she usually doesn't seem to care about what anyone thinks she sounded so sincere. So Karen, Janet and I basically forgave them and we all cried a little. But now we are OK and we get along great. You know this is because of you Angie. You say you are just like everyone else but you're not. Your strong and say things in a way that we touch us deep inside. We missed you so much while you were at home and some of us thought that you might not come back. I was so sad."

Karen said, "It was like something was missing."

Angie sat for a few minutes trying to take it all in. Then she said, "I have never revealed my deep inner thoughts to anyone besides my mother. But you, all of you, have taught me that friends are something we all need. I have not talked to anyone outside of my family about anything personal but," she hesitated for a minute, "For the first week I cried myself to sleep every night after the day this happened. I felt guilty that three people died and one was seriously injured because I came to CDO. I discussed this with my mother and it helped somewhat. Then I had some visitors that brought up my spirits to a level I had not felt since before Mike confronted me the first time. Sherri, Karen and Janet, that was you. I could not believe anyone would come to see me other than my family. I spent an enormous amount of time discussing this with my mother because I did not understand how people I had just met had such an intense effect on me. Then when I thought I was beginning to understand all of you sent me the card, balloon and puppy. I could not read through the card. I cried. You touched me in a place I have never felt before." She had tears in her eyes now. My mother tried to explain the feelings but I still do not quite understand. This is new territory for me. In fact I am feeling very self-conscious today because everyone has been so caring and are looking after me. I feel as if I am under a spot light. I feel ugly because of my face and wrists. I thought I would come today and it would be just like before this happened and other than all of you no one would say anything or notice. I do not know how to deal with this." She was full on crying now and holding her napkin over her eyes.

Of all people to say anything to try to make Angie feel better, Gina went over to her and put her arms around her shoulders. She said, "OH Angie, don't feel bad. Everyone is being nice because they care. You have become very popular. Since this happened everyone has been so concerned about you and no one knew anything. Don't think you're ugly. No one thinks that. Everyone is so happy you are back at school I don't think anyone cares that you still have not completely healed yet. And I wouldn't ever say anything like this before," she paused, "but I still think you are the prettiest girl in the school I....I can't believe I said that. But it's true."

Then another girl that Angie didn't know walked up and asked if she was in pain. She asked if she need Tylenol or something. Angie was able to get a "No, I'm fine. Thank you Ma'am." She didn't realize it was another student. She turned her head and saw that it was just another student. The girl said, "I know that you don't know me but I think you are the bravest person I ever knew. If you need anything just let me know, OK?"

Angie was able to say, "Thank you."

Sherri then told Angie, "See Angie, everyone is just concerned. I think it was very brave of you to even come back to school this early. It is only showing everyone how much dedication you have."

Angie was drying her eyes. "Thank you, all of you. This means so much to me to have you here. I wish I knew you years ago." She was calming down. "Maybe we should eat our lunches, we do not have much time left."

"Yes I agree." Denise said. "Just remember Angie, we are all here for you if you need anything, OK?"

Angie looked at Denise. "Thank you."

Lunch time ended with the bell and they all got up, threw out their trash and went to their next classes. In between one of her classes, Angie dropped one of her books and another student immediately picked it up for her and handed it back. He asked her if she needed help to her next class and he offered to carry her books for her. Angie didn't know what to say so she just said, "Thank you."

He walked with her to her next class. Then he gave her the books back. He told her that is she needed anything to just ask. He said he thought everyone knew that she was in still in pain and he thought anyone would help her if she needed. Angie looked at him and smiled and told him, "I appreciate your help, thank you." Then she walked into the class.

This was her last class of the day which was Composition. As in all of her other classes she was offered help if she needed it. Mrs. White greeted her and welcomed her back. There was only one more day before Christmas Vacation and Mrs. White gave the class an assignment to write over Christmas vacation on a topic that they felt was important to them or an experience that they recently had. She told them the paper needed to be at least 6 pages. As usual most didn't like this assignment but Angie already had picked out a topic. She was going to write about her experiences going to a new school. She thought her experience had been so touching and life changing and as she formulated a mental outline she thought she may need to shorten the subject to possibly just the time after the confrontation with Mike. Then she thought with shortening it to this period may be difficult to only write 6 pages.

By the time school day ended Angie was completely drained, physically and psychologically. She was struggling from the pain from her injuries and from the psychological stress from this day at school. She said goodbye to her friends and went to her car, opened it and sat down. She closed the door and just sat there with her head against the headrest and closed her eyes. She thought to herself, "How could I have been so amiss about returning to school? Today was so draining." She sat there for what she thought was a few minutes when she was startled by a knock on the door window. She turned to look. It was Mr. Lewis.

Angie rolled down the window. "Is there a problem sir?"

Mr. Luis answered, "I stopped to see if you are alright. It's almost an hour after school let out."

"What? An hour? I thought I just took a deep breath and sat back for a few minutes. Maybe I fell asleep? Today was very draining both physically and psychologically for me sir."

"Did you have any problems with other students? Did anyone give you a hard time such as Gina or her friends?"

"Oh, no sir. Quite to the contrary. I did not expect most everyone in the school offering help and welcoming me back. I was just overwhelmed sir. I did not know how to react to this. And, no, Gina and her friends are my friends now. Somehow I said something to them and they apologized to Sherri, Karen and Janet. From what I was told it was very emotional encounter and they are now friends. The 6 of them even sent me a get well card, a balloon and the cutest little stuffed puppy." Angie told him.

"You got them to apologize? There are friends now? How did this happen? They were so much trouble. And the 6 of them sent you a card? Together?"

"Yes sir. And I sat with all of them at lunch today and it got so emotional that I cried and they all tried to console me, sir. And the whole school was like this as well. I expected to come back to just Sherri, Karen and Janet being my friends and everyone else being as before. I never could have thought everyone would be so cordial. I just sat back to reflect before I left. I believe I need to say thank you sir."

"To me? Why?" Mr. Luis asked.

"Because the school is a reflection of you, sir."

"OK, you're welcome. Are you OK to drive Angie?"

"Yes sir. I feel much better now, this little talk has helped. Thank you for your concern, sir. And, even with the things that happened in the past couple of weeks, after discussing it with my mother at length, I believe I made a good choice transferring to CDO. I really need to leave now sir. My parents will be worried."

"Ok Angie. Drive carefully. You will be here tomorrow then?"

"Oh course sir." Angie closed her window, started the Cuda and drove away.

Angie arrived home and told her parents about her day. She looked drained and Lizzy asked, "Would you care to have dinner in bed Honey?"

"That would be very nice mother, thank you. I could rest until then. Then I can finish my homework afterwards."

After dinner Angie completed her homework and began an outline for the paper for Composition. Then she slept.

Chapter 29

In the morning Angie prepared for school, had some break-fast and gathered her things, she said goodbye to her mother and father and left for school. This day was not much different from yesterday other than the expectation that others would show concern and offer help.

She met her friends at lunchtime as usual. Angie told them, "I am very grateful for your support and compassion, ladies. Yesterday I was painfully overwhelmed and I felt unusually vulnerable. I have never experienced these emotions in this manner and I was extremely apprehensive as a result. I could not drive home without first resting in my car. Today I continue to feel these same emotions only to a lesser degree. I do not know how to react to this. I feel as though I have lost my confidence." She had tears in her eyes again.

Sherri replied, "Angie, everyone feels like this sometimes. And you know that we are here to listen if you need to talk. I don't know if we could give you advice but we can all listen. I have never known anyone like you, Angie, you are strong and confident but you have a soft side."

Paula added, "Angie, I think we have all changed, in a good way, because of you. I feel like I am a different person than I was a few weeks ago."

"I know I'm ditsy a lot but you showed me that I should try to think before I open my mouth, if that makes and sense."

Denise said. "I don't know, that thing you said was like a slap in the face. I guess no one ever cared that much before."

Gina said, "Angie, I never really thought about a lot of things I said before. I just blabbed stuff out. I never thought about if I hurt anyone, I just never thought. You made me see what I bitch I was. You getting ticked at us the other day really opened my eyes. I felt more than embarrassed. So it isn't only you Angie, I feel a kind of pain too. And I'm sure I speak for everyone here, we are all in an uncomfortable place right now."

Karen and Janet didn't know what to say. Janet was rubbing Angie's shoulder, she didn't even realize she was doing that.

"I still do not understand how I had such a strong effect on all of you. But all of you have had an immense effect on me and you have shown me that friends are important. When I made the decision to go to CDO I was expecting that the teachers would be exceptional, and they are, but I just expected the students would be easier to talk to. I did not consider how this would affect my life. I understand no one could have predicted what happened with Mike. But meeting all of you and becoming friends, and the emotions I have been feeling," Her eyes were tearing up. "I never considered. I always like to be prepared and I was not prepared for any of this. I feel like I am exposed----almost like I am naked, I feel so many emotions and I do not know how to respond. I do not think I have ever been unprepared for anything." She was beginning to sound like she was losing it and her hands were visibly shaking.

Just then Sherri went over to Angie and put her arms around her. She said, "Oh Angie, you will be OK. A lot happened to you in such a short time it's amazing that you are doing so well. I think most people wouldn't be back at school yet. You are so brave to come back so soon. You should give yourself a break and relax. You are doing great. Tomorrow starts Christmas vacation so you will have more time to heal."

Karen said, "Didn't you say you do meditation when you train? You also worked out too right?"

Angie looked up, "yes."

"Well, maybe missing your workouts and meditation is contributing to how you feel. You said you have been training since you were 7 and that's a long time to do something and just have to stop." Karen said.

"Yea, I didn't think of that. Maybe you were able to use that to help cope with things and now you can't do it." Paula said.

Denise smiled and said, "That's got to be it! Kinda like what happens to a drug addict if they are cut off. Maybe it is kinda like withdrawal."

Angie looked at them and thought for a minute. "That is entirely possible. That is something else I did not consider. I have been so focused on trying to understand my feelings and all of the pain I have that I have forgotten to meditate. The training also helps but the meditation helps me to clear my thoughts. How could I have forgotten that? Thank you, all of you. I feel so much better now."

They all finished their lunches and went back to class. Angie was feeling much better. She thought to herself that she needs to go and see her Sensei after school.

After her last class she met her friends and wished them a very Merry Christmas and a Happy New Year. They all reciprocated. Angie got into her car, started it and drove off. She headed to the Dojo to see her Sensei.

She parked near the Dojo and went inside. Immediately her Sensei said, "Good see you. You better? I talk to Physical therapist. He say you still not work out. Come, we check your leg see how muscles feel." They walked over to a chair and Angie sat down. He took her leg and ran his hand up and down the top and sides of her leg. "Muscles very stiff. You need do stretch exercise. I discuss with therapist. He say I show you proper way stretch to help muscle without hurt. Do you have key for locker? You have workout clothes? You need out of jeans to do properly."

"Yes sir. I have my key I will go and change." Angie got up and went into the locker room. She took out her Gi and changed. She thought it felt great to change into her Gi, it felt like it was so long since she had worn these. She took her cloths and purse into the locker. She took her key and went back to her Sensei.

"Very good Angie. First sit." He told her. He pushed up the leg of her Gi pants then did this thing with his hands she had not seen. He clapped his hands together hard once then rubbed them together fast. (This is not an uncommon thing in the martial arts) Then he put his hands on her leg at the thickest part of the hamstring muscles. When he touched her skin she gasped because it was so hot but it felt good. "Yes hands hot, need warm up muscles first." He did this a few more times. "Stretches make good blood flow and soften scar tissue. You no stretch before heat up muscles, understand?"

"Yes Sensei."

"OK stand. Put heel on chair and slowly bend forward with body and put your hands on leg like this." He showered her. "Bend slow no do until hurts. No want hurt, hurt bad for muscles. Hold 5 seconds. Do 4 times. Now lay on back. Put this leg over other like this." He showed her. "Now slowly pull hurt leg to you. No want hurt, remember. Hold 5 seconds. Do 4 times. No want to bounce muscles, bounce bad. OK, now put legs straight, good. Lean front, ok if bend back. Remember no hurt. Very important. Hold 5 seconds. Do 4 times. Now rest I get rubber band." He got up and walked to a table and picked up a piece of stretch rubber. It looked like spandex. He sat down and put it around the ball of her foot on the leg that she hurt. "Put hands out with arms straight." Then he wrapped the piece around her hands and tied a knot. "Take rubber band in hands when sitting. Pull gently with leg straight. You want stretch muscles on back of leg. Do for 1 minute, relax do again. 4 times. OK stand."

Angie stood up.

"Take ankle in hand behind." He pulled her ankle up and put her hand on it. "Now pull lightly and hold 5 seconds. No pull too hard, no want pain. Do 4 times. Now wrap cold towel around leg muscles." He went and took a towel and wet it with cold water and wrung it out. He wrapped it around her leg. "Do like this. You do this every day for two week then come see me, OK Angie? Remember, every day. We want loosen muscles not hurt."

"Yes Sensei. I will do as you say, every day. I miss working out and I want to get back to it. You know by now, I will follow your instruction exactly."

"Very good. You be meditate?"

"I am sorry Sensei, with everything and all of my pain I forgot. I don't know how but I forgot. I have been in turmoil since this happened. I do not know how I forgot. You have taught me to do it whenever I feel stress but I forgot." She was embarrassed for forgetting and her face turned red.

"No worry just do Angie. Start meditation, it good for healing whole body. See you in two week, OK?"

"Yes Sensei, thank you for your time today."

"No need thank you, just do OK? And meditate."

Angie went into the room that they use for meditation. This room always calms her. It is filled with pillows, mats and low lever lights. The colors are all indigo, white and pink. She sat down and crossed her legs and put the back of her hands on her knees. She closed her eyes and relaxed. Her mind soon began to clear and she felt like she was floating. She held this position until she felt her mind was completely clear. She opened her eyes and took in the colors. She felt serine. She slowly got up. She had to do it slowly because of her rib pain.

She walked to the locker room and changed. As she left she said to Sensei, "Sayonara Sensei." And she went home. As she drove she felt much better than she had since the confrontation with Mike.

She walked into the house and Lizzy said, "Hello Angie. Did you stay late at school?"

"No mother, I went to the Dojo and had a talk with my Sensei. He showed me exercises to help loosen and heal my hamstring muscles. Then I meditated. I realized just how I missed my training and working out."

"You will get back in time Angie."

"Mother?

"Yes?"

"At lunch today I became very emotional again and the ladies reminded me that I had not been training and asked if I was meditating. I was shocked because I have forgotten to meditate throughout this whole ordeal."

"Really? You forgot? I thought you were meditating when you were alone so I did not think to ask. I was so involved in helping you understand. Now I understand why you have been so overly emotional, I thought it was only because of the trauma. How do you feel now?"

"Much better mother. I was tied in knots again after school. Oh, I need to do these exercises every day and go back to see my Sensei in two weeks. Seeing him brought back some of the confidence I felt I had lost during the past two days at school. I am going to go and take a shower before dinner."

After dinner Angie completed her homework and began an outline for the paper for Composition. Then she slept.

Chapter 30

Angie and Sherri talked on the phone the next morning, Saturday, the first day of Christmas Vacation. She told Sherri that she went to the DOJO after school and now has stretching exercises to do and she meditated. She told Sherri how much better she felt afterwards.

Angie then invited her for lunch and she accepted. When Sherri arrived Angie was reading a novel and listening to the Nutcracker Suite. Lizzy brought Sherri to Angie's room and knocked. "You may come in mother." Sherri entered. "Good Morning Sherri, you look lovely."

"Thank you Angie. You look much better than yesterday at school. What is this that you are listening to? It sounds familiar."

"This is the Nutcracker Suite by Tchaikovsky. I love this ballet. The next piece is the Pas de Deux and it is my favorite. This is so passionate it usually brings tears to my eyes"

"Really from classical music? I never really thought about classical like that. My mom listens to it all the time though."

"I love this especially in person as it is performed. The symphony plays and you feel like you are in the music. I have seen it with my family the last few years. It is incredible! Watching the ballet and hearing the music is wonderful. I am always moved from the experience."

"Wow! I never went to the ballet or heard a symphony in person. I sort of know the story of the nutcracker." Pas de

Deux began. "Is that an oboe? I love the sound of the oboe! My mom has music that is just an oboe."

"Yes Sherri, it is an oboe."

"It must be amazing to hear it live. I think I would love that."

"I am going with my family again this year. I would love it if you would join us. I am certain my mother and father would be delighted."

"Really? I would love to. But how much does it cost? I don't have much spending money, isn't ballet and the symphony expensive?"

"Do not worry about the cost Sherri, if you do not have enough I will cover it. I would be elated if you could join us. It is not so much the cost as it would mean so much to me to share your first experience seeing the Nutcracker Ballet your first time and your first experience hearing a symphony orchestra. The first time I experienced the Nutcracker it brought tears to my eyes. You need to experience the music and dance in person to understand why I am so excited!"

"I don't want to be a burden and I think I would be uncomfortable with you paying."

"OK," Angie thought for a minute, "then I will make it a gift to you for the unending support that you have given me since the incident with Mike. It would not be unlike the gifts and card all of you gave me before I returned to school. I very much want to do this for you. And afterwards my grandfather always takes everyone out for dinner to The Palomino restaurant. This may also be something new to you. And you will meet my family. I assure you that you will like them. You already know my cousin Bella."

"Well alright. I am not going to say I won't be uncomfortable because I don't really know anyone besides you. How do I dress for this? And when is it and where is it?"

"We are going Saturday late afternoon. That would be the 21st. It is at The Auditorium at The University of Arizona.

This year I am not going to dress as I usually have done. I have learned many things this year and I found that I enjoy dressing very feminine for special occasions. Do you have a nice dress you could wear?"

"Yes. I have one that I use for special occasions. This is going to be fun! I would love to see you dressed like you say. I can't picture how you would look dressed like that but I would love to see."

Just then Lizzy came and said, "Lunch is served ladies."

"Thank you mother."

Sherri said, "Thank you ma'am" as they walked to the dining room.

They walked into the dining room. "Aunt Maria, I was not aware you would be here. How nice. Aunt Maria may I present my friend, Sherri. Sherri this is my Aunt Maria."

"It is a pleasure to meet you ma'am."

Maria smiled and said, "It is a pleasure to meet you as well Sherri." They all sat down.

Maria looked at Angie and said, "You have been teaching Sherri how to be a lady Angelina, very well done."

"Actually, Sherri has picked this up from interacting with mother and me."

"I am impressed." Marie replied. She looked at Sherri and said, "Sherri your response is very impressive. You have learned the beginnings of becoming lady, my dear."

"Thank you for the complement, Ma'am." Sherri replied.

"Sherri is Angelina's friend from school. I have been impressed by her since the first time we met."

"Mother, I have invited Sherri to join our family for the Nutcracker. I trust you do not mind."

"That is wonderful dear. Sherri, have you been to the ballet?"

"No Ma'am. And I haven't been to the symphony either."

"I believe you will be touched and moved by the performance. It is a powerful experience particularly your first time."

"I am looking forward to the experience, Ma'am. Angelina told me about the reaction she had the first time and I am eager myself. Ma'am, I would like to say this table is wonderful! I have not seen anything so beautiful."

"Thank you Sherri. Since this is the first time Angelina has had a friend for lunch I wanted it to be special. Maria came to assist me."

"Thank you mother and Aunt Maria, this is a wonderful surprise.

Lizzy set the table with her fine china and flatware and linen napkins. She had the napkins in napkin holders on each plate. She had prepared a simple lunch of sandwiches made on French bread; homemade baked sweet potato fries and homemade coleslaw. She made iced tea to drink.

They all talked about many things. Lizzy and Maria learned about how Angie and Sherri met and how Gina, Paula and Denise apologized and then became friends. Sherri said, "I feel so fortunate that I met Angelina and the both of you. It has made a wonderful impression on me and I feel that it has changed me in a way that I never would have believed."

Maria Asked, "How has meeting us impressed on you Sherri?"

"Well, Before meeting Angelina I was just a girl that felt depressed and alone because of what Mike did to me. And meeting Angelina made me understand that this was just me doing this to myself. I feel like she showed me the way by giving me hope. I never knew anyone with such confidence. I love how she is so courteous and understanding and not afraid to express how she feels. She has taught me something I never knew I wanted, and that is how to be a lady. Then I met you, ma'am, the day we came to visit Angelina and I knew then I wanted to learn how to speak properly and act properly. And now meeting you, Ma'am," She looked at Maria, "I know in my heart that it is the right thing to do."

Maria looked surprised, "Angelina, you continually astonish me! And Sherri, I understand now why Angelina is fond of you. May I ask what it was that Mike did to you that caused you so much anguish?"

"You may ma'am. This was why Gina, Paula and Denise had been harassing us. I was afraid to talk about this but it is another thing that Angelina gave me the confidence to put this behind me. Mike raped me at knife point along with my two friends Janet and Karen. And no one did anything about it. So we were left to suffer alone."

"Oh, that must have been dreadful and painful for all of you. I can see how you felt alone. I feel so sad for you dear." Maria said. "And Angelina, you helped her to begin healing." Maria had tears in her eyes and carefully blotted them with her napkin. "You are an amazing lady! There are many times my mother would be so proud, god bless her sole." Maria crossed herself.

"Thank you ma'am and the little Angelina has told me about her, she sounds like she was an amazing lady."

"There is so much you do not know about my grandmother and my aunt and father. One day I will tell you as to me it is not unlike a fairy tale."

"I would like that Angelina. And possibly I won't feel so uncomfortable meeting your family if they are half as accepting, I don't think that is the best word, as your mother and aunt."

"Sherri you are very sweet." Maria said.

"Thank you, Ma'am."

They continued talking and finished lunch. Angie excused herself and Sherri. Sherri said to Aunt Maria, "It was very nice to meet you ma'am." And they left and went to Angie's room.

Saturday came and Angie began dressing. Lizzy let her pick another of her gowns and she looked as beautiful as she did at thanksgiving. At this time she no longer had the dressing on her cheek and the black eyes were mostly faded.

Sherri arrived and she was met by Dominic at the door. He introduced himself and brought her to where Angie and Lizzy were getting ready.

"Hello Mrs. Tucci and Angelina. Mrs. Tucci, you look very beautiful!"

"Angie said she would be out in a minute. She is just brushing her hair. And thank you Sherri, you are very sweet. And you are beautiful as well. That is a lovely gown you have on."

"Thank you Mrs. Tucci, for the complement. This is my mothers and she thought I should wear it because this is the first time for me to go to the ballet and to hear the symphony. She wanted me to feel comfortable with your family."

"Sherri, it is obvious you mother is a lady as well and cares about the impression that you make. I am impressed."

Angie came into the bedroom and said, "Sherri, you look very beautiful! I love the gown."

"Thank you for the complement Angelina, I almost don't recognize you. What an amazing transformation! I don't know what to say besides you look like a model!"

"Thank you that is a very nice complement as well Sherri. And I am beginning to feel that I am beautiful, I never believed it."

"I kind of feel like this is a dream. I am so excited and a little afraid."

"Why are afraid Sherri?" Lizzy asked.

"Well, I have never been to anything like this before and I don't know most of your family. I want to make a good impression. And I am worried that they won't accept me because I am not, ah, rich."

"You need not be frightened Sherri, our family is very excepting and we treat everyone with respect."

"Thank you for your encouragement Mrs. Tucci. But I am still feeling uncertain. This is all new to me."

"You will be fine Sherri, I promise." Angie said. "I understand your apprehension but soon you will see it is unnecessary."

"If you say so." Sherri said. She was beginning to become very apprehensive and was beginning to sweat.

Dominic came in and said that they should be leaving so they won't be late. "My, It is unbelievable, I am surrounded by 3 of the most beautiful women in Tucson!"

Sherry blushed, Angelina and Elizabeth both said thank you. The three ladies then picked up their purses and walked out following Dominic. They got into Lizzy's car and drove to meet the rest of the family at the Auditorium at the U of A.

They parked and went in. Everyone else was there already. Angie took the liberty to begin to introduce Sherri to everyone. Right away Bella came to say hello to Sherri since she knew her from school. Bella said, "Hello Sherri, you look lovely today. I am happy that you could share this with our family. Everyone is excited for you."

"Thank you Bella that was sweet of you to say."

Just then Shelly came up and hugged Sherri and said, "I am Shelly, Angelina's cousin. I am pleased you could come."

"Thank you Shelly." Sherri said. She wasn't sure how to act. She met Rosa and Edward as well.

Angie said, "Try to relax Sherri. It is time to go in and take out seats. You will be able to meet everyone else possibly at intermission."

Everyone began to enter and find their seats. Shelly came up and said to Angie and Sherri that she has the tickets for the two of them, Bella, Rosa and herself. She wanted to make sure that they all sat together. "The music is so passionate Sherri, I brought a small packet of tissues for all of us. Angelina said you have not been to the ballet or symphony. I believe you may be overwhelmed, I was my first time. And do not be afraid to cry, we all do at some parts."

Angie whispered to Sherri, "My whole family is like this, you will see." Just then the lights went down and the Overture began.

Sherri was already feeling the music. The curtain opened and the ballet began. She thought it was wonderful. As it progressed Sherri began to feel emotions from the music and ballet she never felt. She was impassioned. Soon it was inter-mission. Bella leaned over immediately and asked Sherri if she was enjoying it. Sherri almost couldn't answer. She was teary-eyed. Bella smiled because she knew just how Sherri felt.

Sherri looked at Angie and said, "This is so amazing, I, I don't know how to describe it."

Angie said, "I am so happy you are enjoying it, Sherri." The 5 ladies talked throughout intermission. Lizzy, Lilly, Kristina and Maria were all noticing this. Lizzy said that she thought that Angelina has made a wonderful friend. She said to Lilly that it is like a dream come true that all of the women were dressed in gowns for the first time at the ballet, and how Sherri seemed to fit right in.

The lights flashed signaling intermission was ending and everyone took their seats. Act II began. Sherri was completely enthralled. When Pas de Deux began she remembered that this was Angie's favorite. Hearing it played by the symphony in person she understood why. It was so passionate she had tears in her eyes again. She couldn't believe how music could have such a profound effect on her. When it was over Sherri needed to compose herself. She was choked up.

Everyone walked to the lobby and gathered together. When Joseph saw that everyone was there he went over to Angelina and said, "Are you not going to introduce me to your friend Angelina?"

"Don't tease Grandfather. May I present Sherri, my friend from school, Sherri this is my Grandfather Joseph." Angie said.

"I am pleased to meet you sir." Sherri said and held her hand out. Angie had been coaching Sherri on how to be proper with her family.

Joseph said, "It is a pleasure to meet you as well Sherri."

Angie brought her around to meet everyone. Afterwards they got into their cars and drove to the Palomino Restaurant. Sherri had never been to such a fancy restaurant before but watched as everyone was seated. She had never had someone place the napkin over her lap and push her chair in. She thought to herself that she could easily get used to this.

The dinner went well and Sherri was amazed at the extra care that was given at a high end restaurant. She had seen this in movies but never thought that it could be like this in real life.

Angie felt a kind of pride that she had made such a good friend and that she interacted so well with her family. Until this year she had not known what she had missed by not having friends. It was as if her life had never been complete. Then she wondered if she would feel like this again when she met the man she would marry. She hoped it would be something like her mother and father experienced.

Angie had never thought like this before. She knew that one day she would get married and have a family but she never thought of it in this way in the past. The more she thought the more she wondered if this was also another thing stimulated by the whole incident with Mike. Maybe she was thinking more of her emotional future than previously. This would be the subject of another discussion with her mother and the thought came to her, and maybe a discussion with Sherri. She was thinking that it would be nice to hear the prospective of someone her age. Then it dawned on her that this was what her father had told her.

Chapter 31

The Christmas and New Year's Eve holidays went very well. Angie wore a gown for Christmas this year. For Christmas the family rotates which family member has the gathering and this year it was Aunt Maria. This year it too was somewhat different for Angie because she dressed in a gown instead of her jeans and sweater. She had realized she was beginning to love the holidays much more now.

New Year's Eve was another new experience for Angie. She had always celebrated with her parents. This year she celebrated with Sherri; Karen; Janet; Gina; Denise and Paula. Sherri had the celebration at her house. They all had a good time, watched late night movies, ate pizza and slept over at Sherri's.

After Christmas Vacation school was back and the big thing was the papers that were due for Mrs. White's class. Angie was a little embarrassed because she couldn't keep her paper to only 6 pages. When she turned it in to Mrs. White, she told her that she spent many hours trying to shorten her paper. She explained that she began writing about her transition to CDO and her outline was 10 pages alone. Then she shortened it to returning to school after a traumatic experience and her outline was 6 pages. She continued to explain that she felt that the biggest change came from making friends, so she only wrote about this. With it condensed down her paper was 11 pages.

Angie titled her paper, *"How Making Friends Changed My Life."* She told Mrs. White that this was a difficult paper because how emotionally tied she was to the story. Mrs. White told her not to let it worry her, that a few extra pages wouldn't be a problem. She said, "Angelina, from what I know about you from this year so far, I know your paper will likely be the most interesting one to read."

Angie said, "Thank you so much for the complement, Ma'am."

A week later while Mrs. White returned the graded papers, she announced to the class, "I have an announcement to make about one of the papers turned in. I have a friend that works for the Tucson Citizen, and I showed him this particular paper because I was touched by the story. He would like to print it in the Tucson Citizen, of course with the writers' permission.

The students were all looking around wondering whose paper this was. Angie was wondering as well. Mrs. White said, "This paper touched me because it showed me that there is compassion within this school. The title of the paper is, "How Making Friends Changed My Life" and it was written by Angelina Tucci."

Angie was shocked! She knew that she wrote well but never thought her school paper could be published. Everyone looked at Angie and had comments such as, "That's so great!" "Angie you so deserve this." "I am so happy for you" and so on. Angie was blushing. This was another thing that was new to her. She said, "Thank you everyone. And I have to say I wrote this about this school, so everyone really has a part in this story. I wrote about my new friends, how I met them, how I was treated and how I was overwhelmed by everyone in this school when I came back after recovering from my injuries. I would be honored to have my paper published in the Tucson Citizen Mrs. White." By this time Angie was in tears. She couldn't believe it.

Mrs. White also said, "My friend also wanted to know if he could interview you. He would like to write a story to go along with the paper and he said you would determine what would be included. He said he understands that what happened was traumatic and he only wants to get a better view of your time at CDO."

Angie agreed. Mrs. White said she never gave anyone a 100% on a paper but she couldn't find anything wrong with the writing, punctuation or grammar so this is a first for her.

As what generally happens in high school this got around the school very quickly. After class, this was the last class of the day; everyone surrounded her as if she was a big celebrity. Sherri hugged Angie and told her she was so happy for her. Angie was finding it somewhat easier to emotionally deal with the attention she was getting. And Mr. Luis was there and shook Angie's hand and told her that he was proud to have her there at CDO and that this was proud to have a students' paper published.

Angie arranged a time when she was the least busy to interview with the reporter. They talked for over an hour and she left feeling good about what he would write.

Angie discussed her paper being published in the Tucson Citizen with her parents. She decided that she wasn't going to say anything to her family. She wanted to see their reaction from reading it first. She also discussed it with Bella and Rosa. They had already told their mother, Aunt Maria, but were able to tell her that Angie didn't want anyone else to know. She agreed.

The following week there was an article about a student at CDO with her paper printed in whole beginning on the front page. Lizzy began getting calls from family members about the article. And her sister, mother and Aunt Maria said they got all teary eyed when they read Angie's paper. They had not understood just how life changing it was for Angie to make her first friends.

During the first week of January Angie and Lizzy went to the follow up appointment with the dermatologist. He was very happy with how Angie's cheek healed. There was a very faint scar and only from the deepest part of the wound. He suggested that it would take 2 chemical peels to remove it completely. They began immediately. This was the only visible thing remaining from the incident with Mike. You could see very little of the ligature marks on her wrists and ankles. However, her ribs continued to be sore and tender. This would take months to completely heal.

By March the second chemical peal was mostly healed, and Angie couldn't see where the scar was. This made her feel extremely happy. Soon she could put the whole saga behind her. She was back at the Dojo working out, but still was not sparing due to her ribs. She had gained full use of her right leg muscles and was working on her reverse 360 deg. roundhouse again. Her Sensei told her she should not have been hurt if she had done it correctly. He worked with her to tighten up the tone and form of her reverse 360 deg. roundhouse.

The first Sunday in March Angie finally was able to make her first run in the Cuda at the track. Her whole family was there, Sherri, Karen, Janet, Gina, Paula and Denise were all there. And as a surprise, all of the guys from the shop came as well. And Angie didn't know until after the racing was finished that Jim and his mother were also there, but he was in a wheelchair.

Dominic had Angie's helmet painted Panther pink with flames and had "Angelina" lettered on it in script and in gold leaf and pinstriped. He was able to do this without her knowing. When they got to the track and everyone arrived, he presented it to her. Angie got teary eyed and said, "Thank you so much father, I must be the luckiest girl alive!" and she gave him a big hug.

She entered Eliminations (bracket racing) and over the past months she and Dominic made some modifications to the Cuda. They added full length tuned headers with cut outs, hotter cams, modified the carbs and Dominic had the heads cleaned up with pocket porting, manifold port matching and a 5-angle valve job. She ran with slicks, narrower tires in front, open headers and velocity stacks. She was able to make 3 practice runs and dialed in at 12.35. It wasn't a busy day so there weren't many cars.

She did her burnout and staged against a stock 427 Corvette. The lights came down she was first out of the hole and ran a 12:38 @ 121 MPH beating the Corvette. Second, she raced a 1970 383 Demon. She won again with a 12.37 @ 122 MPH. All afternoon no one could beat her. At the end of the afternoon the final race was the two remaining cars. Angie's Cuda and a 429 Mustang. Both of them were running a few tenths of a second above dial in so this would be close. She wondered if the Mustang's driver was worried that he could lose to a girl.

They staged. The lights came down and the Mustang red lighted. Angie ran a 12.35 @ 123 MPH, her exact dial in! Angie won! She got a trophy and some money and pictures with her father and the track owner. Many of the guys racing that day came and congratulated her for running so well. Her family was ecstatic. Even Edward was cheering her on. Later on, Edward told Angie he thought she was just lifting one of the front tires off of the ground when she came out of the hole. He even asked Angie if he could help next time she raced. Angie's family wanted a picture with her beside to her car along with the trophy and her friends had a picture taken with her beside her car along with the trophy. They all wanted a copy. All the guys from the shop wanted their picture with Angie beside the Cuda with her holding the trophy. Later they got the picture blown up and framed and they hung it at the shop in the show-room for everyone to see. Then Angie saw Jim. She walked over and said hello and leaned over and gave Jim a hug. "Thank you for coming Jim."

Jim said, "My mom didn't think I should go anywhere yet, but I wanted to see you race. Do you think I could get a picture of you with your car Angie? It would help me to put everything that has happened behind me. and...." He hesitated.

Angie asked, "And what Jim?"

"Well, I would have a picture of the most beautiful girl in school and someone I now look up to."

"I do not know what to say Jim. Of course, you may have a picture. How about we get a picture of you and me next to my car? It would give me a picture of the person that saved my life. I will never forget that Jim."

"You would do that? I was so mean to you." Jim said.

"Jim, you have changed since then. Admitting what you had done is the first step in your new life. And it would give me a picture of my new friend." Angie said.

Jim looked choked up.

Angie said to Jim's mom, "Thank you for bringing him Mrs. Parker."

"It was my pleasure, Angelina. It was interesting watching you race. I never saw this kind of racing and I found it invigorating." Mrs. Parker replied.

"I am delighted that you enjoyed it Mrs. Parker. Come with me Jim," Angie grabbed the handles of his wheelchair and rolled him to her car. She asked if she could get one additional picture. The photographer said absolutely.

A few months later Angie graduated from High School with a 4.0 grade average. And soon afterwards she took the first of many ASE certification tests and passed. She became the first female mechanic in Tucson to be ASE certified.

From there Angie worked with her father and with the artistic help from Sherri to make up a new ad for the shop. It had a picture of Angie in uniform with the ASE patch visible along with her CUDA in the background with a few trophies on the hood saying, "Come to Dom's Automotive and Performance Center and see me, Angie, an ASE Certified Mechanic, to get your car or light truck repaired properly or for performance modifications." This worked out well. Dominic had this painted on some bus stop seat backs; 2 billboards and a few newspaper ads. People were coming in just to see Angie.

The other shop mechanics didn't want Angie to have all of the attention, so they all began getting ASC certifications as well. Soon Dominic had a sign made up that read "All mechanics ASE Certified" that he had mounted just below the main sign.

When Angie decided to go to CDO she had no idea that this decision would be life changing. Even though she suffered some great psychical and emotional pain from this she also believed that she grew tremendously. And she believed that making friends was the high point of the year and the most positive experience of her life

Chapter 1 (Preview)

Sept 1975

After High School graduation Angie needed to readjust because she no longer needed to be studying every day. She read more books on engine swapping and auto repair in general. This didn't fill much time or really occupy her mind. She read more crime novels but these didn't take much time or occupy her mind either. She needed something more complex to keep her mind occupied as she always wanted to be learning something and did not like to sit idle.

She worked at her Father's shop, Dom's Automotive and Performance Center, from opening to closing Monday through Saturday. She continued Martial Arts training on Monday's and Wednesday's from 6 PM to 8 PM. However she now had quite a bit of time to fill.

The weather had been warm, in the upper 80's to upper 90's and clear to partly cloudy. It was beautiful weather for this time of year as it is the beginning of the monsoon season.

Angie visited with her friends in the evenings during the week every few days. They got together and went shopping, watched TV, went out to eat and talked. One time while they were together and talking Angie appeared to get what looked like an electric shock. This was like when you get a big static shock. Her friends noticed this time. Usually she was able to cover these up but not this time. Gina asked, "Are you OK Angie? You looked like you just got a shock."

"I am fine Gina, thank you. There are times I get a vision of something popping into my head. It does not seem to mean anything however."

"What do you mean a vision?"

"I just saw a screaming adolescent girl that is all. It probably does not mean anything. I was just startled, that is all." Angie replied.

"That's so weird. You just see stuff like that?"

"Yes, it is just a picture and no one I know. I just think it is some memory of something I saw in the past." She was becoming slightly apprehensive about these visions. They didn't show her anything other a distressed young adolescent girl. But she couldn't think of anything that had happened in her life that could contribute to something traumatic. Outside of the incident with Mike she could not think of anything. She felt as though she couldn't have asked for a childhood any better that she had. She kept thinking about this. She had good parents that always supported her and helped her whenever she had a problem. They were always there for her to listen or explain things, so it couldn't be her parents. She thought about her Grandfather Joseph and Grandmother Kristina and could not think of a time that she had been angry at them. She thought the same about her aunts and cousins. She thought this couldn't be it. What could be causing her to see these visions she wondered.

One Saturday afternoon at closing time Angie's Grandfather Joseph stopped by to talk to her at the shop. "Hello Grandfather." She went and gave him a hug. "What brings you here? Car trouble?"

"Hello Angelina, I came to see you."

"You came to work see me? Why?"

"Now that you are working full time I wanted to have a discussion about building a portfolio."

"Grandfather, have you been reading my mind? I had just been thinking about this and thought I would visit you to discuss this."

"Is that so?"

"Yes Grandfather. I know you do so well investing and I know that is how you and Grandmother became wealthy. I have admired your ability to invest since I learned what that means. I thought that maybe you could assist me with this. I know you have been assisting Father and he appears to be satisfied with how he is doing. But I would not know where to begin. I want to build for my future, possible buy my own house and maybe retire early."

"That is wonderful Angelina. I did not know you had thought this way. If I had known that I could have been working with you already. You never cease to amaze me."

They went into the break room and sat down. He went over some strategies and explained that she would need a broker to buy and sell for her. He explained how to watch the market and what to look for to determine when to buy and when to sell. He also suggested that he could show her when she decides to begin. He suggested that she could come to his office once a week after work and they could begin. She told him that she would open an account at the bank and each pay day she could put a portion of her pay into it. Then she would use this for investments only. They agreed on an amount for the deposits. Then she would go to his office and he would begin to show her how to begin.

Angie decided that Tuesday's would be perfect because she trains on Mondays and Wednesdays and received her pay check every Friday. Angie chose the following Tuesday to begin.

Joseph was impressed. He left thinking how forward thinking Angelina was. As he drove home he thought that he would surprise her on Monday night with some money for her to get started. He thought a gift of $1000 would be sufficient to make her first investment.

When Tuesday came Joseph went to his bank and withdrew $1000 to give to Angie when she arrived. He thought that he could go with her to the bank to open an account for her. About 5:00 the doorbell rang. Kristina went to answer it. "Angelina! This is a nice surprise."

"Hello Grandmother." She gave her a tight hug. "I am here to see Grandfather. He is going to teach me about investing."

"That is wonderful Angelina! I did not know you had interest in investing."

"I have admired Grandfather's ability since I knew what it meant to invest and since I am working full time now I have the means to begin." They were walking towards Joseph's office.

"I am impressed! This is another surprise! Your Grandfather will be a good teacher. Do you know he has been helping you father invest?"

"Yes Grandmother, I have known since he began. I have been waiting for the time I would be able to begin as well."

Kristina knocked on the door. "Yes, you may come in." Joseph said.

Kristina walked in along with Angie. "Hello Angelina. Come here. I set a chair for you here next to me so you can see what I am doing."

"I will leave the two of you." Kristina left and closed the door behind her.

"Angelina, I have decided to give you some money to help you begin investing." He opened his center desk drawer and pulled out an envelope and handed to Angie. "This is for you to deposit when you open your account."

"Thank you Grandfather. You are so generous." She opened the envelope. "$1000!" She immediately stood and hugged him and gave him a kiss on his cheek. "I cannot believe this! I opened a new savings account last week and transferred some money from my existing savings account. Here is my passbook." She handed it to him.

"$5000? I wasn't aware you had saved so much."

"I have been saving a little her and there then I began working full time. I only have my car, insurance gas and registration and whatever I need for spending for the week. The rest I have been putting in my savings account. I believe Father pays me almost as much as the seasoned mechanics. He told me I was well worth every penny. I left myself about $1200 in my other account in case I need something. I am very serious about investing. I would love to be in a position such as you and Grandmother later in life."

"Angelina, you have impressed me again. Now you have another $1000 to add. I believe you will do well."

Joseph worked with Angie for about an hour and he showed her some stocks to begin her portfolio. These were stable ones such as AT&T; Kodak; IBM. He started an account with the broker he uses and explained what she should watch and how to determine what to buy. It was almost equivalent to a class in school. She loved this. She had many new things to learn, which was something that she felt she needed.

Joseph could not be more proud. "You know you father has told me quite a bit about your grandparents. I believe they would be very proud Angelina. When I think about it I find it incredible. Just you alone, your grades throughout school, your hard work at you father's shop, your racing and your ability to defend yourself and your overall attitude, I almost cannot believe it."

Angie had tears in her eyes. She looked up to her Grandfather for as long as she could remember. He was always strong and she believed a good role model. She admired him for his ability to manage money. "Thank you Grandfather, I am proud of you as well. You and Grandmother have always been good role models for me. I need to leave for today. Thank you again for your help and for your gift. I love you so much!"

"I love you as well." They hugged. She left and closed the office door as she went out. She looked for Kristina so she could say goodbye.

"Angelina, you're leaving already?"

"Yes Grandmother, I need to get home for dinner. Mother is holding it for me." They hugged each other. "I love you Grandmother."

I love you as well sweetheart." Kristina hugged her back.

Angie also has been thinking about projects she could do related to her passion for cars. She felt that any project could teach her something new, particularly if it was something that they haven't done at the shop yet. She still craved new knowledge and since she was not studying for school she needed another way to learn. One thing she thought would be nice would be to add air conditioning to the Cuda. Now that she is using it as her every day driver and driving it quite a bit more than when she had been going to high school, air conditioning would be a benefit on the 100+ degree summer days and through the monsoon season in Tucson. She discussed this with her father and the guys at the shop and they all thought this could be a nice addition for the car. "A Panther Pink HEMI Cuda with air would be sweet." Eric said. (Eric was the 5th mechanic Dominic hired)

Dominic talked to many of the racers and some of the guys that came into the shop for performance parts. He told them that he was looking for a junkyard Cuda that had factory air conditioning. It didn't take long before Dominic received a list of a few junk yards that had Cudas.

Dominic contacted the junk yards and chose one recommended by a racer friend because he said this place will guarantee to gather every part required. Dominic made a deal for all of the necessary parts including the dashboard, ducting, wiring, compressor, condenser hoses and all of the other pieces needed to convert a non-air conditioned car to an air conditioned car. They would remove all of the necessary parts, package and ship the parts to the shop.

Angie spent quite a bit of time at a Plymouth dealer parts department looking through parts books to determine what all of the parts were and where they would go and how they fit together. The exploded drawings helped her the most. The only issue was that HEMI cars did not come with air conditioning so they would need to modify the brackets for the compressor. The parts they ordered from the junkyard were from a 440 Cuda.

Since Angie was working every day now she was getting to know the regular customers. And there were racers that came in often to buy parts or to get advice on modifications. Usually they talked to Dominic but a few wanted to talk to Angie since she had been running so well at the track.

Every so often one of these guys would ask Angie out on a date but she always politely told them that she wasn't interested in dating at this point. One guy, Rich, asked, "Angie, would you like to get together sometime?"

"Rich, I am flattered that you asked but the truth is that I am not interested in dating now. But thank you for asking."

The next time Rich came in he asked again but differently, "Hello Angie, Would you like to go somewhere after work to just talk cars? I would like to hear about how you launch so hard. I'm really not looking for a girlfriend. I would just like to be friends."

"As I have said many times Rich, I appreciate the offer but I have definite plans for the next few years and they do not include any male friends or boyfriends. I do not want to be tempted which could significantly alter my plans. I trust you can understand this."

"I guess, if you say so." He was disappointed. But he honored her wishes although he didn't understand. He walked away wondering what plans she could have that would keep her from having a boyfriend. He did however talk about this with a few of his friends. They all told him the same thing. A few of them had asked her and they had been turned down as well.

One day Rich was looking through the books in one of the racks as Angie was standing at the counter filling out some paperwork. She appeared to get what looked like an electric shock. Her demeanor changed immediately. She looked at him oddly and he took that as she needed help. He told her he would help her to a chair. She sat and looked lost in thought for a minute.

"Are you OK Angie? Should I get you father?" Rich asked.

After a minute or so she said, "No, I am fine thank you. It was just an odd feeling." She stood, "Thank you Rich for helping me to a chair. I get these sometimes but I do not think it is anything to worry about. I need to get back to work if you will excuse me please." She left him and went back into the shop.

Angie thought to herself that she hoped these visions do not happen too often. She saw a few distressed kids now, but they could be any kids anywhere. She thought it was maybe because she did not sleep well the previous night. She shrugged it off and continued to work.

The shop had been very busy lately which kept all of the mechanics busy. She found that when she was very busy with a job that required her to concentrate she didn't have these visions. She thought about this for some time. She decided that she needs to have a clear head to have these visions. Maybe she could control the visions by doing or studying about something enough to keep her mind completely occupied. She thought that this may be the key to control when she has these visions, especially since she has been getting these at times where she may need to explain herself.

In about a week and a half the crate with the parts from the wrecked Barracuda arrived. Angie and Dominic carefully laid everything out on the floor and Angie cleaned them all up. Angie, Dominic and Scott (besides being a mechanic he is also a fabricator) took the compressor to the Cuda and looked at how the brackets would need to be modified to fit the HEMI. They took measurements and cut the brackets and Angie would then need to make sketches of the pieces that needed to be fabricated. Scott would then show her how to make them and weld them together. Angie remained at work after closing a few nights to clean and paint some of the greasier pieces, make the sketches and verify the measurements for the pieces for the compressor brackets. She had stayed late a few evenings in the past and also the last few nights so Dominic was not worried that she would have any problems. Everyone had left and she was the only one in the shop. She verified that all of the doors were locked and then locked the last one when Dominic went home. Earlier she had parked the Cuda just inside the overhead door and had the hood open to take measurements. She walked over to the Cuda a few times to work on the cardboard cutouts of the new pieces for the compressor bracket that she had made. The last time she was walking over to the Cuda she happened to look around and she felt a little spooked. She looked around again. The shop looked normal except that there was no one else there. She saw movement in the corner of her eye in the shadows. She looked but there was nothing there. She whispered to herself, "What is spooking me tonight? I have not felt like this the last few times I stayed alone." She took the cardboard pieces and fitted them over a few studs that stuck out and they fit. The other pieces fit just as she had visioned. She thought, "That was not that difficult." She picked up the pieces and closed the hood. She turned to walk back to the office and she felt chilled, just enough to make her shiver a little. She had not realized that the shop was damp and she had an eerie feeling. "Snap out of it Angie," she said to herself. "There is nothing here that is not here during the day. Maybe I am just tired." She walked back to the office and shut off the shop lights as she past the switches. She stopped and looked back. "Nothing there." Then she realized she had said that out loud. She shook her head back and forth as she walked into the office.

It was about 9:00 PM when Angie had finished putting everything away, closed and locked the office and stopped in the bathroom. She finished, washed and dried her hands. As she was reaching for the door knob and hesitated. "What is wrong with me?" She shook it off shut off the light and opened the door. She walked out and almost walked into one of two guys that had just broken in looking for things to steal. This shocked both her and them. Immediately the guy that was behind her and grabbed her around the arms and the other was going to punch her to try and knock her out. Immediately she used the first guy's hold on her to lift her legs and she kicked the other guy in the face quite hard with her right foot. He fell backwards across the room into the chairs next to the table and some chairs fell over him.

Then she moved her head forward and slammed it back and hit the nose of the guy holding her. He screamed and let her go. She knew this causes quite a bit of pain and usually makes the eyes water. Angie turned and kicked the guy that just let go of her in the chest and he fell backwards out through the break room door and onto the floor. This knocked the wind out of him. He was gasping for air. She turned to see the other guy start rushing her. His nose was bleeding. He tried to punch her and she blocked it, grabbed his wrist and pulled then slammed her forearm into the guy's arm and broke it. This is a classic Aikido move. He screamed in pain and stepped back a few steps in shock.

The first guy caught his breath, got up and pulled out a big knife, "So you're the karate girl. You can't be that good. I saw the news. I know it was all bullshit. They're two of us you lose. Ha ha." He swung the knife trying to cut her stomach but she quickly stepped back and kicked his arm in the same direction that he swung the knife then grabbed his head to make him continue to spin and at the same time kicked out his left leg. He fell hard and screamed then didn't move. He fell on his knife and she thought it had killed him.

Then Angie turned and the second guy had recovered somewhat from the broken arm enough and screamed, "You killed him! Now you are going to die." He reached into his jacket pocket and pulled out a revolver and Angie kicked his arm to the side with a forward roundhouse using her right foot just as he fired the gun and he shot the wall. She spun around and as she came around she cocked her elbow and snapped it back with all of her strength and hit him directly in his left temple. His head slammed against the wall and knocked a big hole through the drywall. Then he bounced the opposite direction and fell over slamming the other side of his head hard on the edge of a table gashing the skin and tipping it over. He landed with his arms limp and his eyes wide open. Blood was running out of the gash.

Angie ran to the phone and dialed 911. The 911 operator said, "Hello 911 what is your emergency?"

"This is Angie Tucci at Dom's Automotive and Performance Center 847 N. Stone; I am being attacked by multiple armed guys that broke in. Please help." Then she slammed the receiver down. When she returned to the guy that stabbed himself, she found that he had pulled out the knife and managed to stand. He looked at Angie and raised his arm with the knife and she got in position and did a 360 degree reverse roundhouse to the side of his head. He went down slamming the side of his head on a table edge so hard that it cracked the plywood top. As he fell the hand that he was holding the knife hit the floor and twisted. It stabbed him again as he fell. Blood was running out of the gash in his head and from the knife wound. She was positive he was dead now. She thought it was over and began to relax and realize what just happened. She began to shake and her legs were beginning to feel like rubber.

Angie heard sirens and made her way to the light switches for the shop and turned the lights back on. She was shocked to see a third guy running towards her from the back door. She immediately focused and ran towards him, jumped and did a side kick to his face. His head snapped back and he fell backwards onto the floor and skidded a few feet. Just as she landed he sat up, shook it off and started to get up. Angie thought that he must have been high on something because this should have at least stunned him. She ran a few steps towards him then jumped and kicked him in the face again before he was on his feet and he went down again, this time much harder and when his head hit the floor it sounded like a bowling ball hitting the floor. She landed past him and as she turned he sat up, shook his head a little and stood. He reached into his jacket pocket and began to pull out a gun. The instant she saw the gun she spun and did a 360 reverse roundhouse to the side of his head and made certain her boot heal hit him right in the temple. His eyes went blank and he fell over like a bag of potatoes and slammed the other side of his head on the corner of the battery charger. He hit it so hard that it bent the wheel bracket on that side of the battery charger and it tipped over. He landed on the floor with a kind of slapping sound. He didn't move. Blood was running out of his head from the gash he received from hitting the battery charger. She had been working with her sensei on this kick since the incident with Mike almost a year ago and has perfected it. Her spin is incredibly fast, her body tight and she now can deliver a lethal blow to whatever she targets, and without injuring herself.

Just as she was doing the 360 degree reverse roundhouse Lieutenant Edwards came through the back door where the guys had broken in. He witnessed Angie spin and hit the guy and he saw him going down. It made a loud bang when his head hit the battery charger. She turned around and jumped into her stance again ready to attack. Lieutenant Edwards said out loud, "Angie, its Lieutenant Edwards. Angie it's me." Angie took small steps towards Lieutenant Edwards to take aim at him she was full of adrenalin and did not recognize the Lieutenant. She was in her stance her eyes were wide open and had her right hand in a fist cocked back to her side and her left hand in a fist just in front of her face. She had her teeth gritted and was growling. She looked as though she is ready to kill. She wasn't going to let anyone even touch her. Lieutenant Edwards screamed, "Oh Shit!" and then screamed out loud, "Angie it is me, Lieutenant Edwards, Angie, Angie, Angie!"